Dear Reader,

This month we are pr~~~~~~~~~~~ four books with very different themes and settings: Australian author Tegan James's debut *Scarlet* novel is a mixture of mystery and passion with a glorious outback setting; Vickie Moore offers us mystery, too, but her romance is set in a thrilling gothic castle. From Jan McDaniel we have a story which will tug at your heartstrings . . . and we think you'll find the ending thought-provoking and a little surprising. And last, but by no means least, Maxine Barry, one of our most prolific and popular authors, has created a pair of lovers who strike sparks off each other against a beautiful English countryside backdrop.

You'll have noticed that our back covers have changed slightly and for three of our authors this month we're delighted to share with you some of the praise for their previous *Scarlet* romances. We hope you find these review quotes interesting. Let us know if any of them agree with your opinion of a particular *Scarlet* title, won't you?

Till next month,

Sally Cooper

SALLY COOPER,
Editor-in-Chief – *Scarlet*

P.S. UK readers will notice another change this month – a slight price increase. But we're sure you'll agree that *Scarlet* romances are still great value for money.

About the Author

Vickie Moore lives in Wichita, Kansas with her family and assorted pets. A full-time writer, she enjoys the enticing mixture of romance and suspense. Her family has become quite accustomed to finding references to homicidal intent jotted down anywhere . . . including on recipe cards!

When Vickie's not plotting love and murder, she enjoys being outdoors, gardening and painting.

Shadowed Promises is Vickie's second novel for *Scarlet* and we're sure that readers will enjoy the exciting blend of mystery and romance contained in the story.

VICKIE MOORE

SHADOWED PROMISES

Enquiries to:
Robinson Publishing Ltd
7 Kensington Church Court
London W8 4SP

First published in the UK by Scarlet, 1997

A copy of the British Library Cataloguing in
Publication data is available from the British Library

ISBN 1-85487-720-8

Printed and bound in the EC

10 9 8 7 6 5 4 3 2 1

To Pat Randall for your friendship and
your expertise. I have learned so much from you.
And, as always,
to my family for their love and understanding.

To all of you reading my book,
thank you.

CHAPTER 1

'I sense fear in this room,' the young woman said, her eyes closed, clutching an age-yellowed shawl tightly to her chest.

Who wouldn't? Thomas Blackwell thought. The secret artist within him had appreciated the golden highlights in the copper shine of the woman's long hair. He could even admire the delicate structure of her face. But as a man, the psychic mumbo-jumbo she was spouting was giving him the creeps.

She reached her hand out in front of her and began to walk to the middle of the room, her eyes still closed. She stopped, then lifted her face as if listening. Suddenly, she opened her eyes and pointed to a darkened spot on the parquet floor.

'Death . . . murder.' The woman said softly, then tilted her head and frowned. 'A young man.'

'Ah, jeez. This is ridiculous,' Thomas muttered and folded his arms across his chest. He received a quiet shushing and a hard stare from his grandmother, Alicia Blackwell, who stood beside him. Anyone familiar with Kansas lore would know

1

about the infamous murder of David Blackwell in 1865. Surely his grandmother knew that.

He waved his hand toward the so-called psychic, but did lower his voice in deference to the woman who had raised him. 'Grandma, you don't actually believe in this rubbish, do you?'

'Thomas, I'll whack you with my cane if you don't be quiet,' his petite grandmother threatened in a stage whisper.

'Your blood,' the psychic said as she whirled toward him, her long hair swinging around her shoulders with the movement.

'What?' His gaze moved to hers, then he frowned as he glanced to the dark stain the family had never been able to remove from the floor. 'My blood?'

She stepped toward him, her eyes hypnotic and potent. The gold flecks in them warmed the dark honey color of her eyes. She arched a thin brow and her lips quirked into a smile. 'The victim. Was he not an ancestor?'

'Oh.' Thomas felt an unexplained sense of relief. 'Yes, I'm one of David Blackwell's descendants. As I'm sure everyone is aware, the Blackwell family built the castle and it has always remained in the family; hence the name, Blackwell Castle.'

This whole seance thing had gone a little too far, he thought. He rubbed a rough hand over his face and took a deep breath. 'I'm sorry, Ms . . . ?'

'Miss Lark Delavan,' she offered, her gaze hardening to match his.

'Miss Delavan, I have a very hard time believing in this kind of thing. Not to mention the fact that David Blackwell was murdered over a hundred years ago

2

and even if the legend is true and Theorosa did not kill him, it's all a moot point anyway. Wouldn't you agree?'

He had to admire her guts as she folded the old shawl neatly, then placed it on the back of the couch. She lifted her chin and met his look. 'Mr Blackwell, I'm sorry you feel that way, but I must admit I had expected a more open-minded response from a member of the family.'

'I have been more than open-minded as far as this is concerned. Especially considering I let you in the door.'

'Thomas Blackwell,' his grandmother's voice rose with indignation. She whacked him none too gently with her cane on his shin. 'I am appalled by your rude behavior. Miss Delavan came only at my request. She's my guest, and as such, I expect you to treat her with the utmost respect.'

His gaze never left the self-proclaimed psychic's face. 'She's staying here?'

'Thomas!' The elder Mrs Blackwell stamped her cane on the floor, very close to the toe of his boot.

Stepping slightly out of reach of his grandmother, he turned and nodded. 'I apologize.' Then he met Miss Delavan's gaze. 'To both of you.'

'That is better,' Mrs Blackwell said. 'Since you have effectively and irreversibly trashed Miss Delavan's psychic flow, I would like you to show her to her room.'

'Please follow me, Ms Delavan, and I'll take you to the guest room,' Thomas offered as he started to bend to retrieve her luggage at the doorway.

'No, Thomas, I've had Theorosa's room prepared,' Mrs Blackwell said.

He stopped at his grandmother's words, knowing his face registered his shock. The room was one of the spookiest in the castle, second only to the library at night. Theorosa's room had been the source of many late night dares for the young Blackwells as they were growing up. Several family members had claimed to hear her moaning in the room for her lost lover, or, as he remembered from his own experience, the creaking whine of the oak floor boards under her ghostly feet as she paced back and forth within the room. Portraits of the people who participated in the drama so long ago hung in the castle, but Thomas figured the story, or the legend as the family liked to call it, had been enhanced over the years to add to the mystique of the Castle of the Plains.

But as far as he knew, no one had ever slept in Theorosa's room since the day she was executed for the murder of her lover. Or so the family had always claimed.

Thomas recognized his grandmother's stern expression to mean she was completely serious. He glanced to the young woman, then stiffened at her cool, amused slight smile.

'This way, please,' he said. Thomas bent over and grasped the woman's two large suitcases, surprised to find that they weren't that heavy. Too late he noticed a large object shift and fall with a solid whack against his head. Dropping the luggage, he grabbed the thing and found himself staring into the grinning face of a small gargoyle. 'What the hell is this?'

'Oh, sorry,' the woman said as she took the item from him, 'it's an umbrella. I had to pick it up from the canvas shop on my way to the airport.'

Thomas glared at the miniature monster as he rubbed the knot on his head. 'That has to be the ugliest umbrella I've ever seen.'

Her chin rose a fraction, 'Mr Blackwell, despite its appearances, this happens to be a very rare item. My ancestors had it custom made in the late 1800s and it's been passed down ever since. It was even used as a weapon in an altercation where a man lost his life.'

Still rubbing the bump on his head, he continued to frown at her defensive stance. 'I'd believe it. The damn thing almost killed me. If you're anything like your ancestor, I'd say he definitely did need it as a weapon.'

'Thank you,' she smiled. Alicia took the umbrella from her and placed it in the stand in the library. 'I've been told many times I take after my great-grand-mother.'

'Grandmother,' Thomas growled in a low voice, retrieving the luggage and turning to the stairs, 'it figures.'

As he climbed the large staircase, he sincerely hoped Theorosa would put in an appearance for their unusual and, as far as he was concerned, unwanted guest.

'I gather my visit was unexpected?' she asked as they moved up the imposing staircase.

Her voice was soft and smooth, making him think of a fragile and gentle girl. The image did not blend well with the hard look she had given

5

him when he had interrupted her with his blunt statement earlier.

'I guess I've always assumed your profession worked on a "spook and run" basis.'

'I am an accountant by profession, Mr Blackwell,' she responded, her tone crisp. 'And no matter how unwanted it is, my . . . ability is not something I can hide, or ignore.'

He opened the door to Theorosa's room and stepped inside to deposit her luggage by the foot of the bed. Turning, he found Miss Delavan standing in the hallway, her hands clasped in front of her, quiet and under control. A look of reluctance and a glimmer of fear crossed her face. Thomas frowned, regretting his harsh statements earlier. After all, his grandmother had contacted the woman, not the other way around.

He stepped into the hallway and studied her face. 'Is there something wrong?'

She looked at him quickly, then shook her head. 'No, I . . . I was wondering where I might find the portraits of the family that you mentioned.'

He hesitated, remembering his earlier thoughts about the paintings. 'I didn't mention anything about the family portraits, Miss Delavan.'

'Please call me Lark,' she said. 'Perhaps it was your grandmother who told me about them.'

Thomas wondered just how far her abilities extended, then quickly shrugged away the idea. *Keep it up, Thomas,* he told himself, *and you'll be believing her hocus pocus too.* 'You'll find the portraits upstairs in what used to be the old ballroom.'

'Thank you, Mr Blackwell,' she said as she started to move past him. She held his gaze for

6

a moment, then spoke softly. 'I realize it's hard to believe in what most people do not consider normal, but I came only out of respect for your grandmother's wishes.'

Her eyes never wavered from his; seemingly she was accustomed to being scrutinized. A polite stranger with honest eyes, he thought. Yet, Thomas knew only too well how deceiving the combination could be. 'How much is she paying you?'

She allowed nothing to register in her expression. Only her eyes glittered with her anger and, if he wasn't mistaken, pain.

'I have never accepted payment for my help, Mr Blackwell. Now, please excuse me.'

She moved stiffly past him without a glance and shut the door firmly. Thomas remained looking at the closed door for a moment, then chuckled with amusement. He didn't know which surprised him more; the brief glimpse of the fire beneath the cool facade, or the fact that he believed her.

Lark sat on the edge of the bed and took a deep breath, then released it. Thomas Blackwell had caused such intense sensations to wash through her; a white haze of goodness with a dark curl of fear swirling beneath.

Frowning, she tried to focus her thoughts on the source of the anxiety she had sensed. The mist evaporated, however, leaving her with only the remnants of the feelings that had moved within her. What had it meant? she wondered. Once again she felt frustration with the lack of clarity in her ability. The goodness and the fear had been the only strong sensations she could recognize. Everyone could recognize and understand goodness, but was it fear she felt for him? Or because of him?

Lark remembered Blackwell's features as he opened the door, a hesitant, friendly smile on his face till she had given him her name. His expression had hardened then as it seemed to do every time he looked at her. She had never known anyone to affect her as Thomas had. The moment she looked into his eyes, the shadowy features of the man in her recurring dream suddenly became clear. He was Thomas Blackwell.

The dream would come to her occasionally, mostly when she least expected it. She had never been able to will the dream to come to her when she needed it most. It would come without warning. It would slip into her bed and her thoughts like a silent lover. He would look into her eyes and she would revel in the warmth of his gaze. She could feel the warmth of his touch on the back of her head as he pulled her slowly to his kiss. His lips caressing hers were as real as the disappointment she always felt when she would awake from the bliss of the dream. Alone.

Sighing, Lark felt the weight of acceptance settle over her. She had come because of the engaging personality of Alicia Blackwell. Her grandson had the same charismatic energy, but unlike his grandmother, it was apparent what he thought of her and her ability.

She had grown accustomed to the realization that she would be led by the knowledge that would appear without notice within her. That she could not ignore. But never would she become accustomed to the black, shimmering sensation of death.

Taking a deep breath, Lark stood and began to walk slowly around the room. Theorosa's room had been recently dusted and thoroughly cleaned. By the firm comfort, she guessed the old bed sported a new mattress and she knew the linen would also be new. A vase filled with flowers rested on the writing desk by the window. Mrs Blackwell had been gracious with her hospitality. Yet, even with the window raised to allow in a warm spring breeze, there was the unmistakable feeling of the past.

Lark hoped she could help fulfil Mrs Blackwell's unusual request. To free Theorosa.

She closed her eyes and began the relaxation technique her mother had taught her in order to open her thoughts. The feelings. Even with the history of the castle, of the room, she was surprised by the strength of the impressions she felt. Perhaps the sealing of the room had helped the sensations remain strong through time.

Opening her eyes, she focused on the lace curtains. Clean, though stained with the yellow of age, they rolled with the gentle breath of morning. She inhaled the subtle fragrance of approaching rain. Starting toward the window, she hesitated, then stopped. Something within her held her back; kept her from going to the window. Lark turned away and slowly walked around the room.

She touched figurines, sometimes picking them up to see if the contact would give her something more.

9

Nothing. If anything, happiness was associated with the items, although she could not say why, in contrast to the tragic story Mrs Blackwell had told her about Theorosa's brutal death.

Lark stepped toward the wardrobe, then hesitated. The doors were closed, its secrets were held within. She opened one door with its ornately carved oak and studied the contents.

A pale rose linen dress hung stiffly on a wooden hanger. Lark lifted the sleeve to examine the cuff and admired the meticulous skill of the seamstress. An image flashed in her mind of youth. A bright day filled with laughter. Lark smiled and lowered the arm of the garment; she had been worried that Theorosa's tortured spirit would have only bad memories.

She slid the delicate dress aside and began to inspect the other garments. Lark could barely make out the delicate pattern of what appeared to be a lace gown at the very back of the wardrobe. In order to reach it more easily, she tried to open the other door but found it stuck. Probably the humidity, she thought.

Lark slid the other dresses over and reached her hand into the darkness to pull the last garment out. Her finger skimmed the rough stiffness of the fabric. A jolt of fear, icy and sharp, stabbed through her with such an intensity she found herself backing away. A hiss, like the sound of an angry snake's warning, swirled through the room.

Lark looked around her and found nothing. The cold blackness of dread filled her, suddenly at odds with the warm cheer of the room. She felt a sticky sensation pool on her fingers and glanced to her hand.

Lark gasped, her heart beat wildly at the sight. A dark stain covered the tips of her fingers where she had touched the partially hidden garment.

It was blood.

CHAPTER 2

Lark's hands shook as she ran water over them. The dark blood-red color mixed with the water, shifting and swirling like a red snake into the drain. She inspected her finger, hoping to find a cut to explain the sudden stain of blood. As she ran her thumb over the tips of her fingers, she released her breath slowly. Nothing.

Quickly she reached for a towel to dry her hands. Unpacking would just have to wait she thought. She needed to get out of the room and find a little time to organize her thoughts.

Shutting the bedroom door behind her, Lark moved in the general direction of the ballroom where Thomas had said the family portraits were displayed. After opening several doors, Lark realized the second floor consisted mainly of bedrooms.

'Is there something I can help you with?'

A sharp voice startled Lark and she turned to find a woman carrying a set of folded sheets in her arms. Lark's frown matched that of the woman's as she studied her. She was young with mousy brown hair cut in an unattractive bob around her thin elfin face.

She would have made a perfect elf for a chocolate chip cookie commercial, except for the nasty look in her dark eyes.

'I was looking for the ballroom,' Lark answered firmly. 'Mr Blackwell said it was around here. Somewhere. Could you possibly point me in the right direction?'

The woman's eyes narrowed and her lips pursed as she thought it over. 'You're that psychic Alicia sent for, aren't you?'

Lark didn't know how to answer that one, so she didn't. Instead she merely returned the woman's gaze as she waited for her to answer.

'I'm LeAnn. I work for Alicia,' she said. She shifted the load in her arms and nodded toward the staircase at the end of the hallway. 'Take those stairs to the third floor. That's where you'll find the ballroom.'

'Thank you,' Lark answered. She didn't know why it surprised her to see the woman wearing a sweater, jeans, and tennis shoes. Except that the other servant, Maria, had been wearing a conservative, standard maid's uniform. There was nothing conservative or standard about this shrewd woman, Lark thought. She started to turn to make her way to the stairway when LeAnn's voice halted her.

'There's no such thing as ghosts, you know.'

Okay, Lark thought. She met the woman's gaze. 'Logically, I would have to agree with you, LeAnn.'

Lark then continued to the large staircase to follow the beautifully turned spindles of the railing to the third floor. At the top, she found a wide landing and a set of double doors. She hesitated, her hand not quite touching the brass knob, and turned to look back over her shoulder. LeAnn stood at the foot of the stairs watching her with a dark scowl. She held Lark's gaze for a brief moment as if measuring her, then turned and walked away.

Lark shook her head at the sense of unease the woman had given her. And people thought she was spooky.

Opening one of the huge doors slowly, it surprised her that it did not creak or moan as she pushed it. Lark looked around her, then took a deep breath. She reminded herself that she didn't need to feel like an intruder; after all, Mrs Blackwell had said she had the run of the castle.

Lark's breath caught as she took in the expanse of the room. What Thomas had so casually called the old ballroom was an understatement. It wasn't the gilded gold of England, but the inviting warm, dark wood of America. Ornately carved wainscoting and several marble fireplaces adorned the outer edges. The woodwork of the floor moved into an intricate parquet pattern, marking the dance area.

Lark could see several contraptions hanging from the ceiling that she could only guess were used for the drapes or brightly colored fabric to decorate the ballroom when it was used. Around the main fireplace hung the painted portraits of the Blackwood family.

The soles of her low-heeled dress shoes made an echoing click as she moved across the floor to the impressive dominating fireplace. Apparently in chronological order, the paintings ended with Thomas, who would inherit Blackwell Castle.

14

The portrait was an excellent likeness and allowed her to move closer and study him as the flesh and blood man never would have done. Even in the painting there was an impression that he was tall. Tall enough to tower over her own five-foot, five-inch frame. His dark hair was smoothed back from his rugged face in natural waves. His eyebrows were heavy and accentuated the dark fringe of his eyelashes. The artist hadn't missed the faint cleft of his chin or the slight indentations of the dimples that would appear if he laughed. An unexplained pang of disappointment moved through Lark. She knew he would never do much of anything except frown around her.

Her brows drew together as she stepped closer to look at the eyes of the portrait. The hazel-green was a shade darker than that of her own, but the artist had captured what so few could, the spark of Thomas's inner light. Mesmerized, she studied his eyes and remembered the intense feelings he had invoked within her. The light of goodness and the dark curl of fear.

Unconsciously her gaze moved to his full lower lip . . . and she swallowed. Thomas had made her experience the sensation of fear and the almost equally fearful sensation of desire.

Shaking away the unwanted thoughts, Lark moved away from the portrait and glanced over the rest until she spotted the dark eyes of a beautiful woman.

Theorosa.

Everything within her bristled with the knowledge. The painting was hung above her head and hard for Lark to study, but she moved her gaze slowly over the young woman's face. The face of a woman accused of her lover's murder.

Her hair was thick and straight, her skin smooth and supple over finely sculptured cheek bones, a sign of her native American heritage. Her pose was regal and proud, but again Lark was drawn to the portrait's eyes. The dark honey-brown eyes spoke of pain, fear, loss, and cautious happiness.

'That's Theorosa.' A man's deep voice came from behind her.

'Oh.' She jumped, then turned to face an older man dressed in jeans and a shirt that had seen better days. 'I'm sorry. I didn't know anyone was up here.'

'Except for parties, there usually isn't anyone here.' The man smiled good naturedly. 'I was just checking the lion heads on the turret.'

Lark frowned. 'Pardon?'

'Turret. It's like a tower,' he chuckled.

'I know what a turret is,' she assured him with a polite smile, 'but lion heads?'

'I'm sorry, miss,' he said as he extended his hand to her. 'I'm Tim Waslawski, I'm the grounds keeper, or whatever else is needed around here. Since I'm here so much, I sometimes forget that people may not know what I'm talking about.'

'Lark Delavan,' she returned as she shook his hand. 'And as you've already guessed, I'm not from here. In fact, I had never even heard of this famous Castle of the Plains till I spoke with Mrs Blackwell a couple of weeks ago.'

He chuckled. 'Castle of the Plains sounds like a perfect name for a soap opera. Of course, the family history is much like one.'

16

Lark shook her head, 'I really don't know much about the family.'

'I don't want to bore you with the whole household history, but I can at least point out the ones you're dealing with, if you would like?'

'Yes, thank you. I would appreciate that very much,' she said.

The man faced the paintings, then pointed to the first Blackwell portrait. 'That is the original Blackwell of the castle, David. He's the one Theorosa supposedly killed.'

Lark studied the man's face. 'You sound as if you believe she didn't.'

'Obviously I wasn't around then.' Tim shrugged, 'but I know how people can jump to conclusions and judge you guilty before you're even given a chance.'

His voice was steady and low, but Lark felt that the man understood that sort of judgement. He glanced at her, then moved on, skipping a few paintings to point out the more notable people represented. 'The man with the incredible mustache is Alicia's late husband, Harrison. He was a personality. Had to be to marry that woman.'

'Mrs Blackwell seems like a generous and warm person,' Lark said. She truly liked Alicia and admired her energy. She couldn't believe one of her employees would be saying such things to a guest of the castle.

'Oh, don't get me wrong, miss.' Tim smiled as he looked at her. 'I've known Alicia Blackwell for years. No one could help but like that woman. That's her portrait next to her husband. She was a beauty when Harrison married her. Years may have aged her, but

17

she still has that energy that draws everyone to her. Let's see, I think you've already met Thomas.'

Lark almost laughed when Tim made that comment. She had been the focus of Thomas's dislike, had watched her umbrella fall and whack him on the head, and been informed of his doubts about her. All in the span of an hour. Yeah, she had met him.

'You probably haven't met David.' Tim pointed to a portrait near Thomas's.

'Why are there two pictures of him?' she asked.

'This is a different David, he's Thomas's cousin,' he said, then glanced around as if someone might be lurking in the shadows. He lowered his voice. 'And whatever you do, don't mention the similarity.'

'I don't understand. Why wouldn't there be a similarity? He's a descendent, right?' Lark asked. She sensed that the man had begun to feel at ease, yet angry at the same time.

He pursed his lips for a moment as if weighing a decision, then met her gaze. 'He believes he is the rightful heir to the castle.'

Lark wondered if the man wasn't making more out of the story than was really there. 'Mrs Blackwell obviously can leave the castle to whomever she pleases, but I thought it was going to Thomas.'

Tim nodded. 'That's right. You see, everyone knows the legend of Theorosa and there is documented proof of her existence. Yet, she and David were never married and they didn't have any children. When the elder David was murdered, the castle went to his younger brother, Joseph.'

'Who was Thomas's great-grandfather,' Lark finished.

'Exactly,' Tim said, his head bobbing up and down excitedly. 'The elder David was known as a ladies' man and there were stories of an illegitimate child, a daughter.'

'Aren't there any birth certificates?' This story was definitely getting bizarre.

'No and no one really knows what happened to the mother, but apparently she gave the child to one of the younger Blackwells so the baby could be adopted and at least have the father's name. She was never heard from again.' Tim met her gaze. 'I don't have any idea what kind of claim on the estate an illegitimate child would have had back then, let alone a baby girl.'

Lark had to agree. Even after the child had grown, she doubted the daughter would have been allowed to make a claim. Especially when her mother had left her without a heritage.

'So that's probably why he was named David?' she asked.

'His mother, Sheryl, married a Blackwell that didn't care much for work. She had to work hard to take care of the family,' Tim sighed. 'David's almost a year older than Thomas and I guess she really thought everything wrong could be righted if David was made the heir. Sheryl confronted Alicia, and Thomas's father, and demanded her son be given his "rightful' heritage.'

Larks eyes widened. 'What did they do?'

'I have to admit they at least treated her fairly,' he said. 'They were willing to seriously consider her claim, if she had proof. But all Sheryl had was a colorful old story that had been passed down through the generations.'

She could almost imagine the woman's frustration. 'It must have been hard for her.'

'Sheryl refused to be around the family after that.' Tim looked at the painting for a long moment. 'She eventually divorced the bum she was married to and never spoke to the Blackwells again. It wasn't till her death that David really got to know the family.'

'Do you think he really feels he's the rightful heir?' she asked.

Tim shrugged, then faced her. 'I don't know him that well, but I look at him and sometimes I see a lot of his mother in him.'

Lark's gaze moved over the portraits. Compared to her own uneventful family history, the Blackwells did seem like a colorful family with a dark shadow in their past. 'Now I see why you would call it a soap opera. I would have to say this castle is definitely suited to the Blackwell family. I haven't gotten to see much of it, but what I have is beautiful.'

'Then allow me to give you a tour,' Tim offered. He waved his hand toward an arched doorway in the corner of the room. 'The staircase to the roof of the turret is through here.'

They walked across the ballroom floor toward the alcove. Lark glanced to the handyman and studied his lined face, which was creased around his eyes and mouth as if he laughed often. In a way, he too could almost be taken for a Blackwell.

'You seem to know a lot about the family.' She smiled and asked good naturedly, 'You wouldn't secretly happen to be a Blackwell also?'

20

'What?' He stopped, his gaze darting to her. He frowned, his expression a mixture of anger and distrust. 'No, I'm not.'

'I'm sorry, I was just joking.' Lark assured him, surprised by his reaction. What was it about the Blackwells that always evoked such strong emotions?

He continued on and Lark cringed when she realized the staircase Tim had spoken of was little more than an elaborate ladder. She emerged through the opening and joined the grounds keeper. She had never been one for heights, but the view of the rolling green land was worth a few moments of tension. Lark spotted the dark billowing clouds of an approaching thunderstorm, the low rumble of thunder making its way to her a moment later, then she turned her attention to the landscape of the castle around her.

'The first Blackwell had drain spouts installed around the turret and the roof that, as you can see, are lion heads,' Tim explained as he leaned through a small opening.

She shook her head at the man who was obviously comfortable with the idea of perching himself precariously on a turret while the building winds whipped around them.

'They're just below this ledge if you want to take a look.'

'I'll take your word for it, Mr Waslawski.' Lark frowned, swallowing to fight back the fear creeping over her. At his knowing smile of amusement, she lifted her chin and determinedly inspected the lion heads on the roof of the castle. 'I guess you might say it's guttering with teeth.'

He chuckled. 'More or less. One of the other reasons David Blackwell had the turret installed was so his hired hands could keep a better eye on his cattle. Although the Blackwell family still has most of the original land, they don't keep many cattle these days, but at one time the herd numbered in the thousands. It was real handy to have a lookout this high.'

'Well, it is definitely high, isn't it?' Lark murmured.

Tim chuckled, raising his hand to point out another landmark. 'Over there is the family cemetery. The dates go back several generations. In fact, I believe the original Blackwell who brought his family here from Europe rests there.'

Lark followed his direction and could see the small cemetery through a clearing in the trees. The area didn't look as gloomy as she would have expected. The sun shone through the leaves of the trees surrounding the clearing. The sporadic movement of the shadows caused the tombstones and the statues to look as if they were dancing in a ritual frenzy around the large mausoleum that squatted in the center of the graveyard. The intricately carved stone of the building looked formidable with the almost life sized statue of an angel looming from the top. The wings of the figure were fully spread, her arms stretching outward in what Lark assumed was meant to be a gesture of care.

Instead the statue of the angel reminded her more of a gargoyle coiling on its perch before it swooped down on its next unsuspecting victim.

22

The morbid thought caused a shiver to move through her.

The grounds keeper must have noticed her discomfort as he quickly stepped to the stairway. 'Yes, but the best part of the tour is the house. Obviously you've been in the ballroom. Tell me what else you've seen.'

He took her hand to steady her as she stepped down the stairway. Lark felt better at once when her foot touched the wooden floor of the ballroom alcove. She shook the disquieting thoughts of the graveyard from her mind. 'Just about everything. Mrs Blackwell took me through the first floor.'

'So you've been in the library?' he asked as he moved through the arched door.

'Yes.'

'Then I'll take you to see her room,' Tim offered, the 'her' obvious to both of them.

'Oh, no need, Mr Waslawski,' she said. Their footsteps echoed through the room, their voices holding a distant quality like actors rehearsing in an empty theater. 'That's where I'm staying.'

The older man's shoulders stiffened as he stopped at her words. Lark caught a brief glimpse of his face as his gaze darted quickly to the oil painting of the beautiful girl long since dead. He swallowed nervously, then apparently noticed her watching him. He smiled stiffly, then continued on to the doors. She doubted that he had wanted her to hear his words, but the acoustics of the room carried them to her, softly and clearly.

'I hope to hell you know what you're getting into.'

* * *

23

The grounds keeper's tour had filled in the gaps in Lark's knowledge of the castle's layout. After the brief informative session, Lark had thanked Tim, then explained she planned to go for a short walk to take in the grounds around the castle. He waved, then went on his way, leaving her to herself.

Lark took a deep slow breath, inhaling the warm spring air. The grounds keeper had been a nice man and very helpful, but she needed the serenity of the outdoors.

Since she had arrived at Blackwell Castle she'd been bombarded with a variety of intense sensations. Fear, death, and even more disturbing, desire. Lark shook her head as the idea moved through her thoughts. The last thing Thomas believed in, much less wanted around, was a psychic. She'd sensed his distrust of her and the respect he felt for his grandmother, but Lark knew if it weren't for Mrs Blackwell, her grandson would be shoving her out the door as fast as he could, forcing her to try to dodge it as he slammed it behind her. Again Lark shook her head, it was incredible the situations she sometimes let herself get into.

The wind gusted around her as she moved away from the castle. The clipped edge of the lawn slowly gave way to the rougher texture of buffalo grass as she followed a well-worn path toward the trees. Glancing up, Lark frowned as she caught sight of the rough timber of an old bridge ahead of her. Looking back and seeing no road except for the foot path, she realized the structure must have been the victim of modernization. She'd seen them before, bridges in the middle of nowhere, silent reminders of where the past had once been.

Curiosity pulled at her as Lark continued toward the bridge. Slowly, she began to feel the familiar icy tingle move through her like a gradual wave, then jarring flashes of awareness jolted her thoughts. Even as her steps faltered, she still made her way toward the bridge, drawn to it by sudden images. She felt fear. Fear and the dark power of hate.

Her breath caught in her throat, 'Theorosa.'

The name fell quietly from her lips. She heard softly in the distance of time, taunting voices of others no longer alive as they shouted their hatred at the frightened girl. Lark's steps slowed and reluctance enveloped her. Yet she still moved toward the old bridge as if something stronger was pulling her there.

Die, you murderous witch. The shouting of the heated voices grew stronger around her. The flash of an image shot through Lark's awareness. A tall girl, Theorosa, running through the trees as the limbs caught and pulled at her long, white gown.

An incessant pounding worked its way into Lark's thoughts, mingling unnoticed for a moment with the gasps of her fear. The snort of a horse shook her briefly from the overwhelming sensations emanating out of the bridge that were drawing her to it.

Lark ripped herself from the images to find herself standing in front of the bridge. The source of the pounding sound was suddenly there before her. A horse and rider were galloping wildly toward her.

The pair entered the bridge from the opposite side; the pounding of the horse's hooves changed when its metal shoes hit the rough wooden planks. Lark stumbled in her effort to get out of the way, then jumped awkwardly away from the entrance. She fell heavily into the bushes with a groan as the dark blur of the animal moved swiftly past.

She looked up to find the rider, a blonde woman, whirling the horse around toward her.

'You little fool, didn't you hear us coming?' the rider said, spitting out the words angrily as she tried to quiet the prancing animal.

Lark stared at her for a moment, the fear quickly losing its grip on her. Yet she wasn't so sure about the rider. The woman sat comfortably astride the animal, with haughty malevolence filling her eyes. Her cool beauty seemed familiar to Lark, but she could not recall from where.

'You know, you're damn lucky you didn't get your neck broken,' she hissed.

The woman's words, perhaps because oxygen was finally getting to her brain, ignited Lark's temper. She stood, then began brushing debris from her clothes with short jerks of her hands.

'Do you always ride like a bat out of hell?' Lark snapped, stopping to return the woman's glare.

The woman smiled icily, tilting her head to the side. 'You're that psychic Alicia sent for, aren't you?'

Lark didn't answer, knowing the woman didn't expect one. Instead she attempted to bring her anger under control as she picked bits of grass and leaves from her hair.

'You don't look like a psychic,' the rider commented. She let her breath out in a short puff of frustration. What was it with people and psychics around here? she thought. Lark leveled her gaze on the woman. 'I just recently had the chicken bone removed from my nose. Maybe that's what threw you off.'

The blonde chuckled. 'Well, well, testy aren't we?'

'*We* would be too, if *we* had almost been run down by a horse,' Lark said, trying to control her ire.

'Oh, that. Satan likes to take the lead whenever he can. He is a very spirited animal. Thomas picked him because of it.' The blonde's cool gaze moved from the horse to settle on her. 'He likes his women that way too.'

'You mean broad hindquarters and led by a rope?' Lark asked, biting her lip to keep from laughing when the woman's eyes heated from the comment.

'I apparently need to introduce myself,' the woman said as she easily dismounted from the horse. She took the reins and walked toward Lark, then stopped in front of her. 'I'm Natalie Brown and I'm a very good friend of Thomas. He isn't at all pleased that his grandmother brought you here.' Natalie arched a knowing brow at her and smirked. 'Being a psychic you would already have known that, wouldn't you?'

'It is none of my concern what Mr Blackwell thinks or doesn't think of me,' Lark answered, holding the woman's gaze.

Natalie looked away briefly as though noticing

the weather for the first time, then looked back to Lark, her blue eyes dark and threatening like the approaching storm. 'I don't know what your scam is . . . Lark, isn't it? But if you think you're going to spook your way into soaking Alicia out of the Blackwell money you'll only find yourself in a lot of trouble.'

'Is that a threat, or advice,' Lark asked through clenched teeth, 'from experience?'

Lark watched the anger flash in the woman's eyes, then was surprised when she laughed. 'Though I would love to chat with you, I'm afraid I need to get ready for your dinner tonight.'

'My dinner?' Lark questioned dryly, not relishing the idea of having to see this woman again.

'Oh, it must have slipped Alicia's mind. That happens sometimes with people her age you know,' Natalie commented, turning slightly to stroke the silky coat of the black horse. When her gaze returned to Lark, the malice in the woman's eyes was as dark as the animal beside her. 'I will be attending with Thomas, as usual. I hope you brought an appropriate gown, Alicia is known for her grand occasions.'

'I was not made aware of any plans,' Lark commented.

'Don't worry,' Natalie quipped, her gaze moving over Lark's form. 'I'm sure she can dig up something for you. I brought one of Thomas's favorite gowns, in fact he picked it out for me himself.' She hesitated, smiling knowingly. 'Of course I never need to worry about night clothes. After he looks at me, I doubt I would need them anyway.'

Natalie chuckled as she walked past Lark. 'See you tonight.'

Resisting the urge to stick her tongue out at Natalie's retreating figure, Lark swiped at the grass clinging to her skirt. 'I just can't wait.'

'I see you've had the pleasure of meeting the ever charming Miss Brown.'

She turned to find a man standing not far away. From his amused smile, she imagined he'd witnessed pretty much the whole show.

'I don't know that I would exactly call it a pleasure,' Lark commented as she walked to the man.

'I'm Jeffrey Linden,' he said, extending his hand. 'I'm a representative for a historic preservation society. I've been working with Mrs Blackwell on a very important matter. Fortunately, I very rarely have to be exposed to that person.'

She introduced herself, then nodded toward the castle. 'Are you attending the dinner tonight?'

'Yes, I've been graciously invited, though I doubt my presence will be very welcome,' he said, as they walked back toward the castle.

'As you just witnessed, obviously I know how you feel,' Lark offered, feeling the tension start to ease from her shoulders as she opened the large front door. 'I believe Mrs Blackwell is in the library, I'll take you to her.'

Together they stepped into the foyer. Jeffrey automatically removed his hat and held it in his hand. 'Mrs Blackwell had mentioned you were coming. I'd hoped to meet you, Miss Delavan. This castle has such an interesting history.'

'Please call me Lark,' she answered as they walked to the library. 'Since I arrived I haven't really met a friendly face yet.'

She looked beside her to find no one there. Turning, she found Jeffrey staring in awe at the large staircase that spiraled through three floors, the dark wood contrasting with the chiseled stone of the castle walls. 'Mr Linden, is there something wrong?'

'No,' he said, his gaze moving over the interior of the castle. 'No matter how many times I see this place I still have such a strong reaction to it. History fascinates me, Lark, and this castle has such an extraordinary history. To think all this beauty was accomplished by hand without the sterile influence of machinery – it is truly a work of genius.'

Lark watched the man, his passion for the past visible in the animated expression of his face. He looked at her sheepishly and smiled.

'I apologize, I always get carried away,' he said as he moved to stand beside her.

'Never apologize for passion, Jeffrey,' Mrs Blackwell's voice rang with authority. She stepped from the hallway behind them, her cane clicking lightly on the floor. Joining them, she eyed the embarrassed man with an amused expression. 'Passion is a very powerful motivation. It can make you do things from throwing the china at the wall to making love on top of the desk in the library. Of course, if you plan on doing that you really should lock the doors.'

Jeffrey cleared his throat nervously. 'Mrs Blackwell, I don't think I would describe my feelings with such a strong word as,' his voice cracked like a teenager, 'as passion.'

'Nonsense,' the older woman, waved away his comment. 'However, you do need to work on redirecting your passion, young man, from old castles to something much more appealing, perhaps. The old cliché that "life is too short" wouldn't be a cliché if it weren't true, now would it?'

'I suppose so, ma'am,' Jeffrey stammered, his cheeks flushing a darker shade of red. The stain of his embarrassment clashed with the red-orange of his curly hair, giving the man a clownish look.

'Oh, LeAnn, would you be a dear and take Jeffrey to the library?'

The unusual maid had appeared quietly behind Alicia. The woman's gaze never left Jeffrey's face. 'Of course, Alicia. Please come this way, Mr Linden.'

'Jeffrey, I'll be with you in a moment.' Mrs Blackwell smiled as she watched LeAnn close the sliding doors behind the flustered historian before turning back to Lark. 'I wanted to speak to you about this morning and my grandson's behavior,' she said.

Lark shook her head and smiled. 'Mrs Blackwell, you don't need to apologize, I am quite used to people doubting what they don't consider normal.'

'Please call me Alicia, and I wasn't going to apologize for my grandson, my dear.' The old woman smiled. 'After all, it's not my place to apologize. I wasn't the one acting like a pretentious ass, now was I?'

Lark laughed, 'No, you were not.'

Alicia patted her hand. 'It's good to hear you laugh, I have a feeling you don't do it enough. Now what I wanted to speak to you about does regard Thomas, though. He may act quite unseemly sometimes, but he really is a nice man. I hope his doubts about our endeavor won't deter you.'

'I promised you that I would do what I could to help,' Lark said. She noted the expectant look in the woman's otherwise confident face. 'I intend to do just that.'

'Good. Thank you, Lark, this does mean a lot to me.' Alicia smiled, taking her hand to give her a reassuring squeeze.

Lark suddenly remembered the dinner. 'Alicia, about the dinner tonight.'

Alicia frowned, 'Who told you? It was supposed to be a surprise welcome for you.'

'I sort of ran into your grandson's fiancée at the bridge,' she answered. She took a slow breath as she recalled just how close they had come to literally running into each other.

'That damn nuisance of a girl.' Alicia's face darkened. 'And she is not Thomas's fiancée, Lark. Fortunately, my grandson came to his senses and broke off their relationship. The unfortunate thing is they parted on amicable terms which that girl uses as an open invitation.'

Lark was surprised, but greatly amused by the woman's dislike of Natalie. Not knowing how to respond, she chose to skim past that topic. 'She mentioned the party was to be quite formal. I really didn't bring anything suitable for a formal dinner.'

Alicia waved her hand. 'Don't worry about that, dear. Natalie is prone to exaggeration, as I'm sure you will learn all too quickly. However, I hate to admit that perhaps I have put you in an awkward position. Still I do have a solution. I'll send it up to you after I've finished with Jeffrey.'

'Alicia, you don't need to go to such trouble.' Natalie's words regarding 'digging' up a garment came back to Lark. 'I did bring several nice dresses.'

'And I'm sure you look beautiful in them.' Alicia smiled. 'However, there's something about seeing people dressed in their finest that allows us to see the best in them. Goodness knows we could use a boost of that around here.'

The woman patted Lark's hand and nudged her toward the staircase. 'I'll have the dress sent up to you right away. Maria can help you try it on and do any minor alterations that might be needed. With your figure, my dear, I doubt you will need it.'

Lark chuckled as she climbed the staircase. Alicia could probably charm a snake into buying socks. Obviously the matron of Blackwell Castle had been planning this event for some time and Lark felt as if she had been smoothly maneuvered into whatever role the woman had just chosen for her. She didn't know what her part was, and really didn't relish the idea of a tortuous evening with Miss Brown as a guest, but the thought of Thomas in a tuxedo was quite an intriguing image. Not to mention very enticing.

Reaching the second floor landing, Lark shook her head. Apparently her libido was working overtime to make up for so long without any romantic notions on her part. She had to wonder if the mystique of the Castle of the Plains coupled with the legend of love never fulfilled was starting to affect her, causing her to feel and think things that she had forced out of her thoughts for so long.

Chuckling once again at the path her thoughts were taking, she opened the door to her room. Her eyes focused on the interior. The numbing veil of shock moved over her as she gasped at the sight before her eyes.

The mattress lay beside the bed. The curtain rod had fallen from one of its wooden brackets and hung awkwardly across the front of the window. Lark stepped carefully over the lace pools of the dresses from the wardrobe that had been thrown without regard to the fragile condition of the time-worn fabric. She took the end of the rod and started to lift it to replace it in the bracket, when her gaze was caught by a movement outside her window and she sucked in her breath. The rod fell from her hand. The motion loosened the other end which was already hanging haphazardly from its bracket and the entire window dressing fell with a loud clatter to the wooden floor.

Lark's heart beat heavily in her chest as she tried to swallow back the fear clutching at her throat. Someone was making it quite obvious that her presence was not wanted at the castle. She was unable to remove her gaze from the prop planted to scare her. By itself the item could only be considered the work of a juvenile prank, she tried to remind herself. After all, it was only a rope twisted into a knot.

Except this one was obviously meant for her.

CHAPTER 3

Thomas found himself hesitating as he struggled with the strands of his black tie. His grandmother was known for her dinners where participants were encouraged to dress as if going to the Emerald Ball. He took a deep breath and exhaled with frustration as he loosened the tie to his tuxedo to start over for the third time.

It was that *psychic's* fault.

He'd had women remain in his thoughts before, some had distracted him, but he hadn't really had one bother him quite so much. She was a beautiful woman and he had even found himself smiling when he had spotted her talking with the grounds keeper. She had hesitated, then laughed at something Tim said, and her face had lit up with her warm smile as her hair lifted in the wind around her.

Till he remembered what she was and why she was here.

Thomas finally knotted the tie firmly into place. Even though he was worried about the ulterior motives of the stranger, he trusted his grandmother. She had never allowed herself to be swindled out of anything in her life and he doubted she would start now. If Alicia believed in the 'power' of this woman, then he would not interfere with his grandmother's plan.

Thomas opened the door to his room. Maybe, just maybe, he might make it through this evening.

Nearing the parlor, Thomas could hear the muted tones of his cousin David. He opened the door and found that most of the guests had arrived. Natalie was standing near David till she saw Thomas enter, then she shifted slightly away. David was frowning as he spoke to his grandmother. A good friend of the family, Dr Henry Graham, stood near her side.

'Grandmother, it could very well have been your psychic who trashed the room.' David lifted his wineglass to take a sip, then hesitated. 'It wouldn't be the first time one of them has used something like this to add an air of legitimacy to their claims.'

'David, I have to agree with you,' Natalie concurred, then patted Alicia's hand. 'Alicia, sometimes it's hard for us to judge people. I'm sure in the beginning you felt you had a strong reason to bring her here, but surely you can see that she is in this to try and get your money.'

Thomas watched his grandmother carefully, waiting for her to explain what had happened. He could see the anger beginning to seethe beneath her calm exterior. He knew she didn't like to be cajoled by anyone, especially Natalie.

'I know how hard this must be for you, but I'm only telling you for your own good,' Natalie soothed. She placed her hand tenderly on the old woman's shoulder. 'I'm an excellent judge of these things,

Alicia. I feel you should face the facts of this situation and acknowledge that this woman is looking for easy money.'

'For once, my dear, I would have to agree with you,' Alicia said, facing the younger woman. 'You would know a lot about that.'

Natalie removed her hand and tried to act as if she had missed the intent of the statement, but not before Thomas noted the deep anger in her eyes. 'If you'll excuse me, my glass seems to be empty.'

'The glass isn't the only thing empty with that girl,' Alicia murmured as the younger woman walked away.

'Now, Alicia,' Henry Graham chuckled as he moved closer to her. 'You always seem to be misbehaving. I, for one, am looking forward to meeting this young lady. There have been several instances in my experience with this castle when some things have happened that I knew were not natural occurrences.'

'What exactly has happened, Grandmother?' Thomas may have had doubts about the psychic his grandmother had brought in, but it disturbed him to think of anyone being harmed.

'I'm sorry, Thomas, I hadn't realized that you were unaware of the incident this afternoon,' Alicia said as she set her drink untouched on the table. 'Someone ransacked Theorosa's room. A harmless prank I'm sure.'

'I believe Grandmother means that the crackpot she's brought in did this,' David frowned deeply, his dislike registering on his face. 'What reason would any of us have for doing something like that?'

'Perhaps as a warning for me to leave.'

Everyone turned to the speaker standing at the wide doors of the library. Thomas was reluctant to admit, even to himself, that he had never seen a woman more beautiful. Lark stood proudly at the door, her hands clasped calmly in front of her. The dress she wore was of vintage design, but fit her figure as if it had been made only for her. Her hair was arranged in a coil on her head with long wisps framing her elegant features. For a moment Thomas could almost believe she had stepped from the past and into the room.

Lark's gaze slowly met each of those who stood before her. The room remained quiet, hesitant, as if waiting for their unusual guest to conjure a spirit to explain what had happened in Theorosa's room that day. Her eyes met his in turn and Thomas felt something deep within him stir, and he had a premonition of his own.

Lark Delavan was going to be a dangerous lady.

'Are you insinuating one of us is threatening you?' Natalie's blonde brows furrowed with resentment.

'I think it was more of a warning, than a threat.'

Lark took a deep, slow breath as she met the scrutiny of those standing in the room. She felt a momentary sense of envy as she looked at Natalie. The blonde was elegantly dressed in a blue satin evening gown that clung to her every curve. The woman was beautiful, even with the haughty slant of her brow.

If the man standing next to Natalie was her companion, they made a striking couple. Lark recognized David from the painting in the ballroom. Thomas's cousin was tall and his wide muscled shoulders fit smoothly into his evening jacket. His curly, blonde-brown hair framed his tan face and he had the unmistakable Blackwell brown eyes. Those dark eyes so similar to Thomas's met hers.

'I suppose you're going to say it was the work of a poltergeist. That maybe a seance would help us clear this up?' David's handsome face scowled in disbelief at her, then he turned to Alicia. 'Come on, Grandmother, how much is this farce costing you?'

'Miss Delavan is my guest, just as you are, David,' Alicia stated, giving the group a stern look. The burgundy color of her gown trimmed with black lace added an air of Victorian authority to the matriarch of the family as she spoke. 'The weather is becoming quite bad, I would hate for you to drive home in it. You too, Natalie.'

Natalie's mouth flew open in protest, then shut quickly as she thought better of it. David met his grandmother's eyes and Lark watched as the anger softened. She could see that despite his hostility toward her presence, he loved his grandmother. 'I apologize. I'm only concerned for you.'

'I think our grandmother is quite capable of taking care of herself.'

Thomas's deep voice startled her and she looked toward him where he stood in the shadows of the room. He stepped to his cousin's side. Lark felt strong, hot desire spear through her. The defined contours of his muscles may have been clad in the tailored lines of the tuxedo, but the hint of his power simmered underneath. Lark didn't try to mask her appreciation as her gaze moved over him to the silky curl of his dark hair just cupping the tip of his collar. She noted the smooth masculine ridge of his jaw till her gaze stopped on the full curve of his lips. Unconsciously she licked her own as she glanced up and was mesmerized by the golden center of his brown eyes.

'Even if she has an unusual way of doing it,' Thomas added, a small smile lifting the corners of his mouth.

Lark suddenly felt the small heat of embarrassment as her cheeks colored under his look. She wondered if this was how someone else felt when she had used her ability to probe into another person's thoughts. She looked away as she nervously smoothed her hands over her dress.

'Thank you, Thomas.' Alicia laughed and the tension within the room slowly started to dissipate. 'I'll assume that is a vote of confidence.'

'Is this the woman, Aunt Alicia? Is she going to contact Theorosa?' A short pudgy woman in a shabby ill-fitting yellow dress stepped forward. Lark sensed the conflict of the woman's emotions as she moved toward her.

Alicia quickly put her arm around the woman's shoulders. 'Sweetheart, please forgive me. Lark, let me introduce you to my niece Stephanie Tarrant and her husband John.'

Lark nodded to the husband. John Tarrant was almost a duplicate of his chubby wife. His suit, although expensively cut, clung tightly to his portly frame. Lark turned back to the wife and met the woman's nervous gaze before it slipped quickly away. She could feel Stephanie's self-consciousness radiate from her and Lark wanted to reach out to her. Hadn't she felt the same sense of not belonging, even within her own family?

Before she could address the woman, Maria, wearing a formal black uniform with a white apron, appeared in the doorway. 'Dinner is ready at your convenience, Mrs Blackwell, and another guest has arrived.'

'Excellent,' Alicia said, taking Henry's arm. 'I want you to meet this young man, Henry. He's the historical representative I've been telling you about. He has such wonderful enthusiasm for old structures like this. His excitement is quite contagious.'

The old doctor started to speak when Natalie's voice filtered through their conversation. 'Oh no, not him too. Well, this should be a fun evening, a stiff and a psychic.'

Henry raised his brow at the woman's comment, as did Alicia. It was obvious by the uncertain look on Natalie's face when she noticed their expressions that she hadn't really wanted them to hear her displeasure.

'I was just joking,' she said, trying miserably to stumble through her blunder.

'Come along everyone. Let's try to ignore this storm and enjoy what Maria has prepared.' Alicia fixed a pointed gaze on Natalie for a moment longer as she steered the conversation smoothly past the woman's indiscretion.

The older couple moved past Lark and she smiled as Henry leaned toward Mrs Blackwell. 'Alicia, I think you thrive on trouble.'

Alicia laughed ruefully. 'You're a fine one to talk, Henry.'

Lark startled as she felt a hand on her elbow. She became angry with herself when she felt disappointed that the man offering to escort her was not the one she had secretly hoped it would be. It surprised her how much she had wanted it to be a certain dark gentleman with tiger-brown eyes.

Instead she forced a smile as she looked into the angular face of Jeffrey Linden. He offered his arm as he spoke in a conspiratorial whisper. 'I guess you and I are both the "unwanted" guests around here.'

'I'm sure it could be worse,' Lark offered as they followed the Tarrants out of the room. Stephanie hesitated for a moment as she looked back toward Jeffrey, her expression a mixture of shock and unease. She looked as if she were going to speak to him then she turned awkwardly away.

'Yeah, at least they haven't sent for the lynch mob.'

Jeffrey's words sent a chill through her as the image of the noose swinging in the breeze that afternoon flashed quickly into her thoughts. Dread filled Lark and she hesitated momentarily, causing Jeffrey to look at her. She murmured her reassurance to him as her gaze met that of Thomas. Again, she felt the dark pang of fear laced with the sharp edge of desire.

Lark turned purposefully away. Hadn't she learned that lesson all too well? She hardened her resolve even as she found herself seated next to Thomas. Hadn't she learned through first-hand experience that the handsome face of a man often covered a shallow, self-centered personality? That the shallowness also applied to the man's emotions? Lark shook herself as she forced the pain of those thoughts away. She had convinced herself that a particular person wasn't worth her time and she wasn't going to allow herself to give in and think again of the humiliation she had felt at being so easily deceived by a charming smile. Besides she was dressed in a beautiful gown sitting between two good-looking men for a small party . . . well, Jeffrey couldn't exactly be called good-looking, Lark thought to herself as she smiled into her drink. Her smile deepened as she realized a certain specter from the past was starting to lose his power over her.

Lark was enjoying her salad when she caught the nervous movement of Stephanie's gaze as it continually flicked toward her, then occasionally toward Jeffrey. She couldn't help but note the hope within the woman's eyes as she finally mustered the courage to speak to her.

'Miss Delavan, my husband and I were quite ecstatic to hear you were coming. Do you talk to the dead?' Stephanie looked around her quickly as if trying to hide her embarrassment. 'I mean, are you planning on contacting Theorosa?'

John frowned as he watched his wife intently. Jeffrey seemed to take a sudden interest in his salad as he picked nervously at it. Alicia frowned with concern. Lark noticed the sudden tense silence of the people around her and had the impression that something deeper rode on this question.

'I do not contact the dead, Mrs Tarrant.' Lark laid her fork across her plate as she studied Stephanie thoughtfully. She didn't want to hurt the woman, scare her off, or worse yet, offend her. 'I do not talk to spirits. I really don't do anything. Sometimes . . . sometimes I get feelings about something or usually someone. Sometimes I get images. But not always. Mrs Blackwell understands that I may not be able to help her with her request at all.'

She caught Henry's movement and saw him eyeing Alicia with amusement. He placed his elbows on the table and steepled his hands with relish.

'I'm just curious, Alicia. Why are you doing this? This is a bit eccentric, even for you.'

Alicia returned his gaze with a fond smile. She hesitated before she answered. Lark knew Alicia was very intelligent and highly respected within the community. She could feel all those in the room waiting with curiosity for the explanation to Alicia's recent unusual behavior. Everyone looked at the older woman sitting at the head of the table.

'I wish I could say it was because justice was denied to a beautiful, young girl so long ago. That I, at the very least, wanted to give Theorosa the innocence that was taken from her so long ago when she was not allowed to live a full life. But I can't.'

Thomas was sitting to his grandmother's right. He placed his hand over hers. 'We support you no matter what the reason, Grandmother.'

David met his grandmother's gaze. 'Even if I don't agree with it, Grandmother, it is your decision.'

Her face softened and for a moment was somber with thought. 'Thank you, children. It means a lot to me to hear you say so, but I don't know if I can completely explain to you why I feel this needs to be done.' She sighed as she picked up her glass. 'Let's just say I've had a hard time sleeping lately.'

Henry frowned with concern as he touched her arm. 'Alicia, you should have mentioned this to me.'

Alicia laughed, her eyes once again sparkling with humor. 'Nonsense, I'm not ill, doctor. I feel fine, in fact better than I have in a long time. I've only been having some unusual dreams.'

'Such as,' Henry urged.

'I have never really been one to recall my dreams.' Alicia paused, her eyes narrowing as she tried to conjure the memory. 'It was the feeling I had when I awoke that kept me awake. It was an impression really. I felt as if she had come to visit me. The fear she felt worked its way to me. I knew . . . I know she's trying to warn me.'

David's gaze swung to Lark, his look a mix of bewilderment and anger. 'The psychic? She's trying to warn you?'

Alicia shook her head, her thoughts seemed to be miles away. Then her gaze moved to David. 'No dear, Lark is here to help me try to decipher the message. It was Theorosa's fear I felt.'

Lark caught the brief flicker of her own fear in Alicia's eyes before she masked it with a smile. Alicia lifted her drink to take a sip, then she paused, her glass just a breath from her lips. Her voice was soft, but easily reached those sitting at the table around her.

'I believe Theorosa's trying to warn me.'

Dinner had passed with relatively few disagreements. Still, Lark felt tired and wished deeply for a long, hot bath, then sleep. The rain pouring against the windows mixed soothingly with the music quietly drifting through the room and did not help her efforts to focus on what was being said. Sighing with resignation, she smiled yet again at Jeffrey as he spoke of other historical locations in the area. Lark's face felt as if it were straining at the effort of polite conversation. She and the young historian had ended up talking to each other when everyone was gathered in the parlor for an after dinner drink. Even though the two of them were talking among themselves, she noticed the nervous looks of the Tarrants occasionally flicking toward them, just as she saw the uneasy tolerance of David and Natalie. Only Thomas seemed to be oblivious to her presence.

She tried to maintain some sort of focus on what he was saying, but she continually found her thoughts drifting to the sound of Thomas's deep voice. He was talking quietly with his cousin. David's features were hard with the serious expression he wore as he murmured a response to Thomas's question. Thomas spoke, then his face lit with humor as he smiled at something David said. Lark found herself focusing on Thomas as if there were no one else in the room. She took in his handsome face and the relaxed poise of his body as he talked with his cousin. She could admire the sheer male beauty of him even as she felt envy for his ability to interact with others so easily. He turned and his eyes held hers. This time his smile did not leave his face, but softened. Suddenly she could sense his curiosity about her. His desire.

Lark frowned as she turned her head away. It confused her to learn his thoughts. Yet, she had learned long ago that people usually have mixed reactions to others. She shook herself free from the feelings and found Alicia had joined her and Jeffrey.

Jeffrey tugged at his tie as his excitement showed on his face. He seemed more nervous than normal. 'Mrs Blackwell, the castle is beautiful. I admire how your family has kept it up over the years.'

'Why thank you, that is really kind of you to say so.' Alicia smiled at him.

'The upkeep alone must be incredibly expensive.' His eyes never left Alicia's face as if he were trying to gauge her response. Alicia's smile never dimmed as she took a slow sip of her coffee.

'Not really. No more than I was willing to pay.'

Stephanie had slipped quietly to the edge of their little group. Lark wondered if the small woman hadn't lived most of her life in the fringes. She noticed Stephanie's voice usually started out somewhat strong, then ended weakly. 'I remember when the roof needed to be replaced. It staggered me when Aunt Alicia told me how much it was going to cost.'

Alicia looked as if she wished her niece would keep family matters out of the conversation. 'The Blackwells have always tried to maintain the original quality of the castle. Sometimes authenticity may seem expensive. Yet, history is important.'

'I can't tell you how relieved I am to hear that, Mrs Blackwell.' Lark watched in fascination as Jeffrey's enthusiasm ignited within him a flame of energy. The man's normally dull personality sparked and his nondescript, almost comical expression, lit with passion. The stance of his body even changed as he leaned toward Alicia.

'I realize the cost must be astronomical to maintain such an important part of history. I am very pleased to present an exciting proposition to you. My organization is prepared to make what I believe to be a very generous offer-'

Suddenly David and Thomas were both joining their group. David, whose hostility had been simmering close to the surface all evening, moved beside his grandmother as he spoke to Jeffrey. 'Sell the castle? You've got to be out of your mind.'

'It is not my intention to sell the castle, Jeffrey.' Alicia's voice was soft, but firm.

'Especially not to some loony, fly-by-night obscure group trying to save every pile of rock just in case someone important may have slept there once.' David's expression was dark with anger as he stood in front of Jeffrey. Everything about his words, his tone, and his stance were more than intimidating.

Jeffrey unexpectedly did not back away. His cheeks colored red, in clashing contrast to the orange-red of his hair. His eyes flashed with anger as his shoulders stiffened. 'The Kansans for Historical Preservation has been a leading group in saving historical landmarks in our state for over fifty years. That hardly makes us a "fly-by-night" organization.'

Lark could feel the tension that had been quietly present most of the evening growing ever tighter. David looked as if he were ready to take on the historian and Jeffrey looked only too willing to

49

please. Thomas put a hand on David's shoulder. 'Mr Linden, Blackwell Castle is our family home. It has been passed down several generations. I agree it does have a colorful history, but it is not a historical landmark.'

'But it could be, don't you see? The architectural history alone would qualify it.'

Alicia's eyes were hard, her voice strong with her dislike for the turn of the conversation. 'This is my home, Jeffrey. I've lived here all my married life.'

Lark perched on the broad ledge of a window and watched Linden's chin droop as he sulked. She could see him backing down from his confrontation, but he still held tightly to the righteousness of his resolve. 'But you said yourself history is important.'

'And it is.' Alicia agreed. She put her arm through David's in quiet reassurance as she spoke. 'However, I'm not talking about only Blackwell history. We are the Blackwells that are a part of that history. The castle will remain in the Blackwell family.'

Jeffrey shook his head, his small concession to defeat. 'Mrs Blackwell, I really think you should seriously consider my offer. It would make an incredible contribution to the people of this state.'

David stepped forward and grabbed him by the jacket. His face was dark, his eyes bright with anger. 'Do you not understand the meaning of "no"? I believe my grandmother has made it more than clear that Blackwell Castle is not going to be sold. Ever. It will be sold over my dead body.'

Thomas looked ready to restrain his cousin if he had to, but his voice remained calm. 'Take it easy, David. Grandmother has given her answer and even Mr Linden realizes he will have to accept that. There are no options.'

Jeffrey smiled wickedly as if he knew some powerful secret. 'There are always options, Mr Blackwell.'

David tightened the hold he had on the man's jacket. 'Is that a threat?'

Henry's normally jovial voice was tight with anger as he rose from the sofa. 'Wait a minute, young man. Blackwell Castle is not registered as a historical landmark.'

'But it would easily be accepted,' Jeffrey said, his eyes never leaving David's. Linden slowly began to pull himself out of his grasp.

'I am an attorney, Mr Linden,' Thomas said, moving to pour wine into his glass. He appeared to concentrate on the gesture, then turned back toward the man, 'and even you must know a house cannot be registered as a landmark against the owner's wishes.'

Jeffrey's chin lifted slightly. 'Again, I say there are always options.'

David shook his head with disgust as he stepped away. Lark could feel the anger radiating from him as he leaned against the corner of the fireplace. 'And just what are these incredible options of yours?'

'Public pressure for one.' Jeffrey walked to the center of the room. He turned quickly to face them all as he let his gaze move from one to another. 'What would the public think of an affluent family turning their back on the importance of history? Denying it to the little people? A family thumbing their noses at the very people who helped them become what they are, but refusing to give anything back to the community?'

Natalie, who had been surprisingly quiet, rose from her seat in a wing chair and sauntered past Jeffrey to the bar to fill her glass. She didn't even bother to face the man as she bit out her words. 'What would the public think of an organization using their influence to try to force a family out of their home? One that has been in the family for several generations.'

Linden's gaze was hard with anger as Natalie effectively shot down his words. Alicia's brow raised in reluctant admiration. 'Well said, Natalie. Jeffrey, I feel I owe you an apology. I love my home and your enthusiasm was so contagious I enjoyed sharing the castle with you. But it is my home, Jeffrey.' Alicia smiled at him, though her eyes were not yielding. 'I never intended to encourage you. I realize it's getting late, and I think it would be best if perhaps you went home.'

Lark looked out the window as sheets of rain poured against it. 'I think it's a little too late for that, Alicia.'

Natalie turned toward her, the woman's voice filled with sarcasm. 'Does your psychic "power" tell you he should stay?'

Lark met her gaze with amusement. 'No, I would merely call it the power of observation.'

John moved beside her to look out the window. 'She's right. The water is over the lower road and the wind is picking up.'

Stephanie bit at her lip with concern. 'I guess that means we're stuck here too, Aunt Alicia. I hope it's not an inconvenience.'

Alicia took her niece's arm and patted her hand soothingly. 'Of course not, sweetheart. I'll have Maria show you to a room.'

Henry set his drink on the table and moved to take Alicia's free hand. 'It's time for me to take my leave also. Thank you for dinner, Alicia, as always it was invigorating.'

Alicia frowned as her voice rose. 'You can't be serious. It's storming out there.'

'My house is just across the field. I'll be fine. It takes more than a storm to scare me.'

'Make sure you hold your umbrella way up in the air when you see lightning, Henry.' Thomas shook his head as he chuckled. His teasing comment served to lighten the mood of the room.

'We wouldn't want it to miss you, now would we, Henry,' David added.

'Boys! I don't find this the least bit amusing.' Alicia scowled at her grandsons, but Lark could see the twinkle of humor in her eyes. It was as if everyone had silently agreed to put the tension aside, at least for the rest of the night.

'If you want amusement, we could always send the psychic, or better yet, Jeffrey out there. That would definitely eliminate a few problems,' sniped Natalie.

Well, almost everyone, Lark thought as she watched Natalie smooth the tip of her finger on the rim of her glass. Stephanie's eyes widened as she gasped with shock.

'Natalie, sometimes I don't understand how you can be so waspish.'

The blonde's lips purred into a small smile as she studied the timid woman. 'That's awfully creative, Steph. Even for you.'

'That's enough.' John stepped to his wife and put his arm protectively around her shoulders.

Natalie looked ready to pounce again, when Alicia stepped in to head off yet another confrontation, her stern gaze reprimanding the woman. 'That's enough from everyone. My patience has worn thin and I think it's time we all retired to our beds.'

Alicia turned on Henry, her voice leaving no room for disagreement. 'Henry, you'll stay here and don't argue with me. I've had enough of that tonight.'

Jeffrey looked from the window to Alicia as he started to move toward the door. 'I appreciate your offer, but I have a four wheel drive. I've driven through worse weather than this, Mrs Blackwell. Thank you for dinner.'

Alicia took his hand and patted it with her other. Her voice was a quiet offer of peace. 'I've enjoyed your company in the past, Jeffrey, and tonight we had a disagreement. But I cannot in good conscience send you out in weather like this.'

Lark could see Linden's reluctant agreement in his eyes. Alicia squeezed his hand and chuckled good naturedly. 'You can stay till morning and I promise none of us will try to tar and feather you in your sleep.'

Jeffrey didn't look as if he found her joke comforting, but he laughed politely. Lark even found herself smiling at the thought as everyone except Natalie laughed.

John lifted his glass in a mock salute to the young man. He tried to keep from chuckling as he noted the man's nervousness. He winked and grinned at him. 'If I were you, I'd sleep with one eye open.'

They started to drift out of the room and the entire group headed toward the bedrooms. Lark smothered a yawn as she climbed the stairs. The day had been long and the evening tense. The man who had been haunting her dreams didn't want her there and someone had trashed her room in an effort to make her leave. Well, she thought to herself as she opened the door to her room, tomorrow had to be better.

The scream worked its way from the depths of his dreams till it caused him to sit upright in bed. Thomas looked around him, dazed and confused. The shadows of the night storm shifted wildly in his room as he tried to remember what had caused the sudden, intense fear that even now had his heart thudding.

Again a scream echoed through the castle. Only this time he knew it was not part of his dream.

Thomas flipped the covers back and leaped from his bed. He shrugged hurriedly into his robe even as he reached for the knob of his door. Throwing it open, he raced down the hall to the stairs, hearing other doors opening behind him.

Taking the steps two at a time, Thomas felt the fear well up within him. Something was terribly wrong. The air practically crackled with the tension. He reached the bottom of the staircase and listened. He could not shake the effect the memory of that scream had had on his nerves.

It had been a scream of fear and danger.

'Thomas, what has happened?' his grandmother called in a loud whisper. The silence of the night made it sound like a shout of alarm.

'I thought I heard someone screaming.' Natalie moved quickly down the stairway as the rest of the guests trailed behind.

Thomas stood in the hall as he tried to discern what direction the scream had come from. He held his hand up to signal them to be quiet. The sound of sobbing drifted from the library and he reacted immediately. He moved quickly to the closed doors of the library. On the first try of the old knob Thomas found it unmoving. But it was not unusual for the door to stick at times. He twisted the knob harder and felt it give as he opened the door.

Lightning flashed, briefly illuminating the room. Thomas felt the dread wash over him like an icy wave. Part of him did not want to believe the scene before him, even as another part of him wanted to close the door to keep the others from seeing what was inside the room.

The figure still sobbed, the sound a low pitiful moan as the person rocked slowly back and forth. Thomas could see the body partially hidden from view by the person crying. He ordered everyone to stay at the door as he slowly moved across the floor. His heart beat wildly as he looked down at the blank, unfocused stare of the historian. The wound, the blood, the smell of death permeated the room and Thomas knew there was no need to check for a pulse. Jeffrey Linden was dead.

Someone beside the door flipped the light switch on and the room was flooded with light. His grandmother gasped in shock as the others spoke in low murmurs behind him. Lark was kneeling by the body. Suddenly she looked at him as if finally noticing his presence. Thomas felt the revulsion run through him as she held her hands toward him.

'It won't go away.'

His gaze never left her eyes as she showed him her blood-stained hands. Her hair was a mass of tangled waves around her pale face covered with sweat. Lark's expression registered her confusion as she looked around her. She met his gaze again and he noted the dilation of her pupils.

'Lark, what happened?' Thomas watched as she simply stared at him. His words not getting through to her.

'Why won't it go away?'

Her voice was soft, almost a whisper, as she asked the question. Thomas took her by the shoulders and helped her to stand. His stomach tightened as he saw the blood staining the white linen of her nightgown. He started to lead her away from the body when she stiffened. Lark's eyes were focused on the dead man's face and her body began to shiver violently. She looked from the bloody wound of the man's head to the blood covering her own hands.

'Did I kill him?'

The words were quiet, but filled the room like thunder. Natalie glanced at David, then toward Lark. Thomas saw the dismay in his grandmother's eyes and the shock reflected in the eyes of all those looking at the woman beside him. No one answered her question, for it seemed like a rhetorical one.

CHAPTER 4

Lark knew she was dreaming. Dreaming of a haunted house where a bloody specter chased her as she tried to run on floors that lurched and tilted crazily under her. She felt dizzy, disoriented, as she continued to get lost deep in the bowels of the house.

She groaned as a wave of nausea washed over her, then she heard the voices. Disembodied and distant, she could hear them calling to her from the fringes of her consciousness.

She started to turn away from them till the deep sound of a man's voice stopped her. The fear swirling within her calmed and the desire to respond to the voice was overwhelming. He called again and Lark opened her eyes. She blinked, feeling the groggy weight of sleep pulling enticingly at her. She looked around her, momentarily uneasy when she didn't recognize her surroundings.

Then she remembered.

She was at the castle, she was sure, but not in her room. Lark lifted her head to look around her, then let it fall back immediately as, again, dizziness overcame her. Slowly she turned her head and knew that she wasn't in her own bed.

'Lark, sweetheart, you're awake.' It was Alicia's voice. Lark could hear her concern. Something was wrong. She could feel it almost as well as she could the warm comforter covering her.

'What has happened? Where am I?'

'You're in Thomas's room.' Alicia's brow knitted with concern and she looked questioningly away from her as if she didn't know how to answer the other question. It was then she noticed the others standing in the room. Dr Graham stood on the other side of the bed and gently took her wrist in his hand as he monitored her pulse. At the sight of Thomas sitting in a chair studying her intensely, Lark felt a pang of desire stir within her and her cheeks colored with her thoughts. Very easily, in the sleepy state she was in, could she imagine him alone with her in the room.

Thomas broke his gaze from her and looked away with a hint of anger. 'Does this really have to be done now, detective?'

'I'm afraid it does, Mr Blackwell.'

Lark turned a little too quickly toward the stranger's voice. Her vision blurred, then slowly the twinned images flowed together till she focused on a tall man. His ebony eyes fixed on her intensely. She could feel the dislike radiate from him.

'Obviously she's still very disoriented. I don't know that she can even fully comprehend what's being asked of her.'

Lark frowned at the sharpness of Thomas's voice. She moved to sit up and groaned as she clutched her head. The pain. Her head was killing her and she was so dizzy and confused. She couldn't even sense what was going on around her. Nor could she tell if Thomas's anger was directed at her or the man leaning against the bedroom wall.

'Disoriented or not, we have questions we need to ask her. It is imperative we try to get any answers we can as soon as possible,' he said as he pushed away from the wall. He walked toward the bed, then stopped as he once again studied Lark. 'I'm Detective Ron Baker, Miss Delavan, I understand you've had a rough night.'

Lark frowned as she tried to remember what had happened. Obviously she felt very ill, but a sense of foreboding worked through her mind as she realized she could not remember anything of the night before. Doubt clouded her thoughts and tears pooled in her eyes. 'I really don't know. I can't seem to remember anything.'

Lark watched the man's eyes look slightly toward Thomas and his lips tightened. She may still not be feeling well, but she was at least starting to sense things around her. The man standing before her was concentrating on her. Studying her. The intensity of his thoughts enabled her to pick up on him even though she was so ill. She quieted as she started focusing on him, interpreting what she could from him.

Lark's eyes widened as she began to understand and she looked at the man with fear. He was a detective, he had said as much, but she could feel something horrible had happened last night and that the man was convinced of her involvement. 'What has happened? Why are you here?'

She felt Alicia's hand on her shoulder as the woman sat beside her on the bed. 'Sweetheart, something terrible has happened.'

'Mrs Blackwell, please let me continue.' The detective looked sternly at Alicia.

'I believe, Detective Baker, this is my house and Lark is my guest. Do not use that tone with me.'

He leaned toward her, his tall frame looming over the foot of the bed. 'This is an investigation, Mrs Blackwell. Don't try to get in my way.'

Thomas rose, then moved to stand beside Lark. 'Are you charging Miss Delavan with anything, detective?'

Baker studied Thomas's stern face for a moment. 'Not at the moment, Mr Blackwell. I only wish to ask her a few questions.'

'Then I'll ask you to get straight to the point,' Thomas said. 'Obviously she's been through a lot and needs to get her rest.'

Baker's lips thinned with his anger, but he nodded. 'Of course, although I must say I hadn't realized you were now taking on criminal cases.'

Lark looked to Thomas questioningly. Criminal cases? He still was holding Baker's gaze as the two men measured each other. Fear sparked anger within her and she looked to the faces around her.

'What the hell is going on? Why are all of you in here and why is he talking about criminal cases?' Lark asked as she pointed toward the detective.

Henry smiled softly. 'It's good to see some energy out of you, young lady. You were pretty sick last night.'

'What happened?' She closed her eyes tightly and rubbed at her pounding temples with her fingertips. The dizziness seemed to have subsided as long as she didn't make any sudden, large movements. 'Why am I sick?'

'Good question, Miss Delavan. But first tell me what is the last thing you remember?'

Lark opened her eyes and frowned at the detective's question. She searched through her memory and realized with alarm that a large chunk of it was gone. 'I remember helping the girl, LeAnn, clean up my room, then getting dressed for the evening. I had been told that Mrs Blackwell was going to have a dinner party in honor of my arrival.'

'Then what?' The detective lost some of his defensive stance as he listened, but Lark did not miss the pen in his hand quickly, concisely taking notes.

In her mind's eye she tried to push farther into the recesses of her memory. Blurry, confusing images emerged to shimmer briefly in her thoughts, then slid elusively away before she could connect with them. Mentally, Lark shook herself from the images to find everyone watching her expectantly.

'I really don't know. I can recall some things, but I could not tell you whether they were real or not.'

Alicia looked quickly toward Henry, but not before Lark saw the alarm in her eyes. Henry took Mrs Blackwell's hand and patted it reassuringly. 'I can't say that surprises me, dear.'

Lark felt as if the floor was about to crash from under her. She was having a very hard time trying to follow the conversation. The words were not registering with her brain and as she tried to catch them, they skittered away from her.

'I don't understand.' Even to her, her voice sounded almost desperate. She could hear her own fear.

Lark felt a momentary sense of relief when Baker removed his gaze from her. She could tell he didn't like her, but she had no idea why.

'It is my understanding that you were the one to take care of her when she was found?'

'Yes, I was.' Henry did not elaborate, but merely returned the detective's gaze.

'What was her condition?'

'Miss Delavan was disoriented and confused. She was dizzy, light-headed, and drenched with sweat.' Lark watched with a growing sense of disbelief as Henry removed his glasses to clean them with a handkerchief while he answered the detective.

'From a fever?' Baker looked up briefly from his notes.

'No.' Henry put his glasses on with an air of determination and faced the detective as he folded his arms behind him in a deliberate stance of authority. 'I believe it to be part of a reaction. She had considerable trouble focusing her eyes and walking. And I would also say she was somewhat delusional considering some of the things she was talking about.'

'You mentioned reaction?' Baker eyed Henry speculatively. 'Reaction to what?'

'I obviously won't know that till the tests come back from the samples I gave to your technicians, but I strongly believe she was poisoned.'

'What?' Lark clutched at the comforter. Somehow she had awakened from a bad dream only to find herself in the reality of a nightmare. The information was starting to overwhelm her and Lark didn't know whether to laugh or cry because it didn't seem real. It could not be real, she tried to convince herself.

'Who would want to poison her?'

Lark glanced toward Thomas as he spoke and was startled to find him so close to her. He held her gaze as he placed his hand gently on her shoulder.

'Perhaps whoever ransacked her room.' Alicia looked as if she instantly regretted saying the words. She glanced quickly at Thomas and said nothing more.

Baker, however, picked up on her unease and turned his dark gaze on her. 'When did this happen, Mrs Blackwell?'

Lark did not know Alicia well, but she had never seen her nervous till now. Under the detective's hard gaze, Alicia was tense. Lark knew she would normally be able to pick up on why, but at the moment her thoughts were not flowing smoothly enough.

Alicia glanced again to Thomas who gave her a nod of assurance. 'It happened earlier in the day. At the time we didn't think much of it. It pains me to admit, but most of my family was not pleased that I brought Lark here.'

'Why was she brought here?' To Lark the detective's question seemed almost rhetorical, because she could feel that he seemed to already know.

'I'm a psychic.' Her back stiffened at the words, knowing how ridiculous they sounded. To the detective's credit he didn't laugh, but only smirked at her.

A low noise came from Alicia's throat and, if Lark wasn't mistaken, sounded very much like a growl. 'Detective Baker, Miss Delavan has quite a reputation and I had to persuade her to come help me with a very special request. She is here because I asked her to be here.'

Baker studied Alicia for a moment. Lark could see that the detective knew he'd better not push Alicia Blackwell too far. He lost some of his smirk, but apparently couldn't resist one last shot. 'That would explain the animosity of the family.'

'I think animosity would be too strong a word.' She was surprised to hear Thomas speaking in her defense.

Baker's gaze returned to her, causing Lark to take a deep breath. 'So the room was ransacked and you helped the maid clean it up, is that correct?'

'Yes, I do remember that.'

'Has anyone made threats toward you?'

'No.' Lark could feel her thoughts starting to organize and make sense. It gave her a small sense of security to be able to think somewhat coherently because a part of her knew that a lot was riding on this line of questioning. Desperately she wished she were functioning at her full capacity. She truly felt as if she were missing important elements of the conversation going on around her.

Baker's gruff voice broke into her thoughts and reluctantly she returned her attention to him. 'How did you know Jeffrey Linden?'

'The historian?' she asked as she frowned, then shrugged with confusion. 'I met him yesterday. I do seem to remember that neither of us felt exactly welcome here.'

Alicia took her hand in hers and held it tightly. 'I'm so sorry I brought you into this, Lark. It was never my intention to make you feel uncomfortable. And I would never have wanted this to happen.'

There it was again. Lark could feel that something had happened, but perhaps because of her confused state, she could not pick up on even the most obvious nuances. 'Alicia, please tell me what has happened. I know something is wrong.'

Alicia took a deep breath and Lark was startled to see tears in the elder woman's eyes. 'Jeffrey was killed last night, Lark.'

'In the storm?'

Lark felt the dazed disbelief and distress at the death of this man she barely knew, but somehow there seemed to be more. Everyone looked to her with sympathy, till she met the dark gaze of Detective Baker. His lips tightened into a grim smile and, if she didn't know better, she thought he took great pleasure in inflicting his words on her.

'No, Miss Delavan. He was found with severe blunt force trauma to the head.'

She gasped and her heart pounded. Suddenly a very horrible vision filled her thoughts. It was the bloody specter of her dream, but now it was the historian's dead eyes focused unseeing on her. A cold chill moved over her and she shivered. Lark looked around her and noticed they were all looking at her. Watching her.

'What does this have to do with me?'

'Apparently your umbrella was used as the murder weapon.' He leaned closer till she focused on his face. 'And you were found kneeling beside the body.'

'What?' Her voice was a shriek, a terrified shrill noise to her own ears. She looked to Thomas and his face was unmoving as he simply met her gaze. Fear infused ice into her veins and she was suddenly very cold. Her voice shook. 'That's impossible. I don't remember anything.'

'I'd say that was convenient, wouldn't you?' the detective stated with an unfriendly smile.

Thomas reacted quickly. His sudden movement surprised her as he shifted toward the detective, but then stopped as he pulled himself under control. He stood next to the man not saying anything till Baker was forced to meet his angry gaze. 'Detective, unless you're going to charge her, I must ask you to leave. Now.'

'No problem, Mr Blackwell.' Baker smiled knowingly as he slipped his note pad into his suit pocket. He shifted away slightly, his stance seemingly relaxed as if they were old friends. 'Oh, by the way, I want her at the station by tonight.'

Henry snorted at the man letting him know what he thought of his order. 'I don't believe you understand the severity of what she's been through.'

'I'm sure even you, doctor, understand the severity of this crime. She had better be at the station or I'll come after her with a warrant.' Baker shifted his gaze to her, his dark eyes relishing every word. 'I've looked in to you, Miss Delavan. I know something about you. This time you won't beat the charge quite so easily.'

Thomas's brows dipped into a frown and his shoulders stiffened. 'Just what are you getting at?'

Baker smiled, then looked from Thomas to Lark. She hadn't ever truly hated anyone, but at that moment she understood the feeling quite well. Humiliation and fear swept over her as her cheeks colored at his words. She faced him and refused to let her eyes waver from his as she lifted her chin defiantly.

He chuckled as he noted the gesture and her silence. 'This wouldn't be the first time you've been charged with murder, now would it, Lark?'

The detective's words hung heavily in the air. Alicia's hands loosened on her own, but Lark had to admire that she never let go of her hand. She felt the hot tears of the humiliation he was throwing on her sting the corners of her eyes, but she refused to let them see her cry. She could feel their gazes on her and she forced herself to meet them. She saw pity and concern in Henry's and Alicia's eyes, but it was Thomas's look of anger and slight revulsion that sliced through her. She thought she had protected herself from that kind of hurt a long time ago. Obviously some things could still get through to her, she thought. Like the look of distaste on his handsome face. How she wished she could make him understand.

'No, it's not the first time.' Lark held Thomas's gaze. She forced her voice to be strong, even as the tears burned in her eyes. 'What he is saying is true.'

Lark stood in front of the bridge. She did not move toward it. She could feel the sensations of the structure moving through her, but she blocked her thoughts to them. She could not concentrate on the past as she had been brought here to do, but had to remind herself that what was going on now was what could harm her.

After the detective had left and the others had quietly left the room, she had fallen into a very disturbed sleep. When she awoke, she had felt much better, had even regained a lot of her energy, but the memory of the looks on the faces of the Blackwells and Dr Graham had remained with her. She had been the focus of that look more times than her heart cared to remember. In their faces she had seen the shock. In their eyes she had seen the seed of doubt. Images of many other faces with the same look superimposed themselves into her thoughts and Lark closed her eyes against the tears that threatened.

She lifted her face to the wind and relaxed in its gentle caress. She took a deep breath and inhaled the fresh air of the afternoon. The sun was warm and bright, helping to quickly dry the drench of the previous night's storm. When she had wakened, Lark had slipped quietly outside just so she could be alone for a moment. Soon enough they would look for her and she would have to face what she already knew from experience would be a grueling evening.

Lark turned and focused on a stand of tall cotton-woods not far from the bridge. When she first came to Kansas she had been fascinated by the movement of the trees in the wind. When she truly needed to relax, she would focus her thoughts on the movement of the breeze as it gently rocked the blades of grass or the limbs of bushes. The comforting rhythm made her feel cradled, protected, cared for. Cottonwoods had more energy to their movement, a frantic ease that winked and danced in the air like a light melody on a flute. It had pulled from her a smile when she had first seen them. Now she desperately wished they could do the same this time. A man was dead and they said she was found kneeling over him with his blood all over her.

She took a deep breath, unable to stop the sob gripping her. Frantically she tried to search her memory and still she could find nothing to explain how or why this had happened. Lark bit her lip, unable to stop the tears from spilling down her cheeks.

It was happening again, she thought to herself. This time she might understand the feelings, the sensations, the images, coming from somewhere within her, but it did not stop the fear. The fear of being horribly intertwined with murder.

Lark hesitated. She felt him before she heard him behind her and quickly wiped away the tears from her eyes' before he could see. 'Thomas, were you afraid I had run away?'

She turned to face him and felt the incredible pull of his eyes. He said nothing, simply held her gaze as if trying to read her thoughts. Once again, she was reminded that this is what it must be like for others when they were around her. She looked away as if that alone would shield from him what she was thinking.

Thomas stepped forward and took her chin in his hand. He tilted her face up for his inspection. His gaze moved over her face, pausing on her reddened eyes, then stopped for a brief moment on her lips. For an instant, the only small moment she would allow herself, she wanted him to kiss her.

His hand dropped and he gave her a concerned smile. 'I wanted to make sure you were okay, Lark.'

'I feel better, thank you.' Lark cleared her throat and stepped away from him to walk to the edge of the small stream stretching lazily under the abandoned bridge. As she stared into the shimmering rustle of the water she heard him move beside her.

She felt a connection with this man. She didn't know if it was right or wrong, based on the fantasy of her dreams, or the reality of his presence, but she felt an ease with him she had never had with anyone else, including her own family. Somehow she felt a level of acceptance from him for what she was.

Lark grimaced with amusement. What a ludicrous thought. Thomas Blackwell would accept her good bye with more enthusiasm than he would accept her for what she was.

She closed her eyes for a moment and concentrated on the man beside her. She frowned as the sensations washed over her. Lark opened her eyes, then faced him. 'Why are you here? And don't tell me I should already know the answer to that.'

Thomas smiled and looked away from her to study the trees across the stream. By the amused look on his face, she wondered if that was what he had indeed planned on saying to her.

'I probably deserve that.' He turned to study her with those potent eyes of his. 'I'm concerned for you.'

Lark shook her head at his words. She could not recall anything that had happened the night before. It frightened her that her memories had been taken from her, leaving only an empty void of doubt. A black void that made her feel cold with isolation.

'Why?' She simply looked into his eyes as she softly spoke the words. 'Why are you concerned about me? I thought it was your driving desire to get me away from your grandmother.'

'Grandmother takes care of herself as I'm sure you've already figured out for yourself,' Thomas said as he chuckled. Slowly the smile slid from his lips and he became serious. 'I'll be honest with you, Lark, and I hope you will be honest with me. Considering what you're getting ready to face, I think it is imperative that we be forthright with each other.'

Lark quietly nodded her agreement. Thomas noted the movement, then turned back to study the trees across the stream. He placed his hands on his hips and though he seemed relaxed, she could see the concentration on his handsome face.

'I want to help you.'

'Why?' The word was out of her mouth before she could control the shock it had sprung from. She cleared her throat, then shrugged. 'Look, Thomas, I understand you're probably doing this because Alicia asked you to, but really it's not necessary.'

'My grandmother does not know we are even having this discussion.'

Lark watched him for a moment as she let his words sink in. 'I know I keep saying this, but why? You don't know me and till this morning, you couldn't have cared less if I were here or not.'

'I won't deny that in the beginning, I didn't want you here, Lark.' His words bruised her, but at least Thomas was telling the truth. She knew he had not wanted her here. 'But I don't want to see you hurt by this.'

Lark studied him. Waited till his gaze lifted to meet hers. 'Do you think I killed Jeffrey?'

'Grandmother doesn't think so and she trusts you.' Thomas looked to her. 'I respect my grandmother greatly and I trust her judgement.'

'I guess that was meant to be comforting,' she stated flatly.

'I'm a lawyer.' Thomas bent over to pick a few pebbles from the sand. He took one and tossed it into the water as he spoke. 'It's hard for me to make judgements on anything till I review all the facts pertaining to the case.'

'Damn it, Thomas. I'm not a case. At least not yet.' Lark felt her frustration flood through her as she ran her hands through her hair. How could she feel so strongly about a man and he be so totally ambivalent toward her? 'And people have been judging me all my life. If that's all the help you can offer me, then I'll pass on it, thank you.'

Lark turned to walk away till she felt his hand on her arm. She looked at his hand, then to his face as she waited for him to speak.

'I'm sorry, Lark. I always seem to say the wrong thing around you, don't I?' He pulled her back to where she had stood before, but somehow she seemed to be standing closer to him. 'I just want to help you through this.'

Lark hesitated. The feel of his warm hands against her made her reluctant to leave, but it was what she felt from him that made her stay. Thomas was telling her the truth. He really did want to help her.

'I can't remember anything from last night, Thomas. My umbrella was used to kill Jeffrey and they said I was found kneeling over him with his blood all over me. That makes me the prime suspect in a lot of people's eyes and if you throw in my background, you might as well throw in the towel.'

Lark wrapped her arms around herself as a chill ran through her. She had not allowed herself to say the words out loud till now and she was frightened. Spoken in the quiet clearing they stood in, the words took on an ominous tone.

Thomas ran his hand up her arm to hold her shoulder as a sign of reassurance. 'Lark, we haven't seen any of the reports yet. We don't know what the autopsy will reveal about how Jeffrey died and we don't know what the crime lab will come up with when they finish processing their material. I think it's still too early for you to start wondering how you would look in stripes, don't you?'

'I doubt the killer would have been stupid enough to leave his or her fingerprints behind, Thomas.' Lark stopped and forced herself to take a deep breath. She appreciated his effort and gave him a small smile. 'I'm sorry I snapped at you.'

He squeezed her shoulder gently, then let his hand drop. 'This hasn't been the best day for any of us, Lark. I think you're entitled to be a little grumpy.'

She nodded, then took one of the pebbles from his hand. She tossed it into the water and watched the ripples fade quickly into the current. She was reluctant to speak because she knew that they now would have to go talk with the police.

All her life she had been taught to face whatever challenge was sent her way. This time should not be different, she reassured herself, but a part of her remained hesitant as she continued to watch the stream sliding smoothly by. She had no memories of what had happened last night. No sense of security in herself that she did not kill Jeffrey. She had already witnessed the seeds of doubts in these people's expressions. But, it was her own doubt that plagued her most. Dr Graham had voiced his suspicions that she had been poisoned and became very ill because of it.

But had it been enough to make her kill another human being?

Thomas placed his hand on her back. His voice was quiet as he spoke to her. 'It's time to go now, Lark.'

She looked at him and nodded silently. They turned and began walking to the house. 'I know. Let's just get this over with.'

The interrogation room was plain. The walls were a dirty beige and were not interrupted by any windows. A table stood in the middle of the room, the surface pock-marked with cigarette burns. Detective Baker took the chair facing the door, pointing for them to sit across from him as he pulled the tape recorder toward him.

Thomas pulled out the chair for Lark as he gave Baker a stern look. 'I hope we can get this over with as soon as possible, detective.'

'I'm sorry, Mr Blackwell, if this murder has in the least inconvenienced you.' Baker returned Thomas's look with a hard one of his own.

Thomas merely raised his brow with a small hint of amusement. Lark knew he was baiting the man and hoped he wouldn't go too far.

'Let's just say I don't like having strings pulled and having a prime suspect running around loose without a care in the world.'

'She was poisoned, if you care to remember,' Thomas said as he sat down next to Lark.

Baker leaned forward, his face looking ghostly in the pool of light concentrated in the center of the table. 'I guess we won't know till the tests come back whether she was poisoned or not.'

The detective then focused his gaze on Lark, accusing and unrelenting. 'I don't mind telling you, Miss Delavan, that if it were left to me, I would have you dressed in Sedgwick County orange till we've concluded our investigation. I do not appreciate someone using his influence to make sure one of his friends receives preferential treatment.'

He leaned forward, once again the light causing a stark image in the hollows of his dark face. 'Preferential or not, I intend to get to the bottom of this. And I won't let anything keep me from pursuing your involvement in this case.'

Lark did not flinch. Her heart pounded and her palms were sweating as Baker's animosity bombarded her, but she refused to crumple under his pressure. She waited a moment, noting the vein in the center of his forehead pulsing with anger. Her gaze moved back to his; she knew he was angry; he knew she knew it also.

'If you're done now, may we get started?'

He studied her for a moment as if assessing her strength. His lips thinned into a grim line, then he pulled his notebook from his pocket and opened it in front of him. Baker placed a tape in the recorder, started it, adjusted a few buttons, and slid it closer to Lark. He went through the routine opening remarks of the case file.

Baker held his pen balanced between his two hands as he focused on her. 'Let's start with whether you remember our conversation this morning?'

'Yes.'

'Good, then let's go over again what your recollections of last night were?'

Lark hesitated as she searched the fog of her memory. She had tried again and again to conjure up any image, but had not been able to produce anything. 'I can't say that I really remember anything.'

Baker lifted one hand and shrugged. 'No images, nothing?'

'Images, yes.' She slid her hair behind her ear nervously with her finger. 'I don't know if they're real or part of the bad dream I had.'

'What are the images of?' he asked as he glanced up from his note pad.

Lark tilted her head as she looked at a point above his head. She unconsciously squinted her eyes as she tried to remember the horrible images that had assaulted her during the night. 'I was walking, maybe running, down the hallway because of a voice. I remember I kept seeing a face. I didn't recognize it at first till they told me Jeffrey had been killed, then I realized it was his face I was seeing.'

'You said you didn't know the victim well?' Baker asked.

'No, I did not.' Lark felt a little more at ease as the anger seemed to slip from his voice. His stance even seemed to visibly relax.

'When did you last see him alive?'

'I don't know,' she answered with a hint of confusion. She looked hesitantly toward Thomas. 'I would assume that I spoke with him during dinner, then, perhaps, afterward.'

'Mr Blackwell?' Baker looked toward Thomas questioningly.

Thomas slid his arm along the back of Lark's chair and she welcomed his presence.

'Yes, Lark did speak with him several times during the course of the evening.'

The detective nodded, then concentrated on his note pad for a moment. 'Who attended this dinner party?'

'Lark and I.' Thomas shrugged as he started ticking off the names with his finger on the table. 'My grandmother, Dr Graham, my cousin David, a friend Natalie, my cousin Stephanie, and her husband John. And of course, Mr Linden.'

'Of course.' Baker returned his attention to his note pad. A part of Lark wanted to know what was so fascinating about it considering how much time he spent looking at it. She could see it pretty well and knew that the scribble was barely decipherable. The detective focused on her and she could tell by the gleam in his eye that the relaxed pose he had been taking had been just that, a pose. He had let her relax in the unassuming line of questioning and now he was ready to start cutting into her without allowing her much time to prepare herself.

'Lark, would you explain to me why you were found kneeling beside the body?'

'I've told you before I don't know why.' Lark felt her mouth dry with her unease.

She looked hesitantly toward Thomas and he nodded his reassurance. She nervously cleared her throat. 'I do not remember anything.'

Baker tapped his pen impatiently on the note pad. 'Could you explain how your umbrella was used to kill this man?'

'I wish I knew.' Lark again flicked her gaze toward Thomas. Her chest felt as if it were tightening with the fear enveloping her. Baker was effectively backing her into an emotional corner. Thomas, as if sensing her apprehension, slid his hand from the back of her chair to touch her between her shoulder blades. The detective could not see that he was touching her, but the warmth of him that she felt through her shirt reassured her more than words from him would have.

'It's a rather unusual item.' Baker smiled at her. She realized the gesture was not meant to be friendly. She would almost guess it was his unconscious warning. 'Where did you get it?'

She licked her lips hesitantly. 'It was custom made for someone in my family a long time ago.'

The detective seemed satisfied for a moment when he leaned back in his chair and continued to smile.

Lark felt the push of his presence ease off and she slowly exhaled. For the next thirty minutes, he repeated questions he had already asked her, then had her clarify them yet again. The tension started to ease from her as she began to realize that the man was finally winding up his questioning.

Thomas had been quiet so far. Occasionally he would nod his reassurance if she glanced toward him or she would feel the movement of his hand on her back as he soothed her with his touch. She was grateful for his presence and understood the impatience she felt growing from him.

Thomas leaned slightly forward as the detective let a moment of silence fall between them. 'Are you close to being finished, Baker?'

'Not quite, Blackwell. I realize you're probably not familiar with this kind of proceeding.' Baker leaned back in his chair, his pose that of relaxed ease. Lark had a feeling that he was enjoying this entirely more than she would have liked to admit as he focused his attention on her and grinned. 'But you are, aren't you, Lark?'

Thomas drummed his fingers on the surface of the scarred table. 'Get to the point, detective.'

'Sure. Let's talk about the other, what should we call it, Lark? Incident?' Baker placed his hands on the table, then shrugged with amusement as he continued to study her. He tapped the table with his hand for emphasis. 'Yes, incident would be the word I would use. What can you tell me about that?'

Lark gritted her teeth as she held the hateful man's gaze. Again, the pain and humiliation rushed through her, but she had learned by experience how to push it away and distance herself. She took a slow deep breath, then spoke calmly and concisely. 'As I'm sure you have already discovered, I was charged with murder.'

'Murder?' Baker asked in mock surprise. He clutched his hand to his chest and his eyes widened as he regarded her in pretended shock. 'How is it that someone like yourself gets involved in not one, but two murders?'

Lark would have enjoyed telling him what he could do with his heavy sarcasm, but knew it would only provoke him. Instead she settled for a sweet smile. 'Just lucky I guess.'

The detective's gaze hardened and his lips tightened with restrained anger. 'You won't be so flippant when we get done with you.'

Her anger swelled within her and she felt the tears threaten. The man's dark scrutiny belittled her, and she felt ineffective in protecting herself from the enjoyment she saw in his eyes as he inflicted painful humiliation with his countless pointed questions.

Lark slapped her hand against the table. 'Let me ask you this, Detective Baker. Are you even pursuing other avenues in your investigation? What other suspects have you come up with?'

Baker continued with his Cheshire cat smile, his teeth a gleaming contrast to the darkness of his skin, and proceeded with the next question without even so much as acknowledging her outburst. 'You were charged with the murder of a teenage girl back in your home state of California, is that correct?'

Her anger burned her cheeks and she took a few deep breaths as she tried to bring it under control. It was the warmth of Thomas's hand smoothing a small reassuring circle on her back that kept her from bursting into tears. 'Yes, I was.'

'Please explain why you were charged, Miss Delavan.'

Lark ran her hand through her hair as she took a steadying breath to remove the tremor from her voice. Sadness colored her expression as she met the detective's gaze. 'I went to the police with information I had regarding the murder. They took little note of what I had say. I left the station wondering why I had even bothered, but the images would not leave me alone.'

'These would be your so called "psychic" images?'

She glared at the detective and the sarcasm in his voice. 'Yes. I concentrated on the images and the sensations I felt and found the girl's body.'

'If you found the body, then why did they charge you, Lark?' Baker asked, crossing his arms over his chest.

'Because they figured the only way I could know so much about what had happened to the girl was because I had killed her myself.' Lark didn't care what the detective thought of her. She closed her eyes against the memory of the young woman's battered body, then opened them to focus on her hands clasped in her lap.

'How did you beat the rap?'

She looked up and met the dislike in his gaze with that of her own. Her voice was hard as she answered him. 'I did not beat the rap, as you call it, Baker. The girl's murderer confessed after he was captured later for robbing a bank.'

Baker chuckled as he sprawled casually in his chair. 'Do you know where this girl's murderer is now?'

Tiredly Lark shook her head, then rubbed at her throbbing forehead. 'No, but I'm sure you're about to tell me.'

He laughed at her words, then tapped his hand on the table. He looked and acted like he was having a friendly conversation with an old pal. 'He's in the state hospital back in California. He was declared legally insane and has been knitting doilies or weaving baskets since then with the rest of the residents of the cuckoo nest.'

'Baker, I consider your comments insensitive and rude.' Thomas leaned forward, the movement causing him to encircle Lark more within his arm. 'Not to mention that even you know that the insanity plea has enjoyed its height of popularity. Obviously, Lark was cleared of all charges and that "incident", as you call it, has no relevance to what is going on now.'

'I agree, Blackwell, no relevance at all, except for the fact that she's been fingered as the prime suspect twice in two separate murder investigations.' The detective raised his brows as he shrugged, then turned to contemplate a section of the bland wall. 'As long as she was in my house, friend, I would sleep with my door locked.'

Thomas flattened his palms on the table. 'Have you concluded your questioning, sir?'

Baker continued to study the wall as his lips tightened into a small smile. 'Yeah, I think that will do it, don't you? And since you've pulled such influential strings, Blackwell, I'll even let her go home with you, but I'm sure you know the routine about any sudden trips.'

Thomas rose, then held the chair for Lark as she joined him. The detective remained seated, staring with elaborate interest at some imaginary spot on the wall as they left the room without a word. At the door she hesitated for a moment to glance back at the detective. It disturbed her to find him staring at her with such intensity, as if she were a specimen pinned to the board. She felt Thomas's hand on her elbow and she left.

She couldn't dispel, however, the feeling that the detective was toying with her like a cat would a mouse by letting her 'escape' only so that he could, at a later time, 'catch' her.

CHAPTER 5

'Mrs Blackwell, she makes me nervous. We really don't know that she didn't kill Mr Linden.'

'I know she didn't.'

Lark stopped at the end of the long hall, unseen by the two women. The maid, LeAnn, was twisting her hands nervously in front of her as she talked to Alicia. Calmly, Mrs Blackwell took her hand and patted it reassuringly as she smiled.

'LeAnn, I know you had special feelings for Jeffrey. He was a sincere and nice man, but Lark had nothing to do with this tragedy. Do you understand that?'

LeAnn's lips puckered angrily as her eyes filled with tears. 'He wasn't just a "nice" man. He was intelligent and thoughtful. And none of this would have happened if that woman hadn't come here. There is no such thing as ghosts.'

Alicia's brows dipped into a concerned frown as she continued to hold the woman's hand, but her voice became firm. 'Please try to remember that she is my guest, LeAnn. Now you go on and finish up the bedrooms for me. Oh, and could you also run some clean towels to Stephanie's room? She's apparently come down with the flu and is quite ill. I'm going to the kitchen to fix her a cup of broth and see if she can keep that down, the poor dear.'

The thin woman nodded at what Alicia said, but yet still she hesitated. The maid seemed tense as her eyes skittered from one point to the next, but never quite meeting the older woman's own.

Alicia appeared to pick up on her unease. 'LeAnn, is there something wrong?'

LeAnn bit her lip as she finally met Mrs Blackwell's gaze. She looked as if she were about to speak, her mouth opening, then she clamped her lips shut, a dark frown creased her forehead and she shook her head. She quickly entered one of the many rooms on the floor, leaving Alicia to watch her for a moment as she disappeared from view.

Alicia turned to start down the hallway, but stopped when she saw Lark standing there.

Lark knew they had been talking about her. She could even understand why the woman felt the way she did. But it didn't make her feel any better.

Alicia came to her and put her arm tightly around her. To her credit, she didn't even pretend that Lark had not heard what had been said.

'No matter what, Lark, keep your chin up.' Alicia gave her a squeeze as she spoke gently to her. 'We'll get through this.'

Lark nodded to Alicia and gave her a smile of assurance, then the two women went their own directions. Lark let her hand skim down the smooth wood of the stairway as she descended. She could hear Thomas's cousin David talking in a low voice with someone so she bypassed the front door and headed toward the kitchen exit. She breathed a sigh of relief when she didn't encounter anyone and closed the door behind her.

Stepping outside, Lark immediately felt better. The wind lifted her hair and she closed her eyes as she raised her face to the sun. She opened them and put her hands in the pocket of the red sweater she wore over her jeans as she stepped from the porch.

She picked her way across the yard and headed toward the bridge to go for a short walk. As she approached the driveway, she heard footsteps. The last thing Lark wanted to do at the moment was answer any questions the others might have about what had happened. In all truth, how could she answer them? She couldn't remember anything.

Lark stepped quickly behind the sheltering green of the arborvitae that edged behind the garage. The dark wall of the trees extended a little way past the garage also serving to hide the tool shed from the view of visitors. She found herself standing at the back doorway of the garage. She leaned against the door and listened as the voices melted into the sounds of the wind. Whoever it was passed and Lark let out the breath that she had been holding.

Suddenly the door she was leaning against opened and Lark fell backwards. She was caught by a pair of strong arms and she found herself looking into Thomas's amused eyes.

'Were you hiding, Lark?' He chuckled, making no move to help her get back to her feet. 'Or do you just enjoy standing behind garages?'

'No.'

She shifted and he was obliged to help her straighten herself. Lark stood, then realizing how close she was to him, she moved a safe distance away. 'Well . . . yes, I was hiding. I don't know if I'm ready to talk to anyone yet.'

He studied her, a soft look on his face. He lifted his hand and smoothed a strand of her hair away from her face with his finger. The touch of him along her cheek caused seductive chills to move through her and she pulled her sweater tighter around her.

'We aren't going to hang you at the nearest tree, Lark,' he said quietly. 'We aren't that bad.'

'I know. I just really don't feel up to answering questions right now.' Lark found herself staring at his chest. His shirt was unbuttoned more than she would have liked. She cleared her throat and forced herself to meet his gaze. 'I . . . uh . . . can sense the unease of some of the people who are around me. After all, I was found kneeling beside the body.'

Thomas hooked his finger under her chin and tilted her face up to his. His expression was solemn, and full of what she could only hope was understanding. 'Henry thinks you were poisoned, which would explain a lot of things.'

Lark could find herself getting lost easily in his eyes. When he looked at her like he was looking at her now, she could even stop thinking. She could forget what was going on around her. She licked her lips, then moved out of his touch. 'You have an answer for everything, don't you, Thomas?'

'I'm a lawyer, remember?'

Lark chuckled, feeling more at ease with him than she ever had before. 'Which makes you even lower in stature than I am in some people's opinions.'

'Believe me, I know.' Thomas stepped away from her to lean against the trunk of a black BMW convertible with its top down. He looked relaxed as he smiled at her. 'There's even an internet site dedicated to lawyer jokes.'

He crossed his arms over his chest as he grinned at her. 'Do you know what the definition of a "crying shame" is?'

She returned his smile as she thought for a moment, then shrugged her shoulders. 'I don't know, what?'

'A bus load of lawyers going over a cliff and there's one empty seat.'

Lark laughed and Thomas grinned at her amusement. She joined him as she leaned against the trunk and quieted to an occasional chuckle. She shook her head at the idea of him telling her the joke. She studied the tools hanging neatly on their hooks on the wall as she thought about the man beside her.

Lark ran her fingers through her hair, then smoothed it with a flip from her neck. It felt good to be talking with him as a person. Right now, he made her feel almost normal. She didn't feel like a psychic. Just at the idea, she started feeling sensations from the man standing next to her and she promptly shut them out. She didn't want to be a psychic at the moment.

Thomas turned to her almost as if he too could sense the direction of her thoughts. He stood in front of her, almost over her, as he pushed her hair from her face. His fingers brushed her cheek, then moved to cup her neck. He gently caressed the sensitive skin of her throat as his gaze moved over her face.

'It's nice to know you can still laugh, Lark. You're beautiful when you do.'

His voice was as soft as his touch on her. Those incredible, magical eyes of his held her as he leaned toward her. She watched in fascination as his lids lowered when his lips touched hers. He only touched her briefly as his lips hovered over hers, ready to take hers yet again.

Lark put her hand on him and her palm flattened against the smooth skin of his chest. Her heart had started to beat wildly when he'd touched her, now she felt as if it were quivering in her throat. Even her words sounded shaky to herself.

'Thomas, I don't know if this is a good – '

'It's not,' he interrupted, kissing the corners of her mouth, 'but I still want to touch you anyway.'

'You don't even know me,' she whispered as he lightly feathered kisses across her cheek. Her hands rested on the swell of his biceps, enjoying the movement of his arms as he moved closer to her. His body not quite touching hers, but only a whisper away.

'Then how come I feel like I've known you for what seems like years?' Thomas pulled her to him, closing the distance between them as he wrapped his arms around her.

He kissed her, probing deeper till she opened herself to him. Lark slid her hands from his arms to encircle his neck as she reveled in the feel of him pressed against her breasts. Thomas held her with his arm and eased his other hand along the curve of

91

her back to the swell of her hip. The heat of his touch was delicious, she thought, even through the bulk of her sweater and the roughness of her jeans.

Lark had been standing with her legs slightly apart as she leaned on the car, Thomas now took the opportunity to move between them as he pressed himself against her. She groaned as a spear of desire shot through her and she met his kiss with a need of her own. A strand of her hair worked between them causing Thomas to chuckle softly as he pulled it gently from her face with his hand.

The movement pulled her from the desire, the need for him, that she'd let herself fall into. She met his gaze, amazed at the power his look had to affect her. She could see his want for her in his eyes, feel his ease at being with her, but she sensed the small flicker of doubt move through him before he pushed it roughly away. Lark could tell by his expression that he knew she had witnessed it.

'Thomas, I'm sorry,' she said softly. Lark wondered if he would always doubt her. She shifted away from him and he moved to let her by. At another time she might have found it humorous that they had been too distracted with each other to realize they had been practically lying on the trunk of the car.

She took a slow breath as she turned to face him. 'I won't lie to you. I can sense too much from you right now.'

Thomas leaned back against the car, his palms flat on the trunk. He looked darkly handsome with an old dress shirt half-buttoned over his faded jeans. His hair was slightly mussed from her fingers gripping the satin curls. He studied her with a hint of anger. 'What do you sense from me, Lark?'

She answered his question with one of her own. 'Do you think I had anything to do with Jeffrey's death?'

Lark found herself holding her breath as she waited for his answer. She had asked him the question before, but this time she hoped for a different response. When he had touched her with his caress, she felt as if he had touched a deeper part of her. She forced herself to watch his eyes, slightly surprised that he could shut his thoughts from her.

'I don't think so.'

'At least you're honest, Thomas.' Lark looked away. She ran both her hands through her thick hair in an unconscious show of frustration. She lifted the heavy strands from her neck as she rubbed the back of her head, then let it fall around her shoulders. She looked back to him and met his gaze. 'But you should also admit that there is a small seed of doubt planted in your thoughts.'

Thomas's frustration matched that of her own. He lifted his hand and massaged the back of his neck. He let it fall back to the trunk. 'Lark, you were poisoned. I don't have to wait for any tests from a lab. I was the one who found you. I saw the look on your face. You were scared of something and kept saying something about "it wouldn't go away." It was not you talking.'

Thomas's words struck her and an image flashed white hot in her mind. Her thoughts flamed and shimmered within her. Lark frowned as it took over and she tried to grasp it. Keep it. Force it to remain in her memory.

A woman running in terror.

It was her, but not her. The woman's long hair hung in heavy strands over her shoulders and down her back. A gown clung to her body as she ran through a door and into the night. She could see something ahead of her. She had to escape. A sense of relief, maybe refuge, moved through her. It was the bridge she was running toward, she was sure now.

Thomas gripped her arms and shook her gently. He called to her and his voice pulled her from the image. 'What is it? You're seeing something, aren't you, Lark?'

'What?' She squeezed her eyes shut, then shook her head as she tried to dispel part of the fear that held her. Thomas repeated his question and she nodded. 'Yes, I need to go to the bridge. Now.'

Thomas did not ask any questions, but took her by the hand and led her out the door toward the bridge. Lark was distracted by the images, but still noticed that he glanced nervously toward her as they hurried – nearly running – toward her goal.

The sensations started to build within her the closer they came to the bridge and distantly she heard herself say Thomas's name. Her vision fogged, then was superimposed with another shimmering image. Far away she could hear the noise of a horse galloping toward her and she felt resignation and fear.

Hands.

Many hands gripped her, then lifted her onto the saddle of the prancing animal. A part of Lark knew as her feet took her closer that the impression she felt was growing. She could feel Thomas's hands leading her as she blindly followed. His touch was as real to her as the distant reality going on in her mind's eye.

The horse was led to the bridge. The woman Lark seemed to be a part of sobbed with bone-shattering fear. A rope was swung over the rafter of the bridge. The thick knots twisted above the loop fell in front of her face like a slap of cold reality.

Her eyes widened as the anger surrounded her. The rough texture of the rope scratched at the soft skin of her cheek as a man with dirty hands shoved it over her head. She could not see, but felt the many people around her. They shouted their venom at her. Fear and devastation flooded through her.

Then from within herself a woman's voice sang a rhythmic chant in a language unlike her own. Yet somehow she knew the words. Accepted the comfort. Her eyes closed, accepting what she could not change.

The horse sprang with a surge of power from under her. She screamed. The sound cut off as an incredible pressure gripped her throat. She was unable to fight the blackness overtaking her.

The anger faded, then the voices.

Thomas held Lark's hand as he led her toward the bridge. He glanced at her as they trod the thick grass. Her eyes looked as if she were blind. A part of him knew that she was seeing something, but it wasn't what was in front of her. Or him. Her hand in his grew colder as they neared the old abandoned structure.

He watched as the fear grew within her eyes and it sparked a matching fear within his own heart. She said nothing. Just simply stood there with her eyes open, seeing things he could not. He may have doubted her ability at first, but now he worried that the images might take her.

Thomas moved to stand in front of her and, even though he was directly in her line of vision, she never acknowledged him. Her eyes looked at him, through him. He said nothing to her while she was in this trance-like state. He didn't know what to do or if he should speak to her. Would it hurt her?

Thomas stiffened when her face paled. Lark suddenly screamed, the sound cut off as she grabbed at her throat. He yelled to her, taking her by the arms as she went limp. He lowered her to the rough planks of the bridge, then pulled her hands from her throat. Her skin was cold to the touch. She was struggling to breathe, but yet he could find nothing hampering her.

'Lark,' Thomas said, then called to her again as he cradled her in his arms. He shook her gently and felt the relief flood through him with an intensity he would not have expected when she started breathing more evenly. Lark blinked, then frowned as her gaze focused on him. He smiled and smoothed her long hair from her face. 'Lark, are you all right?'

She looked at him for a moment, then slowly glanced around her. He could see her recognition of the surroundings. 'I'm okay now. It's gone.'

Thomas's heart still pounded with the apprehension of what he had witnessed. He wanted to keep holding her in his arms even as he watched the color return to her face. He touched her cheek to see if her skin was warming up. 'What the hell happened?'

Lark met his gaze and he wondered if she were trying to pick up on his thoughts. He'd seen the look before. It was almost as if she were mesmerized and he could feel the pull of it. She blinked, then focused on his chest by her face. Thomas enjoyed watching her reaction as she realized he was still holding her. She sat up, then scooted nervously out of his hold, but not before he saw her desire for him.

Lark remained sitting on the bridge beside him. For a moment she didn't say anything as she finger-combed her hair away from her face. He could see by the frown on her face she was thinking about the images she had seen.

'What is it, Lark?'

She shifted, then stood. She studied the old structure around them. 'They hanged her, didn't they? They hanged her from this bridge.'

'Yes, they did,' Thomas answered as he rose to stand beside her. He watched as she seemed to be looking for something.

'Well, at least you got rid of it,' Lark murmured as she turned away from him to walk to the railing of the bridge.

'Got rid of what, Lark?' Thomas walked with her, then leaned his forearms on top of the rail as he watched the stream below them move with snake-like precision over the sand.

She turned her face to him. 'The hangman's noose.'

'Lark, Theorosa was killed over a hundred years ago. The noose has been gone for decades.'

He watched something move through her expression. Was it fear he saw, or realization? Realization of what? he wondered.

'I'm talking about the noose I saw hanging out here the other day,' she said quietly.

'When did you see it?' Thomas felt an unnerving sense of apprehension move quickly through him.

'The day Jeffrey was killed.' Lark exhaled slowly and shook her head. She turned away from the railing and leaned back against it with her arms crossed over her chest. 'When I found Theorosa's room ransacked, I began straightening things. The curtain rod was hanging from the window so I picked it up. That's when I saw it. Here.'

She lifted her arm to point directly over the spot that only moments before she had been lying under. 'It was hanging right there.'

Chills rippled icily through Thomas. He rolled his shoulder to loosen the tension caused by the spooky thoughts flowing through his head. 'Why didn't you mention this earlier, Lark?'

Lark shrugged, then looked toward him. 'I didn't even remember it till now, Thomas. Anyway, I figure whoever wrecked my room probably did it.'

Thomas pushed from the rail and stood in front of her. His expression was dark and he clenched his hands with the anger he felt for whoever had played the cruel prank. Lark continued to look at him, but he refused to let her into his thoughts.

'What is it, Thomas?' she asked softly.

'Whoever did it, Lark, could have also killed Jeffrey,' he answered.

'What kind of stunt are you trying to pull here, Blackwell?'

Baker's voice boomed through the room causing other detectives to turn and look at them as they sat in front of his desk piled with folders. Lark could easily ignore the questioning stares, for she had been doing it most of her life, but Thomas seemed to grow uneasy under their scrutiny.

'We are trying to give you information pertaining to the case,' he said, his voice purposely low. Thomas did not acknowledge the people watching him, but Lark knew he could feel their eyes on him.

'A rope?' Baker snorted, then leaned back in his chair as he studied them. He ran his hand distractedly over his wiry hair. 'You're trying to tell me I should stop our investigation and concentrate on some punk kid playing a prank?'

'You don't know that it was a kid playing a prank.'

The detective met Thomas's gaze as he bent forward. 'You don't know that it wasn't.'

Lark could see the frustration and anger working in Thomas's gaze. His jaw stiffened and his eyes grew hard.

'Don't you think it's too much of a coincidence that the noose was hung on the bridge and Linden was killed that very same night?' Thomas said the words slowly and patiently as if he were dealing with a stubborn child.

'Let me put it to you this way, Blackwell.' Baker learned forward in his chair and folded his arm on the desk top, ignoring the folders he displaced with the movement. 'How much coincidence would you say it was that the main suspect was not only found kneeling over the body, but has also been charged with murder before? I'd say it's a more plausible theory than a rope, wouldn't you?'

Thomas exhaled and shook his head. He bit his lip as he concentrated on his closed hands in his lap for a moment. When he looked back to the detective his determination had returned. 'Detective Baker, we're just trying to cooperate with you.'

'I understand and appreciate the effort.' Baker raised his hands to show that there were no hard feelings on his part, then he turned toward Lark. 'Have you remembered anything else, Miss Delavan?'

'No, I haven't,' Lark answered, without feeling. She knew they had received what little cooperation they were going to get from the detective.

'Has anything been determined from the forensic tests?' Thomas asked, still doggedly trying to gain something from the encounter with the man.

Baker laughed as he rose from his chair. It was his signal to them that the conversation was over. 'Blackwell, you know I can't share that information with you.'

Thomas stood and waited for the detective to turn back toward him before he spoke. His voice was low and sincere. 'Come on, Ron, we're just trying to get things cleared up.'

Baker chuckled and shook his head as if Thomas had told him a particularly crude joke. 'Give us some credit for investigative ability, okay?'

When the detective started to walk away to escort them to the door, Lark touched his arm and held his gaze when he turned to meet hers. How could the man be so flippant? she wondered.

'Detective Baker, we're talking about my life here. You can't expect me to sit back and wait to see what happens.'

'Then I suggest you start finding answers,' he muttered, his gaze cold and unfeeling. Lark let her hand drop and the detective walked away.

She felt the tears sting at her eyes at the helplessness threatening to swallow her. 'I guess that was a wasted effort.'

'Not really,' Thomas said, his expression distracted. He stared after the detective, lost in thought for a moment, then slowly he smiled. He took Lark's hand and started heading toward the elevators. She followed in silence, too shocked to think of anything to say. At the elevator, he turned to her. His dimples deepened as he chuckled, the sound a little too devious for her comfort.

'The detective told you to start finding some answers. That's just what we're going to do – find some answers.'

Thomas pulled to a stop in front of the castle, then turned the engine off. He played with his keys in the ignition distractedly as he gazed toward the bridge.

'So what do we do now?' Lark asked quietly, her voice breaking into his thoughts.

He let his hand drop as he leaned back in the seat and rested his palm on the headrest behind her. Shrugging, he smiled at her, 'You're the psychic, you tell me.'

'You're the lawyer,' she retorted without anger.

He chuckled softly, then let the silence fall comfortably between them. She didn't look away from him, but merely held his gaze. Thomas gave in to the temptation to touch her skin as he lifted his hand from the headrest to stroke the smooth contour of her face with his thumb.

Lark leaned toward him and tentatively touched her lips to his. Thomas closed his eyes and let himself fall into the sensations she stirred inside of him. He inhaled the soft scent of her, moaning lightly as her fingers touched the skin of his chest exposed at his collar. Raising his hand to her hair, he stroked the silk of its length, then cupped the back of her head as he moved his lips over hers.

She pulled back, just a breath away, and leaned her forehead against his as she shook her head. Her voice was quiet and just a little shaky. 'I don't think this is going to get us anywhere.'

He kissed her cheek, then moved to nuzzle her neck. 'No, it won't. But . . .'

More than half aroused, he felt the frustration move through him when the activity around the stables caught his attention. He frowned and shifted to get a better look over Lark's shoulder.

Her face was flushed and very close to his. She scanned his face as if trying to read his expression. 'What is it, Thomas?'

'I wonder why Jim's here?' he murmured more to himself than the woman beside him. Lark turned to follow the direction of his gaze.

'Who's he?'

'He's our veterinarian.' A sense of unease drifted over him. There were no scheduled visits for any of the animals. 'Come on, the way things have been going lately, it makes me nervous to think of why he's here.'

Getting out of the car, they started walking to the stable. Thomas could see Jim standing in the outside pen with Satan, examining a spot on the animal's back. He seemed to be talking with someone, but Thomas could not yet see who it was.

'It looks like a pretty nasty cut. It should heal without much scarring though.' The vet stroked the glossy coat of the black horse. 'He'll need to be on antibiotics for a while, at least till the scratch heals.'

Natalie ducked under Satan's head as she moved around the horse to stand beside Jim. 'I've already started him.'

'You missed your calling, Natalie.' Jim chuckled as he smiled with open admiration toward Natalie. 'You would have made a good vet.'

'The first time I came across a case of neglect or abuse of an animal,' she said, unaware of the audience behind her, 'I would have to kill someone.'

'Who would that be, Natalie?' Thomas asked, taking great satisfaction in watching her jump at his words. 'The animals, or the owners?'

The woman turned automatically toward him with a smile. It dimmed, however, when she found Lark standing beside him. Her expression remained bright, except for the small indentation of a frown between her eyebrows.

'It was just a joke, Thomas. Of course, you knew that.' She laughed. Her gaze moved to Lark and her eyes darkened. 'I see they decided not to put you in jail.'

'Innocent until proven guilty, and all that jazz. You know how that is.'

Thomas watched in amusement as the two women squared off with each other. Lark seemed to be fighting the urge to cross her arms and tap her foot, while Natalie looked like she would love to take the psychic on for two out of three rounds.

'No, I'm sure I wouldn't.' Natalie never let her eyes waver from Lark's. 'If you'll excuse me, I need to go freshen up.'

Natalie turned away and sauntered off toward the castle, leaving the three behind her silent for a moment. Jim cleared his throat, then looked uncomfortably toward Thomas.

'Did I stumble into a rattlesnake pit, or what?'

'No, don't worry about it, Jim,' Thomas said as he shook his head, then clasped the vet's shoulder with his hand. 'You know how Natalie can be.'

Thomas turned toward the horse and moved closer to the fence so he could pet the animal as he looked the wound over. 'What happened to Satan?'

'I really don't know,' Jim answered and moved beside him to show him the wound. 'Natalie called and said he had been cut. It's really not as bad as it looks and hopefully it shouldn't scar him. By the time I got here, she'd already cleaned the cut and worked some salve into it. He'll be fine.'

Thomas frowned. 'And she's already given him his antibiotics?'

Jim nodded. He studied Thomas for a moment. 'I hope that's all right. As I'm sure you know, Natalie does have quite bit of experience with animals.'

'It's not a problem, Jim. Don't worry about it.' Thomas smiled at the man as he shook hands with him and thanked the vet for coming out.

Thomas took Lark by the elbow as he escorted her toward the house. They both turned to wave as Jim drove away.

'That was interesting,' he said thoughtfully.

Lark glanced toward him, then shrugged. 'In what way?'

'I didn't realize that Natalie was quite so knowledgeable about veterinary medicine.' Thomas moved up the steps of the castle, then realized that Lark was no longer beside him. He turned to look at her questioningly and found her with her hands on her hips staring at him. 'What?'

'She was your fiancée, Thomas,' Lark supplied with a twist of her lips. 'How could you not know?'

'Never officially,' he muttered. He couldn't understand why he suddenly felt the need to explain that to her where he'd never felt it before. He knew he just didn't want her looking at him like she was now. He'd seen that 'just-another-typical-male' look before. 'I'll admit I knew she was good at caring for animals, but I didn't know she was so good at treating their illnesses.'

'Go on,' Lark prompted, her brow arched with wariness.

'It stands to reason that if someone knows how to treat someone when they are . . . sick,' Thomas began patiently. He could see by the change in her expression that she was starting to follow what he was saying. 'Then they also know how to make someone sick.'

'Oh.'

Lark nodded her concession to his statement. He chuckled as he put his arm around her shoulder. 'And you call yourself a psychic.'

She opened her mouth to answer his retort when the front door opened and Alicia hurried out to them. He'd never seen his grandmother so agitated. She may have noticed his arm around Lark, but she said nothing, only motioned them to hurry into the house.

'It's all over the news,' she stated with tight-lipped, barely controlled animosity. 'It's horrible what they will do these days for ratings.'

'What is it, Grandmother?' Thomas felt a sense of dread move over him as he looked toward Lark. She met his gaze, her eyes wide with fear. He already had a sense of what they were going to see.

'It's Lark,' Alicia answered as she took the girl's hand and pulled her beside her in a show of support. 'The media found out about the other murder. They're pointing out the connections between the two.'

CHAPTER 6

Lark's face was everywhere on the television. All the local stations were running the story and, flipping through the channels, they found a cut-down version on the national cable news. Thomas picked up the remote and changed it back to one of the local channels. The murder and her involvement were at the top of the news.

The segment started with a brief update of the investigation into Jeffrey's death, then launched into the 'psychic' connection of the local case with that of the murder of a teenager in California. Lark felt her face flush as they showed footage of her being escorted from the jail wearing the standard issue uniform.

'I wouldn't say that was one of your better colors, would you?'

Lark turned to glare at Natalie as she walked into the parlor. The blonde had the nasty ability to look elegant in anything she wore, even the faded flannel shirt and jeans she had on.

'Natalie, bite your tongue,' Alicia warned her with a pointed look.

The report showed a picture of the murdered girl's body covered with a forensic lab sheet on the side of a wooded hillside. One foot stuck out from under the cover. The stockinged foot, minus a tennis shoe, looked small and frail in the damp undergrowth of the forest.

Lark squeezed her eyes shut against the picture as it caused more vivid images to spring into her thoughts. As the reporter went on with the alleged 'similarities', which were practically non-existent, she rose and turned away from the television.

Alicia took her hand as she stood to stand beside her. 'Sweetheart, I know this is so upsetting, I'm sorry. Are you all right?'

Lark's gaze went unwillingly to Natalie's. The blonde studied her, part of the haughtiness gone from her expression. Lark did not want her sympathy. Right now, she didn't want it from anyone.

'I'm fine, Alicia. Please excuse me.'

She moved past Natalie and into the hall before she took a slow, calming breath. Damn, she hated this. Images from the girl's murder superimposed themselves onto the nightmarish ones from her dreams. She shook her head wishing she could simply dispel them, or force them as effectively from her mind as she could block people's thoughts when she needed to. Better yet, she wished fervently there was a surgery that could remove the haunting ability from her very existence.

'Are you all right?'

Lark startled at the sound of Thomas's voice. It unnerved her that the man had developed the ability to approach her without her knowing it, or sensing it.

108

She turned toward him and tried her best to give him a smile, but found she could manage only a shaky one.

'I'm fine, really.' She ran her hand through her hair and looked away from him toward the stairs. 'I think I'll just go upstairs for a while.'

She started to move away from him when he surprised her by taking her hand in his. She looked at him and he gave her a small smile. 'I think I'll go with you.'

A flippant remark about him tucking her in entered her thoughts, but caused even more disturbing images of being alone with him and stopped her from voicing it. She hesitated a moment, not knowing what to say. Or think, for that matter.

'Don't worry, Lark,' he chuckled softly, appearing to notice the thoughts moving through her expression. 'I just want to talk to you. I promise.'

She nodded and let go the breath she was holding as she accompanied him up the stairs. A tension with a delicious edge tightened through her when they walked past several bedroom doors. Lark frowned as they kept moving till they reached Thomas's room. She bit her lip nervously as she looked from his hand holding hers to his profile.

Thomas opened the door and released her to allow her to go before him. Lark looked around the room curiously as she had been too sick the last time she was here to take in the furnishings of the room. She glanced quickly back to him as he shut the door behind him.

Lark quickly avoided those beautiful eyes of his as she moved in a circle to study the room. It was comfortably masculine and tidy, she noticed without much surprise. After all, the man did have a maid. It was also large with a sitting area to the side where Thomas waited for her beside a fireplace. A small fire glowed within, casting its warmth toward her. He waved his hand toward a large wing-back chair, and watched as she took a seat before he sat on the ottoman in front of her.

Thomas leaned his forearms on his knees as he studied Lark. The rich glow of the fireplace reflected partially in his dark eyes, deepening them with a heat Lark felt move through her with a seductive flare. He smiled slowly as he watched her face, then he leaned back almost as if he were allowing the air to cool the space between them.

He held her gaze as his face became serious. 'Lark, will you tell me what happened back in California?'

She looked away as a quick stab of panic moved through her. She had tried her best to shut those memories away, but there always seemed to be something, or someone, forcing her to face them, over and over. Lark swallowed the tears threatening in her throat and nodded silently to him. Maybe it would be best he did know. Then, when this was all over, she could leave. If she was allowed to.

Lark knew it would be too easy to find herself becoming deeply enmeshed with this man. Better he did know this part of her past so he would let her just simply walk away.

Lark took a deep, steadying breath as she turned her thoughts back to that time. It had been several years since it happened, but it never failed to amaze her how fresh the memories were. And the hurt.

She clasped her hands in her lap in front of her as she studied them. Her skin was cold to her own touch. Lark forced away the fear, the humiliation that always accompanied these memories and was thankful her voice sounded even and unemotional.

'I was a junior in college. One day I was sitting in the campus activities center studying between classes. I remember there was a television set in the corner of the room and a couple of guys were watching a soap opera.'

Lark shook her head as she smiled at that part of the memory. The last few minutes of her normal life before 'it' happened.

'The show ended with a news break and the lead story was about a teenage girl who had been missing for a couple of days. Her car had been found and there were signs of a struggle, so even at that time they believed there had been foul play of some kind. I wasn't really watching the television, just sort of listening in on it as I studied.'

She hesitated as she remembered the graphic nature of the images that flashed into her thoughts. The vividness with which they had appeared to her as she heard the words of the news story.

'Part of me heard the reporter talking about the woman,' Lark's voice faltered, but she pushed on, not allowing herself to stop. 'Then these pictures took over my mind. It was like I had been transported from the college campus to where the girl's car had been found. I was with the girl whose picture had been on television. I recognized her, but she wasn't pretty and smiling like she was in the photo. She was scared. Terrified.'

Lark took a deep shaky breath and welcomed the steadying warmth of Thomas's hands as they covered her own. 'She was screaming as she was being pulled from the driver's side of the car. I could see her. I could feel her fear. Somehow it had become my own. But I was only a shadow, there was nothing I could do to help her.'

Lark let her head drop to Thomas's hands as she cried the tears she had cried many times for the girl she had been unable to save. He pulled her to him as he moved them both so he could sit in the chair, then he lifted her to his lap. He held her tightly in his arms as he stroked the hair away from her tear-stained face.

'What happened then, sweetheart?' His voice was low and calming as he spoke with his cheek leaning against the top of her head.

'I guess I screamed and passed out,' she sniffled. She thanked him as he handed her a tissue. 'I really don't know what happened. I woke up on the floor with a bunch of people staring at me as if I had grown a horn in the middle of my head or something.'

'Did you know what you were seeing at the time?' Thomas asked.

Lark shook her head. 'No, not at first. I guess the shock of it made me block it out. I still could remember the images, but not the reality of them.'

Thomas gently stroked her cheek and she offered him a weak smile as she continued her story. 'I tried to push the memory of that first "glimpse" out of my mind, but it stayed with me. Later, it would reappear to me. It was like a movie, it would start where the last image had left off.'

'You saw what happened to her,' he said softly.

She gave a vague nod of her head. Her eyes widened as she remembered. 'I only saw glimpses of the man. I could "see" the long, shoulder length of his hair and I could "feel" the rough material of his army jacket, but I really could not focus on his face. She had stopped for whatever reason, to give him a ride or offer him help, it was something she knew she should never, ever do. She knew better than to do it and I could feel this with as much conviction as I would know something about myself. But she stopped anyway, I don't know why, I don't think even she knew why. She knew she'd made a mistake as soon as she saw his face. His eyes. That's when she tried to drive away.'

Lark rubbed her hand across her forehead at the headache starting to pound. 'She really never had a chance. He hit her in the mouth with his fist through the open window and the force of the blow stunned her for a moment. It sort of stopped her thought process, only for a small moment, but just long enough for him to open the door and try to drag her out.'

She shrugged, then looked toward him. Thomas's eyes were gentle and understanding. She could feel it from him, he truly did understand the anguish the images had caused her.

'I didn't know what to do, Thomas. At first, I thought maybe I was going crazy. But the visions were so real. I was there. I could feel her.'

'Is that when you went to the police?' he asked.

'No.' Her answer was quiet and she shoved her hair away from her face. 'I still really didn't know what was going on. I did know that I needed to find where the car had been found. I followed the newspaper articles and they were very explicit with the description of the location, so it wasn't hard to find.'

'Was it like what happened with you at the bridge today?' Thomas frowned slightly as he studied her face.

Lark nodded. 'As soon as I stepped out of my car on the road side I could feel it start to come over me. It's like a tingling shower that envelops me and I lose awareness of my surroundings. The closer I walked to where her car had been, the stronger the sensation became. The images started flashing in front of me with a strength that was almost overpowering. They came quicker and quicker till I was suddenly there.'

'With the girl?'

'Yes.' Lark shivered as she remembered the trees scratching at the teenager as she was forced to walk through the woods. 'I saw where he was taking her. I saw . . . I saw what he did to her. Then I saw him . . .'

The man had savagely raped the teenager. Then when she curled into a ball and sobbed after the brutality he had inflicted on her, he had stared at her with a look of hatred. Evil, vile hatred. The image refused to be stopped and Lark was once again forced to witness the murder of the teenage girl. The repeated blows still caused her to flinch as they flashed in her mind.

Thomas tightened his arms around her and pressed his lips to her forehead. 'Lark, baby, I'm sorry. I'm so sorry I asked you about this.'

She shook her head. 'I'm not. I never had anyone I could tell this to. I had to tell the cops, but they weren't the best of listeners.'

Thomas squeezed his eyes shut and frowned as if recalling Baker's animosity. 'It must have been horrible.'

Lark shrugged away the thought. She had learned that dwelling on the bad things that had happened to her would never help. 'After I saw . . . what happened to the woman, I passed out. When I came to, I got back in my car and went straight to the police. The images had been so vivid to me, I guess it never occurred to me that they wouldn't believe what I was telling them.'

'What did they do?'

'Nothing,' she answered. 'One detective would give the other one a pointed look, like I was crazy. I even heard one guy telling another that it wasn't unusual for women to come in after a story about a horrible crime because the lady wanted a little "official" attention. They didn't know I could hear them and it humiliated me to think they thought I was a cop groupie. I made them listen to the whole story, mainly to ease my own conscience. I guess I thought that if I did the best I could, the images would go away.'

'And they didn't,' Thomas stated. He smoothed a section of her hair behind her ear as she continued.

'I think I said before, these visions were like a movie. Except now the "movie" was stuck on the last scene. Her death was looped in my mind, it played over and over. It wouldn't leave me. It started affecting my sleep and my studies. Finally, I knew

I would go crazy if I didn't finish whatever had been started within me. I filled my car with gas and started in the area where the girl's car had been found. I drove the back roads searching for something familiar. I wasn't following any maps, just letting my senses take me where I needed to go. At first I felt nothing, then I started to sense it. I could "feel" that I was going in the right direction. I ended up following this little path barely wide enough for my car. It was obvious that it was an old path, rarely traveled. Soon I had to stop the car and continue on foot. I walked and walked till my legs ached, but I knew I was going in the right direction. I knew it.'

'Weren't you scared of what you might find?' Thomas asked. 'Or that the killer might still be around?'

Lark chuckled softly at the amazed look on his face. It suddenly occurred to her how comfortable it was to merely sit on his lap and talk with him. No pretenses or tension. She touched the already darkening shadow of the beard on his cheek.

'I think I knew what I would find, but I wouldn't allow myself to dwell on it. And yes, I was scared, but not because of the killer. I knew he was gone. I was more afraid of the normal things you might scare yourself with in a forest as it starts getting dark. You know, things like bears and snakes. Werewolves.'

He smiled at her humor. 'So you kept going on?'

'I had to.' Lark's face fell solemn as she lost her amusement. There could be no room for jokes at this point. 'It was twilight. It was starting to get hard to see where I was going. I remember being surprised when I found her. Maybe shock does that to you. Of

116

course, I had never seen a dead body before, except at funerals. He had tried to hide her body, but her feet stuck out from under the branches he had used. I had to remove a couple of them to see her face and it was the same face that had been haunting me for days. What struck me at the time, however, was that her shoes were so white. They were so clean compared to the rest of her. Somehow it just didn't match in my mind.'

'Lark, what did you do?' Thomas prompted.

'It finally hit me, really hit me what I was looking at and I ran. It wasn't long till I had to stop because I become violently ill. Finding her had not had the calming effect I thought it would.'

Lark reached for Thomas's collar and began playing with the corner of it. Her lips tightened as the tears welled in her eyes. 'It was dark by the time I got back to my car and I was scared out of my mind. I had imagined every horrible and vile thing following me as I ran back to the car. I looked like hell and was covered with dirt because I had fallen down a couple of times on the way back to my car, but I didn't care, I was determined that the cops were going to listen to me this time.'

'Did they?'

'Yeah, right.' She chuckled without humor at the thought. She looked to the ceiling for a moment, then met Thomas's questioning gaze. 'I had to practically get hysterical with them till they finally gave in and came with me out there. Fortunately, I did not have any problems finding the place again, considering I had left in such a hurry. The detectives really didn't have much to say. They called in people to work the scene and I had to stay there for a couple of hours. Later when they had taken me back to the station and were questioning me, it didn't occur to me what was going on. Even as they were fingerprinting me, I don't think I really had a clue because I was so exhausted from everything that had happened. I was so tired that I hadn't realized they had read me my rights and were placing me under arrest. When they put me in that cell and closed the door on me, it all hit me at once. I did not know what was worse; knowing what that woman had gone through and watching her die, or being charged with her murder when I knew what the real killer looked like.'

Thomas stiffened, his expression hard. 'The woman had been raped. The physical and trace evidence alone, should have cleared you. Any lawyer worth his pay would have had you out of there within the first twenty-four hours.'

Lark stroked his cheek with her thumb. 'I know, but the case had received a lot of media exposure and to some people it was enough that they had put me in jail. I knew what had happened. I knew how she had been killed. Hell, I had led the police to her body. Some people thought I was making up the "alleged" killer.'

'I suppose they thought you "made up" the alleged rape too,' Thomas snapped. Lark knew his anger was not directed at her.

'That can be done,' she answered, 'and, yes, some believed I had done it to throw suspicion off myself.'

'Idiots,' he muttered, his eyes dark. 'You might have been able to alter the physical aspects of it, but surely they took samples. That alone should have proved that you didn't do it.'

Lark smiled at his anger. He may not have realized it yet, but he had allowed himself to believe her and was now firmly on her side. 'They did take samples, but they also took their sweet time in processing them. Even if the tests confirmed a man had been involved, to some it would have only meant that I had had a partner.'

Thomas exhaled slowly as he shook his head. He stared past her to the flames of the fire that helped knock the chill from a beautiful spring day. He stroked his thumb across the soft skin of her hand, then turned to study her for a moment.

'Lark, it just seems so incredible.' His voice was subdued as he reached to gently brush the ridge of her cheek with his fingertips. 'What did you do after they released you?'

'I tried to get on with my life.' Lark looked into his eyes and did not feel the need to look away as the memories of that time of her life moved through her expression. It had been hard. Sometimes devastatingly hard to try to maintain some sense of normalcy in a town where people constantly stared at her. She had read the disbelief and dislike in their eyes, but what had been the hardest to accept was the fear. It hurt her deeply to remember the times when she would walk past a family at the mall and the mother would grab her children's hands and pull them closer to her. Away from Lark. Away from the person that some people still believed had killed the girl.

Lark smiled and shrugged away the pain as she had learned to do. 'Fortunately, I was close to finishing my degree. I stuck it out till I was done, then I moved and tried to start over.'

Thomas flipped his finger teasingly under her chin. 'And became an accountant. That sounds like a life of excitement.'

'That from a lawyer.' Lark chuckled softly, then took a deep breath as she let out a sigh. 'I really was lucky, though. I found a boss that is very understanding. In fact, he was the one who helped me work through my experiences with that case and direct my ability elsewhere. Kevin very much believes in turning a negative into a positive.'

Thomas leaned his head back comfortably against the chair as he looked into her eyes. 'Sounds like good accounting logic. So what did he do to help you?'

'He told the local cops about me.'

'What?' Thomas asked. His thick brows drew together as he frowned. The man was incredibly handsome no matter what his expression, she thought as she watched his look of concern.

Lark giggled as she propped her elbow on his shoulder and rested her face on her palm. Their faces were not far apart and she enjoyed the leisure of studying the dimples of his cheeks as he waited for her to continue. She reached to his mouth and flipped his lip with the tip of her finger, laughing at the surprised look on his face.

'A young boy had wandered away from home one day and became lost. Kevin went to the police and told them I could find him.'

'And, did you?' Thomas's question was cautious.

'Well, yes,' she answered matter-of-factly.

'But was he . . . I mean, did they find his . . .'

Thomas was obviously at a loss for words and Lark could tell that he assumed that the poor child had been found dead. She smiled as she remembered seeing the child huddled by a tree. He'd been scared and cold, but safe.

Safe. She had been able to help the child before something bad could happen to him. It had lifted a terrible weight from her and she had started being able to accept the part of her that made her very different from everyone else.

'No, he was alive. It was one of the few times I was glad that I had this ability.'

'It must have been very rewarding for you,' he offered.

'It was,' she answered softly. Lark touched his cheek with her thumb and down to the ridge of his dimple. 'But it happens very rarely. I seem to be able to pick up on the negative more than I can the positive.'

'How do you live with all this?' He turned his head toward her as he held her gaze.

Those eyes, she thought. He could mesmerize her with only his eyes. Part of him had come to accept her, but she wanted him to try and understand also. 'It's a part of me I can't change. Believe me, if I could get rid of it, I would.'

'But it's a part of who you are, Lark.' His voice was low, gentle as a caress. His gaze moved over her face, then hesitated on her lips and she felt the warmth of it glide through her. He lifted his eyes slowly back to hers. 'Can you sense what I'm feeling now?'

Lark studied him. She simply wanted to feel his skin beneath her fingers. To be close to him as she was now. She wanted to touch him. She concentrated on him, and felt nothing. Nothing, but her desire, her need for him. 'No, I can't. You're different somehow. I usually know when someone is near me that I know. Except you. I never know about you.'

'Hmm,' he murmured as his gaze dropped back to her mouth. 'Can you tell me what I'm thinking now?'

Lark chuckled as she leaned toward him, her lips a breath away from his. 'No, but I can tell by the look on your face that it's probably X-rated.'

Thomas murmured his agreement as he touched his lips to hers. He raised his hand to cup the back of her neck as he pulled her deeper to his kiss. Lark unfolded her arms and wrapped them around his neck. Her hand slid into the thickness of his hair as naturally as if it was made for her touch. She moaned softly with pleasure as his hand moved up her ribs to cup her breast under her sweater. She felt herself harden as he rubbed his finger over the satin material of her bra.

Lark was quickly losing herself to the heat of his touch as his lips moved to the sensitive skin of her throat. The sensations he could create within her overcame any number of reasons why they should not go on. Lark touched his cheek with her hand as she drew his mouth back to hers. She kissed him with the desire she felt for him and moaned as he responded.

The door opened suddenly, causing Lark to yelp with surprise. Natalie stepped through the door, at first not seeing them sitting together.

'Thomas.'

'Oh.' The words seemed to die in her throat as Natalie focused on the couple, her mouth remaining open. She recovered quickly and snapped her mouth shut with a disapproving frown. Her elegant features hardened with anger as she put her hand on her hip. 'I guess I hadn't realized you two had started keeping company.'

Thomas's hand tightened against Lark's stomach as he leveled his gaze on the blonde. 'What is it, Natalie?'

She met his look with a glacial one of her own. Her brow lifted and she refused to acknowledge Lark's presence, or her position on Thomas's lap. 'Alicia decided we all needed a change of pace. She asked me to invite everyone out to dinner. Her treat.'

'We would love to come,' Thomas answered, emphasizing the 'we' as he included Lark in the invitation. 'Thank you, Natalie.'

Natalie paused at the door, her eyes remaining on Thomas's. Never did her gaze shift toward Lark. She looked as if she would love to throw something at the two of them.

'Is there something else?'

Thomas's nonchalant dismissing words caused the woman's lips to tighten with her frown. Lark didn't think Natalie would frown like that if she knew what kind of lines it would cause on her face. Of course, Natalie probably wouldn't be too receptive to anything she had to offer at the moment, she thought.

'I can't believe you'd stoop so low, Thomas,' she bit out between clenched teeth.

123

Natalie swung away from them and slammed the door loudly behind her as she left. For a moment the two of them simply stared at the closed door, then Lark chuckled softly. The elegant, blonde sexpot hadn't looked so sultry when she'd frowned like a school marm at them. The expression had been somewhat comical. Thomas looked at her, then joined her.

Lark tried to smother her giggle as she cleared her throat. 'I didn't think you two were still an item.'

'We never were much of one,' he answered as the chuckle faded from his voice. He eyed her cautiously, obviously concerned about what direction the conversation might go. 'Do you really want to discuss this?'

'Not really.' Lark could think of a lot of other things more appealing than the thought of Thomas with the Ice Queen. Like an audit by the IRS, for example.

'Good,' he said with firm relief. He swatted her on the bottom as he lifted her off him. 'We'd better start getting ready for dinner.'

Thomas walked with her to the door, his hand resting warmly on her lower back. He put his hand on the door knob, but didn't open it as he leaned over and kissed the tip of her nose. He remained leaning close to her as he held her gaze. 'Lark, I appreciate you telling me about what happened before. I know it was hard for you.'

Lark nodded, but did not say anything. For just a moment she let herself get lost in his eyes as he simply looked at her. She didn't need to sense what he was feeling. She only had to look into his eyes. The pleasure stirred within her at the soft look he was giving her.

But would it last?

Some lessons learned are hard to forget. Lark looked away and Thomas, as if sensing the change in her, opened the door. She didn't look at him as she passed through the doorway and started down the hall toward her room. She heard the soft click of Thomas's door as he quietly closed it and she released a small sigh of relief that he had not asked any more questions.

As she neared the door to her room, Lark frowned as she started to feel something. She felt as if someone was watching her. Her shoulders stiffened with tension as she realized that she'd heard Thomas close his door.

Lark turned quickly to look behind her. The grounds keeper, Tim, stood at the other end of the hall and watched her without apparent concern for her nervousness. Then he turned and went around the corner without saying a word to her or acknowledging her presence.

Exhaling slowly, Lark stared at the spot where the man had stood only seconds ago, then shrugged the unease from her shoulders. There had been no anger or dislike in the man's expression. Just a look of question. It was as if the man was trying to come to a decision about her, Lark thought as she recalled his face.

Like whether she was a threat or not.

Maybe the grounds keeper was taking his job a little too seriously, she thought. Lark shook her head at her thoughts. 'Now you're getting paranoid. Morbid and paranoid.'

Lark opened the door to her room and stepped inside. She swung the door closed behind her as she moved toward the bathroom. She had plenty of time to fix her hair and freshen her make up before it would be time to go to dinner. Then she could just relax for a few moments so she' could hopefully let some of the tension of the day dissipate before she had to face stern looks of disapproval from David and Natalie.

'Well, well, if she isn't back so soon.'

Natalie's voice stopped Lark cold. A wave of apprehension moved through her as she turned slowly to find Natalie leaning against the wall beside the door. Obviously she had positioned herself behind the door so Lark would not see her as she walked in.

Too bad she hadn't flung it open, Lark thought dryly.

'What the hell are you doing in my room?' she asked instead as she crossed her arms over her chest.

Natalie pushed away from the wall and walked slowly toward her with her hand on her hip. 'That's funny. I was going to ask you the same thing about Thomas's room. You two looked to be pretty cozy with each other.'

The woman's eyes were hard with anger. The unusually light blue of her eyes made them look icy and unfeeling. She waited for Lark to speak. Her mouth tightened when Lark refused to acknowledge her rude comment.

'Nothing to say? Fine, then I'll do the talking.' Natalie looked Lark up and down as if she were an undesirable subsitute that paled in comparison to her own Nordic beauty. 'Don't even think that anything more is ever going to develop between you two but maybe cheap, sweaty sex.'

Mee-oww, Lark thought. 'It's really none of your business, is it?'

Natalie moved to stand in front of her. She tried to intimidate Lark by leaning over her. Her voice was low and threatening. 'Nothing is going to happen between you two. I won't let it.'

'Considering what's happened lately, Natalie,' Lark said as she held the woman's gaze with a hard look of her own, 'I would consider that a pretty strong statement.'

'I wasn't the one found with blood on my hands, now was I?' Natalie's lip curled with disgust as she looked at her. 'Oh, I forgot. You don't remember.'

'I want you to leave this room. Now.' Lark's hands balled into fists as her anger shot through her. Natalie remained where she stood as if testing Lark's determination. Lark lifted her chin and she sniffed her dissatisfaction. 'This really reminds me of a "clichéd" scene from an old, bad movie, Natalie. Surely, even you have more imagination than this.'

Natalie's brows rose in mock surprise, although the anger never left her expression. 'And what are you? The poor, defenseless heroine waiting for her man to save her from the authorities?'

Lark moved past her toward the door. She took the knob in her hand and opened the door, holding it open as an obvious invitation for her unwanted guest to leave. 'I'd say that at least beats the hell out of being the peroxide blonde who's only good for one thing. Wouldn't you?'

Natalie's lips tightened and her eyes narrowed at the comment. Then the woman pulled herself under control and relaxed her features. She walked to the door and stopped in front of Lark. The woman was a good couple of inches taller than Lark and emphasized the detail by leaning slightly over her while looking regally down her nose.

'How cute. Just remember what I said.'

The woman walked past her into the hallway and did not look back. Lark leaned into the hall slightly as she called to her. 'Don't worry, I'll remember every clichéd word of it.'

Natalie did not acknowledge her. She walked to her own room and opened the door as if she hadn't heard a word Lark had said. Then she slammed it shut behind her.

Lark chuckled as she softly closed her own door. She smiled as she shook her head at the thought of the woman. What incredible nerve. She stopped at the doorway to the bathroom, her hand resting on the frame. Lark frowned as Natalie's words came back to her.

Nothing is going to happen between you two. I won't let it.

At the time she had told Natalie they were strong words, but as she thought back on it, they seemed to become even more ominous. The woman had obviously not liked Jeffrey's presence at the dinner party that night. A part of Lark wondered if Natalie had taken it upon herself to have a little 'talk' with Jeffrey later in the library.

Just how far, she wondered, would the woman go to make sure nothing ruined her plans to be the lady of the castle?

CHAPTER 7

Dinner went surprisingly well, Lark thought as they walked through the door of the castle. Thomas had undertaken the role of her escort and had been attentive to Lark's needs. Alicia and Henry had, of course, kept the conversation flowing smoothly with practiced ease and, thankfully, had steered it away from any awkward subjects. David had been civil and even Natalie had at least decided to be nicer than her normal nasty self. Instead, she had spent most of her time showering a bewildered David with her attention in an obvious attempt to better Thomas. John had remained at the castle with Stephanie who was apparently still ill.

All in all, the Ewings couldn't have done better with a barbecue at South Fork, Lark thought with wry amusement. She'd always enjoyed watching the television series *Dallas*, she just never thought she would be living it.

'Alicia, thank you for dinner,' Henry said as he led the way into the family room located in the basement of the castle. 'I feel like I've been stuffed for the oven.'

'That wouldn't be the first time, now would it, you old bird?' David chuckled as he clasped the doctor's shoulder with a friendly shake.

Henry gave him a lopsided grin. 'Sarcasm from one so young.'

Alicia put her arm through Henry's as she joined them. 'You're welcome. How about joining me in a game of pool?'

'No, my dear,' he answered as he patted her hand good naturedly. 'Not that I don't enjoy playing against you, but you always win. I think I'll just sit over here and let my dinner comfortably settle.'

'Chicken. And I don't always win,' Alicia smiled ruefully, then she turned to David. 'How about you? Are you too chicken to play a game of pool with your grandmother?'

'You are on,' David said as he leaned over to kiss his grandmother's cheek, then tweaked her nose with his fingers. 'I'll even let you break.'

David flipped the frame between his hands, then set it on the green surface of the pool table. With quick ease he shuffled the balls into the wooden rack as Alicia picked her pool stick from the rack on the wall.

Natalie sauntered to the edge of the table and placed her hands on the ledge. 'Alicia, how about Thomas and I play partners against the two of you?'

Thomas frowned at Natalie's suggestion as he looked toward Lark. 'Perhaps it would be more appropriate if we invited one of our guests to join us.'

Natalie turned toward Lark and leaned her hip against the edge of the table. She crossed her arms over her chest and leveled a cool smile on her. 'I'm sure Lark wouldn't mind. Would you, Lark?'

Refusing to rise to the bait, Lark smiled sweetly as she took a seat on the overstuffed couch. 'Of course not. Please go ahead.'

Natalie's gaze hardened only slightly before she shifted away from the table to retrieve a pool stick. Thomas looked toward Lark and she gave him a reassuring smile till he joined his grandmother.

Alicia broke with a resounding whack and the pool balls scattered in an excellent break. Lark's eyes widened with surprised humor. Who would have guessed Alicia Blackwell was a pool shark?

Henry poured himself a glass of ice water at the bar, then moved across the room to join her on the couch. The family room had been renovated from the original root cellar to a modern, comfortable addition to the house. The room differed from the rest of the castle, not only because of its separation, but its furnishing and decor. The original narrow stairs had been replaced with a wider carpeted stairway. The walls were painted in a camel color with vivid paintings. In contrast, Lark was highly amused to see the infamous, tacky reprints of dogs playing poker, at one end of the pool table. Of course, no game room would be complete without it. The room even sported a pin ball machine in the corner.

The room had been decorated to be cozy, inviting, and fun. Lark relaxed against the couch and smiled as Henry sat next to her.

'I'm sorry I haven't had the chance to speak to you since the other morning.' He lowered himself with a groan to the seat and leaned back with a lazy quirk of his lips. 'How are you doing, Lark?'

'I'm fine, Henry. Thank you for asking,' she answered politely. Lark liked the retired doctor, but had not come to feel completely at ease with him yet.

'Good. That's very good.' He nodded.

Lark looked to the others and was thankful to see the four engrossed in the game of pool. It looked like Alicia and David were beating the other pair pretty easily. She was glad to see them occupied and hoped to talk with the doctor about her encounter with Tim. The grounds keeper's behavior earlier in the afternoon when she had seen him in the hallway had made her uneasy and she wanted to ask Henry about the man.

'Henry,' she started, keeping her voice low as a sign to him that she didn't really want the conversation to be heard by the others. 'I was wondering, well, more like hoping that I could ask you about something.'

'Go ahead, Lark. I'll try to help you if I can,' he answered, with a worried frown. 'What is it?'

'Well.' Lark hesitated. Tim really hadn't done anything that afternoon, but his actions had unnerved her. 'I wanted to ask you about Mr Waslawski, the grounds keeper.'

Henry met her gaze, his expression guarded, 'What about him?'

'I really feel like a fool for mentioning it,' Lark licked her lips nervously, 'but he was standing at the end of the hall when I was going to my room this afternoon and he seemed to be watching me. I guess, considering what has happened, I wondered if he . . . should I be nervous?'

The old doctor studied her for a moment, then tried to give her a reassuring smile. 'No. There is nothing for you to worry about.'

'Henry, I've sensed things about him,' Lark said as she held his gaze, trying to read his expression.

'I hope you don't mind if I ask what you've sensed about him?'

Lark lowered her voice even more to match the older man's. 'I think he is hesitant to trust, because he's been betrayed before. And I think he understands what it's like to be wrongly judged.'

Henry remained silent for a moment. Finally he nodded slowly as he clasped his hands in front of him. 'You're very good, Lark. Very good indeed.'

Lark did not say anything. She knew he'd come to a decision and was now collecting his thoughts before he spoke.

The retired doctor took deep breath and released it on a sigh. 'Tim does know very well what it is like to be judged. He grew up in an orphanage and was very poor. He also had a learning problem that today would have been dealt with. Back then, well, he was considered not worth the effort. His life was very hard and he didn't trust easily till Alicia hired him. Alicia is a very natural person and it took her several years, but she finally won him over. He's very loyal to her, and the rest of the family in a sense, but very much so to her. I'd assume he was just keeping an eye out for Alicia. I really wouldn't worry about it too much, my dear. He's really a harmless man.'

'Thank you,' Lark said. She knew herself what being different was like and about suffering from a reluctance to trust. 'I won't worry about it.'

Henry smiled into his drink, then looked as if he had suddenly remembered something else and his voice raised with excitement. 'Oh, I wanted to let you know that I received the test results back from the lab today.'

She swung her gaze toward him. 'What did they find?'

'Mushrooms,' he answered as he raised his thick brows and pursed his lips in a comical look of surprise.

'What?' Alicia looked at him as she held her pool cue in front of her. 'The only mushrooms were in the salad. We all ate the salad.'

'We all may have eaten the salad, but Lark was the only one to eat Panther Mushrooms.'

'How can that be?' Alicia asked. She stepped away from the table, the game momentarily forgotten as she frowned at Henry's answer.

He shrugged as he fiddled with the condensation on the side of his glass. 'No one else became sick, Alicia. Believe me, they would have become very sick too. You saw yourself how bad Lark was.'

'So how did this mushroom get in her salad and not everyone else's?' David asked as he finished his shot. His eyes followed the movement of the ball as the question hung in the air. Lark thought of her room being ransacked and wondered if he again thought that she had 'staged' her illness to add validity to her claim. Surprisingly he did not look toward her, but directed his attention to Henry.

'Good question.' Henry's gaze moved to Alicia. 'Who made the salads that day, do you remember?'

'Well, I did,' she answered. Alicia paused as she considered the question further. 'But I used fresh mushrooms from the store.'

Henry rose and walked to Alicia to put his arm around her as he reassured her. 'Of course you did, Alicia. I did not mean to imply otherwise. Someone obviously put the mushrooms in Lark's bowl later.'

Thomas had been quietly following the conversation, a look of concern on his face. He pursed his lips at Henry's comment, then turned his attention to his grandmother. 'What did you do with the salad after you prepared it?'

Alicia thought for a moment. 'I put it in the refrigerator, then came upstairs to get ready for Lark's dinner party. At serving time, Maria dished it into the salad bowls and set . . .' Her eyes widened as she clutched at her collar. 'Oh my.'

'Then she set the servings at the table,' Thomas finished for her, 'where anyone could have had access to them.'

The unspoken implication hung heavily in the air. Natalie looked pointedly toward Lark with a smirk on her face. 'How very convenient, wouldn't you say?'

Alicia's gaze snapped toward Natalie with a dark frown. 'Lark couldn't have done it. If you remember, Natalie, she was talking with you as I was preparing dinner. You two had "run" into each other at the bridge.'

Natalie rolled her eyes and pushed away from the edge of the pool table to study her shot. Alicia continued. 'Then she brought Jeffrey in and I watched her go on up to her room myself. From that point on she was never by herself.'

Lark felt an almost uncontrollable urge to run to Alicia and hug her. She hadn't given it much thought, but Alicia was right. There had been no way she could have planted the mushrooms in her own salad, even if she had wanted to. Lark couldn't help but grin at Natalie's look of disgust at being an unwilling part of her alibi.

'It's very possible that whoever poisoned Lark could have killed Jeffrey,' Alicia finished the thought.

If the subject had not been so serious, the reactions of those in the room would have been comical. Like the classic mystery story, everyone eyed each other with new, nervous interest.

Natalie snorted at the thought, then leaned over the table to shoot. 'Who says the mushrooms have anything at all to do with his murder?'

'What?' Thomas frowned as he shook his head. 'Are you suggesting that someone poisoned Lark and Jeffrey just happened to get murdered the very same night? In the same house? That's ridiculous.'

Natalie straightened and put her hand on her hip as she boldly met his hard look with one of her own. 'Do you think someone would go to such extremes as poisoning her so she would freak out and kill him? They wouldn't have known how she would react to the mushrooms.'

'I can't believe we're even discussing this as if it were an Agatha Christie novel.' David scowled angrily as he chalked the tip of his pool cue. 'At least we no longer have to worry about Linden trying to sneak the castle right out from under us.'

'David,' his grandmother admonished him.

Lark heard footsteps tread down the stairway and turned to see who it was. John padded down the steps, then stopped as he noticed the looks on everyone's faces.

'Did I come at a bad time?' he asked with a nervous smile, looking from one face to another.

Alicia moved toward him with a thankful laugh as she took his arm and pulled him into the room. 'No, John. In fact, you've given us a wonderful excuse to change the horrible conversation we were having.'

'Good. Then I won't ask what you were talking about,' he said with a relaxed grin.

Alicia chuckled, then offered him a drink. 'How is Stephanie? I went up to see her earlier and she was asleep.'

'Much better, thank you,' he answered. He gave her a tense nod, then looked away. 'I think the "incident" upset her greatly.'

'I think it's upset all of us,' Henry added before taking a sip of his water. 'I can look in on her in the morning, if you would like?'

John shook his head quickly, then cleared his throat. 'That's not necessary, Henry. She'll be just fine.'

'Well, if you need me, John, just give me a call,' Henry offered as he rose. He took his glass to the sink of the bar to empty it. He walked to Alicia and patted her hand. 'Thank you, again, for a wonderful dinner, Alicia. As usual it beats a frozen TV dinner.'

'Oh, as if you would eat one,' Alicia laughed as she met his gaze. She threaded her arm through his. 'I'll walk you to the door.'

Henry turned to say goodnight to everyone, then walked with Alicia to the stairs. The sound of their friendly bantering grew softer as they headed to the front door.

David replaced his pool stick back in the rack on the wall. 'I think I'll follow their lead.'

'I'll go with you,' John said as he joined him.

Lark rose from her seat on the couch as she prepared to take her leave also. Thomas started to move toward her as if he was going to walk with her when Natalie stepped in front of him, effectively blocking his way.

'Thomas, we haven't finished the game yet. You can't leave,' she purred with a silky smile as she touched one of the buttons of his shirt with her fingertip.

'In case you haven't noticed, Natalie, our competition left.' Thomas met her look with a polite smile.

Lark knew exactly what the blonde was up to and she refused to take part in the woman's little game. She did not care to try to compete for Thomas's attention. The woman had a lot more ammunition than she did, Lark thought. Nasty attitude aside, Natalie was a very striking woman.

Too bad her attitude almost drove someone to strike her.

The catty thought caused Lark to chuckle and she grinned at the perplexed look on Natalie's face. She said goodnight to them with a slight wave and gripped the railing to head up the stairs. As she started up the stairs, she turned her head to look back toward them and the smile froze on her face.

Thomas was now standing with his back to her, while Natalie stepped closer to him. Her eyes met Lark's over his shoulder and she smiled with wicked triumph as she put her hand possessively on Thomas's arm.

Lark's steps faltered for a brief moment, then she continued up the stairs. She shoved away the anger and the hurt caused by Natalie's look and headed to the stairway leading to the bedrooms. She'd been played the fool too many times to remember and this was one time she was not going to allow it to happen again.

It'd have to be a pretty damn cold day in hell, she thought as she climbed the stairs, before she would let Thomas ever touch her again.

December in hell had never been so delicious.

Lark could feel his hands touching her, sliding up her rib cage to hold her breasts. He cupped her softly as his fingers worked their magic on her till she moaned with pleasure. He smoothed her hair from her neck and his lips were hot and greedy as he nipped at her throat. The sensations he was building within her caused her to shiver, but not from being cold. She turned toward him and tasted his skin with her mouth as her eyes opened. Her movements stopped, her body froze as she met the ice cold gaze of Natalie over his shoulder. The woman's lips were twisted into a knowing smirk as she advanced toward them carrying a clown doll dressed like Jeffrey Linden.

Lark's eyes focused on the face of the doll. Its eyes were open, staring at her with a dull expression. She recognized it for what it was. The dull face of the dead.

Lark shook herself from the dream with a gasp. She opened her eyes and stared at the ceiling as she reoriented herself to her surroundings. She suddenly felt too warm as she realized she was sweating from the grip the nightmare had on her.

Shaking the covers off, she sat up in bed with her feet crossed in front of her. Lark had to laugh at herself. Here she was sitting in the middle of the bed because she was too afraid to put her feet down on the floor. She turned on the lamp next to the bed and shifted cautiously to lean over the edge so she could peer underneath.

'You are such an idiot,' she said to herself as she rolled to sit on the edge of the mattress. 'I can't believe you just did that. Looking under the bed as if something would be there.'

Knowing sleep now would not come easily, Lark picked her robe from the end of the bed and shrugged into it. She yawned as she tied it and shuffled to the door. She thought warm milk was disgusting, but had always found chocolate a nice substitute for not being able to sleep. Opening the door, she stepped through and closed it with a quiet click.

She did not want to wake anyone by accidentally bumping into something so she stood for a moment to let her eyes adjust to the darkness of the hallway. Soon she was able to see quite well and started to make her way quietly down the hall toward the stairs.

Padding silently across the carpet, her steps hesitated outside Thomas's door. She couldn't help but wonder if he was alone. Lark shook her head, angry at herself for even thinking of the question, let alone

141

caring about the answer. She began to move past the doorway when she stubbed her toe into a small table.

Lark swallowed the groan that had threatened to escape her lips and she bit into them to keep from crying out. Or cussing at herself for her stupidity. The table had shifted slightly, not making much noise, but in the quiet of the night it sounded overly loud to her own ears. Lark waited a moment, then relaxed slightly when she heard no movements or sounds come from the rooms. Not even Thomas's.

'Probably too damn worn out to hear anything,' Lark muttered softly as she bent over to examine her toe. It wasn't bleeding and the pain was starting to ebb away. She ran her finger gingerly over the bruised digit and found no scrapes either.

'Do you always make such a racket in the middle of the night?'

Thomas's voice startled her and she jerked up, automatically reaching for the back of her robe. The length of the garment barely skimmed her thighs and the very unladylike position she had been standing in must have given him an incredible view. Lark nervously looked at his face and found him smiling comfortably and wickedly at her.

'Of course, if this is what I'm going to find when I check to see what's going on, I guess I can't say that I mind.'

'Jerk,' she snapped as she closed her robe tighter in front of her. 'I couldn't sleep and I was going downstairs to get something and I stubbed my toe.'

'Outside my door,' he stated, matter-of-factly.

Lark gasped at his insinuation. She put her hand on her hip as she stiffened, her voice an angry whisper. 'Yes, just outside your door. It is on the way to the stairs, in case you haven't noticed.'

'So it is,' Thomas said softly. He looked down the hall toward the stairs, then back to Lark. His eyes were sleepy, yet aware as his gaze held hers. 'Why couldn't you sleep, Lark?'

'I . . . I just couldn't. That's all.' Lark knew it sounded feeble even to her own ears, but she was not about to admit to him the extent of his participation in her dreams.

'Why don't you come in for a moment?' he asked, his voice low and inviting. At the look of fear and surprise on her face, his brows raised in humor. 'To talk, Lark. To talk. My, you have a dirty mind.'

'No, I won't and no, I don't,' she said, crossing her arms over her chest.

Thomas studied her for a moment as he leaned against the door frame. 'Is it because you're afraid of me, Lark?'

'My, someone has a pretty high opinion of himself, doesn't he?'

She took a deep breath, her heart pounding, and walked past him into his room. Once inside, she let the breath go and couldn't help looking around her at the contents of his room.

'Looking for something?' he asked, his hand resting on the door knob. 'Or should I say someone?'

'It's none of my business what you do or who you see, Thomas. Or is it whom?'

Lark moved away from him toward the fireplace, which glowed with a low flame. There was still just enough of a chill out in the spring night air that the fire felt good. She stood in front of it and let the warmth caress her skin. At Thomas's silence she looked back toward him.

She frowned at the serious look on his face. 'What is it?'

'Lark, I've never felt the need to explain my actions to anyone before, especially when it concerned women,' he said. He moved away from the door to stand beside her. She met his tiger eyes as the glow of the fire flickered over his features. 'But you are different.'

She shook her head, 'I don't understand.'

'It's important to me that you understand there is nothing going on between Natalie and me,' he said, his voice dropping to a soft whisper.

'Thomas, as I said, it's none of my–'

Thomas leaned toward her, kissing her gently as he effectively silenced her. His fingers skimmed lightly across her cheek. He pulled back only enough to leave a breath between them as he looked into her eyes. 'That makes it your business.'

'Thomas, I don't know–'

She started to protest, but again he silenced her with his lips. Thomas cupped her cheek as his kiss deepened, his lips moving deliciously against hers. Lark opened herself to him as he pulled her closer, his arms moving to tighten around her waist.

Lark sighed huskily as his lips skimmed across her cheek to her ear. He traced her lobe with the tip of his tongue and the slow moistness caused shivers to shimmer through her body. She slid her hand into his hair, through his hair, caressing the short, silky length of it. Thomas's hands slid over her back, down her hips, then back to her waist as he pulled her against the length of him. His lips found hers and he kissed her, leaving no doubt in her mind that he hungered for her. Needed her.

Needed her? Did he truly need her? Lark frowned as she pulled slightly away from him. She knew the answer to that question. Knew it too well. No, Thomas did not need her. He wanted her. She'd learned the difference a long time ago.

'I can't do this,' she said quietly, her voice no more than a whisper.

Thomas stopped kissing her neck and leaned back to study her. His eyes were heavy-lidded with desire. 'What's wrong, Lark?'

She licked her lips nervously as she smoothed her hand along his chest in a last forbidden caress before she pulled herself from his embrace completely. 'I just can't do this, Thomas.'

'I'm sorry, sweetheart,' he said softly as he skimmed his fingertip along her chin. 'I didn't mean to rush you like this. Please forgive me.'

Lark chuckled softly without humor as she turned away from him and moved to stand in front of the fireplace. 'Please, don't say anything more. You'll actually make me think you're a genuinely nice guy.'

'Who says I'm not?'

She shook her head. He shifted to stand beside her. She looked toward him and fought back the hunger she felt for him as she studied his face. His strong, handsome features were highlighted with the flickering light of the fire as he returned her quiet look with a thoughtful one of his own. The curve of his lips and the warmth of his eyes were deliciously inviting to her. Her fingers ached to reach out and touch the strong ridge of his cheek. To touch the soft indent of his lower lip.

Lark sighed as she moved her gaze to what she thought would be a safer focus, his eyes. How could she forget the heated potency of his eyes? His gaze was so open, inviting as a gentle caress. She cursed her traitorous body for responding to him as she turned away from him and closed her eyes against the memory of his handsome face.

'Oh, Thomas, why can't anything ever be simple?' she asked quietly, the question more for herself than for him.

'Most things usually aren't easy,' he answered as he moved behind her. He touched her shoulder softly. The feel of his hand more reassuring than seductive. 'If they weren't, would they be as much fun when you overcame them?'

She smiled as she shook her head. 'Typical lawyer, always have an answer for everything, don't you?'

'It's required by law,' he chuckled as he put his arms around her in a tender hug. He kissed the top of her head, then laid his chin on her hair.

And that was it.

Lark frowned as he continued to hold her, his hand rubbing her arm with gentle reassurance. Thomas did not attempt to make any masculine, macho, magnificent moves on her, or seduce her with his sexual prowess, or try to sweet talk her with a silver tongue. He simply held her.

She closed her eyes as she shook her head at her thoughts. How could he have sensed that instead of trying to overcome her defenses, he should wait and let her take them down? Logically, she knew when

146

she took his hand and drew it to her lips to press a soft kiss on his skin that she was making a mistake. But her body remembered the feel of his body against her, the heat of him. And her heart remembered the sense of security she felt within his embrace. The sense of belonging.

Lark knew with every shred of reason within her body that going any further with this man would be a mistake. Yet, she still turned in his arms, her gaze meeting his.

'Lark, I-'

She stretched up on tip-toe and silenced him with her mouth. She held his face in her hands as her lips moved over his deliberately. When he relaxed and his hands moved to encircle her waist, she sighed into his kiss.

Thomas took the opportunity to voice the seed of doubt that continued to nag at his thoughts. Her lips softened against his, then moved to his cheek. 'Lark, I won't deny I want to be with you. But only if you want me in the same way.'

'Thomas, be a good lawyer and shut up,' she quipped. She traced the contours of his lips with her tongue, then deepened her kiss as he opened to her.

Lark sighed, the sound husky with desire. She circled her arms around Thomas's neck and allowed herself to get lost in his kiss. He gripped her waist with his hands and pulled her closer to him. His lips moved across her cheek, then down to her neck.

Thomas's shoulder dipped as he shifted to pick her up in his arms. Lark gasped in startled surprise and unexpectedly found herself giggling. She'd never been carried before. The curve of her breast rubbed against his chest as he moved toward the bed. His arms, his warmth, his strength enveloped her, awakening something very primal deep within her. Her lips curved in a sultry smile as she decided she liked being carried.

'What are you thinking in that mind of yours, you little minx?' Thomas chuckled. She could feel the vibration of it move against her breast and her smile deepened.

'You can torture me and I'll never tell,' she answered. Lark tilted her head back to meet his gaze. Perhaps at another time it would have surprised her to find herself acting in such a brazen manner. But Thomas seemed to know how to break all her rules. The rules that had protected her, kept her heart safe from hurt for many years.

'Damn, I love a challenge,' Thomas said with relish as he moved toward the bed.

He put his knee on the bed, then draped Lark across the quilted cover. She raised herself to her elbows to pull the length of her hair from under her. She watched his eyes, fascinated, as his gaze moved over the length of her body.

Thomas took his robe off and let it fall to the floor. Lark licked her lips nervously as he joined her on the bed, wearing only his briefs. There were no words as he held her gaze, then let it drop slowly to her lips. His own touched hers, briefly, lightly. Lark sighed into his kiss and arched toward him to press herself against him.

He leaned over her, to pull aside her robe with his hand. The satin chemise she wore beneath it shimmered in the light of the fire. She watched, mesmerized, as he nipped at her breast through the material with tiny, gentle bites. He caressed the smooth skin of her thigh as his mouth moved from one satin peak to the other. Lark let her head fall back, a groan of pleasure on her lips as Thomas brushed aside the thin fabric to expose her tender skin to the heat of his mouth. She held his head in her hands as he drew her nipple into his mouth, sucking the peak softly.

'I should have known a lawyer would be good with his mouth,' Lark said, her voice catching as desire speared through her.

Thomas's chuckle vibrated against her skin, causing her to groan with pleasure. 'Don't knock a lawyer till you've tried one.'

They laughed easily together like time-tested lovers. The tiny lines at the corners of his eyes only accentuated the tiger-strength potency of his gaze as he met hers. Desire replaced the humor in his eyes and he shifted to help her remove the last of the filmy fabric from her body. He rolled slightly away from her and removed his briefs. Before her skin could cool from his touch he was beside her again, touching her, cupping her, holding her.

Lark ran her hands slowly over the defined muscles of his chest. The expanse of it was bare, the feel of his smooth skin moving against hers caused the heat within her to flare into flame as she continued her exploration of his body.

Lark's hands moved of their own will to his shoulders, then down the bulge of his biceps. Here they hesitated, basking in the power of his arms as he moved over her. Thomas's body almost covered her as his hands dipped lower, his thumb trailing the length of her rib cage to skim over her navel to the dark mat of her hair. He dipped his finger into the moist warmth of her, then gently caressed her. He barely touched her, slowly working the tiny bud with the tip of his finger in slow, delicious movements.

Her head fell back as her mouth opened with the moan that escaped from her. Lark's legs tingled and pulsed with the arousal he was so carefully building within her. The white hot spears of pleasure coiled within her, tighter and tighter, till it sparked and flared into flame. The heat of it, the intensity of the pleasure building caused her to grip his shoulders as her mouth sought the skin of his neck. She tasted him briefly, before the hot arousal of her climax spiraled through her and she was left clinging to him, the energy of it flowing away in delicious waves.

Lark's breath came in short pants as she lay limp beside him, feeling heavy with spent passion. She found the energy to move her hands over his arms as he rose above her. His muscles moved beneath her fingertips and again she found herself smiling with vivacious pleasure at the strength of him.

Thomas's eyes never left hers as he moved between her legs. His arms were braced on each side of her as he lowered his mouth to hers. Lark lifted her chin to meet his kiss and felt a momentary sense of frustration as he remained just out of reach. His lips hovered a breath above hers as he entered her slowly, till she held him completely.

Lark didn't know she could want someone so desperately as she did now. It was not the physical joining with him. Simply him.

He took her lips with his own, his kiss deepening as she felt the strength of his need. He lowered himself to her as he cupped her face in his hands.

Thomas's lips moved over hers, nipping at the small dip of her lower lip. He lightly trailed the moist tip over the indent before pulling it gently into his lips. His mouth continued to feather teasing, heated kisses over her cheeks and lips as his hands worked into the length of her hair.

Slowly he moved within her. The delicious feel of him over her, in her, caused the pleasure to build within her again. He sensed the need growing in her as she moved against him and he responded, instinctively moving with her.

Lark wrapped her arms around Thomas's neck and buried her face in the hollow of his neck as the fulfilment rocked through her. Thomas continued to move over her for a moment. He moaned huskily into her ear as he joined her.

His breathing matched hers as he lazily lifted his head to kiss her softly on the lips. Thomas moved beside her and pulled her into the crook of his arm as she laid her head on his shoulder. The bedspread was beyond being straight on the bed, so he pulled it around them, their bodies generating more than enough heat to keep them warm.

Thomas squeezed her gently in his embrace and planted a kiss to the top of her head. Lark tilted her face toward him and returned his smile as she kissed him tenderly, letting the intensity of her feelings flow through her and into her embrace.

Thomas murmured his pleasure, then leaned back as he studied her face. 'What was that for?'

'Nothing important,' she answered, ducking her head to rest it on his shoulder before he could see her expression.

'Liar,' he said.

'Accountants don't lie,' she quipped.

'And neither do lawyers,' he chuckled as he lazily traced his finger up and down her arm in slow gentle strokes.

Lark laughed, 'Yeah, right. And you know where you'll go for saying that.'

'I doubt I'll be alone,' he replied. Thomas shifted, tilting her head till she met his gaze. He studied her for a moment. 'Lark, I don't want you to take this lightly.'

'What?' she sputtered. 'You think I do this on a regular basis?'

She started to shift away from him when he caught her with his arm. She leveled her gaze on him. 'Let me go.'

'No,' he smiled casually. 'I know what you're trying to do. You're feeling awkward, maybe even feeling a little tenderness toward me and it scares the hell out of you. Rather than deal with it, you're going to try to pick a fight so you can get out of here and blame everything on me.'

'You're not the psychic, remember? I am,' she muttered as she continued to lie stiffly in his arms.

'Right now, I would say that is probably a good thing,' he chuckled good naturedly. 'Because I have a feeling by the look on your face that I probably would not want to know what you're thinking at the moment.'

'Does a tower and a high-powered rifle conjure any images for you?' she said through gritted teeth. It irked her to know he was right. She felt her anger slipping away from her, but a part of her still remained hesitant. It surprised her that someone, a man no less, understood how she felt. Still she could not open herself to him completely. Not yet anyway.

She studied his eyes as she bit her lip in thought. Lark sighed at the conflicting emotions warring within her. One night, she promised herself. It was just one night with the man who had haunted her dreams for so long and now would never leave her thoughts.

She gave him a tentative lopsided smile as she gave in to the urge to nestle back beside him. Thomas again stroked her arm with his fingertips as he pressed his lips to her forehead.

'Thoughts like that could get you in trouble, little girl,' he said softly, his mouth brushing against her skin.

'Thomas, you have to be the first man in history who actually wants to talk after making love,' she murmured against his chest as she closed her eyes and snuggled deeper into his embrace.

'There's just something about you, Lark,' he said softly. 'I plan on figuring it out.'

'Maybe it's my charming personality,' she yawned. 'Or maybe you're being drawn to my aura. If you believe in that kind of stuff.'

'A skeptical psychic?' Thomas chuckled. 'Isn't that a contradiction in terms?'

'Thomas?' Lark said. She had to stop to yawn yet again, and found it hard to keep her train of thought as sleep threatened to take over.

'What is it, sweetheart?' he asked softly.

She draped her arm over his chest as dark edges of sleep started to envelop her. 'Shut up.'

CHAPTER 8

The sweetest sensations moved through Lark as she started to stir from her dreams. In the mist-like place between sleep and morning she experienced a sensation she'd rarely had before. Contentment.

Lark knew she was dreaming. Knew that soon the light of the morning sun would intrude upon her secret wishes and force her eyes to open. She turned her back to the reality morning threatened to bring and savored the last few moments of her dream.

There Thomas held her within his embrace. He held her gaze with those beautiful eyes that could so easily mesmerize her. His hard body was pressed against her and she could feel the heat of him warming her soul. Here in this tranquil state, Lark knew they could be a normal couple doing normal things. Here there were no psychic feelings, no bodies wanting to be found, no people who refused to believe she was a person with needs just like theirs.

Lark sighed, snuggling closer to the warmth surrounding her. Reality crept into her thoughts like an unwelcome visitor and she opened her eyes. Slowly she raised her head to look beside her. She met Thomas's gaze filled with humor.

'Good morning,' he said cheerfully.

'Oh no,' she muttered, rolling to her stomach to bury her face in the pillow. 'A morning person.'

'What's that?' he teased as he leaned over her to stroke her back with his hand. 'The pillow sort of muffles things.'

Lark lifted her head slightly and spoke slowly as she enunciated each word with feeling. 'I hate morning people.'

'I'd say it would be more accurate to state that you hate mornings,' he chuckled.

'I don't have a problem with mornings when I've gotten some sleep the night before,' Lark growled. She shifted to her side, her hair falling like a dark curtain over her face. 'You wouldn't know anything about that, would you?'

Thomas shrugged with mock surprise, then grinned wickedly at her. 'I couldn't help it if you threw yourself at me.'

'Jerk,' she muttered.

'I think you called me that last night too,' he laughed. He smoothed the hair from her cheek and Lark squinted sleepily at his cheerful face.

'If you're interested, I can show you something that will really wake you up,' he offered suggestively.

Lark gave him a dry look. 'Only if it's a suitable replacement for a caffeine-packed cup of coffee.'

Thomas chuckled against her skin as he leaned over her to nuzzle her neck. 'It must be pretty good if you're complaining about not getting any sleep last night.'

'You know, I was serious when I said I hated morning people, Thomas.'

'I guess I can take that as a tentative no,' he said without losing an ounce of his good humor, Lark noticed with a grimace.

'Take it any way you want it, but leave me alone.' Lark nestled into the pillow and closed her eyes, more than prepared to go back to sleep.

'You're cute when you're being reluctant, you know that?' Thomas said, his hand dipping lower under the blankets.

'Kittens are cute, Thomas,' Lark answered without opening her eyes. 'Now remove your hand from my breast before I break every one of your fingers.'

Thomas cupped her breast in his hand as he teased the peak with his thumb. He ignored her remark and smiled as she did nothing to stop him. The dark bud tightened beneath his touch and he watched as her expression lost much of its scowl.

Lark shifted, giving him better access to her and he did not hesitate to take full advantage of the situation. Thomas started to lower his mouth to taste her when a scream pierced the tranquil morning stillness.

He stiffened at the sound. 'What the hell was that?'

'It came from downstairs,' Lark answered, her heart beginning to pound in her throat.

They fell silent, their breathing the only sound in the room as they listened for any noise from below to confirm what they had heard. A woman's voice could be heard sobbing as she cried out first for Mrs Blackwell, then Thomas. He swung from the bed and shrugged into his pajama bottoms, then into his robe. Lark matched him for speed as she pulled her

157

chemise over her head. She was tying the belt of her robe as Thomas pulled open the door of his room.

He stepped through the door with Lark close behind him when they met the more than curious stares of the others standing in the hallway. Lark's gaze first settled, unfortunately, on Natalie. The woman looked as if she could do some screaming of her own when she saw her obviously leaving Thomas's bedroom and the immediate implications it offered.

Before more curiosity could be stirred up regarding their presence together, a voice from the bottom of the stairway focused everyone's attention below. Lark and the others raced to the landing to find Maria clutching the decorative newel post at the foot of the stairway. Her white-knuckled grip matched her pale face as she stared up at them, her mouth quivering with shock.

'Maria, what has happened?' Thomas called to her.

'I can't believe it. I walked into the room and I . . . I found her.' Her gaze swung to him. 'She's dead.'

Then Maria fainted, falling into a crumpled heap at the bottom of the stairs.

Maria's dramatic statement had momentarily stunned everyone. Thomas was the first to pull himself from his shock and move into action. He ordered David to notify the police immediately, then asked his grandmother to attend to the still unconscious maid. It didn't occur to him till later that Henry stood by his grandmother, wearing one of her ruffled robes.

He turned to Lark, 'I need you to come with me.'

She frowned at him, 'Why do you need me to come with you?'

Thomas stepped closer to her and lowered his voice so that the others could not hear him. 'Would you rather stay here and keep Natalie company?'

'Good point,' she murmured as she started toward the stairs.

Maria had not been specific as to where she had found the body, so they decided to start with the kitchen. There they found the young maid, LeAnn, lying on the floor against the island in the kitchen.

Thomas knelt beside the woman and felt for a pulse even though it was obvious there would not be one. He stood and exhaled slowly. 'Damn it.'

Lark ran her hand nervously through her hair. 'We probably should get out of here till the police come. The less traveled the scene is the better for their technicians.'

He looked toward her with a frown. She sensed that he was seeing a different side of her. Her experienced psychic side that dealt regularly with death, natural and violent. She had the uneasy sensation that he didn't know how to accept this part of her.

'You're probably right.'

Thomas turned away from her and headed toward the library where the others had also decided to go. Everyone was still dressed in their night clothes and the room was silent as each person appeared lost in their own thoughts.

Lark felt uneasy and alone as she hugged her arms around herself. Alicia, now dressed, sat on the sofa with Maria, who was timidly sipping a glass of water. Henry was also dressed in the clothes he had been wearing the night before and hovered near Alicia, his worry showing in his tight expression. David and Natalie sat in chairs side by side, but neither seemed to notice anything around them. Stephanie sat in a wing-back chair with John standing behind her. The pudgy woman looked ill and unkempt, an obvious sign of the illness she had been fighting. John's gaze kept flicking nervously from his wife to the door as he fidgeted behind her.

Even with the group seated in the room, Lark still felt isolated. They were all clumped to one side while she leaned against the desk across from them. Thomas stood apart from the others as he stared out the window at the growing light of the morning. But he also stood apart from her.

Everyone's attention turned toward the windows as the first wail of the sirens started up the long driveway. Two police cars pulled to a quick stop in front of the house and Thomas went to open the door for them. He escorted the policemen to the kitchen.

The activity started immediately. Officers radioed the call in to notify homicide and the coroner. Lark moved behind the desk and sat down with a heavy sigh. She let her head drop to her hands and started to massage her temples as the headache started to pound through her forehead.

'This is all your fault, you little bitch.' Natalie's voice was vehement and filled with accusation as she stood and walked toward the windows.

'Natalie,' Alicia barked, her face a rigid mask of disapproval, 'I truly don't think this is the time or the place for this kind of outburst.'

'When is the right time, Alicia?' the blonde spat as she spun toward the older woman. Her hard gaze remained on Alicia's as she jabbed an accusing finger toward Lark. 'After she kills someone else?'

'What?' Lark cried as she jerked her head up to look at the two women. 'You can't possibly think I was involved in this?'

'Knock it off, sweetheart,' Natalie snapped, her mouth twisted into an ugly frown. Her blue eyes were dark with loathing as her voice continued to rise with her building anger. 'Your little innocent act may have got you into Thomas's bed, but it doesn't work with me. You show up and two people are murdered. You were even found kneeling over the first body. Who's next?'

'Stop it,' Stephanie screamed, clutching her hands to her face as she started to sob. 'Please stop it.'

Alicia immediately rushed to the woman's side and put her arms around her as she tried to give her comfort. 'Shhh, sweetheart,' she crooned softly, brushing the tears away with her fingers. 'I'm so sorry this has happened. It's obviously upset all of us.'

'Give me a break,' Natalie snorted as she turned her back on the group.

Alicia's gaze hardened as she glanced toward the tall woman, a striking contrast to her gentle voice. She ignored her for a moment as she focused on taking care of Stephanie. 'John, why don't you take her back upstairs. Henry, would you mind taking a look at her? She doesn't look well at all.'

'I agree,' John answered. He took his wife by the shoulders and helped her to stand. 'Come with me, Stephanie. I'll help you back to bed.'

Alicia stood with her hands clasped in front of her as she watched the trio leave. Stephanie leaned heavily against John, but her sobbing had quieted to sniffles as they climbed the stairs.

Alicia turned from the door and faced Natalie. The matron of Blackwell Castle looked every bit the queen as her gaze focused on the blonde standing by the window. Her voice was cool and poised. 'Natalie, I've about had enough out of you. What you just did is intolerable. As soon as this situation is resolved, I think your visit should come to an end. For good.'

'That is just fine, Alicia,' Natalie said, her voice heavy with bitterness. She turned to face Alicia, her expression dark. 'But if you're going to boot people out, you might think about booting your psychic out as well. The mortality rate around here would drop immediately without her.'

She turned to glare at Lark for a moment, then stalked from the room. Alicia watched her go as she slowly exhaled. When she faced Lark, her face was lined with fatigue. 'Lark, honey, please try to understand that this is very upsetting for all of us.'

'I do understand, Alicia,' she said quietly as she stood. Lark walked to the older woman and took her hand and tried to offer her a smile. 'Now, if you will please excuse me, I would like to get dressed before the detectives arrive. They'll want to talk to all of us.'

Lark left the room, leaving Alicia to watch her with a worried expression. The older woman frowned as she rubbed her forehead tiredly with the tips of her fingers.

David moved beside his grandmother to put his hand gently on her shoulder. His expression was soft with concern. 'Grandmother, as much as I hate to agree with Natalie's outburst, part of what she said might be true. Maybe it would be for the best if that woman leaves. At least till things are cleared up.'

Alicia glanced quickly to her grandson. Her voice was gentle, but firm. 'David, that woman's name is Lark. She has a good heart, and I refuse to believe she has had anything to do with any of this. I think she is being used as a convenient scapegoat because of who she is and she wouldn't be involved in any of this if I hadn't brought her here. I'd sooner believe you or Thomas killed them than Lark.'

David held her gaze for a moment, then acknowledged his understanding of her belief as he gave her hand a reassuring squeeze. 'For your sake, I hope you're right, Grandmother. But I think you are looking through rose-colored glasses when it comes to her. Someone in this house killed these people. I think it's time we started opening our eyes and looking at the facts.'

David hesitated a moment, hoping to let the impact of his words persuade his grandmother to stop feeling so responsible for this unwanted stranger. He gripped her hand as his voice hardened with conviction. 'The fact remains that all the evidence points toward your psychic.'

Lark dressed, then sat heavily on the edge of the bed as she let her breath out slowly. All energy had left her and she felt empty and drained as she waited to go downstairs and face the detectives. She looked around her at the room and realized how Theorosa must have felt as she waited for her execution. This time there wouldn't be a rope, just a jury and a possible death sentence.

She stared at the floor, lost in her thoughts, trying to make sense of what was going on. A knock at the door startled her and she pushed from the bed to open it. The astonishment must have registered on her face when she found Thomas standing in the hallway, because he smiled at her as he gently touched her cheek.

'Why do you look so surprised?'

'I just am,' she answered as she stepped into the hallway, closing the door behind her and their conversation. She allowed herself a small smile, she wasn't about to tell him how happy she was to see him. Her eyes focused on the deputy standing behind him in the hallway and all thoughts of happiness fell away like an icy rain.

'It's just procedure, Lark,' Thomas said, answering the silent question in her eyes.

'I know, Thomas.' She gave him a small, forced smile. 'Remember, I know the routine.'

They walked without talking to the library where Detective Baker waited for them. He rose without smiling when they entered the room.

'It seems death follows you wherever you go, Miss Delavan,' Baker said, his gaze fixed steadily on her.

Lark refused to rise to his bait. Instead, she continued to meet his stare.

'No flippant remarks this time, I see.' His lips thinned into a straight line, a grim semblance of a smile. 'Maybe you'd like to tell me what happened?'

'There is nothing I can tell you, detective,' Lark said, her voice void of emotion.

'Surely you've had time to think of something,' he said, his brows dipping into a thick frown.

'Baker, that's uncalled for.' Thomas's voice may have been quiet, but there was no mistaking the authority surrounding him.

'I have no answer, because I do not know what happened last night.' Lark folded her hands in her lap. They were cold with fear, but she refused to let that man see her shake. 'I did not kill her. I really didn't even know her.'

'Who did it then?' Baker asked without pausing.

'Baker,' Thomas barked, his expression thunderous.

'Cool it, Blackwell.' The detective stood, his hands on his hips. 'I've about had enough out of you, and your girlfriend.'

The detective walked to the window and looked out for a moment, letting the silence fall heavily into the room. He turned back to them, looking from one to the other.

'Now, Miss Delavan, would you like to explain just what you did do last night?' he asked, his voice filled with mock patience.

Automatically her gaze met Thomas's and she wished with all her heart that she could remove him from all of this. It surprised her to see his gaze remain steadily on hers. It held no remorse or anger.

'She was with me,' Thomas answered, his face a mask as he turned to look at the detective.

Baker's brows rose and his lips twisted into a smirk. 'All night?'

'For the most part.' Thomas took a seat on the couch beside Lark.

Baker nodded, chewing on his lip as he seemed to consider the statement. 'Okay,' he started, as he walked to stand in front of them. 'She went up to your room with you and was with you most of the night. Is that what you're telling me?'

Thomas's jaw clenched and Lark could see the anger building in his eyes. The detective instantly picked up on his silence.

'Did I get it wrong then?' he asked, his voice thick with sarcasm. 'Which part?'

Lark watched the two of them as they glared at each other. She felt the anger rise within her. How dare the man treat them as if they had had a sordid affair.

'I did not go with Thomas to his room,' she blurted, her face heating with her embarrassment. 'It wasn't until later in the evening.'

'I see.' The detective rocked back on his heels as he studied her. 'Go on.'

Lark took a deep breath and exhaled slowly as her nerves tightened. As she said the words, even she could hear how incriminating they sounded.

'I woke up from a bad dream and knew I couldn't get back to sleep, so I decided to go downstairs and get a snack. I stubbed my toe on a small table in the hallway and that's when Thomas opened his bedroom door to see what was going on.'

'What time was this?' Baker crossed his arms over his chest as he waited for an answer.

Lark shrugged, 'I don't know. I didn't look at the time.'

'So you heard a noise, Mr Blackwell, and opened your door to see who was in the hallway, correct?' The detective shifted to take a seat in a chair across from them. He leaned his forearms across his knees and lifted his brows in question when he finally looked toward Thomas.

'That is correct.' Thomas's face remained impassive.

Baker lifted his hands in front of him and shrugged. 'And?'

'And what would you like to know?' Thomas asked.

Baker's expression darkened and he looked as if he would like to snarl a few foul words at the remark. He paused as he studied Thomas, then narrowed his eyes. 'You say a noise woke you. What kind of a noise was it?'

'I don't really recall.' Thomas was obviously reluctant to discuss the evening, but Lark knew that his nature would not allow him to do otherwise. 'I jolted awake and I started listening to see if I would hear it again and figure out what it was.'

'And what did you hear?' Baker prompted.

Thomas shook his head. 'I heard soft footsteps, then nothing for several moments. I could hear them continue and I knew that someone was walking down the hall. The person hesitated outside my door, then bumped into the table in the hallway. I opened the door and found Lark outside my room.'

A smile barely touched the corners of his mouth and she knew he was thinking of her bending over

167

checking her toe and Lark had the incredible urge to whack him.

Baker rubbed his chin thoughtfully as he again chewed on his lip. 'Did you actually see Miss Delavan leave her room?'

Thomas stiffened and she could see his reluctance to answer the question. They both knew the answer would not look favorable to her already incriminating position. His voice was tight as he finally spoke. 'No, I did not.'

Baker's gaze never even flicked in her direction. 'So you wouldn't have been able to tell if she had come from her room, as she says she did, or if she had just come up from the stairs?'

Thomas's expression was hard as he returned the detective's look. 'No, I would not.'

'What time would you say it was when Miss Delavan just happened to show up in front of your bedroom door?'

Thomas's jaw was working as he tried to gain control over his temper. He said nothing for a moment, then answered the question. 'It was around one o'clock in the morning.'

'How did you know this?' Baker asked.

'I looked at the clock.' Thomas's expression showed how frivolous he thought the question was.

'Ron, I realize you're busy,' a man interrupted from the doorway of the library. 'But Sid is here. He's ready to get started.'

Baker nodded his thanks to the man as he rose. He turned back to them. 'You two would probably be interested in this, why don't you come with me?'

Lark met Thomas's gaze and she could tell that he too did not feel comfortable with the detective's suggestion. Thomas stood and offered her his hand. She took it and welcomed the strength and support he gave her.

They followed Baker as he made his way to the kitchen. The large room was busy with law enforcement. A police photographer and a couple of forensic technicians had already worked the grid around the body and were searching toward the outer edges. At a glance, it could have been mistaken for a party as people milled around the room, but the uniforms were a dead give away that it was a crime scene.

So was the body.

A man with the beginnings of a pot belly knelt beside LeAnn's body. His glasses looked as if they continually perched on the end of his bulbous nose as he tilted his head to examine the woman lying before him. He studied the neck and face of the corpse, then attempted to lift her hand. The limb did not move easily and the dark discoloration on the bottom of her arm remained somewhat fixed when he pushed at it with his finger. He made several noncommittal noises, then rose awkwardly to his feet.

The man looked toward them, nodding an acknowledgment to the detective. His eyes seemed small and protruding behind the thick glasses as he looked at them without much interest.

'What do we have, Sid?' Baker asked as he knelt beside the body to look it over.

'Well, the lab guys have obviously already been in this area,' he stated as he pulled a handkerchief from his pocket and dabbed at the sweat beading on his

169

upper lip. 'Of course, I can't tell you much till I get her on the table, but her wounds are consistent with blunt force trauma. I can give you something a little more accurate later.'

Baker looked up at him as he laid his forearm across his knee. 'Time of death?'

Sid pursed his lips as he raised his brows in an unconscious comical expression of thought. 'Rigor mortis is just beginning, lividity is just starting to become fixed, and she's cool to the touch. It's a rough estimate, but I'd say she hasn't been dead very long.'

Baker's face showed his frustration at the non-committal statement. 'Can you be a little more specific, Sid?'

'Oh. Well,' the man puffed and shrugged, obviously reluctant to commit to a time. 'I can give you a rough estimate, of course, but I need to get her in so I can pinpoint a more exact time for you. And, as you know, even that would be a rough estimate.'

'Rough estimate would be fine,' the detective prompted.

Sid again shrugged as he puffed, then groaned. He dabbed at his lip, then cleared his throat. 'Somewhere between twelve and one o'clock. Very roughly speaking, of course.'

'Of course,' Baker murmured. His gaze fixed on Lark with steady determination. 'Wouldn't you say that is interesting, Miss Delavan?'

Man, she did not like this guy, she thought as she remained silent in response to his statement. She frowned as he continued to study her, then she turned to look at Thomas. She could see by his grim expression that things were definitely not going well for her. Lark shook her head at the disturbing thoughts starting to appear from the dark recesses of her mind. When would the good detective arrest her and haul her in to question her over and over?

How was she going to get herself out of this one?

Fear. Bone chilling fear moved through her at the control she had lost over her life. Unseen, unknown forces were moving her, herding her where they wanted her to go. If ever there was a time she could use her ability, it was now. Now she wished fervently that she could call up a vision that could help her find her way out of this situation.

She closed her eyes and concentrated. A small moment passed. Nothing. Her thoughts remained silent and black.

Lark exhaled slowly as she opened her eyes to look around her. Thankfully, the detective was lurking elsewhere and only Thomas stood with her.

He touched her shoulder gently with his hand. 'Are you all right?'

'I'm fine,' she murmured.

Lark gave him an encouraging smile as she reached to take his hand and gave it a reassuring squeeze. She glanced away from him toward the body of LeAnn. She started to look away when something caught her gaze and she returned to it.

She frowned as she studied the body. She started with LeAnn's face. Death had not been kind to the woman. Her eyes were open, staring into the eternity of the afterlife. Nature's stiffening of her muscles gave her expression a startled, fearful look.

171

Lark tilted her head as she continued her inspection. Something had caught her attention, but she hadn't quite figured out what it was. She narrowed her eyes as her gaze moved over the lifeless form.

'Dust,' she said softly.

Thomas looked at her. 'What?'

'Dust,' she repeated. She started to step closer, then thought better of it. She lifted her hand to point at the smudges on the body. 'Look, Thomas. There's dust smudged on her face, her arms, and the back of her legs. She lives here doesn't she?'

He nodded. 'Both she and Maria have rooms downstairs. Tim lives in the carriage house above the garage, but I still don't get what you're talking about. It could be dirt.'

'I don't think so.' Lark did not step forward, but knelt so she could get a better look. 'Dirt looks different. She lives here, what need would she have to go outside? Maybe it is dirt, but it reminds me of what you'd find someplace that hasn't been open in ages.'

Lark stood as she put her hands on her hips. Her expression was thoughtful as she pursed her lips, trying to attach meaning to this new finding.

Thomas's brows rose and he shook his head. 'How can you tell the difference between dust and dirt?'

Lark turned to him, giving him a dry look. 'When is the last time you held a dust cloth in your hand?'

'Okay,' he murmured. 'Point taken. Still, I can't think of a place around here with that much accumulation. Even the attic and garage are fairly clean.'

'Mmm.' She heard his words, but they sounded distant to her. Surreal.

Lark's gaze had fixed on the dead woman's eyes and they seemed to draw her toward them. She did not move forward, her body did not physically move, but still she felt herself being pulled toward the dead woman's stare, the eyes growing larger till she felt as if she were being absorbed by them.

She forced herself to continue despite the fear enveloping her. The sensations showered over her, the tingling feeling washed through her. Lark felt LeAnn's grief, then her curiosity mingling with apprehension as she moved forward in a dark, stale hallway. The scene changed with a flaring of color, then a figure stood before her. It beckoned to her with its hands. Lark frowned as she held the dark gaze of the woman standing before her, then she recognized her.

It was Theorosa. And she was calling to her.

Lark shook her head. She could not understand what was wanted of her. The figure disappeared in a glitter of brilliance to be replaced with images flashing in bursts of light, faster and faster, till she felt assaulted by them.

Turning away, she closed her eyes in an effort to stop the images, but they continued, speeding through her thoughts. Lark heard Thomas calling to her, felt his hands on her arms as he shook her. Instantly, the images were gone and she felt herself returning.

Opening her eyes, she had never felt so relieved to see his face even as she worried over the concern in his expression.

'Damn it, Lark. Are you all right?' The tension showed in the rigid mask of his face.

'I'm fine,' she answered, moving her hands to grip his arms. She shook her head in an effort to dispel the lingering sensations of fear and warning still sifting through her when she caught Baker's hard gaze. Her heart pounded heavily and her breath shook, still she lifted her chin and returned his look.

She needed to talk to Thomas, but not here. Not where that man might overhear what she had to tell him. She turned back to Thomas and tried to give him a reassuring smile. 'I'm fine, Thomas, but I would like to go to my room and lie down for a little bit.'

Thomas put his arm around her shoulder and walked with her through the door. Lark did not feel any easier till they started climbing the stairs toward the bedrooms. Still, she felt as if she were being watched. At the top of the stairs, she turned to look down toward the kitchen, half expecting Baker to be standing there watching her. He always seemed to be watching her.

There was no one.

Lark took a slow shaky breath, but felt no relief. She had sensed a presence, but had found nothing to explain what she felt. She rolled her shoulder to ease the tension knotting itself between her shoulder blades as they came to Thomas's door.

His hand hesitated on the door knob and he turned toward her. 'If you would rather be alone, I can take you to your room.'

She shook her head as she wrapped her arms around herself. She felt cold and the sensations of the images still lingered within her and she didn't want to be alone. 'I could use the company if you don't mind.'

He smiled and opened the door for her, softly touching her shoulder as she passed into the room. 'Of course not. It saves me from having to convince you otherwise.'

Once inside she hesitated at the sight of the bed. She didn't go near it, but instead moved toward the fireplace. It wasn't that she held remorse for what had happened last night. Oh, on the contrary. The way she was feeling at the moment, the iciness shivering through her, she knew it would be all too easy to succumb to the heat he could ignite within her.

Thomas moved to the wing-back chair to sit down, then held his hand out to her. She paused only a moment, then smiled as she took his hand and lowered herself to his lap. He wrapped his arms around her and gave her a gentle squeeze as he kissed the top of her head.

'I know you saw something down there.' Thomas's voice was low and filled with understanding. 'But I also realized you probably did not want to talk about it in front of an audience.'

'Not so much an audience,' she stated, 'but that audience. Baker is not the most sensitive of people.'

'That he's not,' Thomas chuckled, laying his chin on her head. Lark nestled closer to him, enjoying the warmth of him, the smell of him, the feeling of his voice vibrating through his body to hers. 'Tell me what you saw down there.'

Lark nodded absently as she mulled the images through her mind. She rubbed her forehead against the dark shadow of Thomas's beard, then nestled her head in the crook of his neck. She took a deep breath, inhaling his spicy aroma. Placing a small kiss on the smooth skin of his chest, she stroked small circles there with her fingertips, just happy to be touching him.

Finally she spoke, her expression losing the soft look to be replaced with her determination to see the images through. 'I could feel her sadness, then I could see a . . . place. I hesitate to call it a hallway, but it was like one, long and narrow. But I don't think it was, because it was dirty.'

Lark hesitated as the smudges on LeAnn's body finally made sense. 'Dusty.'

Thomas rubbed her arm with his hand as he nodded slowly. 'That would explain the stains. But where would she have gone to get them? She couldn't have been too far away.'

'I don't know,' Lark shrugged as she stared tiredly at Thomas's statue of a small gargoyle. 'I don't think she was familiar with the place. I sensed curiosity and fear, as if she had been drawn there by something.'

Thomas's hand stopped its gentle movement. 'Or maybe followed someone.'

She shifted to lean back and meet his gaze. 'I can't say for sure, but I think you're right.'

He hugged her closer, drawing her back against his chest. 'Was that all of it?'

Lark shook her head. 'The last part didn't make sense to me.'

'What?' he asked.

She bit softly on her lip as she recalled the flashing intensity of the images. 'It was Theorosa. She was beckoning to me to follow her.'

Thomas remained silent and she welcomed it. Before, in the kitchen, the image of Theorosa had melted into a bombarding brilliance of scenes that she had been unable to grasp. Now in the warmth and security of Thomas's embrace, Lark was able to recall the pictures flashing through her mind, still she didn't quite understand them.

Faces of death. Lark had recognized Jeffrey's face, then LeAnn's as they superimposed one onto another. But she hadn't recognized the first one. She concentrated on the features as it clarified itself in her thoughts and she sucked in her breath.

It was David.

'Come on, I need to look at something.' Lark pushed away from Thomas's chest and stood from the chair. She didn't wait for him. Did not say a word, but went to the door and opened it. She started toward the staircase to the third floor and quickened her step.

Thomas was close behind her. 'What is it, Lark?'

'I have to go look for myself,' she said, moving quickly up the steps. 'I don't know if I'll be able to explain it.'

At the top of the stairs, she practically flung the side door open. She ran to where the portraits of the Blackwell family hung. Her gaze moved frantically back and forth till she located what she wanted.

The portrait of Thomas's cousin, David.

Lark moved closer and studied it, noting the subtle differences between the portrait and the image trapped in her thoughts. She shook her head and moved quickly toward the beginning of the portraits. There she stopped and exhaled slowly. She had not seen Thomas's cousin in her vision.

It had been the other David Blackwell. The man who was to marry Theorosa, but had been murdered in his own home.

Lark raised her hand. It shook slightly as she pointed to the portrait of Thomas's ancestor. 'It was him. I saw him in my vision. First I saw him, then Jeffrey, and finally LeAnn's face.'

Thomas was uneasy as he looked from the painting to her. 'What does David Blackwell have to do with these murders?'

'I don't know exactly,' Lark said, nervously licking her lips. She shook her head as she tried to decipher the message, then swung her gaze back to Thomas. 'I can't figure it out, they have nothing to do with each other.'

Thomas studied the painting, then frowned. 'Except the similarities.'

'What?' she asked.

He pointed toward the painting. 'LeAnn's death doesn't fit, but David Blackwell was found murdered in the library, so was Jeffrey. The legend says Theorosa was innocent, that she was wrongly accused of David's murder, but still she was executed . . .'

Thomas's voice trailed off, the following silence thick with tension. He turned slowly to face her. 'You were found standing over Jeffrey's body and certain people would very much like to see you accused of his murder.'

Lark swallowed hard as she followed what he was saying to her. 'And if I was found guilty of the murders I could face a life sentence.'

Thomas ran his hand through his hair, his face showing his apprehension as his gaze returned to her. 'In this state we also have the death penalty.'

CHAPTER 9

In this state we also have the death penalty.

The words echoed through her mind. Lark's eyes widened and she clutched at her shirt. Thomas's statement seemed to bounce around and grow within her thoughts till she felt it would drown out the pounding of her heart.

Although she had not been charged with anything, the realization finally sank in to Lark that the idea of her being tried for these murders could become an all too real experience.

In this state we also have the death penalty.

Her hands felt icy. Numb. She looked around for a place to sit and found nothing near, so she sat on the floor. Her face paled at the thought of this new found reality.

'Lark.' Thomas moved to stand in front of her. He started to reach his hand toward her, then let it drop to his side as if he didn't know what to do for her. Slowly he knelt in front of her. 'Are you all right?'

'You seem to ask me that a lot lately,' she murmured, her gaze distant and unfocused.

Thomas smiled softly as he looked away for a moment. 'Yeah.'

'Damn it.' It was happening again, she thought. What were the odds, she wondered of being accused of two or three different murders and actually be innocent? Then she frowned. She didn't remember anything of the night Jeffrey had died. She had been found with his blood on her hands. Even if she had been poisoned and suffering from delusions, did she kill Jeffrey? What possible reason would anyone have to drive her to do such a thing?

Lark ran her hands through her hair in frustration, and slowly blew her breath out. 'Damn it.'

'Is that all you have to say?'

She lifted her gaze to meet his and gave him a dry look. 'No. I could say a lot more, believe me.'

'Like maybe I should feel sorry for you?' Thomas simply looked at her, his face registering nothing.

Anger flared within her and she could feel it harden her expression. Her jaws clenched and she drew her knees in front of her, then placed her forearms across her legs. Her eyes narrowed. 'What?'

'I'm sorry, did you not hear me?' he asked, raising his eyebrows.

Lark started to open her mouth to say something and realized she could not think of a single thing to say, she was so mad. She could not believe the audacity of the man.

'Feel sorry for myself?' she finally stuttered angrily. 'If you were the one facing possible murder charges, not to mention the death penalty, don't you think you would be a little mad?'

'So what are you going to do about it?' he asked. Thomas's tone and his actions were so nonchalant, she felt like hitting him.

'What am I going to do about it?' Lark sputtered incredulously.

Thomas chuckled good naturedly. 'You keep repeating everything I say, Lark.'

'Repeat this,' she retorted, lifting her foot to push him on his backside. Lark stood, putting her hands on her hips as she glared down at him. 'I know one thing I'm not going to do, and that is sit here and listen to you goad me.'

Thomas stretched his legs lazily in front of him, then leaned back on his hands as he smiled devilishly at her. 'Good.'

Lark looked at his expression, his eyes, then she realized what he was doing. He wanted to make her angry. Angry enough to fight the nightmare threatening to overwhelm her.

She crossed her arms over her chest and smiled. 'You are a jerk.'

His smile widened to a grin. 'You know, I'm beginning to think you mean that as a term of endearment.'

'Not on your life, Blackwell.'

She moved to him, then stepped over his legs to stand over him. She sat on his lap and leaned forward till she was a breath away from his face.

Thomas's eyes twinkled with mischief. And more. His gaze held hers and she saw the desire flare in his look before he focused on her lips. Lark's lips quirked in a devilish look to match that of his. She shifted on his lap, fully aware of the movements she was making. Pressing herself softly against him, she brushed his lips with hers, touching him ever so slightly. She held his gaze, watching his beautiful tiger eyes darken. She feathered the ridge of his lip with the tip of her tongue as she traced the contours.

Thomas moved to deepen the kiss. Lark pulled out of his reach as she brushed against his lap.

He groaned as he again leaned forward. 'Now who's being a jerk?'

She chuckled wickedly, the sound low and throaty. 'Paybacks are truly a bitch, aren't they, Thomas?'

'I didn't torture you,' he murmured as he met her kiss movement for movement, trying to touch her more.

Lark framed his face with her hands as she stilled his movements. 'When will you realize that never, I repeat, never will a mere man be able to out-do a woman? Even if he is a lawyer.'

Thomas put his arms around her and pulled her against his chest. He kissed her. She opened herself to him and he stroked his tongue against her soft crevices till she moaned with pleasure.

He pulled back just enough to meet her gaze. Her lids were heavy with promised passion. 'When will you learn I'm no mere man?'

Thomas lowered his mouth to reclaim her. His hands tightened around her back and she reveled in the callused heat of his palms as he slid them under her shirt. His lips moved across her cheek to taste the softness of her neck. She let her head fall back so he could touch more of her.

'I know. You're my dream man.' Her words were softly spoken. Lark hadn't realized that she had said them out loud till Thomas paused, his lips hovering a fraction above her skin.

'What, sweetheart?'

In response she turned and her mouth found his, working against her till she thought she would want to rip his clothes off with her teeth. Thomas smoothed his palms across her skin till he found the rounded curves of her breasts. He cupped her, rubbing her nipples with his thumbs through her bra. The feel of him, the heat of his touch against the satin material brushing against the sensitive tips caused them to deliciously harden.

'Oh, Thomas,' she said quietly, her voice sounding almost absent minded, 'what is it about you?'

He removed one hand from her shirt to stroke her hair as he nibbled on the silk of her throat. He tangled his fingers in the satin length of her mane, gripping it to him as his desire speared through his body.

Lark moaned as he shifted under her and pressed the hard evidence of his need against the now sensitive area where she sat. She wrapped her arms around his neck and cradled his face as he lowered his mouth to the valley between her breasts. He hooked the collar of her shirt and pulled it away to allow his mouth the freedom of tasting her skin.

'Lark,' he murmured against her.

She giggled softly in his hair, 'Oh, Thomas.'

'Lark.'

'Thomas.'

She fell against him as they joined together laughing. Thomas hugged her to him as he pressed his mouth to her neck with a loud, friendly smack.

'You're the life of the party.'

'I am the party.' Lark leaned back and again framed his face with her hands. Her gaze softened as she looked into his eyes. Never would she be able to think of his eyes as anything but beautiful. The golden centers of his hazel-brown eyes were electric and vibrant. She stroked the stubble of his cheek with her fingertip. 'Thank you.'

'For what?' he asked.

'You know what,' Lark chuckled, reaching to tug playfully at his ears. Her face stilled as she became serious. 'For not letting me give in to feeling sorry for myself. For making me mad enough to see that.'

'So what are you going to do about it?'

Lark chewed her lip thoughtfully, then shrugged when nothing came to mind. 'I don't know. You're the lawyer. What do you think we should do?'

'First of all,' he stated with a slight grimace as he swatted her bottom, 'I think we need to get off this floor, the load isn't exactly light and my butt is about to go to sleep.'

'Jerk.' She popped him lightly on the arm, but obliged him by getting off his lap, then turned back to him. 'Now what?'

Thomas rolled to his knees, then pushed away from the floor to stand. He held him arm out, an invitation for her to go before him. 'Well, I don't think we're going to get too much accomplished by just sitting around waiting for something to come to us.'

'Yes. We've determined that, go on.'

'And, I think it's a pretty safe assumption that our good friend, Detective Baker, will probably not be the most helpful of people in regard to getting us the information we need.'

'Remind me to not invite him to my birthday party,' Lark said with a dry look.

'Really.' Thomas walked with her across the ballroom floor toward the double doors. Their footsteps echoed through the large, empty room and their voices sounded overly loud. Distorted. 'I think we need to take the advice Baker so wisely supplied to us not too long ago.'

' "Wise" and "Baker" do not really go together in the same sentence, Thomas,' she said, stopping to face him.

'That's true, more than likely a fluke.' Thomas laughed good naturedly as he nodded his agreement. 'But, he did unwillingly give us the next step in our plan of action.'

'What's that?'

He reached for her cheek and cheerfully tweaked it with his fingers. 'We're going to start getting some answers.'

'You can't tell us anything?'

'You know I can't, Thomas.'

Jim Morton crossed his arms over his chest obstinately as he shook his head. He leaned against a ultra-clean counter in the county crime lab. Thomas had thought they could glean, cajole, or bully some information out of the short, balding man, but now Lark wasn't so sure. Every time Thomas even started to open his mouth, Jim would automatically start shaking his head as if he needed to continually physically remind himself to assert a negative response to any of his questions.

Thomas ran his hand through his hair as he exhaled loudly. Lark could see by the furrowing of his brows, he was frustrated with the little man's lack of response. He put his hands on his hips as he studied the floor, stopping to think of yet another way of trying to convince his friend to help them. His gaze was distant, then slowly his eyes started to twinkle with satisfaction and his lips widened into a slow grin as he lifted his face to look at Jim.

'No, Thomas,' Jim stated immediately at the look on his face.

'Yes, Jim.' He leaned forward and clasped the man on his shoulder. 'Yes, you can. You won't get in trouble. And you won't get hurt.'

'I notice you didn't promise that,' Jim said with a wry twist of his lips.

Thomas shrugged. 'Lawyers never make promises.'

'Well, I can't tell you how much that comforts me,' he snorted.

'Look, Jim,' Thomas started, leaning closer, holding his hands in front of him as he worked to change the man's mind. 'Let me ask you this; wouldn't you have to supply this information to the defense attorney anyway, when they ask for disclosure?'

'I guess,' Jim started, then continued before Thomas could speak. 'But, you know it's not the procedure around here for me to give the information to you. She's a suspect, for goodness's sake.'

'So am I, for that matter,' Thomas countered. 'They haven't charged her with anything. Besides, it's information you have to supply anyway.'

'Damn it, Thomas,' he snapped, pushing away from the counter to pace back and forth in front of them. He raked his hand through his hair nervously as he shook his head and grumbled under his breath. The movement spiked the short, sparse hair making him look comically insane. 'I don't know about this, I just don't know.'

He paced away from them for a moment and Thomas triumphantly gave her the thumbs up sign as he grinned, then immediately resumed his earnest, solemn expression when Jim turned back toward them.

'Thomas, I could get in trouble for doing this,' Jim said, sounding as if his decision was starting to sway the other way. His face looked like he had just eaten a bad batch of cayenne peppers.

'Jim, your boss is very good friends with my grandmother. They serve on a couple of community service committees together,' he coaxed, using his family's influence in an obvious attempt to change his mind.

'Yeah, I know.' Jim stopped his tense pacing and clasped his hands behind his back thoughtfully. 'He likes to drop names whenever possible. Especially, if it can benefit him in any way.'

'Don't we all,' Lark murmured under her breath. Thomas gave her a pointed look, then swung his attention back to the lab technician.

Jim rubbed his hand over his mouth, then exhaled loudly, 'If I do this . . .'

He paused and Thomas leaned forward to give him an encouraging look. Jim lifted his gaze to meet Thomas's eyes and pointed a finger at him as he gave him a stern look.

'If. If I do this, you promise me no one knows where you got this,' he stated, wagging his fingertip at both of them. 'Deal?'

'Deal.' Thomas straightened, giving the man a proud smile. 'Boy scout's honor, Jim.'

Jim gave him a dry look, snorted, then turned to shuffle away from them. He disappeared into an office and they could hear the metallic sound of a filing drawer open, then, after a moment, close. He stepped out of the small room to the copier and made copies of several pages.

He came back to them, handed Thomas the pages and sighed loudly. 'Here. Now get the hell out of here before I change my mind and burn them.'

'Thanks, Jim,' Thomas said, shaking his hand. 'I really appreciate this.'

'Yeah, yeah,' he snorted again.

Lark had remained quiet so far, letting Thomas exude his force, or his charm, depending on how you looked at it, but now she stepped forward and offered Jim her hand.

'Thank you, Mr Morton,' she offered, her face showing her sincerity. Because of this man's help, reluctant as it was, she truly felt things were starting to perhaps turn in her favor.

Jim frowned as he looked at her hand, then took it slowly in his. 'You're welcome.'

She gave him a quick nod and a small smile, then turned away. She strode into the hallway to wait for Thomas to join her.

'Let me ask you something,' she asked, giving him an amused look.

'Shoot.'

'Were you ever a boy scout?' she asked, one brow raised with question.

Thomas's smile widened into a slow, devilish grin. 'No, I was not.'

Lark chuckled as she shook her head. They started walking down the hallway towards the elevator.

'That's what I thought.'

They stopped to pick up a quick lunch and headed toward a park. Thomas pulled his BMW into the parking lot and they took their sacks with them. He pulled a French fry from the bag and popped it into his mouth, then pointed toward a walking trail.

'Let's head this way. There's a neat little area not too far from here.'

Lark nodded and they stepped onto the path. As they entered the trees, she fell in behind him as the path narrowed into the low branches of scrappy elms mixed with cottonwoods and maples.

They walked a short distance to a clearing where a bench was nestled in the sun-warmed grass. Thomas took a seat beside her and they dug out their cheeseburgers. He took a bite and pulled the papers Jim had given them out from under his arm to take a look at them. He munched as he scanned the neatly typed pages.

'What did he give you?' Lark asked, taking a sip from her pop.

Thomas looked at her skeptically. 'Are you sure you want to discuss this while you're eating?'

Lark leveled her gaze on him. 'You are kidding, right?'

'Oh,' he said, realizing the absurdity of the question. After all, she was a psychic. Was, in fact, well known for finding dead bodies. 'Yeah. Sorry.'

Lark shrugged her shoulders without concern and leaned toward him to read the report with him as she nibbled at a French fry. 'Jeffrey's autopsy report. What does it say?'

'Nothing much. Death caused by blunt force trauma.' Thomas frowned as he looked the findings of the report over. 'This is interesting, though.'

'What?' she asked, sliding her hair behind her ear to keep it out of her cheeseburger.

'It says the wounds are consistent with being struck, but cannot say conclusively that your umbrella was the weapon used to kill him.'

'What? Are you saying maybe something else could have been used?' She shook her head. It didn't make sense. 'I thought they found blood on the umbrella.'

He shuffled through the papers. 'They did, but apparently nothing else.'

'Nothing?' she repeated.

'That's what I said,' he answered, handing her the paper. 'Nothing.'

Thomas picked his cheeseburger up and took a bite. Lark read the report and refused to let the excitement within her grow. 'They found his blood, but no fingerprints.'

'And no hair or skin fragments,' Thomas added. Finished with his burger, he wadded the wrapper and put it in the sack. 'Like I said, isn't that interesting?'

Lark started to smile, then quelled it, but couldn't stop the small amount of excitement from building no matter how much she tried. 'Hot damn, do you know what this could mean for me?'

Thomas leaned back and put his arm across the back of the bench and met her gaze. 'That maybe the umbrella was planted as a diversion tactic? That maybe he might not have been killed in that room? That maybe someone found you and took advantage of your condition, which may or may not have been related, to cover up what they had done?'

She returned his look for a moment as her heart started to pound. ' "Maybe" being the operative word here.'

'Yeah,' he said, his dimples creasing with his smile. 'Maybe.'

Lark rose from the park bench and moved to the trash can. Dropping the sack into the container, she took a last sip of her pop, before tossing that in too. 'Okay, so far we have figured out that maybe, hopefully, my umbrella was not the weapon used to kill Jeffrey, and that, based on the smudges we noticed on LeAnn's face, she may or may not have followed the killer.'

'Well, more accurately that she had been somewhere dirty around the time of her death,' Thomas offered with a shrug of his hand. 'We don't know that she got them "following" her killer. She could have got them while going into some place. Or it was smudged on her after she was dead, possibly when the person moved her body to the kitchen to be found.'

'It was found, wasn't it?' Lark ran her hand through her hair as she chewed on her lower lip.

She paced for a moment, recalling in her mind the scene in the kitchen. LeAnn's body slumped against the island, her outer arms and the back side of her calves smeared with a thick coat of dust. Narrowing her eyes, she remembered the blood pooled beneath LeAnn's head. What little of it there was.

'You're thinking of something, aren't you?' Thomas leaned forward, putting his forearms on his knees.

Lark nodded absently, tapping her chin with her finger. 'Yes, I am.'

Thomas watched her pace back and forth on the path covered with wood chips. His lips quirked into a slow smile. Lark noticed the movement out of the corner of her eye. She stopped in front of him, taking in his amused expression.

'Well, are you going to share your theory with me?' He lifted his brows in question and smiled, the movement bringing out his dimples. 'Or do I get to guess it?'

'Ha. Ha.' She smirked at him. Moving to the bench, she sat back beside him. 'Let's assume LeAnn's body was moved. Why put her in the kitchen?'

Thomas looked at her with a small amount of surprise. 'That is a very valid question.'

She smiled warmly at his open praise. 'Thank you, counselor.'

'You're welcome.' He gave her a quick kiss on the tip of her nose, then his tone became all business. 'Okay, we'll assume she was killed elsewhere. She couldn't have been murdered too far from there.'

Lark watched the sun wink through the leaves of the trees and its shadows skittered playfully on the ground. 'The person would not have wanted to risk being seen taking her body upstairs. The same goes for the ballroom and the turret. The stairs would have been too risky.'

'So we're left with the downstairs,' Thomas finished.

Nodding, Lark's eyes widened as she stared absently at the wooded path. 'Yup.'

He touched the tips of his fingers together and steepled them. 'I think it would have been too dangerous to bring her in from the outside. Both LeAnn's and Maria's rooms are down there. They are both early risers.'

'Did Maria see or hear anything that night before she found LeAnn?' Lark flicked a glance toward Thomas.

'I don't know, I didn't have a chance to talk with her.' Meeting her gaze, he stood and offered his hand to her. 'But I think maybe we should.'

Lark took his hand. 'Sounds like a plan.'

Thomas pulled his BMW to a stop in front of the castle and put the vehicle in park. Lark noticed Natalie's red Mustang still parked beside the house and she fought the urge to grit her teeth in frustration. She did not look forward to another confrontation with the nasty tempered woman.

Thomas quirked his brow as if he could read her thoughts. 'I guess we should take advantage of Natalie still being here and talk to her before we approach Maria.'

'This is one of those few times that a root canal seems like a fun thing to do,' she said, frowning at the idea of having to be in the same room with the woman. She didn't even bother to hide her displeasure at the idea.

He gave her hand a friendly pat, before getting out of the car. When Lark remained obstinately sitting in the front seat, he leaned in the open door. 'Come on, Lark. You're not afraid of her, are you?'

She turned to glare at him. 'Hardly.'

He grinned wickedly at her. 'Don't worry, you won't have to be exposed to her all that long. Just long enough for us to talk to her. She'll be leaving today, remember?'

'Not soon enough if you ask me,' she muttered as she got out of the car.

Lark had schooled her face for what she hoped resembled a calm expression. She felt that evaporate the instant Natalie informed them that she would be staying at least for a couple more days.

'Oh, yes, Alicia and I had a nice little talk this morning. To clear the air, so to speak,' she said, waving a glass of ice tea as she spoke. She eyed Lark with spiteful relish. 'I apologized for my behavior. She, of course, understood how terribly upset I was and as a peace offering she asked me to stay for a couple more days.'

Natalie stood across the room from them and did not hear Thomas mutter his thoughts to Lark under his breath.

'Remind me to thank my grandmother.'

Then again, maybe she did hear them as her eyes narrowed and she looked speculatively at the two of them. 'With pleasure.'

'I hope that doesn't upset any of your plans.' Natalie's blue eyes were ice cold as she looked at Lark. 'I know how well you two seem to be getting along these days.'

'Oh, it will not affect our plans at all,' Lark smiled sweetly, clasping her hands around her knee. 'In fact, we are very pleased to hear that you're staying.'

'Yes,' Thomas continued, giving her an amused look before he turned his attention back to the leggy blonde. 'We'd also hoped to talk to you about a few things.'

Natalie arched her brow. 'What things?'

'To start with, we wanted to talk to you about the night of Jeffrey's murder.' Lark shrugged as if she didn't have a care in the world. 'I don't remember anything, and I was wondering if you had seen or heard anything unusual that night? Maybe you had trouble sleeping and heard something?'

She watched Natalie's reaction. Her hard expression crystallized to ice with her loathing as her gaze remained locked on Lark. The woman's back stiffened and her lips thinned into a line. Her knuckles whitened around the glass she was holding and she looked as if she would like to throw it.

Lark thought about reminding her that she would get some pretty ugly lines on her face if she kept frowning like that. Nope, she chuckled inwardly, better not. She didn't think Natalie would appreciate it very much.

'Just who do you think you are?' Natalie's voice was low with fury.

'I simply would like to get some answers,' Lark replied.

The blonde strode from the other side of the room to the bar. She opened the cabinet door to pull a decanter out. Splashing a small amount of the dark liquid into her glass, she replaced the bottle, then leaned against the cabinet to study Lark. She took a swallow of the drink, the alcohol apparently doing nothing to ease her temper as her eyes remained icy with dislike.

'I see,' she murmured, pausing to swirl the contents of the glass in her hand. 'You've come to realize you are standing in a pile of something really deep, so you've decided to play the detective now, have you?'

'I just want answers.'

'Natalie,' Thomas said the woman's name as he moved to a chair to sit down. He faced her, his expression businesslike, his tone that of a lawyer. 'I would think that, unless there is a reason you would rather not discuss that night with us, you wouldn't mind answering a few questions.'

Her mouth tightened and she flipped her hair back with her hand. 'Of course not.'

'Good.' He studied her for a moment as he steepled his hands in front of him. 'You don't have to go over the dinner since I was there, but what did you do when we all headed upstairs for the evening?'

'I talked briefly with you, as you recall.' Natalie's chin lifted a fraction of an inch and her expression changed just enough that Lark got the idea the woman had tried to do more than just 'talk' with

Thomas. And the slight reddening of Natalie's cheeks showed the answer had not been as positive as she would have liked. 'Then I went to bed.'

'And you did not hear anything?' he continued.

'I slept like the dead,' she said, shaking her head, then took another drink of her 'tea'. 'No pun intended, of course.'

'You did not leave your room?' Thomas's voice was unemotional, but his gaze was stern and demanding as he leveled it on Natalie. He raised his brow in question. 'At all?'

'No, I didn't.' She seemed to squirm under his scrutiny. The silence that fell into the room seemed to needle her and she paced like a tiger trapped in a cage. She turned to Lark, her lips twisted into a smirk. 'You're looking for a scapegoat, aren't you? Conjure up your spirits, or whatever you do, to help you. Hell, for all I care you can call up Theorosa herself, but don't expect me to stand around here and let you try to pin this one on me.'

Natalie swung away from them and strode to the door, closing it with emphasis as she left. They both watched her go, then turned toward each other. Lark bit at her lip trying to suppress her grin, but failed miserably.

Thomas chuckled at her expression. 'I think she's mad.'

'No wonder cops like examining witnesses. That was fun.' Lark wiggled her eyebrows at him. She leaned back against the chair and studied the door the blonde had stormed through. A small smile still lingered on her face as she propped her head on her chin. 'I had the feeling though that she wasn't quite telling the truth about leaving her room, didn't you?'

'Yes, I did.' He rubbed absently at the more than a day's growth of beard darkening his chin. 'We'll wait a while and talk to her again later on.'

She nodded, then stood from the couch. 'Next witness, counselor.'

CHAPTER 10

The next person they decided to talk to was Tim, but that proved to be harder than they had envisaged. They found the grounds keeper working on the tractor behind the large barn. As they walked up to it, the only things they could see of the short, suspicious man were his legs and feet sticking out from under the engine.

Thomas put his hand on the wheel and leaned forward to peer underneath. 'Tim, I was wondering, if you have a moment, could I speak to you please?'

Tim held a wrench to something within the belly of the tractor; his movements stilled when he looked toward Thomas, then his gaze fixed warily on Lark. His eyes flicked back to Thomas, the movement dismissing her in his mind. 'Sure, let me finish tightening this up and I'll be right with you.'

Lark watched as Tim's arms easily maneuvered the wrench. His small stature deceptively hid his strength and she saw the thick muscles of his forearms flex with the movement. Gravel crunched under him as he twisted from under the engine.

He rose, once again looking toward Lark, then turning away without acknowledging her.

'What can I do for you, Thomas?' he asked.

Thomas placed his hands on his lean hips. His tone of voice and his stance looked more as if he were discussing the weather, instead of trying to find answers for two murders. 'I was hoping you could help me with something, Tim.'

He shrugged, 'Sure. If I can.'

'Good.' Thomas crossed his arms as he leaned against the tire of the tractor. 'I was wondering if you could tell me if you heard or saw anything the night of either one of the murders?'

Tim glanced toward Lark, then bent to drop the wrench in the tool box sitting on the ground beside the tractor. He pulled a rag from the tray and started rubbing at the grease on his hands. 'No, I didn't.'

'No lights or sounds?'

'Nothing,' Tim repeated. He continued wiping at the palms of his hands as he spoke. 'I told all this to the police.'

'I understand, Tim, and I appreciate your talking with me,' Thomas said, unfolding his arms. 'We're just trying to get some answers, that's all.'

'My apartment in the carriage house is behind the castle. I really don't have a view of the castle at all.'

Thomas did not say anything till Tim met his gaze. 'Did you leave your apartment at any time, either of those nights?'

The grounds keeper's hands stopped and his jaw clenched as something cold, hard filtered to his eyes. 'No, I did not.' He dropped the rag into the top tray of the tool box and snapped the lid shut. Picking it up, he straightened to face Thomas, his expression once again under control. 'I promised Mrs Blackwell that I would get that upstairs window fixed for her today. Excuse me.'

Lark turned as she kept her gaze on the grounds keeper. She had sensed something darker in his reaction, though she could not put her finger on it. He was obviously reluctant to talk to them, understandable if he'd learned from experience not to trust anyone.

She sighed as she looked to Thomas. 'I really didn't sense much from him. He's reluctant, but he never seemed to be a man who would trust openly anyway.'

Thomas nodded. 'Grandmother has known him practically all her life. I grew up with him, but I couldn't tell you much about him at all.'

'Do you think he saw anything those nights?' Lark asked. 'Or left his apartment?'

'I don't know.' Thomas raised his brows as he shrugged. 'It's not like most killers wear signs admitting what they did. But I would have a hard time believing that Tim could do such a thing. He's really devoted to my grandmother.'

'Maybe he killed because of that devotion,' she added.

'It's hard for me to think of anyone that I know being capable of committing such an act,' he murmured. His gaze seemed far away as the reality of the thought made him solemn. Then he looked at her and attempted to give her a smile. 'It wouldn't be realistic for me to think that it could not happen, would it?'

202

The twist of her lips may have resembled a smile, but Lark felt no humor. 'As a little girl, if you had asked me what I thought my life would be like, I couldn't have foretold what's happened to me in my wildest dreams.' Her eyes widened as she shook her head. 'I wouldn't have wished for it either.'

'Me neither,' Thomas said as he put his arm around her shoulder and gave her a comforting squeeze. 'Let's see who else we can find.'

As they walked toward the house, Lark thought it did seem sort of strange to talk to the people who were present on the nights of the murders. That all odds pointed toward the killer being one of these people and that person still being here among them.

Lark sighed at the irony of it all. She had come to help put a spirit to rest. A story more suited to a romance novel than her life. Over a hundred years ago a girl was found standing over her lover's body and she was hanged. Lark had been found kneeling over Jeffrey Linden's body and remembered nothing of how or why she had got there.

Thank goodness lynch mobs no longer exist around here, she thought. Then she remembered Detective Ron Baker. One did not seem to be much of an improvement over the other.

At least she was doing something, she consoled herself as they climbed the front stairs of the castle. She didn't feel as if she were standing around waiting for the police, or anyone else for that matter, to do something. She felt productive, even if they weren't making any headway at the moment.

Thomas pulled the door open for her and they entered the castle. As they neared the library, they could hear David's voice.

'I guess we've found our next witness, counselor,' she said.

They stopped at the door and looked in. David was pulling a sheet from the fax machine as he cradled the telephone receiver on his shoulder. He scanned the page and answered the caller's questions. He gave a brief smile as he listened to the person on the other end and Lark was surprised at how it transformed the other Blackwell's face. Like Thomas, he was handsome even when he was scowling, but a smile lit David's angular face making him look as if he had just stepped from the silver screen.

David glanced up and caught sight of them. As most people around here seemed to do whenever they saw her, he frowned. He murmured his good bye and hung up the phone.

'Am I to assume that I am next in your little investigation?' he stated without preamble as he sat on the edge of the desk.

'I see you've talked to Natalie.' Thomas briefly touched Lark's elbow as he motioned toward the couch with his hand.

'I guess you could say that,' David said as he watched them enter the room and sit across from him on the couch. 'She blew in here not too long ago and railed for a good twenty minutes on the injustices of it all.'

'Only twenty minutes?' Lark murmured, giving Thomas a sideways glance.

'No one has ever accused Natalie of being subtle.'
David looked at Lark. 'She blames you for all of this.'

'I'm not responsible, David.' Lark held his gaze, her expression firm. 'Whoever killed Jeffrey and LeAnn is. I don't intend to sit around and be accused of something I didn't do.'

'You said you could not recall anything of the night Linden was killed,' David started, his brows dipped into a frown. 'How do you know you aren't responsible?'

Lark shrugged, clasping her hands around her knee. 'I do not remember anything, but I was completely aware of what was going on around me when LeAnn was killed. And I know I did not kill her.'

David placed his hands on the edge of the desk and leaned forward. 'I think everyone around here knows what you were doing at that time.'

She could feel the heat tingeing her cheeks at his insinuation. Thomas leaned forward and planted his forearms on his knees. The movement put him closer to her, a physical show of his support.

'What we are interested in, David, is what you did those nights,' Thomas stated.

Lark knew the two men cared for each other. They were, after all, cousins, living in the same house. But the others had hinted at David's desire to be the head of Blackwell Castle. The alleged rightful heir. They held each other's gazes as they measured one another. She could sense the conflict within Thomas. He did not want to think David capable of such an action.

David crossed his arms over his chest, his expression angry, but controlled. 'I realize why you feel the need to ask me that, Thomas, so I'll excuse the crudity of it and answer it anyway. I was in my room and did not leave it till I heard the screams on both occasions.'

'Did you see anyone either night?'

'Well,' David hesitated as he rubbed his chin. His anger seemed to dissipate to be replaced with embarrassment. 'To be honest, I did.'

'Who?' Lark asked quickly, leaning forward on the couch.

He looked from Lark to Thomas and apologetically held his cousin's gaze. 'Natalie came by my room the night LeAnn was killed.'

'Oh.' Lark and Thomas looked at each other, then back to David. She had a pretty good idea what the blonde had wanted.

As if reading her thoughts, David nodded. 'Yeah. We talked for a moment, then she went back to her room. Sorry, Thomas.'

'Hey, David, there's nothing to be sorry about,' he assured his cousin, holding his hands in front of him. 'Really.'

'I know,' David said with a shrug. 'I know you guys haven't been seeing each other in a long time, but I still just couldn't.'

David may have had a tendency toward anger, but at least he shared a sense of decency with his cousin. Or, since they were talking about Natalie, the younger Blackwell may have had a strong survival instinct.

Thomas clasped his hands together. Lark sensed his reluctance even as she watched him grimace slightly before taking a deep breath. 'David, I have

206

something I need to ask you and I don't exactly feel easy about it.'

David's expression hardened. 'That doesn't seem to have stopped you so far.'

'No, I guess it hasn't.' Thomas rose and walked to the window. He lifted his hand to the pane and stared out the window as if he were trying to word what he was going to say. He shook his head and frowned as he turned away from the window with a look of disgust. Lark had a feeling it was more directed at himself than anyone in the room.

He walked up behind the leather wing-back chair and rested his hand on its broad back. With no small amount of frustration, he raked his hand through his hair. 'Look, David, I see no way around this, so I'll be straight with you. As I'm sure even Lark has heard since she's been here, there are some people in the family who feel you should be the next heir of Blackwell Castle. Your mother made it quite clear at one time that you are the direct descendent of the first David Blackwell and therefore should inherit the family responsibility.'

David rubbed his hands across his face. He looked tired and young as he met Thomas's gaze. 'And you wonder if I would do anything to make sure that the castle does not leave the family because I might have something to gain.' The statement was not meant to be a question, his voice flat and unemotional.

Lark felt her nerves tighten. Murder had such a nasty way of hurting more than just the victims. Because of a stupid, mindless act, these men, cousins, were watching a rift grow between them.

'You were quite angry with Mr Linden that night,' Lark said, the truth of the statement not making her feel any better.

David lifted his brows in acknowledgment, his lips tightening to a thin line with the grim semblance of a smile. 'Yes, I was. But not enough to murder him.'

David pushed away from the desk and stepped to the other leather chair flanking the couch. He sat heavily, letting his head drop for a moment as he simply stared at the floor in front of him. He leaned back in the chair, the energy seeming to drain out of him. Slowly his gaze moved to meet Thomas's.

'I cannot deny that my mother was perhaps obsessed with the idea of me inheriting the castle. Or more to the point, the family fortune,' he said, with a dismissive wave of his hand. 'She'd had a hard life. What little we had was what she worked day and night to provide for us. As you know from family gossip, my father wasn't much into the work ethic. The Blackwell family and the castle was something she truly coveted.'

'Perhaps I am the direct descendent of David Blackwell. Perhaps some traditionalists in the family feel that I should be the rightful heir. Perhaps.' David shrugged, his face held none of the righteous anger of one denied his inheritance. Instead he looked calm and accepting. 'But that was my mother's fight, Thomas. Not mine. I would never want to take anything away from Grandmother or you. Yes, I do care for Blackwell Castle. But, I care more for my family.'

Thomas continued to hold David's gaze. He nodded thoughtfully as his expression softened. 'I appreciate you being so candid with me. I hope we can put this behind us.'

Lark could feel the tension between the two cousins and felt partly responsible. She spoke softly to David. 'I realize how hard this has been for everyone and I truly appreciate your helping Thomas and me with this.'

David turned his head to look at her as he gave her a small smile. 'I feel like I should be the one to apologize, Miss Delavan. I haven't exactly been the most welcoming of people since your arrival. And if I were in your position, I would probably do the same thing.'

Lark returned his look warmly. David had a lot of the Blackwell charm, she thought as she matched his grin. 'Well, I can't exactly say this has been one of my better trips.'

They thanked David for talking with them. Lark felt some of the air had been cleared after their discussion and she was much relieved to see the two cousins shake each other's hands with genuine affection.

They left David in the library and stepped into the hallway, closing the door behind them. Lark was just about to ask Thomas what their next step was when John appeared at the top of the stairway. He seemed to be lost in thought as he descended toward them and was practically on top of them before he finally noticed them.

He jumped slightly as a small groan escaped, his shaggy eyebrows raised in surprise. 'Miss Delavan. Thomas. I'm sorry I didn't see you. My thoughts were elsewhere.'

'How is Stephanie doing?' Thomas asked.

Lark caught just a tiny hint of nervousness in the older man's expression before he looked away. John cleared his throat, his gaze continually flicking toward the top of the stairs. 'She's still quite out of it, I'm afraid. I was on my way to the kitchen to get her something to eat.'

'I hope it's nothing serious,' Lark said.

'Oh no, it's not,' John answered, his voice wavering as he brushed absently at his stomach. He fidgeted from one foot to another. 'Touch of bronchitis. Our doctor has her on some pretty strong medication, so she tends to talk in circles sometimes.'

'Is she awake at the moment?' Thomas asked.

'Yes. Yes, she is. Why?' The question was out of John's mouth before he realized how it must have sounded. 'I'm sorry, yes she is awake at the moment.'

'Good, we were hoping we could talk with her.' Thomas gave his cousin's husband a reassuring smile as he started toward the stairs without waiting for an answer from the older man. 'Don't worry, we won't wear her out.'

Lark hurried to follow Thomas up the stairs to the couple's room. 'Was it me, or did he seem nervous to you?'

Thomas glanced over his shoulder at her. 'John's always nervous.'

'Oh.' She shrugged and stood behind him as he knocked on his cousin's door.

Stephanie's high pitched voice was thin and quiet as she called to them to come in. Lark frowned in surprise when she saw Thomas's cousin propped against a mound of pillows in the center of the bed.

The older woman wore a baby doll nightie edged with thin, filmy feathers and a matching band for her hair in a color that Lark could only describe as 'whore-house red'.

Stephanie's pudgy face was pale and drawn from the illness which had kept her confined to bed for the past few days. She fixed a somewhat glazed look in their general direction without raising her head.

'Thomas, how good to see you,' she murmured, then her eyes met Lark's and fevered energy filled them. Stephanie started to raise herself with her elbows as she practically gushed, 'Miss Delavan, I didn't know you would be coming.'

'Oh, Stephanie, please stay where you are.' Lark held her hand up to silence the woman as she rushed to her side and pressed her gently back to the pillow. 'We're so sorry to disturb you.'

Stephanie's eyes remained locked on Lark, her lips quivering in a nervous smile. 'You're not disturbing me at all. I had hoped so much to spend time with you, but John says I'm too sick. He says I have to stay in bed.'

'You know I'm only doing what the doctor said we should do,' John said as he strode quickly into the doorway. He carried a plate of crackers and a glass of water. His face was red with exertion as if he had run all the way from the kitchen.

Stephanie gave her husband a sideways glance as she pouted. 'I don't like that man.'

Thomas's brows rose in surprise. 'Henry?'

'It's not like that,' John shook his head, flicking a nervous glance toward his wife. 'She's referring to our family doctor.'

211

'Crazy old coot,' Stephanie snorted as she pulled the blanket up to her chin.

Thomas kept a concerned eye on his cousin as he spoke to John. 'We were wondering if either of you had heard anything the nights Mr Linden and LeAnn were killed?'

Shaking his head, John spoke quickly as his glance flew to his wife. In her obviously medicated state, she merely looked at him as he answered Thomas's question. 'No, we didn't. In fact, that was the night Stephanie started coming down with this.'

'Hmph,' Stephanie sniffed, then turned to Lark. Her expression transformed almost instantly to a glowing radiance as she reached her hand out toward Lark. 'Miss Delavan, is that why you're here? Did you talk to them?'

Lark glanced nervously toward Thomas as she shook her head. She felt no choice but to take the woman's hand in hers. She winced at the clammy feeling of moisture coating the nervous woman's palms. 'As I've explained to you before, I do not talk to the dead. I don't know if I even believe in ghosts.'

'What?' Stephanie looked both hurt and incredulous as her mouth hung open. She gaped at Lark for a moment, shaking her head in silent denial. 'No,' she stated as if she were changing Lark's mind herself merely by saying the word. She frowned, acting like she was dealing with a wayward child. 'You can't think that. You might not be able to see them, but they are there. I know my daughter is still with us.'

Lark looked back to Thomas, not knowing what to say. She had no idea what the woman was talking about. John looked as if he were gritting his teeth, his eyes practically bulging from his head as he leaned nervously forward.

She frowned as she turned back to Stephanie. 'I'm sorry, I really don't understand what you're talking about.'

She smiled sweetly at Lark. 'Melissa is my daughter. She would have been fourteen years old this year, isn't that right, John?' Stephanie clutched Lark's hand. 'That's what I wanted to talk to you about. I've missed her so much and I was hoping you could help me talk to her.'

Stephanie looked at her as if she were asking no more than to borrow a cup of sugar. Lark almost felt mesmerized by the woman's unblinking gaze. Her pupils were large, dilated, giving her an alien look as she tilted her head to await Lark's response.

Lark's eyes widened as she shook her head, unable to find anything to say to the woman who was obviously too sick to comprehend what she was saying at the moment. John had said she'd been prescribed pretty heavy duty medication. From personal experience, she knew how disorienting an illness and the remedy required to help could be.

John seemed to sense her unease on how to deal with the situation and leapt to her rescue. He moved to the side of the bed to deftly remove Stephanie's hand and gave her an awkward apologetic smile. 'Sweetheart, I think you need to rest now. Perhaps Miss Delavan might discuss this with you later.'

His wife obediently allowed him to arrange her pillows so she could go to sleep. John held his arm out for them to precede him into the hall. He closed the door behind him with a quiet click. Hesitantly, he licked at his lips, the nervous gesture making Lark feel sorry for him as he faced them.

'I'm sorry about that,' he started. He lifted his hands in front of him as if showing he didn't know how else to handle his wife's actions. 'You have to understand my wife is allergic to codeine, but it's one of the few things the doctor can give her to effectively treat her bronchitis. As a result, it tends to cause her to . . .'

John's voice trailed off and he shrugged his shoulders as if to suggest that her thoughts were less than coherent at the moment.

Thomas nodded his understanding. 'I know losing Melissa was hard on her. Hard on both of you. She was a very sweet girl.'

'Yeah,' John said, his voice soft. 'She was.'

He turned back toward the door. His hand rested on the knob as he looked back over his shoulder at them. 'I'm sorry we couldn't have been more help.'

'John, I'm sorry we had to bother you when Steph's not feeling well,' Thomas replied.

Lark watched as John opened the door and stepped back into the room to take care of his wife. They started walking down the hall toward the staircase. She touched his arm briefly as they neared the stairs. 'Thomas, I gather Melissa was their daughter, but what happened to the little girl?'

Thomas placed his hand on the railing, then leaned to rest his forearms as he seemed lost in thought for a moment. He took a deep breath, then looked toward her, his eyes filled with sadness.

'She accidentally drowned.'

Lark clutched at the neck of her shirt, her eyes widening with understanding. Now Stephanie's earnest question began to make sense. 'How horrible for them. How did it happen?'

'It was just one of those things no one could ever expect to happen to them,' Thomas said, looking away, his gaze becoming distant, his voice shaded. 'She was seven years old when it happened. They had finally bought their dream house, complete with big back yard for Melissa to run wild in. And she was a hellion,' he murmured, his gaze softening with a small smile. 'It was summer and she was playing in the back yard. She was at that age a parent could feel comfortable letting her play outside by herself.'

Thomas stood, gripping the banister and leaning back as he talked. 'Toward the back of the property there was a stream. It wasn't very deep and didn't run very fast.'

He hesitated, glancing back toward the room where John and Stephanie were. 'It's the story you've heard a million times. Stephanie went inside for just a minute to answer the phone and Melissa took advantage of it. She apparently went down to the stream to wade.' Thomas's voice trailed off and he cleared his throat as if trying to dislodge the emotion welling within him. 'When Stephanie came back out just a few moments later, she called for Melissa and didn't get an answer. She immediately started looking for her.'

Lark watched his handsome face as his voice wavered, and he paused. She knew it was such little comfort, still she placed her hand on his arm.

He met her gaze, his voice barely over a whisper. 'Stephanie found Melissa face down in the stream.

215

She apparently had fallen and hit her head, knocking her unconscious. She was still alive, but not breathing when Stephanie found her. She ran her back to the house and called an ambulance. Stephanie worked on Melissa till the paramedics arrived.'

Lark gave his arm a gentle squeeze. 'It had to be hard for all of you.'

He nodded. 'Yes, it was. They were able to resuscitate her for a little while, but she shut down again once they made it to the hospital.'

'How did they do?' she asked.

'As well as could be imagined, I guess,' Thomas shrugged. 'I truly admired John for the incredible support he gave my cousin during that time. He didn't blame her for the accident as sometimes happens in a case like that. Hell, Stephanie was doing that pretty good all by herself.'

'Leaving a seven-year-old alone in the back yard is something that a thousand different parents have done,' Lark offered, knowing it would mean so little. 'She could not have foreseen what would happen that particular time.'

'I know that and you know that.' Thomas shook his head as he pushed away from the railing to head toward the stairs. 'But Stephanie will always wonder what she could have done differently. Melissa's death changed her drastically. She's only a shell of what she used to be. If John hadn't been there for her, I don't know how she would have taken it.'

'None of us knows how we would take it, Thomas,' she said as they descended the stairs.

Lark fell quiet. She didn't have children. Honestly didn't know if she wanted them, but it didn't stop her

216

from trying to understand the pain Stephanie must have felt. The sensations she had received from the woman now made much more sense to her. Her unease, her nervousness. The feeling that so much more rode on the questions she had asked.

She knew the woman must have experienced an incredible sense of guilt because of her daughter's unexpected death. Still probably felt the heavy weight of it pressing her till this day, even after so many years. If she had experienced the remorse, thought herself guilty, there would have also been those who thought the same of her. What hell it must have been for Stephanie to hear their whispers of speculation every time she turned her back.

How could one cope with such a tragedy?

If there were any easy answers, life would have definitely been easier, Lark thought with a humorless laugh.

She shook her head as she blew out her breath. 'Sometimes you wonder how people can deal with such a brutal blow, then try to go on to lead a normal life.'

Thomas looked at her with a hint of admiration. 'Coming from you, that surprises me. Considering everything you have had to deal with, you have coped well.'

'I'm sure any mother would tell you it would be nothing compared to the loss of a child,' she murmured. He was looking at her if she were a virtuous saint and she did not feel comfortable with the comparison.

'I suppose so,' he said letting the subject drop. He took her by the arm. 'Let's get something to eat. I'm starving.'

She grinned, very relieved at the change of topic. 'You are such a typical man, Thomas.'

'Because I said I'm hungry?' he laughed, clutching at his chest with mock pain. 'I am crushed.'

'Yeah, right,' she joked. 'Come on, I'm pretty hungry myself.'

'Then you should have nothing to complain about.'

Lark stopped, propped a hand on her hip as she raised her brow in a look of mock severity. 'Then I wouldn't be a typical woman.'

Thomas placed his hand at the small of her back and she smiled at the ripple of warmth that rushed through her at his touch. He leaned close to her ear. 'Lark, you'll never be a typical woman.'

They headed for the kitchen and were startled to find Alicia giggling like a school girl with Henry. Alicia looked up at them when they entered. Her cheeks were tinged a becoming pink and her face held a look of surprise.

'Oh, Thomas. Lark. How are you?'

'Hungry,' Thomas answered, trying to hide his smile at his grandmother's embarrassment. 'We decided to fix ourselves something for lunch.'

Lark pinched him, not wanting him to make Alicia more uncomfortable by his obvious amusement. If she didn't know better, she would have thought Alicia looked as if she had just been caught like an eager school girl kissing the retired doctor behind the proverbial barn.

'Oh, well you're just in time then,' Alicia murmured as she gave them a distracted glance. 'Uh, Henry and I were just fixing something for ourselves and Maria.'

'How is she doing?' Lark asked.

'As well as can be expected,' Henry offered, pulling two more plates from the cabinet. He set them on the counter and gave a grim shake of his head. 'She thought of herself as a substitute mother for LeAnn and feels somehow responsible for her death.'

Lark again thought of Stephanie and her daughter, Melissa. It never ceased to amaze her, the human psyche's ability to continually accept guilt as a coping mechanism.

'She's lying down,' Alicia said with a sigh as she fixed the sandwiches. 'I wish there was something we could do to convince her that she couldn't have done anything to stop what happened.'

Thomas frowned, but said nothing. Lark saw his look and instinctively wished she knew what he was thinking. Then, she turned to his grandmother. 'Did she say whether she had heard anything?'

Alicia shook her head. 'I was with her when she spoke with the police. Maria woke as usual and went to the kitchen to start breakfast and, instead, found LeAnn on the floor.'

'Did they ask her about the night Jeffrey was killed?' Thomas asked.

'Yes, and she said she was unaware that anything had happened till she heard Lark's screams.'

The mention of that night never failed to make Lark feel uneasy. People would talk of her actions and she felt as if they were discussing someone else. A stranger. They were her actions, yet she did not recall anything from that night.

'What about you?' Thomas said. The question broke into Lark's thoughts and she turned toward Alicia.

The older woman looked nervous and kept casting uneasy glances toward Henry. 'Whatever do you mean, Thomas?' she asked with a nervous laugh.

He frowned at his grandmother's unusual reaction. Henry seemed to be slightly uncomfortable as he cleared his throat.

'I was just wondering if you had heard or seen anything the night Jeffrey was killed?'

'No,' she started, suddenly becoming absorbed in the process of making a sandwich. 'No, I didn't.'

Lark and Thomas exchanged perplexed looks. Lark tried to figure out how to smooth the tension as she ran her hand through her hair. She touched the older woman's hand, her voice apologetic. 'I'm sorry, Alicia. We did not mean anything by the question and we surely did not mean any offense to you.'

'Of course not, sweetheart.' Alicia gave her a reassuring smile. 'None was taken.'

As his grandmother fell silent, Thomas leaned forward slightly and Lark could all but feel the question burning in his thoughts. Why was his grandmother acting so strangely?

Henry watched the scene before him and gave a disgruntled murmur. He leaned toward Alicia. His gaze was soft as he met hers. 'You might as well tell them the truth.'

Lark watched the shock ripple through Thomas's expression. His reaction was so intense she could sense it without any effort. A part of him was terrified at what he thought his grandmother was about to tell him.

'Henry, really,' Alicia admonished. 'I don't think it's exactly an appropriate topic to be discussing with my grandson.'

'Who is more than old enough to understand,' the doctor stated matter-of-factly, his lips twisting with a hint of wry amusement. 'Hell, look at his face, Alicia. He looks like he is afraid you're going to confess to that poor boy's murder.'

Thomas's brow raised as he looked to one, then the other. 'Tell me what?'

'Alicia, tell him,' Henry ordered with mock sternness as he gripped her hand softly. 'Or I'll tell him myself. And . . . give him all the pertinent details.'

Alicia gasped, yanking her hand away from him. She picked up the dish towel and smacked him on the arm. 'You wouldn't dare.'

Henry grinned wickedly and looked as if he were more than ready to back up his threat.

'Okay,' she practically shouted. Her cheeks turned crimson as she took a deep breath, then turned toward her grandson. 'I do not want you to think I took offense to your question, Thomas. Either of you.' Alicia hesitated, giving Henry a stern glare at his prompting grin. 'I was simply uncomfortable because I had not wanted you to find out that . . .'

Alicia's voice drifted out and Henry leaned his elbows on the counter, obviously enjoying her discomfort. 'Tell him, Alicia.'

She growled at the man, causing them to smile. 'I didn't hear anything that night, Thomas, because I was with Henry all night,' she said, the words coming out in a rush.

Thomas's mouth fell open in a comical look of disbelief. 'What?'

His grandmother's features stiffened and her chin lifted defiantly. 'You heard exactly what I said.'

Thomas said nothing for a long moment. He simply stared at his grandmother as if she had suddenly became a stranger with three eyes. Or a libido. Suddenly he recalled that Henry had been standing with them in the hallway wearing one of his grandmother's ruffled robes. Henry was supposed to have gone home. Thomas shrugged his shoulders temporarily at a loss for a words, then waved his hand with ineffective emphasis as the words started to stumble out of his mouth. 'As in . . . with him?'

'Don't look so damned shocked, Thomas,' Alicia barked, her fine features frowning at his look of doubt. 'It's not as if I'm too old for sex, you know. As far as I'm concerned, too old is dead. And in case you haven't noticed, I'm not dead.'

Thomas continued to stare at her. 'I've never heard you say a cuss word in my entire life.'

'Well, you just did,' she retorted, slapping a plate in front of Henry. 'And I am sleeping, as your generation would put it, with the old doctor here. Heaven knows at the moment, I have no damn idea why.'

Henry chuckled good naturedly. 'I can't tell who's more shocked, you or Thomas.'

'I'm not shocked,' Thomas stammered, as he worked to recover. 'Just surprised, that's all. After

222

all, she obviously had . . . I mean, I knew she wasn't . . .'

'Thomas,' Lark interrupted before he could dig his hole deeper. She slid a plate in front of him and patted him reassuringly on the shoulder. 'Eat your sandwich. Remember, you're hungry.'

'Oh,' he murmured distantly. 'Yeah.'

Lark smiled and was forced to bite her lip to keep from giggling. Alicia looked none too pleased with Henry and ate her sandwich in silence. Henry, on the other hand, occasionally chuckled as he ate.

He watched Thomas for a few moments, then leaned toward Lark, giving her a conspiratorial wink. 'I'd have to say this is the first time I've ever seen a lawyer struck speechless.'

'Me too,' she giggled, unable to restrain herself. 'Give him time though. I actually think he may recover soon. Who knows what he will say then?'

'Probably the lecture about safe sex, and all that,' Henry laughed.

Lark fell against him as she joined his laughter. Thomas and Alicia looked at them with bewilderment.

'You know, Henry.' Lark calmed enough to add her suggestion between bursts of laughter. 'If you get her pregnant, you might want to marry her before the baby is born.'

'And make an honest woman out of her?' he chuckled a deep, throaty sound. 'I doubt she'd let me.'

They turned toward the Blackwells to find them watching with stern expressions, their arms crossed over their chests. Only the glint of humor in their eyes gave away their charade.

Henry and Lark cleared their throats and smothered their smiles. Alicia's expression lost its sternness. She put her arms around Henry's shoulders and gave his grizzled cheek a kiss. 'After all the sadness that's weighed this house down lately, it's good to finally find humor in life again, and laugh.'

'Amen,' Henry said as he returned Alicia's embrace, kissing her full on the mouth.

Thomas and Lark blushed and looked away with a smile. For just a few precious moments, the castle rang with laughter. Lark's smile dimmed as an unwanted feeling stole its way into her thoughts.

Just how long would it last?

CHAPTER 11

Thomas remained quiet after their more than enlightening lunch with his grandmother. And her boyfriend? He shook his head at the very thought. Who would have believed it?

They ran into David on their way out. At first David frowned at them, then took one look at Thomas's bewildered expression and asked him what had happened.

Thomas met David's gaze, his voice still held a hint of his shock. 'Did you know our grandmother has been seeing Henry?'

David's face looked as comical as Thomas's had been. His cousin's eyes widened, his mouth fell open, and he stammered, the words seeming to fall from his mouth like lead bricks. 'You mean . . . as in . . . *seeing* him?'

'Yes,' Thomas blurted as he gave David a curt nod. 'She's also been having sex with him.'

'Thomas,' Lark admonished, popping him on the arm as she smiled. 'Do you think you could put it any more crudely?'

David choked. Literally. Lark thumped him on

the back for good measure. He sputtered as he looked at Thomas with mild shock. 'Sex?' he croaked. 'At her age?'

'Geez, guys.' Lark looked from one to other as she planted her hands on her hips. She couldn't help but laugh at their juvenile expressions. 'It's not as if we are talking about an "inexperienced" woman here. She obviously gave birth to both of your fathers. How the hell do you think that happened? By simply shaking hands?'

'I know that, Lark,' Thomas snapped. He looked slightly peevish at her humor. 'It's just that she's our . . .'

His voice drifted as if he couldn't finish the thought. David's expression matched Thomas's and he finished the sentence for him. 'She is our grandmother.'

'So what?' She looked at them as frustration started to stifle her humor. She waved her hand in front of their faces. 'What's that supposed to mean? You're his cousin, David, does that mean you can't have sex?'

He frowned, taken aback by her statement. 'Of course not. But that's entirely different.'

'How?' she demanded, raising her brow as she waited for an answer. She waited for either one of the Einsteins to enlighten her, but words seemed to have escaped them. 'I thought so. I believe that is what you would call a double standard, wouldn't you, gentlemen?'

Carrying a laundry basket, Alicia walked from the kitchen past them, then hesitated as she looked back at the three of them with an ornery smile. 'What are you children up to?'

'Grandmother, you're seeing Henry?' David asked. His voice cracked like a teenage boy going through puberty.

'I just can't believe you two.' Alicia rolled her eyes and growled with frustration at her two grandsons. She gave Thomas a piercing look. 'I can't believe you are still talking about my sex life, Thomas, let alone discussing it with your cousin.'

Alicia strolled up to them, planting herself in front of David and Thomas. She glared from one to the other, then her expression widened into a grin. 'Just who did you boys think you inherited your libido from?'

Thomas and David both gasped with shock causing Alicia to cackle with wicked laughter. She winked at them as she continued on her way. 'Serves you both right.'

'I couldn't agree more.' Lark spun on her heel and walked away from them, leaving the two Blackwell boys to stare at each other in silence. Thomas finally recovered himself enough to ask where she was going.

'For a walk to clear my head. There's so much testosterone buzzing around in here, it's starting to make me feel aggressive,' she said as she spared them a brief glance over her shoulder. 'And I'm afraid I would end up punching one of you two Neanderthals.'

She flipped the length of her hair over her shoulder as the smile returned to her face. She hadn't really been mad at them, but they had desperately needed a wake up call regarding their grandmother's sex life. 'Men are such juveniles.'

Pushing through the doors, she moved across the wide porch and practically skipped down the steps. Alicia had been right, Lark thought. It had been a much needed break to simply laugh at something. Anything would have done. But, she had to admit with a wry smile, the Blackwell boys' response had been incredibly comical.

Too late she spied Natalie walking toward her. Lark didn't bother to scan around her for any concealing bushes to jump into. After all, the woman had already spotted her and had altered her path so they would be forced to meet.

'What are you looking so smug about?' Natalie smirked, as she looked Lark up and down with a slight air of disgust. 'Or do I really want to know?'

'Natalie,' Lark started, hesitating to chuckle as she realized that not even this peroxide viper could spoil her good mood. 'Take a hike. Jump off the bridge, there is one over there by the way. Bite me. Do one, or all of the above. It's your pick, sweetheart, but get the hell out of my way.'

Natalie gasped, the whoosh of it a shrill whistle as her mouth pursed into a pucker. Lark's brow arched as she almost doubled over laughing at the vivid picture Natalie's face made. Talk about a Freudian image.

'How dare you?'

Lark still laughed as she waved the blonde off and walked away. She headed toward the bridge, deciding it would be nice to simply sit and stare at the water for a while. She wanted to let herself be hypnotized by the shimmering movement of the stream. Let the fears and doubts that had been plaguing her unhinge from her thoughts like a leaf and be cast into the water and swept away.

Her footsteps made light thudding noises as she stepped onto the wooden planks of the bridge. The railing was secure and about waist high, but there was enough room to sit under it and hang her feet off the edge. Lark moved to the rail, placing her hands on it to lean into the wind as it caressed the heat of her face. She closed her eyes and leaned her head back to softly shake her hair as the breeze moved through it.

This is what she needed, Lark thought. Taking a deep, cleansing breath she opened her eyes and looked at the banks on either side of the stream. A cardinal's throaty whistle broke the air around her. Lark searched till she found the brilliant red of the male clutching the thin limb of a tree as the wind bounced his perch under him.

She smiled, watching him for a moment, then when he flew away she lowered herself with an agile swing to sit on the edge of the bridge. The wooden planks were sun warmed and hard under her, making her feel secure enough to swing her legs back and forth like a school girl.

Lark raised her arms to hold the rail above her head as she sat. She leaned her cheek against her arm and watched the sun glimmer across the water in a playful dance. Goodness knows, she didn't have much to feel good about. Unless something significant happened, there was the all too real possibility that she could be facing charges within the next couple of days.

She expelled the thoughts with a shake of her head. No, she didn't have much to feel good about, she repeated to herself. Except for Thomas, she thought as she envisioned his smile. The power of those mesmerizing eyes. The feel of his lips on her.

And that was enough for her.

The warmth of the sun fell on her, soaking into her muscles. The heat making her relaxed and sleepy as her eyes fluttered. Lark yawned in a very unlady-like fashion and stretched her back. She chuckled softly as she recalled just why she was so sleepy. And if she had her way later, and she didn't think that would be too much of a problem, there wouldn't be too much sleep for her tonight either.

Lark was too tired to walk back to the house. She scooted back and stretched out on the bed of the bridge, letting the sun fall over her like a blanket. She yawned again as she laid her hands beside her head. She would just lie down in the sun for a few moments, then head back to the house for a nap, she thought sleepily.

Sleep stole over her like a whisper. Lark could feel it sneaking up on her, but it felt so good to hear the sound of the wind in the trees around her like a soft song. The day's tension drained from her and she sighed.

A noise. A snap? Maybe the crunch of a footstep, speared through her dreams. It yanked at her and she sensed something was intruding on the comfort she had surrounded herself with.

Lark had no idea how long she had drifted off. Yet, something had forced her to snap back from the dark depths of slumber. She opened her eyes, blinking at the blinding brilliance of the sun. Lifting her hand, she shielded her eyes and was unable to see anything that had caused her to awake so suddenly.

She squinted as she tried to orient herself from her short nap. She was on the bridge. Raising her hand, she tilted her head to look back above her head and was rewarded with a burst of bright sunlight. Tears came to her eyes and she blinked them away as she scanned the scene around her.

Frowning, she relaxed and wondered what had awakened her. A shadow moved across her line of vision and she looked above her. Her eyes widened at the sight of a figure, blackened by the blinding rays of the sun, standing by her head.

Lark started to lift her hand to see who it was when the figure shifted quickly, the movements short and jerky. She knew the split second before the object hit her head that she should have responded to the slight moment of doubt she had experienced when the noise awakened her. Pain shattered through her head causing numbing blackness of unconsciousness to shower over her.

Thomas chuckled to himself as the image of Natalie's fury flashed back into his thoughts. He shook his head as he opened the front door to search for Lark. Natalie had practically stormed into the house ranting and raving about 'that bitch' and how the hell anyone put up with that psychic was beyond her. She marched up to him and David where they still stood by the staircase and planted her hands on her hips, then proceeded to tell them how 'that bitch' had said all sorts of rude things to her and just what the hell were they going to do about it?

They had not meant to be rude when they both had started laughing. The blonde's mouth had flown open as the sputtering sounds leveled into a growl. After calling them a few choice names, she had ended up stalking past them to her room.

Thomas had turned to David with a grin. 'I'd better go find Lark and see if she is still in one piece.'

Shutting the front door behind him, Thomas walked across the porch to step lightly down the steps. If he had any idea where she would be, he thought easily, she would probably be at the bridge. Thomas headed toward the old structure as the smile remained on his face.

Nearing the abandoned bridge, his smile froze and his heart started pounding within his chest. Some of Lark's talents must be rubbing off on him, he thought as he quickened his step toward his destination. Something uneasy slid past the good humor he had been feeling to grip him in its clutches. His nerves tightened as he neared the bridge and still could not see Lark. He didn't know what had come over him, but he experienced an unfamiliar sense of urgency. He had no idea what it was. He simply needed to find Lark.

The bridge came fully into view, and his heart buckled with fear when he saw her lying on the wooden floor of the structure. Thomas started running, his breath coming in quick gasps, but not entirely from the exertion. He ran to her, then knelt slowly beside her quiet form.

'Lark' he murmured, his voice filled with apprehension.

Her eyes were closed, but she was still breathing. Her hand was beside her head as if she had tried to protect herself, but she bore no marks from a struggle. Lark was lying with her head turned to the side. Thomas gently tilted her face and grimaced at the blood glistening on her scalp above and behind her ear.

Picking her up into his arms, he adjusted her light form and headed as quickly as he could to the castle. As he climbed the steps, he shouted to David, his grandmother, anyone to come help him. He thanked goodness that Henry was still at the house. He came to the door and shouted again as he knocked on the thick wood with the toe of his boot.

Alicia opened the door with a dish towel in her hand. 'What is so important, Thomas, that you . . . Oh, goodness.'

'I found her unconscious on Theorosa's bridge,' Thomas answered gruffly. 'It looks like she's been hit on the head and she's bleeding. Please get Henry for me, Grandmother.'

'Of course.'

She shoved the door back for him to carry Lark in and they hurried toward the stairs. Alicia went to fetch Henry and Thomas took the stairs as quickly as possible. Without giving it a thought, he took her automatically to his room and laid her gently on the bed.

He could hear the commotion of Alicia and Henry as they approached the bedroom. The old doctor had not carried a black bag since he had retired, but had always insisted that Alicia keep a well stocked first aid kit on the premises. The kit was in his hand as he hurried to the bed. Alicia followed closely behind with towels and a bowl of water.

Reluctantly Thomas stepped out of their way, but not far as he clung to the bedpost at the foot. 'Is she going to be all right?'

'I've got to have a look at her first before I can answer that, Thomas.' Henry's voice was calm and business-like as he leaned over Lark to inspect the small gash on her scalp. He murmured softly to himself and to Alicia who stood beside him acting as his nurse.

Henry gently parted Lark's hair and dabbed at the wound with the clean cloth. He rinsed it thoroughly, then asked Alicia for the hydrogen peroxide. 'Well, this ought to wake her up, if nothing else.'

He poured a small amount of the clear liquid over the cut and instantly it foamed white as it killed bacteria. At the sting of the medicine, Lark jerked slightly and stirred.

'Lark, sweetheart,' Henry called to her as he continued to clean the wound. 'Can you hear me, Lark?'

Lark groaned and moved beneath his hands. She lifted her hand to her forehead, then rubbed it slowly over her face as her eyelids fluttered. She narrowed them and slowly blinked her eyes open.

Looking around her, Lark started to lift her head, then let it fall back as she moaned. 'What happened?'

'Thomas found you lying on the bridge,' Henry answered, he kept his voice soothing as he lifted her lids to peer cautiously into each of her eyes. 'Do you know how you ended up there?'

Lark frowned as she appeared to think the question over. Thomas gripped the bedpost as he waited for her answer. 'I went there to relax for a little bit, I guess.'

'Did you see who did this to you?' Thomas blurted, earning a look of reproach from both Henry and his grandmother at the anger competing with the fear in his voice.

She licked her lips as if her mouth were dry. Carefully she shook her head. 'The sun was so inviting and made me drowsy so I lay down for a few moments. I guess I drifted off to sleep. The next thing I knew a dark figure was standing over me with the sun behind them. The sun was so bright I couldn't see anything.'

Thomas's knuckles whitened as he gripped the bedpost. The horror at the sight of her lying there had ripped through him. It had torn even more within him when he found the wound still bleeding on her head. Who would have been so angry with Lark to try to harm her this way?

Instantly Natalie came to mind. Thomas ignored the pointed looks of Henry and his grandmother and leaned over the foot of the bed. 'Do you think it was Natalie?'

'I don't know.' Lark gave it some thought, then shook her head as she sighed. 'I ran into her when I was headed out to the bridge and I didn't feel in the mood to be nice to her.'

'So we heard,' Thomas murmured.

'I wish I could say for sure it was definitely her,' she answered as she released a deep breath. 'But I honestly can't. After we talked she headed toward the castle and I did not see anyone walking toward me.'

Henry sat on the bed beside her as he continued his examination. He poked and prodded, then took her pulse. Finally he folded his hands in his lap and gave her a reassuring smile. 'You definitely could be worse, my girl.'

'How bad is it?' Thomas asked quickly.

Henry chuckled at his worried expression. 'Relax, Thomas. I think the "perp," or whatever the police call hoodlums these days, only meant to get her attention. She does have a nasty cut, but fortunately she's not suffering from a concussion. But she is going to have one hell of a headache,' he said.

'Nothing like a hangover without any of the fun, right, Lark?' Henry joked as he gave her a quick pat on her hand. 'I'll get you something for your headache, but you'll be just fine. However, I would recommend if you decide to take another nap, you might consider a bed next time.'

Lark smiled at his comment. 'I would have to agree with you on that.'

Henry stood, then gently took Alicia's arm. 'We'll leave you two alone now while I go fetch some aspirin for you.'

The older couple stepped out the door just as David poked his head in. His gaze moved from Lark to Thomas. 'I called the police, they should be here pretty quick.'

'Thanks,' Thomas said as he returned his attention to Lark. He moved to the door and closed it quietly. He headed back to the bed to sit beside her and take her hand in his. 'Okay, we've heard Henry's opinion . . . how are you doing?'

Lark smiled at the tenderness in his voice as she gave his hand a squeeze. 'I'm fine, Thomas. I just wish the sun hadn't been in my eyes and maybe I would have defended myself better.'

Thomas lifted his hand to trace the ridge of her cheek bone with his finger, wanting nothing more than to touch her. His gaze dropped to her lips. He started to lean toward her to fulfil his need to kiss her when a soft knock at the door stopped him.

'Damn,' he muttered. Turning toward the door, he called for them to come in.

Henry looked only slightly apologetic as he entered carrying her aspirin and a glass of water. Thomas couldn't help but think the older man was relishing the interruption, considering their earlier conversation regarding his passion for his grandmother.

'Here we go, dear.' Henry stepped beside the bed and handed the pills to Lark. She dutifully took them and thanked him for the glass of water. With a pointed look to Thomas, he gave her one last order. 'Make sure you rest now.'

'I heard our little psychic was up to her tricks again.'

They turned in unison to see Natalie standing at the doorway with a smug expression. She sauntered into the room and stood at the foot of the bed to take her time in looking Lark over.

'She doesn't look hurt,' she said, her voice filled with sarcasm. 'So what has allegedly happened to her now?'

'Someone took a whack at her while she was on the bridge.' Thomas stood and turned to face the blonde, his expression hard. He leveled his gaze on her as he gave her a pointed look. 'In fact it happened shortly after her conversation with you. And, if I remember correctly, when you stormed into the house, you were quite upset with her. Does my memory serve me correct?'

Natalie gasped, her expression registering her shock. Angrily she waved her hand toward Lark. 'You can't possible think I had anything to do with this?'

'I don't know, Natalie.' Thomas's voice was unrelenting and stern. 'Did you?'

She sputtered, her face looking wicked with her outrage. She spoke barely above a whisper as she shook. 'Thomas, I can't believe you would say such a thing. After she sniped at me, I came straight here and talked to you and David, if you remember correctly,' she said, mocking him with his own words. 'Then you saw with your own eyes that I went up to my room. How the hell was I supposed to get back down to where she was, unless I scaled the side of the castle?'

Natalie spun on her heel and stalked from the room. Henry watched her go, trying to hide the amusement in his expression. He sighed softly as he started toward the door. 'I think I'll go back to the kitchen to help Alicia. I would have to say that it is definitely safer there.'

Henry tactfully closed the door behind him and Thomas looked at Lark. She smiled at him. 'I hate to admit it, but I do think Natalie has a point. Only a few minutes had elapsed before whoever it was hit me.'

Thomas rubbed his hand over his face, his lack of sleep catching up with him. He felt tired as he frowned at the truth of what she was saying. How nice it would have been to think Natalie had done it. How easy, he thought. At least he could think it had been the petty revenge of a petty woman, but he knew it wasn't.

There could only be one person who would have sought Lark out to hurt her. What caused Thomas's chest to tighten the most with fear was the realization that the person had already killed twice. What was to stop that person from seeking to do the same with the only person who could possibly identify him or her as the killer?

Another knock at the door, this time more forceful, interrupted Thomas's disturbing thoughts. He rose to answer it. 'Is there a line out there, or what?'

He opened the door to find Detective Ron Baker giving him a not so friendly smile. 'Mr Blackwell, I understand we had another little "incident" today.'

'I didn't realize you made house calls, detective.' Thomas's voice was hard as he tried to control his anger at the man's intended sarcasm.

'I just happened to be in the neighborhood.'

'Lucky us,' Thomas muttered. He made no effort to let the man in.

Baker held his gaze, seeming to enjoy the slight confrontation. 'Are you going to let me in?'

'We reported an assault, not a homicide, detective.' Thomas enunciated Baker's title to make his point.

'Now that *would* be unusual, wouldn't it. Considering what has happened around here lately.' Baker merely shrugged and offered another unfriendly smile. 'I heard the call and decided to come here myself, since it may or may not be related. If you would prefer a unit to come out here, that is your prerogative.'

'I would prefer you to allow Miss Delavan to get some rest,' Thomas said, making no attempt to mask his dislike for the man.

'Thomas, really it is all right,' Lark called softly from behind him.

Thomas said nothing and did not move as he continued to hold the detective's gaze. Baker returned his look for a moment, then turned to slip past him. Thomas clenched his jaws as he left the door open and returned to stand beside the bed.

'Thank you, Miss Delavan,' the detective's voice was kind, a direct contradiction to the hard gleam in his eyes. 'It seems that every time I come here, you are lying in Mr Blackwell's bed. I wonder if it has become a habit.'

'Baker, I've had just about enough of your crudity,' Thomas announced. His voice was tight, barely civil as he spoke through gritted teeth. He could feel the animosity in his gaze and knew that Baker could see how much he would love to remove his badge for him. 'If you've come to insult us, then go ahead and get your ass out of here. At this point I have no qualms in using my influence to keep you out.'

'Such an eloquent threat, Mr Blackwell,' he said, his brow arched.

Thomas stepped slightly forward. 'Not a threat at all, detective. Just the facts.'

'Thomas,' Lark said quietly as she took his hand. She gave it a gentle squeeze before she folded her hands back in her lap. She looked at the detective. 'What is it you want, Baker, because I happen to agree with Thomas? Either get on with it or I'll dial the phone for him myself.'

Baker jammed his hands in the pockets of his inexpensive suit and pursed his lips as he studied her for a moment. 'Sure, no problem. What allegedly happened today?'

Allegedly. This time it was Thomas touching Lark's shoulder in a gentle restraining action. The fury in her expression made her eyes glitter. 'I suppose I "allegedly" whacked myself with a rock too?'

The detective shrugged his shoulder as if he didn't care one way or another. 'It wouldn't be the first time someone had a self-inflicted wound.'

Thomas admired the valiant way Lark ignored Baker's comment and went on. 'To answer your "alleged" question, I was sitting at the bridge when I decided to lie down for a moment and enjoy the sun. Someone came up behind me and hit me on the head. When I awoke I was here.'

'And I suppose you did not get a good look at this person?' The detective's tone of voice showed his lack of belief and his contempt for her answer.

'It was the middle of the afternoon,' Lark snapped, her fists clenching in her lap. 'The sun was behind them, so no, I did not see the person. I saw only a black silhouette.'

241

'So you have no idea who supposedly did this?'

Lark ran her hand through her hair in frustration. She felt so angry, tears were threatening to well in her eyes and she'd be damned before she'd let that man know he had gotten to her. 'No, I did not.'

'So you have, again, no idea why someone would supposedly want to harm you?'

Lark glared at him thinking to herself that if there were any justice in the world, someone would *allegedly* hit him on the side of his head. 'No, I do not.'

Baker pursed his lips and nodded as he took his hands out of his pockets. 'Well, I guess that should just about do it.'

'That's it?' Lark practically yelled, instantly regretting the move as pain pounded unmercifully through her skull.

'You call that an investigation?' Thomas demanded.

'No,' Baker said with a feral smile as he sauntered toward the bedroom door. 'I call it a dead end.'

Thomas watched the man go, wishing desperately he had physically shown him the way out. His stance was tense with anger and he noticed for the first time that not only had he balled his hands into fists, but that he was also baring his teeth. He unclenched his fists and willed himself to relax. He tried to dissipate the anger by reminding himself that Detective Ron Baker was a down to the bone jerk.

Of all the people in the world, why couldn't that

man be taken hostage by terrorists and never be seen in the free world again?

Thomas took a deep breath to ease the tight band of anger clutching him before he turned back to Lark. She was studying him, looking into his eyes. He wondered if she were using her ability to probe within his thoughts.

'You shouldn't let that vile man bother you,' she murmured as she patted the bed beside her.

He arched a knowing eyebrow at her. 'And he provokes no reaction within you, I suppose?'

Lark chuckled, then grabbed quickly at her head. 'I've got to stop doing that.'

Thomas sat beside her on the bed. He leaned across her form with his arm. Lifting his left hand, he smoothed a lock of her long hair from her face, letting his gaze watch the length of its satin texture slide through his fingers.

Lark's eyes remained on his face. 'What is it, Thomas?'

He shook his head at first, unable to speak. Tried to give her a smile, failed miserably and was forced to meet her gaze. He could see by the widening of her eyes that she recognized the fear in his expression.

'I can't tell you what tore through me when I saw you lying there.'

Lark softly murmured his name as she touched her hand to his cheek. 'I can't tell you what it means to me that you care about me.'

Thomas slowly leaned toward her, his eyes on her lips. Those lips that could drive him to distraction. He hungered for her and sought to at least pacify part of his need by tasting her. He lowered his mouth to hers, lightly pressing his lips to hers. She parted under him, inviting him and he needed no second invitations.

Lark sighed huskily, the sound of it vibrating deep within him, sparking a heat that threatened to consume him if he didn't back off quickly. Thomas pulled away from her, forcing himself to remember her injury.

Lark had just taken his face in her hands to pull him to her when yet another knock sounded on the door. Thomas dropped his forehead to touch hers as he groaned in frustration.

'What the hell is this? Grand Central Station?' he muttered, under his breath.

He gave her an apologetic look, even though he didn't feel too sorry. Whoever it was had probably saved him from letting his body override his better judgement. She had been hurt, after all. Thomas shook his head with a little laugh at the simmering, saucy look Lark was favoring him with as he headed toward the door.

He stopped with his hand on the door knob as he turned slightly to wave his finger at her. 'You've been injured, remember. So behave.'

'Who, me?' she feigned innocently.

Thomas was smiling when he opened the door. The look turned to confusion when he found his cousin Stephanie nervously twisting her hands as she waited.

'Steph, sweetheart, should you be up?' he asked, his concern showing on his face as he eyed his cousin's pale expression.

She licked her lips as her gaze flitted from one spot, to him, then on. 'I . . . I was wondering how she was doing? Is she all right?'

Thomas nodded as he placed his hand reassuringly on her shoulder. 'Of course. She's doing fine.'

A look of relief flooded Stephanie's expression, though the nervous tension remained. 'Good. I was so concerned.'

Footsteps on the stairs caused them to look in that direction. John rushed toward the second floor, his breath coming in short gasps from his quick climb. His gaze was frantic till he spied Stephanie with Thomas and he, like his wife, visibly relaxed.

'Stephanie,' he said, his voice calm as if he didn't have a care in the world. 'I've been looking for you. When I didn't find you in your room, I became worried. As ill as you are, I was afraid something had happened.'

'I'm fine,' Stephanie said in a small voice. 'I do think I would like to go to my room now.'

'Of course, dear.'

John took his wife gently by the shoulders as he steered her toward their room. He looked over his shoulder back at Thomas and gave him a reassuring smile. 'She'll be fine, Thomas. Don't worry.'

Thomas frowned. 'She's still very pale.'

John nodded his agreement. 'She's been pretty sick. The problem is she thinks she feels good enough to start roaming around again. I keep trying to tell her not to rush it.'

'You better listen to John, Stephanie,' Thomas

called to his cousin. 'Or we'll set Grandmother on you.'

The couple continued down the hall as Thomas stepped back to close the door. He turned to find Lark looking at him. The gleam in her eye and the knowing twist of her lips tried to entice him, causing very suggestive thoughts to cloud his mind.

He shook his finger at her again, even as he fought the urge to give in to her. 'You need your rest, young lady.'

She studied him for a moment, then scowled when he refused to give in to her. 'You should be pampering me, damn it.'

He walked to the bed and gave her a peck on the cheek. Thomas pulled the covers up around her as he tucked her in. He lifted his gaze to hold hers. He did nothing to hide the heat of desire within his eyes.

'Don't worry, love,' he said huskily, his gaze traveling from her lips to her eyes. 'I will make love to you.'

Thomas held her gaze for a moment more, then turned to leave the room. Shutting the door behind him, Thomas hesitated with his hand on the door knob. He hated leaving her. Hated even more that someone had attacked her on his family's property. His expression hardened with determination as he strode to the stairway.

The detective may not have felt the need to investigate the old structure where Lark had been attacked for any telling clues. But he did.

Thomas studied the bridge and the surrounding area for over an hour. During that time, his expression changed from a frown to a dark scowl. Nothing. He had found nothing. No matter how much he denied it, Baker's words came back to haunt him. Baker had called this incident yet another dead end.

CHAPTER 12

Lark followed the woman. She was tall with regal bearing. Her dark, almost ebony hair flowed over her shoulders, down her back to end just at her waist. The gown she wore was linen with heavy lace sewn into the sleeves, bodice, and the fluted ends of the skirt, giving it a fitted look which emphasized the woman's figure.

The woman walked away from Lark causing her to frown as something about the image nagged at her. Moving down the long, dark, fearsome hallway filled with the cobwebs of time, the lady turned her face slowly to look over her shoulder at Lark, as if checking to make sure she was following. The beauty of the woman struck Lark, as she recognized her face.

She was following Theorosa.

Theorosa smiled when she found that Lark was dutifully following her and turned back to watch the path ahead of her. Lark studied the tall frame moving in front of her and realized that the figure's hips did not sway with the movement of her walking. She glided as if on a cushion of air toward their destination. Where they were headed, Lark did not know. She knew only that there was an air of determination, a sense of urgency to their journey.

Lark called to her, wanting to know where they were going. Theorosa glanced back at her at the sound of her voice, but still she continued without speaking. The fear built within Lark, making her want to stop. To turn away and head to the safety of the castle and Thomas. Wherever that was.

Lark tried to look around her to decipher where she was, or where she was going. She felt that this could be important, but the confining hold of the dream would not allow her to look, as if some unseen force wanted to keep the secret away from her.

Trying to swallow her growing fear, Lark continued to stumble over the rough path as she followed the beautiful woman. Their footsteps echoed off the dark cavernous walls and they moved on. They finally reached a dark room filled with the gruesome stone figures of statues more suited for the adornment of tombstones than even this formidable area. She hesitated when Theorosa slowly turned till she faced her. The woman silently beckoned to her to join her with a graceful wave of her hand and a small, knowing smile.

Lark was unable to remove her gaze from Theorosa as she continued to walk towards her. She forced one foot in front of the other, even though somewhere in the darker regions of her mind she knew it was a mistake.

Theorosa's smile widened, her eyes gleaming as she beckoned to Lark yet again. She held her arms out to Lark as if to embrace her within their security. Lark frowned at the dark shapes that loomed behind

Theorosa. The shapes shifted, then unfolded behind the woman. The wings carved from the cold heart of stone protruded from her shoulders to give Theorosa an almost ethereal quality as her long hair fluttered in the light breeze flowing around them.

As if sensing Lark's reluctance, Theorosa reached her hand out for her to take. Lark looked from her hand to her eyes as she nervously licked her lips, then decided to continue. She had no other choice.

Lark stepped cautiously forward mimicking the woman's gesture. Reaching to Theorosa's hand, their fingertips almost touching, Lark felt the ground suddenly give way beneath her. She could hear her heartbeat pounding within her dream. It seemed to slow, just as time did. Lark looked from the ground opening beneath her with a crumbling crevice back to Theorosa's small smile. A scream ripped from her throat as she fell into blackness.

Lark sat up in bed with a start, instantly regretting the movement. Clutching her head with her hands, she groaned as she tried to relax the grip of pain. Slowly the ache subsided and allowed her to open her eyes at last. She looked around her to find the room empty. Lark scooted to the side of the bed and gingerly put her feet over the edge. Standing, she was relieved to find that the dizziness she had felt earlier had disappeared and, other than the occasional throbbing from too quick movements, she felt only the dull discomfort of a headache.

Lark looked down to find that she was still wearing her now very wrinkled clothes and she gave a disgruntled sigh. She decided it would best to freshen up and change before she faced the rest of the Blackwells. Shuffling to the door, she opened it and gave a quick peek into the hallway to make sure no one would witness her derelict-looking state. She moved semi-quickly to her room and entered it.

Lark sat down for a brief moment on the side of her bed and let her throbbing head rest for a moment. Glancing toward the night stand, she found that someone, probably Alicia, had guessed what her intentions would be when she awakened and had left her a bottle of aspirin.

She took a couple and swallowed them down with a glass of cool water, then headed into the bathroom to start her shower. It would make her feel significantly better to remove the crust she felt covered her. She stripped her clothes and threw them into the laundry basket before stepping into the warm spray of the water. She had to shampoo her hair gingerly, especially around the area where she had been hit. It was only a small wound, but it was sensitive to the touch, causing her to grit her teeth as she worked the lather through the length of her hair.

Finishing her shower, she stepped out and toweled off. She slipped into her terry cloth robe, then wrapped her wet hair in a towel. Lark returned to the bedroom to look through the wardrobe. Shifting items around her closet, she tried to decide what to wear.

She had just moved one of her shirts when something called her attention to the back of the old wardrobe. The nagging thought from the weird dream she had had, suddenly became clear. The dress Theorosa had been wearing was one of those from the wardrobe.

On the first day of her arrival at the castle, the room had been ransacked and the old dresses thrown without regard around the room. At the time, she had been too disturbed by the act to really take notice of the beautiful gowns, but she remembered earlier that day when she had reached to a dress hidden within the wardrobe, and the strong reaction it had provoked.

Lark shifted the hangers out of the way and started to reach toward the back. The door was still stuck, making her twist partially into the wardrobe to retrieve the dress. She hesitated as her fingers brushed the stiff fabric, waiting for the reaction, but it didn't come. Slowly she slid the garment toward her till she could pull it easily from the closet.

She held it in front of her, letting her gaze move over the familiar design. The sleeves were puffed, the heavy lace enhancing the shape. At the elbow the material slimmed to hug the wearer's arm. The bodice looked fuller with the design of the lace and the small waist of the dress flowed smoothly to the knee where the full skirt fluted out even more with intricate lace ovals. Yes, it was the gown Theorosa had worn in her dream.

But, what did it mean?

Clutching the dress to her, Lark frowned as she bit her lip in thought. What *did* it mean? She closed her eyes as she ran her hands over the stiff fabric. Opening her thoughts, she tried to pick up any sensations or images the dress may still hold.

Nothing.

Lark sighed in frustration. She put the dress back in the wardrobe at the back where she had found it. Returning to the task of deciding what to wear, she put the dream and its hidden message to the back of her mind. It had worked well for her in the past. Simply by ignoring the problem for a while, the solution would sometimes make itself known to her. There was something to the dream and the dress, but at the moment she was unable to put the ideas together in her mind.

Lark had come here to help Theorosa's spirit find rest after more than a century of disquiet. Instead of peace, she had become embroiled in the investigation of two murders. So many questions and so few answers, yet it seemed as if several fingers were pointing in her direction.

Just as it had happened with Theorosa so long ago.

Lark shook her head, then ran her hand through her hair. She picked a shirt and a light skirt, then tossed them to the bed. Reaching for a brush, she began the task of brushing the wet length of her hair as another thought pushed into her mind.

There was also Thomas.

She frowned as her body automatically reacted to the thought of him. Her lips yearned to taste him, just as her body ached to feel him against her. Somehow her traitorous heart had reluctantly succumbed to the charm and spirit of Thomas Blackwell.

Standing in Theorosa's small room that held only the bare necessity of furniture, Lark thought she could understand how the young woman must have felt. To come from such a common background, then to be thrust into the elegance of the

Blackwell Castle. How out of place she must she have felt. Like a plain robin perching with the bright beauty of the cardinals.

Thomas was a wonderful man with a warm heart and a charming personality. He was a lawyer and how she wished she could say she was just an accountant. But she was also a psychic. He might wish to spend some time with her, but Lark refused to fool herself. A man of his position could not attach himself to such a 'notable' person as herself. One who was not only known for her unusual abilities but who had also been involved in more than one murder investigation. Three to be exact.

Lark sighed as she ran the brush through her hair. A soft knock at the door shook her from her thoughts. She went to the door and cracked it, more than a little leery of who it might be. With her luck it would be Natalie calling on her again for yet another bitchy reason.

Peeking through the door, she found Thomas smiling at her in the hallway. She opened the door, stood to the side and waved him in.

'You look surprised to see me,' he said as he moved past her.

'Pleasantly surprised, would be more accurate,' she murmured as she turned to face him.

'I guess I'll take that as a compliment,' Thomas said as he moved to put his hands on her arms. He stroked her with his thumbs through her robe as he studied her for a moment. 'How do you feel?'

Lark smiled up at him. 'Much better after my shower and now that you're here, I feel almost as good as new, thank you.'

He chuckled as he kissed her on the tip of her nose. Lark inhaled the spicy scent of him. She started to tilt her head to nuzzle him for a kiss when he stepped quickly away.

'Good, then you'll be ready for dinner soon.'

Raising a more than frustrated brow, she gave him a look of disbelief. 'Dinner?'

'You are hungry, aren't you?' he asked, his dimples deepening with his smile.

'Well, yeah,' Lark answered as she shoved her hands into the pockets of her robe. 'I just thought . . . that we . . . Oh, never mind,' she practically growled the last word.

'Thought what, Lark?' Thomas watched her, his expression showing his amusement at the direction of her thoughts.

'Nothing,' she muttered as she turned away and started rummaging through her drawers for underclothes. Her movements were an obvious dismissal.

Thomas moved toward her. She sensed his presence and straightened. He took advantage of the movement by pulling her to his chest. He smoothed the hair back over her shoulder to expose her neck to his touch as he stood behind her. Circling his arms around her waist, he nuzzled her neck with his mouth. He nipped lightly at the sensitive flesh with his teeth as he slid his hands under her robe. Smoothing his palms along the ridge of her rib cage, he moved up to cup her breasts.

Lark moaned with pleasure as the heat of his mouth branded her neck. His thumbs tortured the sensitive peaks of her nipples, rubbing them into tight buds. She arched against him as one of his

255

hands slid down her stomach to unbelt her robe and push the fabric aside allowing him unhindered access to her body.

Thomas caressed the contours of her body with his hand, tracing the swell of her hip, then cupping her buttock to give it a gentle squeeze. He slid his hand back to her breast as Lark pressed herself against him.

She felt on fire with the need to be touched by him as she turned toward him. The robe dropped slowly from her shoulders to be caught in the crook of her arm. Lark shrugged out of the material as she smoothed her palms over Thomas's chest. Circling her arms around his neck, she captured his mouth with hers and kissed him with the greedy need she felt for him.

Thomas's arms tightened around her as he pressed the length of her against him. Slowly he pulled from her kiss to meet her gaze. 'I'll come get you for dinner in about fifteen minutes,' he said, his voice husky with desire.

'What?' Lark couldn't believe what she was hearing. 'You're thinking of food at a time like this?'

'Of course,' he answered her with a wide, dimpled smile. His gaze moved boldly up and down her nude body. 'What were you thinking about?'

'A cold shower,' she snapped as she turned away from him to grab her underclothes from the drawer. She stalked around him to the bed.

Thomas chuckled behind her and she heard him cross to the door. Opening it, he started to go through and she looked over her shoulder to see him meet her gaze. 'Oh, by the way, we won't be eating with the others tonight and you might want to put some clothes on, although I wouldn't complain too much if you didn't.'

'Jerk,' she muttered as she threw her panties at him. He quickly shut the door and material hit the wood and fell to the floor. Lark walked to the door, then bent to retrieve them. She moved back to the bed and started to get dressed. 'Damned if I'm not going to make him pay for that.'

'Damn insufferable man,' Lark muttered, between gritted teeth. She sat on the side of the bed and pulled her hair back into a pearl clip that matched the golden tones in her skirt. She mumbled a few more rude observations about the man as she slid her feet into her sandals.

Every time she thought about Thomas's unusual, and highhanded, invitation she didn't know how to react. Whether she should be mad, amused, or flabbergasted. It was all very mysterious, and new to her.

'Damn insufferable man.'

She startled at the sound of the knock on the door. Looking at her watch, she rose and walked to the door and opened it. She found Thomas smiling at her with his devilish dimples.

'You are late,' she announced.

Thomas had been holding his hand behind his back and he brought it forward with a flourish. Lark looked bemusedly at the yellow rose in his hand. She was stunned for a moment, then felt herself almost give in to the urge to return his smile. Biting her lip, she forced herself to give him a stern look, even though the gleam in her eye surely gave her away.

'I hope this makes up for being late,' he said softly, his eyes holding hers.

'No, it doesn't.' She could no longer resist. Finally she gave in and gave him a smile. 'But it's a start.'

Thomas held his arm out for her. Lark felt herself blush as she took his arm. He placed his hand warmly on hers and led her down the hallway. As they continued past the stairway, she glanced to Thomas with a questioning look.

He simply smiled at her. 'I told you we would not be eating with the others.'

They moved on till they came to the stairs that led to the ballroom. Thomas waved with his hand and started up the stairs. At the door Thomas leaned toward her and gave her a gentle, lingering kiss that promised her so much more in store for the evening ahead of them.

Opening the door, he stepped inside and held his hand out to her in invitation. 'Close your eyes,' he ordered softly.

Lark did as he asked as she took his hand. Their steps echoed through the room as he led her across the wooden dance floor. He stopped and gave her hand a gentle squeeze.

'You can open your eyes now, sweetheart.'

Lark gasped, clutching her hand to her chest at the sight before her. Candles. Thomas had placed white candles everywhere. An assortment of sizes burned across the top of the mantle as did many others that were gathered in a circle in front of the fireplace. The yellow-white flames of the fire matched the smaller, flickering beads of the candles. The area before the fireplace glowed with a golden hue from the romantic lighting.

Her eyes widened at the sight of the thick blanket spread in the center of the shimmering circle, complete with two place settings. She turned a questioning gaze to Thomas, unsure that her voice would sound steady.

He stroked her cheek softly with his thumb. 'I wanted to give you a candlelit dinner.'

Lark moved toward him and wrapped her arms around his neck tightly as she gave him a resounding kiss of appreciation. She pulled back slightly with an amused look in her eyes. 'Okay, now I forgive you for being late.'

Thomas laughed as he took her hand and led her into the circle where they seated themselves on the blanket. Lark tucked her legs under her and watched him remove the silver covers from their plates. The meal was simple, light, and elegant.

The silence between them was comfortable, intimate, seductive. Lark was nervous as she cleared her throat. Her gaze moved toward the paintings, softly illuminated along the wall till she automatically found Theorosa's.

The girl's warm, brown eyes looked to her in a sad, beautiful way. It reminded her of her unusual dream. She frowned as she studied the painting for a moment.

Thomas noticed the direction of her gaze. He wondered if she were being held by another vision. 'What do you see, Lark?'

She turned toward him with an amused expression, knowing what had gone through his mind. His concern for her pleased her greatly, in a feminine way, adding to the already seductive air moving around them.

'A painting,' she smiled, giggling at his surprised look at her 'normal' answer.

'Oh.'

'I shouldn't tease you like that,' she added softly, as she placed her hand over his. 'Seeing Theorosa's painting reminded me about an unusual dream I had.'

'What was it about?' he asked, then took a bite.

Lark shrugged, 'It's kind of hard to explain. You know how dreams can be. How they can be weird and you have no idea why things appear in it. In my dream I was following her, but she was like an angel moving through this tunnel. See what I mean? An angel underground. That doesn't make sense.'

'Unless it means you're going to hell,' he offered with a wicked grin as he gave her a bawdy wink.

'Well,' she answered primly as she smoothed her hand over her skirt. 'If I am going there, I doubt I'll be alone when I get there.'

They laughed together comfortably, then settled back into their silence. Lark's body was as aware of Thomas's proximity as if he were touching her boldly.

She felt shy, almost like a teenager as she took a bite from her sandwich. Thomas seemed unable to take his eyes off of her. Finally she gave him a pointed look. 'Will you quit staring at me? I feel like I'm unbuttoned or something.'

Thomas chuckled as he shook his head. 'You are not unbuttoned, otherwise I would be taking advantage of it as much as I possibly could.'

'Then what is it?' she asked.

He held her gaze and a part of her shook with unfamiliar fear as she saw a depth of emotion that she was afraid to name within her heart. 'I was right.'

'Right about what?'

'When I planned this dinner for you, I wondered how you would look in candlelight.' Lark said nothing, her chest tightened with desire and an unexpected need to fulfil his wish. He continued, his voice low and husky, 'I thought you would be beautiful.'

Lark couldn't seem to quit smiling as Thomas topped her glass up with more wine when they finished their dinner. He looked up and held her gaze, now it was his turn to ask the same question. 'What is it?'

Lark shook her head, then lowered her gaze to take a sip. Thomas stood to remove their plates, taking them to a side table by the wall. Returning to the blanket, he stretched beside her and once again studied her with those beautiful eyes. His gaze was piercing, hypnotic. Part of her wanted to turn away, to hide from him what was in her heart. The other part of her could not resist him and wished for nothing more than to hold his gaze.

Thomas took her wine glass and set it beside his. He patted the blanket beside him in an invitation for her to lie beside him. Lark scooted next to him and relished the warmth of his body by hers. She lay on her back with her hair fanned around her as he leaned on one elbow beside her with his body turned toward her.

He stroked the soft skin of her cheek before kissing her with an undemanding touch. He pulled only a breath away, his voice nothing more than a whisper. 'What is it, Lark?'

She turned her head to meet the heat of his gaze. 'Why are you doing all of this?'

'Because I wanted to be with you and I didn't want to share you with the others.' The corner of his mouth turned up in a lopsided smile as he resumed touching her. 'Because you've become very special to me.'

'I don't understand,' she murmured as he touched his lips to the corner of her mouth.

'I don't either.'

Thomas cupped her face as he drew her to his kiss. His mouth was firm and insistent against her as he moved over her lips. Gently he drew the soft fullness of her lower lip into his mouth and tasted the sweet texture of her. After a moment he stopped, his forehead falling to hers.

'What, Thomas?' she asked, unusually nervous that something about her had pushed him away.

He slowly shook his head as he groaned. 'I kissed you and this image of my grandmother and Henry kissing popped into my head.'

'Is that all,' she said, giggling against his neck. She nipped at his ear with her teeth as she grinned wickedly. 'I'm sure Alicia wouldn't be happy to hear about that.'

'Are you kidding?' he retorted. 'She's my grandmother, why wouldn't she be happy about ruining "it" for me?'

'Because she is your grandmother, Thomas.' Lark laughed, giving him a tight hug. 'When you were a teenager, yes, she would have been pleased to know she had stymied your adventures, so to speak. But you're a grown man now. It would appall her to think that you were having trouble with sex.'

'I do not have a problem with sex.' Thomas was indignant as he pulled back to glare at her. 'I have a problem thinking of my grandmother having sex, that's all.'

'Good,' Lark roared with laughter as her head fell back against the blanket. 'Otherwise, I would be worried.'

Thomas chuckled, then laughed with her. He squeezed her tightly in an affectionate hug. 'You are wonderful, you know that, Lark?'

He held her gaze. His eyes that before had been filled with humor now darkened with passion as he studied her. His grin softened into a smile as his gaze moved to her lips. Slowly he lowered himself to her.

Lark wrapped her arms around his neck, her hand sliding instinctively into the silky curls of his hair. She gripped it in her hand as she held him to her, deepening his kiss till his tongue slid along the ridge of her lip in an enticing tease. She moaned as he refused to give in to her, kissing her lightly, softly, nipping at her skin as she tried reaching for him again. Then he took her, his mouth working against her as she sighed into his kiss.

She ran her hands over the hard mass of his arms, then moved between them. Her hand slipped beneath the fabric of his shirt to caress the smooth skin of his chest. Thomas shifted till his body pressed against her, half over her as his hand skimmed boldly over her curves till he reached the smoothness of her thigh. Hiking her skirt up he moved upward, dragging the material away from her legs.

Thomas shifted again as he opened her legs with his own and wedged his knee between them. Lark ceased to think, letting her body take control of her actions. She arched the aching center of her against the rough denim of his jean-clad thigh in an enticing movement. Thomas answered with his lips, his teeth, as he tasted and nipped the sensitive skin of her throat. He pulled his hand from her skirt to drag her blouse from the waistband.

Shoving the material out of his way, he sought her nipples with his mouth as he sucked the tight buds gently through the thin satin of her bra. The twin texture caused a spear of heat to shoot through her and settle with a tingling in the center of her hips. Lark arched against him, offering him her body if only he would continue to touch her with his hands, his mouth, with every part of him.

Thomas pulled away just enough to help her remove her shirt and throw it safely out the reach of the candles. His hands slipped beneath her to unhook her bra. As he drew the material from her breasts, he sucked teasingly on each hard peak, then blew on them till they tightened even more. Quickly her skirt and sandals joined the rest of her clothes as he left only her panties on.

Lark impatiently tugged at his shirt as she too wanted to feel the branding heat of his skin against her. He rose to his knees as he undid his jeans and started to slide them down. She knelt in front of him, helping him slide the rough fabric down, caressing his buttocks as she pulled.

The pile of clothes grew as Thomas removed the last of his and lay back beside her. He shifted to lie half over her, his hand searing her skin with the heat of his touch as he cupped her breast. Taking the nipple into his mouth, he suckled greedily at her as she arched against him. He moved from one to the other as her body sought more of him.

Lark nipped at his throat and shoulders, wherever she could touch him, taste him with her tongue as he drove her deeper and deeper into the incredible sensations that only he seemed to be able to evoke in her. He slid his hand across her trembling stomach to touch the wet, heated core of her. Dipping his finger into her, he caressed the center of her, then moved to the aching bud demanding his attention.

As he gently stroked her, driving the electric torrent of her desire higher, hotter, she thought she would burn from the intensity he created. Thomas abandoned her breast as his mouth moved slowly, exquisitely, over her stomach to settle over the bud. He started the flame within her with the firm tip of his tongue as he flicked it over the button, again and again. As the sparks shot faster through her, jolting her as it built white hot till he drew the center into his mouth. Her body shuddered against him as he cupped her buttocks with his hands and refused to let her go. The heat of his mouth ignited her and she flared against him, crying out his name as she arched against him with her climax.

Lark collapsed on the blanket, smoothing her hair from her sweaty brow as the tremors surged through her. Thomas moved over her, taking advantage of her breathless state to cover her open mouth and plunder it with his tongue.

Lark pushed at his shoulder with her hand till Thomas lay on his back and she reversed positions with him. She knelt over him, her energy returning quickly, her eyes darkening with devilment as she sought to give him as good as he gave.

Sliding the tip of her tongue over his skin, she nipped and caressed the hard plane of his chest as she worked lower. Thomas groaned as her lips moved over his navel, then down the ridge of his hip. She took the hard length of him in her hand, stroking him as her eyes met and held his with relish. Lowering her lashes, she took him in her mouth, taking great pleasure as his hand jerked unsteadily toward her. He arched against her and she caressed him as she gave him the most womanly of touches.

Thomas moaned, then grabbed her hands pulling her from him. 'I want to feel myself deep inside you,' he whispered, his voice gruff with desire.

Lark smiled knowingly and put her leg over him as she again took him in her hand. She straddled his hips, then lowered herself on him slowly. She had hoped to torture him with the movement, but groaned herself at the exquisite feel of him. Leaning forward she found his lips with hers and kissed him deeply as again the passion started to build within her.

As she moved, she was forced to raise her head, gasping with the pleasure shooting through her. Her long hair rained over him like a curtain as it slipped over her shoulder to fall forward and she reveled in the feel of him.

In one swift movement, Thomas gripped her buttocks and rolled with her till she was beneath him. He folded one of her legs up beside his hip as he cradled himself against her. His chest pinned her beneath him as his breath came quicker, matching hers as their mouths sought and tasted each other.

Lark felt the hot coil of her climax unwind and she cried out. She gripped the slick skin of his back as she shuddered against him. Thomas found his release only a moment after hers as his body jerked and collapsed with a groan.

After a moment, Thomas lifted himself to his forearms over her and tiredly nuzzled her neck with his lips. 'Am I dead?' he asked, his voice husky with spent passion. 'I feel like I am.'

'Why?' Lark drew his earlobe into her mouth as she nipped it lightly.

'Because that had to be heaven,' he murmured hoarsely against the skin of her shoulder.

'If that was heaven,' Lark sighed, 'then surely you are the devil for driving me there.'

She could feel Thomas smile against the skin of her throat. He shifted slowly, lazily to lie beside her. Instinctively she curled toward him, cuddling her arms in front of her as she nestled against his chest. He pulled the blanket around them and she sighed softly. The heat he had created cloaked them, the blanket cocooning them in their own little world.

Lark sleepily rubbed her forehead against the smooth skin of his chest. Her eyelids felt heavy, drugged with passion as she started to drift. Making love, she thought sleepily, not only was it an aphrodisiac, so to speak, but the cure to insomnia.

And nightmares . . .

CHAPTER 13

'Thomas.'

Lark was leaning on one elbow beside him. When he continued to snore ever so lightly, she poked him in the ribs.

'Thomas, wake up.'

He nodded at her request as he rolled toward her. Draping his arm over her waist, he cuddled his face against her arm. Insistently she nudged him, then she smiled at the frown crinkling his features.

'Thomas, wake up. It's after midnight.'

'So?' he murmured, his voice husky with sleep. He pulled her closer. 'What's your point?'

'My point is I don't think we should be spending the night sleeping on the ballroom floor. It's not exactly comfortable.'

'You weren't complaining too much earlier,' he said, moving to nip at her shoulder.

'Well, earlier I was occupied,' she answered, poking him in the ribs to back him off a little. 'Now I'm not and I would like to sleep on a real bed.'

'I can fix that lack of being occupied.'

During their lovemaking, and their brief nap, they had worked themselves to the edge of the blanket. Thomas's large frame rested half on the blanket and half on the floor. Lark flipped the cover back and stood. Grinning with relish as her unsuspecting lover attempted to go back to sleep, Lark grabbed the edge of the blanket and gave it a hard pull.

Thomas rolled comically off the blanket with a thump to the floor. He flung his arms out from his sides in an attempt to catch himself and his eyes widened with surprise as he yelled, 'What the hell?'

'I told you to wake up,' she offered sweetly. She shook out the blanket and wrapped it around her naked form.

'I didn't know you meant right at that instant,' he grumbled as shifted to stand.

Lark bent to gather her clothes. She scrunched the items they had discarded earlier into a ball under her arm. 'You didn't tell me you snored, Thomas.'

'I don't normally snore,' he said with a defensive tone. He nonchalantly picked his clothes up and draped them over his arm. He stood before her without any apparent concern for his nakedness. 'I must be getting a cold.'

She boldly looked him up and down, with an appreciative gleam in her eye. She gave him a slow wink. 'I just bet you are.'

'No, really.'

'Yeah, right, Thomas,' she chuckled. She tossed her hair over her shoulder and headed across the ballroom floor toward the door.

Thomas called to her and she stopped. She watched as he blew the rest of the candles out and walked toward her. His lips spreading into a slow grin, he pulled the blanket from her hands and wrapped it around both of them.

'Didn't your mother ever teach you to share?' he asked in a low whisper as he nuzzled her neck with his lips.

Lark giggled as his beard tickled the sensitive skin of her throat. 'I doubt this is what she had in mind.'

She let him kiss her. When she pulled away she started toward the door. Thomas was forced to stick himself to her as they shared the somewhat small blanket. They giggled like teenagers as they sneaked down the stairs. Lark hesitated at the corner to peek around it. Thomas took the opportunity to grab her derriere.

'Hey,' she snapped in a sharp whisper. The thread of humor in her voice took the sting out of the words. 'Stop that.'

'Stop what?' he asked, his lips pressed against her ear.

'Isn't the man supposed to protect the woman?'

'I'm here aren't I?' he returned with a chuckle.

'Yes,' she answered as if speaking to a stubborn child. In this case she'd say very stubborn. 'But shouldn't you be in front?'

'I don't know,' Thomas offered as he rubbed her bottom again. 'I kind of like being in back.'

Lark muttered a crude remark that caused Thomas to laugh softly. She peeked around the corner again. 'I think it's safe, come on.'

Without warning she started forward. Thomas was forced to step quickly with her or lose the blanket. Too bad he hadn't been a little less responsive, she thought. It would have served him right to be left behind without any cover. Literally. With that thought in mind she quickened her pace.

'Where's the fire, Lark?' Thomas muttered from behind her.

Lark hurried to Thomas's door and opened it. They shoved through the crack in the door and she didn't let go the breath she'd been holding till it closed with a soft click behind her.

She leaned against the door for a moment, then focused her gaze on Thomas. As soon as they had entered the room, he had stepped from the blanket and casually started to get the bed ready for what was left of the night.

Lark watched with appreciation the movement of the muscles in his arms and back as he folded back the quilt. 'What are you doing?'

Without looking at her, Thomas climbed into bed and sprawled lazily on his back. 'Going to bed. What does it look like to you?'

'Going to bed,' she stammered. She realized how nervous she sounded and cleared her throat in an effort to regain a little of her composure. It wasn't the thought of sleeping with the man, after all, she had 'slept' with him before, but she blanched at the idea of staying the night with him.

Thomas gave her a knowing look as he attempted not to smile at her nervousness. He seemed to guess what was going on in her head. 'Lark, honey, everyone knows we've been together. You sleeping with me won't change that.'

'I know.' Lark couldn't think of a logical way to explain her nerves to him.

'Hell, my grandmother is probably sleeping with Henry right now,' he offered as he rolled to his side and propped himself on his elbow to look at her. 'Lark, weren't you the one telling me I should realize that my grandmother is a woman and has the needs of a woman, just like the rest of us?'

'Well, yeah,' she conceded reluctantly. Still she lifted her chin defiantly. 'That's different though.'

'How?'

Unconsciously she raised her brows at that simple question. Truth be known, she didn't have a ready answer. She searched her thoughts trying to justify herself and realized it came down to one simple truth. 'Because it bugs me, Thomas.'

'Honey, we've made love together,' he started, his voice soft and coaxing. 'Simply sleeping together is pretty innocent in comparison, don't you think?'

'I know, Thomas, and I don't expect you to understand either.' Hell, she didn't even understand it, she thought. Lark shook her head at her nerves. 'I guess it's my nineties moralistic sense of guilt. I just don't feel comfortable staying here tonight. Besides, my clothes are in my room, and I would have to wear what I wore last night, and they're wrinkled, and as soon as anyone sees me, everyone would know–'

'Okay, Lark,' Thomas interrupted her puny litany. He swung his long legs over the edge of the bed and walked toward her. Lark couldn't help but admire the sheer beauty of him as he moved toward her. He stopped in front of her and gently placed his hands on her shoulders to give her a reassuring squeeze. 'I understand.'

'You do?' she searched his eyes, looking for any amusement he might have regarding her unusual opinion. She found none. What she did find was his concern for her as he held her gaze, then placed a soft kiss on her nose before he moved to her lips. She opened her lips to him and returned his kiss as she circled her arms around her neck. He pulled her to him and held her close.

Thomas finished kissing her, then pulled back only enough to look into her eyes. 'I do.'

'I have to say I like the way you think then,' she murmured as she pressed her fingertips to her lips. She could still feel the touch of him and knew she would probably more than regret leaving him before morning arrived.

She reached behind her and opened the door before she tip-toed to give him another quick kiss. 'I'm sorry, Thomas.'

'Don't be sorry, Lark,' he murmured against her lips. 'I'll see you in the morning.'

'Sweet dreams, Thomas.'

Lark held his gaze for a moment, drinking in the sight of his beautiful eyes. Would she ever tire of looking into them? She doubted it.

Slowly she backed out of the room and closed the door behind her. Her lips turned up at the corners into a small smile and she felt quite serene as she walked toward her room. She opened her door and entered and immediately felt the stillness, the emptiness of it without Thomas's presence.

Lark walked to the edge of the bed and let the blanket drop into a pool around her feet, then tossed the clothes she was carrying on top. She started to sit on the edge of the bed when she decided to grab her night shirt and put it on. Shrugging into it, she realized she wasn't putting it on in deference to where she was, but more who she was not with.

She sighed as she walked around the foot of the bed. In the bathroom she filled a glass with water. She started to take a sip when a flash of light from the window caught her attention. Lark moved to the window and looked around the well tended grounds beneath her. Frowning, she noticed the wind picking up as it whipped through the trees and thunder rumbled in the distance. It must have been lightning, she thought. She started to turn away from the window when this time a movement caught her attention.

Shifting closer to the panes, her eyes narrowed as she searched the darkness for the cause of the motion. Her gaze moved over the foliage whipping in the wind and finally settled on the black iron of the fence around the cemetery. The moon was full that night and the light fell on the marble statues of the grave-yard, bathing it in a ghostly white. The large mausoleum squatted in the center like a watchful bulldog, its scroll work and carvings imposing in the ashen moonlight.

Lightning flashed in the distance from the fast approaching storm. Lark gasped when the brief light illuminated the stark face of the statue perched on the top of the formidable building. The angel with her serene face looked soulfully down at the past Black-wells resting around her. Her carved wings protruded stiffly from her back and she held her arms out from her as if she were about to embrace and hold those around her within her care.

Theorosa.

Her dream about the Indian maiden now made sense. She remembered the way Theorosa had reached out to her. The wings that had appeared to be a part of her were actually those of the statue from the mausoleum.

Lark bit her lip as she tried to decipher the message. In some cultures, she remembered from one of her college classes, people believed that if you dreamed of the dead, you were in fact communicating with them in a spiritual sort of way. Others believed that dreaming of the deceased could allow you to become susceptible to the control of the person you dreamed of. She truly doubted that Theorosa was trying to take control of her in her dreams, or her waking moments, for that matter. The tragedy that happened to the young woman more than a century ago could not be undone and no one was left to face justice for the murder she was falsely accused of committing.

No, she thought as she shook her head, it was something else.

Lark continued to lean with her hand against the window frame and looked below to the Blackwell cemetery. Hadn't Alicia said that Theorosa had been coming to her in her dreams? That's when the matron of Blackwell Castle had sent for her. Then the murders happened.

She stewed over the thoughts for a moment as she tried to work things out in her mind. What if Theorosa's appearance in her dreams and the murder charges that might be brought against her were connected, Lark wondered as she sat the glass on the dresser by the window.

Theorosa had beckoned to her to follow her in the dream. She didn't know about the cavernous-looking hallway, but the statue of the angel definitely now made sense to Lark. An idea sparked into her thoughts. It flared and started to grow, and with it the apprehension also grew. It coiled and tightened around her as her heart started to pound and Lark swallowed in an attempt to fight back the fear threatening to overtake her. She knew within herself what she needed to do.

She had to follow Theorosa.

She had to go to the cemetery. And she would have to go now. Lark had no idea why she felt the urgency within her, but as soon as she had realized that the cemetery was where Theorosa was leading her, something within her prodded her on. The sensation she felt was stubborn, willful. It would not allow her to rest till she did what the woman of her dream wanted her to do. Go to the cemetery.

Lark took a deep breath and pushed away from the window. She paced back and forth in front of her bed as she tried to decide what to do. It was not a reasonable thing to go to a cemetery in the middle of the night with a storm coming on.

Thomas was going to kill her.

That phrase echoed through her mind. Yes, he was going to do away with her if he found out that she had been there by herself. But what harm could it do? she asked herself earnestly.

Before she could change her mind, Lark pulled her night shirt off and threw it to the floor at the foot of the bed. She moved to her dresser and rummaged till she found her clothes. Dressed in jeans and a t-shirt she had picked up on a trip to Los Angeles, she laced her tennis shoes with a firm knot.

Taking a deep breath, she stood from the bed and walked back to the window to look below. Her gaze moved to the approaching storm which was quickly rumbling in. She would have to move quickly to beat it. Thunder boomed behind her as she turned toward the door and twisted the knob. She quietly opened the door, then peeked into the hallway. It was silent.

Stepping through, Lark licked her lips, and softly pulled the door closed behind her. All the bedroom doors were closed, giving her a little better feeling about sneaking out of the house in the middle of the night. She had no idea why she was about to go by herself to a cemetery in the middle of the night with a storm coming on.

But here she was doing it anyway.

'Thomas is going to kill me,' she muttered to herself as she neared the stairs. She grasped the rail and padded softly down the steps. The house was quiet and filled with dark shadows. Hurrying to the kitchen, Lark found a flashlight and checked to make sure the batteries were still good. She left it off as she moved to the back door.

Pulling the door open, Lark winced when she stubbed her big toe on a wooden box on the floor. She bit back a few expletives, then stepped out onto the back porch. Coming off the steps, she sighed with relief, started jogging quickly across the grass toward the cemetery hidden within the trees.

The wind whipped her hair around her as she turned to look back toward the darkened windows of the castle. She felt a sense of isolation at the sight of all the black windows. Thinking of Thomas asleep in his bed, she regretted for a small moment having not stayed with him, but she knew it wouldn't have changed what she had to do.

For some reason, Theorosa wanted her to go to the cemetery. To discover what, she did not know, but she had a feeling that it was more for herself than for the girl who died so long ago.

The whisking movement of the wind moved through the trees with a high pitched whistle. Lark had to grip her hair with her hand to keep it out of her face. She slowed her pace, then stopped at the edge of the trees. Again, she wondered why she was doing this.

With a deep breath and a silent prayer, she started through the trees. The dark of the night turned black as she entered the foliage. She flipped on the flashlight and kept the beam steadily in front of her. She had never been so thankful in her life when the edge of the little clearing for the cemetery appeared through the band of trees.

Edging around the fence, she headed toward the gate and found it unlocked. Of course it would be unlocked, she scolded herself in an effort to keep her mind busy and away from all the other frightening things she could be thinking about. The Blackwells wouldn't need to worry about vandals, considering the size of the acreage they owned.

The gate opened with a whining creak and she left it that way because she didn't want anything in her way should she decide to leave in a hurry. For whatever reason, she thought with little humor as her gaze moved over age worn tombstones of the Blackwell ancestors.

'Looks pretty lifeless to me,' she mumbled, just so she could hear the sound of her own voice. 'Pun fully intended of course.'

Lark's heart pounded and her skin prickled with goose bumps as she made her way through the tombstones toward the mausoleum. The night was cool, but that wasn't what was causing the reaction. It was the face of the angel as she approached the formidable building in the middle of the cemetery. The smooth stone eyes watched her with a look of sadness as she approached. The angel's hands reached to her in beckoning silence.

'Why do I let myself get in such stupid situations?' Lark grumbled as she flicked the beam of the flashlight toward the face. The stark illumination changed the sad, serene features instantly to a malevolent scowl. The sudden transformation caused her to jump and squeal at the same time. 'Damn it.'

She looked around her to see if anyone had witnessed her scaring herself, then shook her head as she realized what she was doing. 'I can't believe you just did that. Who the hell is going to be watching you? You are standing in a graveyard in the middle of the damn night, for heaven's sake.'

She moved the beam of the flashlight back toward the angel to prove to herself that there wasn't anything to be scared of. Muttering a few more cuss words for good measure, Lark stepped through the cold stone columns to move toward the door.

The mausoleum was large by cemetery standards and the doors looked huge and immoveable. The thick doors looked to be made of steel, although she really had no idea what they were actually made of. A small part of her fervently wished that the doors were bolted. Or better yet, sealed shut. She lifted the big, ornate loop of one of the doors and pulled. Lark almost smiled with relief when the door didn't budge. Knowing she had to give it at least one more try, she gripped the loop and pulled again, this time throwing her weight into it as well.

The heavy door groaned with a metallic sound, then swung slowly open toward her.

'Just my damn luck,' Lark muttered. Her heart pounded at the incredible blackness of the interior of the mausoleum and her skin crawled at the thought of what might be 'crawling' in there.

She took a shaky breath as she shone the flashlight inside. Dusty. Lark felt that was an appropriate word to describe the entrance of the mausoleum. A fine layer of dust from time clung to the walls and settled like a sheer blanket over scrollwork and carvings of the room. Vases protruded from the walls next to each of the markers where a Blackwell resided. As her gaze moved over the stillness of the morbid room and she breathed the musty, stale air, a few more unflattering adjectives came to mind, but she didn't voice them. In this building which served as a final resting place for the corpses of long dead loved ones, words spoken out loud did not seem appropriate.

Lark swallowed as she slowly moved into the room. Apprehension shivered through her as she stepped deeper into the cool blackness of the mausoleum. The dark shadows fell behind her, around her, enveloping her till she felt that only the white beam of the flashlight kept it at bay.

Scanning some of the names, Lark looked around her and realized that she was in an older section. She found the first David Blackwell's marker, then moved on. She wanted to look for Theorosa's, but realized that the good people who had hanged her, would not have allowed her to be entombed with the man they thought she had killed. No, more than likely, if she was allowed to be buried on Blackwell land, she was somewhere at the outer fringes of the graveyard. She decided she would have to ask Thomas tomorrow where the woman had been buried.

Lark continued to scan the room with her flashlight, then happened to shine across the stone floor as she moved deeper into the mausoleum. She frowned at the sight of tracks in the dust covering the floor.

'Whatever it is, it looks fresh. Someone has been down here recently.'

LeAnn's body. An image of the woman's body propped against the island in the kitchen flashed in her mind. There had been dark smudges on the woman's clothes. She had told Thomas it didn't look like dirt, but dust. And if there was anything abundant around here, besides dead Blackwells, she thought without humor, it was dust.

Dread worked its way up her spine and Lark wondered again why she was doing this. She could very well be walking to where LeAnn had been killed. Had LeAnn been doing the exact same thing she was doing now? Had her curiosity killed her like the proverbial cat?

'No wonder I'm allergic to cats.'

Fear slowed Lark's movements and it took great effort and stubbornness on her part to make one foot move in front of the other. She didn't try to kid herself that it was her incredible courage carrying her through this. Hell no, it was plain stubbornness that was egging her on. How many times had her mother told her that her stubbornness would get her in trouble one of these days?

The original part of the mausoleum was a rectangular room that at one corner turned into a hallway. Lark leaned around the corner a little to point the flashlight down the hallway. It led to yet another chamber.

'Great. More stiffs.'

She moved slowly down the corridor, gripping the flashlight like it was her lifeline. The next chamber folded back against the other so that the mausoleum was almost a U shape. This addition was obviously the new part of the building and by looking at the dates, she surmised that these Blackwells were the more recently deceased.

Looking down, Lark frowned when she found the floor in here didn't have the signs of traffic that the other side did. Turning, she back-tracked toward the hallway to find the tracks in the dust. She was almost in the middle of the hallway again, when she spotted them. Turning slowly, she trained the beam of her flashlight on the floor and followed the marks. The tracks and scuff marks stayed in the center of the hallway till she reached a section of the wall. She followed the marks till they turned sharply. And disappeared.

The tracks simply disappeared into the wall. Feeling a little confused, Lark chewed her lip as she searched the wall with her flashlight. Finding nothing, she started again, but this time poked and prodded with the tips of her fingers for any levers or catches to a hidden door that may have explained why the tracks stopped so suddenly.

Smoothing her fingers along the wall, she ousted a huge spider from its little cubby hole and she screamed. Slapping the eight-legged beast off her hand as she screeched and jumped, Lark started swiping at her arms and hair, feeling as if spiders were now crawling all over her.

'Yuck. I don't need spiders. Do you hear me, Theorosa?' Lark whispered fiercely into the darkness. Damn the ghost, she thought, for bringing her out here like this. 'I do not need spiders crawling on me while I'm doing this.'

She brushed at her face, then at her hands. She could still feel it crawling on her skin and she couldn't stop the shivers of repulsion each time she thought about it. Taking a shaky deep breath, her stubbornness now turning into a sheer act of will to keep going, Lark hesitantly lifted her hand toward the wall again. Stopping just a breath from the wall, she closed her eyes and cursed herself, then Theorosa, before she opened her eyes and continued.

The rough grit of the wall slid under her hands as she now cautiously explored the crevices and curves of the designs on it. She had worked her way from the top of the wall almost to the bottom when her finger smoothed over a rise and it moved. Lowering herself so she could get a better look at it, she held the light on it and could see that the rise was definitely a button of sorts.

Cursing herself, yet again, for her stupidity, Lark pushed it. At first the device was solid and unmoving, then, as she continued the pressure, it slowly sank into the wall.

Lark's eyes widened as a section of the wall started moving with a scraping noise, stone against stone, then opened away from her. She had never seen anything like it. It was an honest to goodness hidden door, just like in the movies. She had heard of some places around Kansas having secret passages and rooms because of bootlegging back in the prohibition age, but in a mausoleum?

She had not walked around the exterior of the mausoleum, so she could not have given a good guess on the size of the interior in comparison. Because it was a mausoleum and there were chambers for the bodies, Lark had to assume it would be easy to conceal a hidden area. But for what purpose?

The area inside the door was pitch black. Stepping into the darkness, the air seemed to cool around her. Lark waited a moment for her eyes to adjust, then realized that the complete darkness would remain beyond the reach of a beam of light.

Shining the beam in the hidden door, she illuminated a small set of stairs that led downward. The steps were chiseled into the ground and below the floor line the passageway turned into an underground tunnel.

Lark hesitated, then forced herself to start down the steps to follow the passage to its final destination.

Her footsteps scraped against the stone of the steps in an eerie echo that reverberated through the tunnel that was just wide enough for her to pass through. Thank goodness she wasn't claustrophobic, she thought, then realized as the slant of the ceiling dropped slightly that she could very easily become so if she didn't find what she was looking for in the next several minutes.

Thick cobwebs hung from the ceiling like heavy lace and swayed ever so slightly with her movements. She ducked under a large strand of the spooky curtains that hung low from a rough beam which shored the tunnel.

'Why am I doing this?' Lark whispered, her voice sounding harsh against the stark silence of the tunnel.

Why was she doing this? she wondered again. Because of a dream? No, she thought, there was something more to it. More than just the cryptic message of a dream unraveled. She could feel there was a purpose for her coming to the mausoleum. A reason for her to find the hidden door. A destination for the underground tunnel.

The air was stale, musty, causing her to wrinkle her nose at the strong scent. Maybe it was because of the cemetery around her, but she felt like the air, the walls, the atmosphere was permeated with the cold finality of death. Lark shivered with her fear, but continued on.

The narrow tunnel started to widen and opened up into another chamber. The circle illuminated by the beam of the flashlight moved over the rough earthen wall. At the edge of the circle a corner of a hole appeared. Lark moved the beam toward the crevice cut into the wall.

The bleached white teeth of a skeleton grinned at her. The blackened holes of the eye sockets stared toward her as wisps of mildewed blonde hair fell across its bony cheek.

Lark gasped, the sound slicing through the silence as swift as a blow against stone. Unconsciously she clutched at her heart, completely unaware of the pounding under her palm. The shivers started with a tremor, then thundered through her as she moved the light over the small skeleton. It was fully dressed, including the thin strips of bones that peeked from the black patent leather shoes on the feet.

The shaking became so bad, the beam of the flashlight jumped and jiggled over the opening in the wall. The frantic movement caused the illusion that the skeleton was convulsing on its stone slab.

Lark turned away and squeezed her eyes shut. Her stomach rolled with nausea. Her heart pounded within the tight band of fear that clutched her chest, making it difficult for her to breathe. She took several deep, shaky breaths as she tried to regain a small amount of the control that had been ripped from her at the gruesome image before her.

Leaning slightly forward, she planted her hands on her knees as she took a moment to calm herself. The circle of light from the flashlight now illuminated the rough grain of the earthen floor and helped her slow her breathing. She opened her eyes and straightened, making sure not to point the beam toward the horrific figure lying only a few feet away from her.

'I see she sent you. I'm not surprised.'

The shrill whisper erupted from the darkness behind Lark. The unexpected voice startled her, upsetting the flashlight from her grasp. Lark's lifeline to light fell from her hand and she tried to grab it, but failed. The flashlight rolled with a clatter across the ground till it bumped against a small stone. The beam whirled unsteadily across the small chamber, then flittered to a stop. The circle illuminated the ghoulish form like a spotlight in a freak show.

Lark turned away from the image, her nerves tightening as she tried to discern where the voice had come from. 'Who's there?'

'I knew you would come.'

Lark twisted toward the sound. She was at this person's mercy. She tried to search the blackness but was unable to see anyone in the void that surrounded her. She could hear someone moving around her and she tried to track the sound, knowing that it would only serve to confuse her more.

'You came to help me didn't you?'

'I will help you,' Lark called softly, as she spun toward the sound of the scraping not far from her. 'Tell me who you are. If I know your name, I can help you.'

'Did she send you?'

Lark frowned at the question. The words caused the image from her dream to flash through her mind. She answered the voice, her own nothing more than a whisper. 'Yes, she did.'

'I've waited so long.'

Lark could not tell if the voice was that of a man or a woman. She only knew that the person seemed to be very familiar with the cavern and the darkness. She sensed no fear of the black void that surrounded them. Only pain and loneliness.

'Waited for what?' Lark asked quietly, holding her hands in front of her to try to sense where the person was.

'For you.'

The voice was ragged and soft. Lark could not tell if the person was tall or short. Harmless or menacing.

'Why me?'

The voice hesitated. A gurgling sound erupted lightly from the blackness and Lark realized the person was sniffling, trying not to cry. When finally the voice answered, it was hoarse with pain. 'Because you can bring her back to me.'

The pain she heard in the voice caused Lark to pause. Whoever the person was, he or she was suffering. Images flashed through her thoughts of Theorosa's terror as she was being hauled toward the bridge and her death. Images of her dead lover's face as it was lit by a flash of lightning. Jeffrey Linden lying in a pool of blood in the library. LeAnn propped against the work island in the kitchen.

So much suffering over the century. So much pain dealt against those who had loved. Too much death.

'I don't understand,' Lark whispered. She shook as fear draped over her like cool satin.

'You don't need to.'

The voice had spoken calmly as if reasoning with her. Lark sensed more than heard the swift movement of the person. She could not tell where it was coming from, only that it was coming at her.

Her only warning was a guttural gasp, then a swift slice of pain. Flashes of color seemed to explode from the blow to the back of her head. Lark felt the grit of the ground bite into her hands as she fell to her knees. Then nothing.

The voice stood over her. Slowly the voice moved to the flashlight and picked it up. The beam pooled over Lark's still form, illuminating the small drop of blood that trickled down her cheek. The voice relaxed at the sight of Lark's even breathing.

Lark was too important. The voice hadn't wanted to hurt the psychic and after what had happened the last couple of times, worried that the blow had been too much.

'I knew you would come. She told me she would send you.'

The voice smiled. Turning the light off, the black void swallowed them all. The tunnel was all too familiar to the voice from numerous visits. The figure turned away from Lark and left.

Finally the pain would be gone.

CHAPTER 14

Thomas stirred, then rolled over. His hand automatically reached beside him for Lark. Hitting the cool sheet, he remembered she had decided to go back to her own room. He smiled softly at her unexpected shyness. He didn't know if it was because she didn't want to be caught spending the night in his room again, or out of deference to his grandmother, who was probably sleeping with Henry, he thought dryly.

Lark had lived most of her life under the scrutiny of others, some of it not too pleasant. It was good to see she still cared about the feelings of others.

Opening his eyes, he stared out the window at the egg shell blue of the morning sky. He could just hear the sharp chirp of a male cardinal. During the storm last night he had only roused long enough to note it wasn't one to worry about. After the rain of the night, the day promised to be a beautiful one. The sun was already bright and strong as it rose in the sky.

Thomas rolled to his back and rubbed distractedly at his chest. He thought about the sweet love he and Lark had made last night in the warming circle of the candles. When she was cleared of all the charges, and he would make sure she was, there would be nothing to keep her here. She would return to her job as an accountant. Live her safe, secure life. At least till another call came. Someone looking for a lost loved one. A lost body.

It shocked him to be thinking of such . . . permanent things. Natalie had only started 'thinking' about commitment and it had scared him off. Quickly. Of course Natalie could scare even the strongest of men off if she set her head to it, he thought without humor.

But Lark was different.

He loved the way she looked at him. The way she responded to him when he touched her. He loved the feel of her body against him. He loved . . .

'Whoa,' he admonished himself, with a puff of air. 'Wait a minute, Blackwell. It's a little too soon to be thinking in that direction.'

Thomas refused to allow himself to go in that direction as he sat up. Swinging his legs over the edge of the bed, he rose and headed to the bathroom. He needed to take a shower and hit the coffee because obviously he wasn't thinking quite straight yet.

He showered and shaved before he stepped back into his bedroom. He pulled on a pair of faded jeans and a dark turtleneck sweater. He tugged his boots on, then ran his hand through his hair a couple of times to achieve some order, and finally headed out his bedroom door.

Glancing toward Lark's room, he found the door closed and thought briefly about knocking on it or, better yet, surprising her by waking her up with a nuzzle against her silky neck. The corners of Thomas's lips turned up in a smile as his body immediately responded to that thought. Very powerful and erotic images leaped into his mind of their bodies tangled in the flickering circle of candles.

Thomas groaned, turning away from her door before he did knock, or knock it down. He ran his hand through his hair again, this time in frustration as he started toward the stairs. They had been up pretty late last night and considering everything she'd been through lately, Lark needed the rest. He was just going to have to control his urges till she had the energy to handle them, he thought with a lecherous wiggle of his eyebrows.

Going down the stairs, Thomas was again smiling as he headed toward the kitchen. There he found his grandmother helping Maria with breakfast.

He walked to her and gave her a soft kiss on her cheek. 'Good morning, Grandmother. How did you sleep?'

Alicia gave him a speculative look as her brow rose. She looked as if she wondered what he was trying to get at. 'I slept just fine, Thomas. Thank you.'

'And Henry?' he asked with a grin.

'None of your damn business,' she chuckled even as she swatted at him with a dish towel. 'You'd better start watching your manners, young man.'

Alicia blushed as Maria looked from one to the other with a smile on her face. The two women worked well together as they finished putting breakfast together.

'This looks wonderful, Maria.' Thomas thanked the woman as she handed him a plate of omelet, sausage, and toast. He started to take a bite when he remembered something. 'Oh, I almost forgot to thank you for the dinner you prepared for us last night. Lark and I really enjoyed it. I'm afraid we didn't clean up the mess though, but I'll take care of it as soon as I'm through with breakfast.'

Maria turned from the stove and smiled widely at him as she gave him a slow wink. 'That's okay, Thomas. I'll do it.'

He shook his head at her kindness. 'You've already done so much, I don't mind doing it.'

She walked to him and swatted him playfully on the arm. 'I will take care of it. You can take that pretty girl of yours for a ride. It's such a beautiful morning.'

'That sounds like a great idea, thank you.' He smiled back at her as a few enticing ideas filtered into his thoughts.

'I meant horse back riding, Thomas,' Maria said with a pointed look, working to suppress a grin.

Thomas almost choked on his bite of omelet and Alicia gasped at the completely unexpected return from their housekeeper. The two looked at each other, then started laughing.

Alicia wiped the tears from her eyes as she quieted to an occasional chuckle. 'I live in a house full of sex fiends.'

'That's rich, coming from you, Grandmother,' Thomas stated good naturedly.

He turned back to his breakfast when the front door bell rang. Thomas wiped his hands on his napkin as he rose from his chair. 'I'll get it, ladies.'

Thomas walked to the foyer and frowned as he saw the tall shape distorted behind the glass of the large front door. He twisted the knob and opened it to the early morning visitor. His frown deepened to a scowl when he found Detective Ron Baker standing on his front porch.

'Good morning, Mr Blackwell,' the detective smiled, the gesture anything but friendly.

'It was,' Thomas murmured, not offering to invite the officer in. 'What can I do for you this early in the morning?'

'Well, it would be nice to be invited in.' Baker rocked back on his heels as he paused for a moment as if waiting to see if Thomas would refuse straight out. 'These spring mornings are still a little chilly.'

'Of course,' Thomas opened the door wider as he gestured toward the parlor with his hand. 'Would you like a cup of coffee?'

'Yes, that would be nice. I take mine black.'

Thomas left the detective milling around the parlor as he headed back toward the kitchen. The scowl remained on his face as he entered the door. Both of the women turned toward him and stopped what they were doing when they saw the expression on his face.

'What is it, Thomas?' Alicia asked, her voice filled with concern.

'The detective has decided to pay us a visit,' he stated. He moved to the cabinet to pull a couple of coffee mugs from the shelf. He filled one for the detective and another for himself, then started back to the parlor. 'I don't think, however, this is going to be a social call.'

Alicia dried her hands and followed Thomas to the parlor. The detective turned from the book shelf where he had been scanning titles. He smiled widely at the matron of Blackwell Castle, then walked over to her to offer her his hand.

'This is quite an unexpected visit, Detective Baker,' Alicia said, seating herself on the couch. 'Please don't think me rude for asking why you are here. I have to assume that it is not of a social nature.'

'No, it's not, Mrs Blackwell.' Baker moved to a wing-back chair and sat. He held the cup in both hands as he met her gaze. 'I don't think it's rude at all of you to ask. Believe me, there have been some occasions when people have actually thrown things out the window at me in an attempt to get rid of me. A cup of coffee and polite conversation is an excellent alternative.'

Thomas's gaze immediately moved to the large wooden end table beside the detective. He knew from experience that it was heavy, but not impossible to move. Or throw. He imagined it would make a spectacular crash too.

The detective held his gaze when he glanced toward him as if he knew where Thomas's thoughts had been. The man's answering smile looked as if he dared him to try it. Thomas shifted forward in his seat causing the detective's brow to raise speculatively.

Alicia looked from one to the other, then rolled her eyes to the ceiling as she shook her head in frustration. After taking a deep breath for patience, she returned her attention to the officer. 'So to what *do* we owe this visit?'

'I really was not trying to avoid your question, Mrs Blackwell.' Baker looked to Alicia. 'I just had a couple of questions that I wanted to ask Miss Delavan, that's all.'

'Have there been any new developments?' Thomas asked quickly.

Baker met his gaze and paused. Thomas couldn't help but wonder if the detective was trying to play head games with him. If that was the case, then Baker was already at a disadvantage. Thomas smiled at that thought.

At the unexpected gesture, Baker seemed even more hesitant as his smile lost some of its wattage. 'None that I can really discuss at this time, Mr Blackwell.'

'I see.'

'What about the fact that there were no traces of skin fragments or hair found on the umbrella?' Thomas asked, without showing any emotion. He leaned his forearms across his knees and clasped his hands together as he studied the detective.

Baker's eyes hardened and his lips thinned into a tight frown. Thomas could see the dislike and anger the man felt, but only for a moment. The detective quickly suppressed his emotions behind a cool mask of disinterest. 'I won't even bother to ask how you found out such information.'

'I'll take that as a verification then.' Thomas let the humor reach his eyes. Pausing for a moment, he waited to see if the statement would again penetrate the detective's armor. Baker remained cool and Thomas let his expression match that of the officer. 'The lack of evidence would not build much of a case against Miss Delavan. In fact, one could argue that the killer found her in an incoherent condition, then took advantage of her illness to mask their involvement in the murder.'

'I guess one could argue that, Blackwell,' Baker's voice became icy as he returned Thomas's look. 'However, the fact still remains that she was found kneeling over the dead man's body with his blood covering her. Not to mention her lack of alibi for the woman's murder.'

'Which brings up another good point, detective. Thank you.' Thomas smiled warmly at the man as if Baker was trying to help. The action caused the reaction he expected. Baker's jaws clenched before he forced himself to relax and take a sip of the coffee. 'Were your lab technicians able to discern where the smudges on LeAnn's body came from?'

'The tests have been conducted, but as of yet, they have not proved conclusive.' Baker returned his attention to the mug he held as he sipped.

'What do you mean by "inconclusive"?' Thomas asked with forced patience.

'The point my grandson is trying to make is we would like to help,' Alicia interrupted, giving Thomas a pointed look. By her look of censure, he knew she didn't think by goading the detective that they would be able to procure any more information from him. He had heard his grandmother use on more than one occasion the old cliché about catching more bees with honey, than vinegar. Alicia smiled apologetically to the detective. 'This has been a very trying time for all of us. As I'm sure it has been for you also.'

'Yes, it has, Mrs Blackwell.' The detective looked as if he were reluctantly warming to Alicia's solicitous charm.

In a very natural act, Alicia leaned toward the detective and kindly patted his arm. 'I'm so sorry, Detective Baker. If there is anything we can do, please do not hesitate to ask. It is our complete desire to cooperate with your department.'

'And you have been, Mrs Blackwell,' Baker added quickly. 'It's just that the preliminary tests on the smudges found on the maid's body are just that, preliminary. It will take a little more time to develop more conclusive results.'

Alicia bestowed a genuine smile on the officer in reward for his helpful answer. The detective quickly looked disgruntled as he realized he had allowed himself to succumb to her infamous and engaging grace. 'May I get you more coffee, Detective Baker?'

Baker shook his head as he grumbled something Thomas could not make out. Thomas decided to press his advantage. 'There's still the incident of the attack on Lark at the bridge to consider, don't you agree?'

Baker frowned. 'No, I don't. If Miss Delavan is guilty of the murders, wouldn't it be logical that she would stage such an "attack" in an attempt to clear herself or make herself a less likely suspect?'

'You're forgetting the wound, Baker.' Thomas leaned back in the chair. His pose appeared relaxed, something which he did not feel. 'How could she have hit herself with the force that it would have required for her lacerations. The angle is impossible. She could not have done that to herself.'

'I've been on the police force for over twenty years, Blackwell,' the detective started with an unfriendly smile. 'One thing I've learned in that time is nothing is impossible. I'll agree that it would have been hard for Miss Delavan to strike herself in such a manner, but I refuse to say impossible.'

'Were you able to find anything from the bridge where she was attacked?' Alicia asked, her gaze innocently holding the detective's.

Thomas truly had to admire his grandmother. Alicia looked every bit the trim idea of a stereotypical grandmother. She was known for her compassion and dedication, just as much as she was known for her intelligence, diligence, and keen mind. His grandmother was always gracious and well mannered, but that did not mask the fact that she was a powerful influence in the business community. She had an easy smile on the outside and the tenacity of a barracuda on the inside when it came to anything she believed in.

Baker shifted before he met Alicia's gaze. By the darkening of his scowl, Thomas surmised that he had finally decided to remove the kid gloves when it came to dealing with his grandmother.

'I did not feel it necessary to review the scene,' he stated, lifting a finger to stop the protest Alicia started to make. 'I do not feel that an attack actually took place.'

'I believe the law requires you, as police officer, to investigate regardless of how you feel, or do not feel about a suspect.' Alicia's smile hardened as she gave the man a direct gaze of censure. 'Is that not correct?'

Baker remained silent. Thomas knew the detective had been called on the carpet. If they, or Lark, decided to press the issue, the detective would find himself in an incredible amount of trouble for not responding properly to the situation.

The silence hung thick between the three of them for a moment till Baker set aside his coffee mug on the end table. The gesture signaled the end of the pleasantries and the beginning of business. His business.

'I came here to ask Miss Delavan a few questions,' the detective stated coldly. 'Is she available?'

'She's up in her room,' Alicia answered. She rose, then paused as she gave the officer a sharp look. 'I'll go see if she's awake yet. We did not expect unannounced visitors quite so early in the morning.'

The detective held her look without blinking or making an apology. Thomas watched as his grandmother turned, then left the room to fetch Lark. Returning his attention to the detective, he found the man apparently studying the books along the shelves of the case. He frowned in thought as he tried to understand the workings of the man's mind.

He had no doubt that at least one of the reasons the detective was so gung ho against Lark was because of the Blackwell family name. Baker had let him know in his actions, his insinuations, and his sometimes outright belligerence that he was a man who had little need for people who'd never had to work for what they had. Thomas had learned Baker had worked his way through the ranks, been married and divorced twice because of his dedication to his profession. Somehow he wished he had this man on their side. It would definitely make life a little easier for them all.

Thomas rose, and moved to the window. He let his gaze move over the yard. The emerald green of the grass glistened in the rising sun. By noon, most of the moisture would be gone.

Thomas turned back toward the detective as he leaned his hip against the window frame. Crossing his arms over his chest, he fixed his gaze on the detective. 'You have a hard time dealing with people like me, don't you?'

'In which category would you classify "people like you," Mr Blackwell?' The detective met his gaze with a look of disinterest. Only the tightening of his jaw and his neck gave away the tension that had threaded through him.

'I wouldn't,' Thomas stated matter-of-factly. 'However, I think you would classify me as the spoilt rich who was given all the opportunities in life just because of my name.'

'Sometimes I'd say that's how it works, wouldn't you?' he asked with a lift of his brow.

'Sometimes,' Thomas agreed. He could name too many examples to deny what Baker had said. Unfolding his arms, he flattened his palms on the window sill on each side of him. 'In case you haven't noticed, my grandmother isn't exactly the kind of person to just hand out money, even to her own family. She's very generous to charity, but she expects those around her to earn an honest wage for a day of honest work, just as her grandfather did.'

Baker chuckled without humor as he flipped his hand in a dismissive wave. 'Look, Blackwell, you don't have to explain how you, or your family for that matter, came by their wealth. I don't care. Regardless of what you have been "taught", it doesn't change the fact that you and your kind use your

301

influence when it suits your needs.' His gaze hardened as he gave Thomas a stern look. 'For example, you used your name to keep your girlfriend out of jail. She may be out now, but she is our prime suspect and if any more tests turn against her favor, even the brass won't feel comfortable in accommodating your family's influence.'

Baker finished with a slight smirk on his face as he held Thomas's gaze. Thomas felt his body stiffen in instant response to the detective's belittling tone, then reined himself in as he realized that was just what the man wanted him to do. Baker wanted to goad him into losing his temper. If Thomas had lost his temper, it would only serve to justify what Baker already felt about him. The man may think he was only a spoiled Blackwell, but Thomas refused to play right into his hands.

Instead he lifted his chin as he gave the detective a small smile. He let Baker's threat hang stiff and awkward between them. The officer stood, his scowl deepening, then he turned away from Thomas to walk to the other side of the room.

Thomas contemplated how he would handle the situation if the detective proved correct. Alicia, gesturing to him from the hallway caught his attention. He flicked a quick glance toward Baker and found the man still ignoring him. Pushing away from the window sill, he walked as casually as he could, even though every fiber in his being was taut from the worried expression on his grandmother's face.

Once in the hallway, she pulled him into the dining room. Alicia peeked back into the hallway, then returned her attention to Thomas.

'I can't find her,' she whispered.

Thomas's reaction of confusion and shock must have registered on his face. Alicia shushed him quietly as she gripped his arm with both her hands. He took a slow breath, then lowered his voice to match hers.

'What do you mean you can't find her?'

'I believe I made myself quite clear, Thomas.' Her eyes flashed with worried anger as she frowned. 'When no one answered my knock, I opened the door. I was afraid her wound had been more severe than we first imagined, but she wasn't . . . isn't anywhere.'

Alicia's low voice trailed off as she shrugged her shoulders helplessly. She gripped Thomas's tighter, her concern filtering from her to him, causing his jaws to tighten. 'Her bed hasn't been slept in either.'

'What?' Thomas wasn't questioning what his grandmother had said. He had heard her perfectly, but his thoughts raced at her statement. Lark had left him to go to her room to sleep. How could her bed not have been slept in?

'I hope there's not a problem?'

The cold voice behind them flared their apprehension as effectively as a lit match thrown on aged kindling. Thomas placed his hand reassuringly on his grandmother's as they both turned to face the detective.

The man was quiet, Thomas had to give him that. He stood only a few feet behind them in the hall. The temperature of his scowl matched that of his voice as he fixed his steely gaze on them.

'Where is Miss Delavan?' he asked, his tone authoritative.

Alicia forced herself not to glance questioningly toward Thomas. Her stance became rigid as she released Thomas and stepped forward. 'I'm afraid Miss Delavan is not available at the moment.'

'I did not ask if she was available, Mrs Blackwell,' Baker said stiffly. 'I asked where she was?'

This time Alicia did give in to the urge to look at Thomas. Thomas put his hand on his grandmother's shoulder. 'Is this an official request?'

Baker's scowl deepened. His lips thinned with his anger. 'Yes, it is.'

Alicia cleared her throat as she quietly clasped her hands in front of her. 'She is not here.'

'What about her room?' he asked.

His grandmother pursed her lips together, obviously reluctant to answer the tightly controlled anger of the man before her. 'When I checked her room, I found it empty.'

'May I see it?'

'Of course,' she said with a wave of her hand. She only spared Thomas a quick look before she started for the staircase with the detective behind her. The officer followed her, then stopped a moment as if he suddenly remembered something.

He looked over his shoulder at Thomas. 'Would you mind accompanying us, Mr Blackwell?'

Thomas's jaw tightened as he unclenched his hands. He gave a curt nod, then trailed behind them. He stepped one foot in front of another as he climbed the stairs. Forcing away the doubts that were creeping to the edge of his thoughts, he concentrated on the action at hand. At the moment he could not allow himself to ponder the reason she was missing.

Missing.

He had to believe that she was missing. After the way she had held him last night, she wouldn't have left him. Not like this.

Alicia led them toward her room. Pausing only long enough to twist the knob, she pushed it open for the detective to enter, then stepped to the side of the room.

Baker let his gaze roam meticulously over the room. Thomas mirrored his action as he tried to look for any clue that may explain her absence.

The surface of the bed was smooth, no wrinkles marring the folds of the quilt. The room was undisturbed and immaculate. Except for the blanket with the clothes she had been wearing last night piled on top. By the placement of the blanket, he could tell that she had let it fall around her ankles on the floor before stepping out of it. Then she had thrown her clothes on top of it.

Noises from the bathroom caught Thomas's attention and he frowned as he watched the detective poking around the contents of a couple of the drawers with a pen. Baker scowled as he looked over the surface around the sink. The man stepped back into the bedroom and stood with his hands on his hips.

'She's gone,' he murmured.

'I think we've figured that one out, detective,' Thomas stated matter-of-factly. 'The question is what happened to her?'

'I think that's pretty obvious, don't you?' Baker met his gaze with a cold stare. 'The heat was getting a little too close and she decided to take off to try to protect her own skin.'

Thomas shook his head, his voice vehement. 'Lark would not do that.'

'When are you going to get it through your head?' Baker asked, practically shouting as he waved his hand at Thomas. 'It's all been a scam, Blackwell. She got off once for murder already. Then the moment she shows up at this place, two more bodies pop up. She may look and act innocent, but that's all a part of her act. Hell, she probably put out just to get you on her side.'

Thomas lunged at Baker and grabbed him by the collar. His teeth were bared as he growled his denial. Baker simply held Thomas's fists and leaned into his face till they were only inches away. 'Give me an excuse to throw your ass in jail, Blackwell. Nothing would make me happier.'

Alicia tugged at his sweater and Thomas noticed for the first time that she held him by the shoulders. Her voice was soft, but a steel thread of determination ran through it. 'Thomas, don't give him the satisfaction.'

Thomas pushed the detective away as he glared at him. Baker's eyes were cold and hard as he bared his teeth in an unfriendly smile. 'Wise decision.'

Alicia stepped in front of her grandson before he could wrap his hands around the offensive man's throat. 'Detective Baker, I think it's time you left.'

Baker's eyes glinted as his lips tightened. 'May I remind you that I'm here on official business, Mrs Blackwell?'

'I don't give a damn if you're here on official business for the President of the United States.' Thomas had never seen his grandmother so livid in his entire life. Alicia practically shook with rage as she planted her hands on her hips and faced the stern detective. Her cheeks colored with her anger in contrast to the rigid ice of her voice. 'I will not tolerate this in my own house, now get your ass out of here before I call your department and file a complaint.'

'Have it your way, ma'am.' Baker showed no outward reaction at all to Alicia's outburst. His hard gaze simply held hers for a brief moment before he flicked a pointed look to Thomas.

Walking away from them, Baker made a show of pulling his cellular phone from his pocket and nonchalantly punching in a series of numbers he was obviously familiar with. He paused at the top of the stairway as he greeted his caller on the other end.

'Yeah, I need you to get a warrant for a prime suspect that's missing.' Holding the phone to his ear, he listened to the other party, then turned toward them with a triumphant gleam in his eye as his lips twisted up in an expression that was anything but a smile. 'Tell the judge we need the warrant for the arrest of one Lark Delavan, one alleged psychic extraordinaire.'

'The charge?' he repeated, his gaze holding Thomas's. 'Tell him she's charged with murder.'

Thomas stood alone in Lark's room. Alicia had followed the detective downstairs to make sure he left as quickly as possible.

He didn't know how long he had been standing there. He did not look about the room for any clues to

Lark's disappearance. Not wanting to admit it to himself, he hadn't wanted to touch anything, afraid that some of her psychic ability may have rubbed off on him. Afraid of what answers he might be given by a simple touch.

He only stared at the pile of her clothes on top of the blanket so casually discarded after what had been a very special evening for him. If Baker was to be believed, then Lark had left because of her involvement in the murder cases. Shaking his head, Thomas refused to allow himself to believe it.

Lark would not have done that to him.

Thomas had to believe that about her. His mind searched back and found several instances to support his claim. The way she had felt the pain and fear of the girl she had found back in her home state. Despite everything, and everyone, telling her that the images she had witnessed in her thoughts were nothing more than just that, images, she had pressed on till she had found the body of the poor girl. She had taken time off from her job to help his grandmother put to rest the legend of a woman wrongly accused over a century ago. Merely because Alicia had asked.

His hands hung limp at his side. He had to believe she was missing. He would not believe that she had suddenly felt guilty and left. The very thought caused a tight band of panic to constrict around his chest, making taking a breath difficult. His heart thudded within his chest. If she had left for that unlikely reason, he was angry, not only at himself for being such a fool, but with her for using him so thoughtlessly. Or, as he felt within his heart, she was missing, and very possibly her life was in danger.

The two possibilities bounced around in his thoughts, making him indecisive.

'Thomas.' His grandmother gently touched his shoulder. Taking him by the arm she drew him from the room. She looped her arm through his and they walked slowly down the hall toward the staircase. Instead of descending, they went to the long beveled window at the end. She wanted to speak to him in privacy and knew this location would give it to them.

'Thomas, I know this has to be hard for you.' Alicia paused as she pursed her lips together. Her expression was a mixture of concern and anger. His grandmother knew him too well, he thought as he patted her hand. She knew how upset he was. 'It's true we haven't known Lark all that long, but I don't think she would do this to you.'

'I know, Grandmother.' Thomas offered her a lopsided grin to try to ease her worry, but could tell by the frown in her eyes that she could see right through him. 'But why would she just disappear?'

'I don't know,' Alicia answered honestly. She shook her head as she waved her hand in front of her. 'I would almost rather think she had deceived us and run away. Not only would it be easier to accept, but at least we would know she was safe.'

'So you feel it too?' Thomas asked. At his grandmother's words that had mirrored his own thoughts so closely, his spine stiffened with apprehension.

Alicia searched his eyes before she spoke. 'Perhaps I just don't want to admit I could have been so wrong about her, Thomas. But this time I don't think so. It's all so coincidental. Too convenient. Maybe one has nothing to do with the other, but I would be surprised if it didn't.'

'So would I.' Thomas ran his hand through his hair in frustration as he turned his gaze to the window. The day had fulfilled its promise. The sun was bright and kissed the leaves of the tall cottonwoods framing the old bridge. The vivid hues of the landscape was an odd contrast to the bleak darkness that weighed down his thoughts. And his heart.

Frowning in thought, he mulled over what his grandmother had said. She had felt it also. Lark would not have left here willingly. Not at this time, anyhow. She had too much of a sense of responsibility regarding the investigation. She also had a strong sense of pride. She would never have left without proving that she was innocent of the charges.

Thomas turned from the window to face his grandmother. 'I think both of us are right. Lark wouldn't have left. That only leaves one explanation for her disappearance.'

'The killer.' Alicia stated. Grim distaste thinned her lips into a line of disapproval.

'Yes.' He paced a couple of steps from her as he tried to form a plan of action in his mind. Baker had already made his mind up about Lark so obviously there would be no help there. Someone had taken her. At this very moment she could be in a considerable amount of danger, he thought. At that notion, his hands tightened into fists. He would do what he could to help her.

He had to find her. And soon.

Thomas pivoted on his foot back toward his grandmother and grabbed her hand before she had time to do more than gasp in surprise. 'Come on, Granny, we have to find Lark and if we're right, we probably don't have much time.'

Alicia followed him with a dark scowl on her face. 'Just who are you calling Granny, you snot-nosed brat?'

He glanced to her over his shoulder with a mischievous twinkle in his eye. 'That tenacity is exactly what I'm counting on, Grandmother. Lark is depending on it.'

'You didn't have to make me mad to help her, damn it,' Alicia muttered, her lips turning up in a smile as she quickly followed him down the stairs. 'What are we going to do?'

'Well,' he started as he headed into the study. 'As I said before, I don't think we have much time. We need to figure out where to start.'

Thomas sat at the desk and opened a drawer to pull out a file where he had placed the reports he had 'received' from the coroner's office earlier in the week. He flipped through the pages, quickly skimming the contents.

Nothing. The report hadn't changed from the last ten times he had studied it. Nothing new that he may have missed leaped out at him. He closed the file with a slap and ran both his hands through his hair. Leaning back with a loud sigh, he slumped in the chair and stared at the manila folder wishing he could conjure telling information from within it.

Alicia paced back and forth in front of the desk, her gaze distant and studious as she tapped her finger on her chin in thought. Her repetitive movement finally broke into Thomas's thoughts and he watched her pace. She looked like a more elegant version of Miss Marple as she pondered their problem.

As if sensing his attention, she started voicing her thoughts as she continued to pace. 'We can assume there is nothing in the physical evidence, at the moment anyway, to help us. Correct?'

'Yes,' Thomas answered as he placed his elbows on the arms of the chair and steepled his hands in front of him. 'I think there are some tests being run, but we really don't have a way of finding out the results. Or when they are going to be done, for that matter.'

'So,' Alicia mused, clicking along on her thoughts. 'What we have left are the people involved.'

'Pretty much everyone who was present on the nights of Jeffrey and LeAnn's murders are still here. Lark and I had talked to all of them individually yesterday.' Thomas unclasped his hands as he pushed from the chair. 'However, I think it would be in Lark's best interest if we talked to them again.'

Alicia followed him as he reached the open door of the study. Thomas paused as he looked back to her, meeting her gaze with a determined look of his own.

'This time we won't be so damned nice about it.'

CHAPTER 15

Lark opened her eyes and blinked. Squeezing her eyes shut again, she opened them and stared wide eyed around her. Nothing. Blackness, nothing but inky blackness surrounding her like a dark wall.

Giving herself a moment to try to orient herself, she tried to rationalize what was happening to her. Images flowed back into her mind on a swift current that brought with it the throbbing pain from the wounds on her head. The revelation of the dream had lured her to the cemetery and the beckoning arms of the stone angel on the mausoleum. Then there had been the tracks in the thick dust covering the hard floor and the hidden door.

The gaping black holes of the skull's eye sockets grinned at her in the underground chamber. Lark's hands had been resting on the ground beside her till that image flooded her mind and she yanked them to her chest as she drew her knees up in front of her. Was she still in the same cavern?

Lark started to look around her in question, but instantly realized the movement was futile without any source of light to help her. Heart pounding thickly in her chest, she forced herself to swallow her fear as she tentatively reached her hands out beside her to skim the area around her.

Rough grit met her palms and the occasional jagged corner of rocks and gravel bit into her hand, but still she continued. Feeling that there was just enough room for her to raise to her knees, Lark shifted till she was on all fours.

Her hands in front of her, she moved them in slow sweeping motions as she slowly crawled forward. The tips of her fingers bumped the hard surface of a wall and she continued feeling her hand up it to a ledge that was at shoulder height.

Lark's eyes were widened and she felt the desperate helplessness of being blind in a treacherous and unfamiliar terrain. Shifting closer to the wall, she continued skimming the surface before her till her hand caressed a smooth scroll-like surface. She started to close her fingers around the object, when the frigid realization of what it was stabbed through her thoughts freezing her hand.

The object was the sleek ridge of a bone from the skeleton.

Jerking her hand back, shivers of repulsion thundered through Lark and she automatically wiped her palms across the pockets of her jeans.

'Damn it, why do I always get all the fun,' she muttered with distaste.

Sitting back on her bottom, she let her breath out in a shaky puff. She was still in the same chamber where the faceless voice had left her. Lark knew from memory that there were two ways out of the room, but in the total darkness, it would be near to impossible to navigate her way in the unfamiliar tunnels.

Running her hands through her hair in frustration, her lips curled in distaste and slight pain as her palms skimmed over the crusted blood from where she had been struck earlier. There had to be a way out, she thought to herself. But if she started wandering on her own, would she only get herself more lost? Just how extensive were the tunnels that ran under the Blackwell land? Or was it just under the cemetery?

So many questions rattled through her racing thoughts and now she had a pounding headache. It was turning out to be a damn fine day for her. Or was it night? Lark had no way of knowing how long she had been unconscious or what time it now was.

Hopefully if any time at all had elapsed, someone from the Blackwell household would notice her absence and start looking for her. Or would they?

Lark shook her head when the sliver of doubt worked its way into her reasoning. What if they didn't look for her? Baker, and Natalie for that matter, already thought the worst of her. What if they convinced the family that she had run off to escape the punishment of her crimes? Would the Blackwells David and Alicia, even consider the notion of her innocence?

Would Thomas?

She felt the tears welling in her eyes as she forced those thoughts from her mind. After the special evening they had spent with each other, she had to believe that he would have faith in her. Desperately she clung to that single hope because it was all she had left.

'Are you awake yet?'

The shrill whine of the sexless voice behind her startled Lark. She jolted and instinctively scooted away from the disembodied sound emanating from the blackness. The sound of her jeans scraping along the grit of the floor inadvertently disclosed her location.

'Thank goodness,' the voice said softly with relief in a breathy whoosh. 'I was worried that I had killed you.'

Like Jeffrey and LeAnn she wondered, but wisely left that question unasked.

Lark could hear the person moving around the earthen room with a sense of slow ease and she wondered how often this person had traveled the tunnels. From the sounds around her, Lark thought the figure may have been trying to move around her in a wide circle. She tried to understand what this individual wanted with her.

'I was scared that I had killed you when you didn't move after I hit you.'

The voice spoke to her in a low, conversational manner. Lark could not tell if the person was trying to disguise his or her voice. Somehow she wished she could discern whether she was dealing with a man or a woman. Not that it would help her in any way, but at least she might be able to feel like she knew who she had to protect herself from.

'I'm not really a bad person, you know. I didn't even try to bring you down here, even though I could have quite easily. I didn't try because I knew you would come here on your own and I was right, wasn't I?'

The voice chuckled. The sound was a wheezing, happy sound, but disturbed Lark deeply. The personality her life was depending on was not a healthy one. There was a certain element of what she could only describe as insanity that wove its way through the person's thoughts causing what they said, how they acted, to seem off center.

Goose bumps prickled across Lark's body as she continued to listen to the sing-song quality of the voice as it tried to make her understand. For some reason the voice wanted her to know why she was there.

'None of it should have happened, you know. But it just did and there was nothing I could do to stop it. Believe me, I tried.' A humorless laugh fluttered through the darkness toward Lark. She could hear the sorrow in the words. The regret. 'It just happened. Then there was that man. Then the woman. It just wouldn't stop. No matter how hard I tried, it would not stop. I didn't know what to do. Then there was you.'

The noise of the figure's feet shuffling toward her frightened Lark. Involuntarily she gasped as she scooted quickly away from the person's approach. At the sound of her fear, her captor stopped, the strange voice dropping to a coaxing croon as it continued to reason with her.

'I knew when I first saw you that you could help me. Even when things became worse after that man and woman died, I felt you could help me.'

'I don't understand.' Lark broke the silence, unable to keep her question to herself. 'How could I help?'

'You can bring them back,' the voice stated matter-of-factly from the cloak of blackness that enveloped them. 'That's why she brought you here.'

'Who?' Lark shrugged as she scanned the darkness for an answer. 'Who brought me here?'

'She did, of course.'

Lark squeezed her eyes shut as she gripped her head. She pulled her knees up in front of her, then moved her arms to hug her legs as the chills again settled over her body. The person was crazy and fear filled Lark as she realized that no amount of reasoning would change that fact.

At Lark's silence, the voice rose into a childish whine. 'She brought you here, didn't she?'

Shaking her head, Lark felt the hot tears fall down her cheeks. She didn't know how to answer the question of the faceless voice. If she answered honestly, or said what she thought the voice wanted to hear and guessed wrong, would it cost her her life? Had Jeffrey and LeAnn been asked the same thing?

'Did she bring you here?' It asked again with an insistent squeak that caused Lark to jump.

'I don't know who you mean,' Lark whispered, then trembled uncontrollably when she had spoken out loud what she had been thinking. Her body tensed as she waited for some sort of negative reaction from the figure.

The voice paused as it seemed to consider her statement. The tone of the answer was mildly surprised, causing Lark to exhale in relief.

'Why her, of course.'

There was a soft click, then the circle from the beam of a flashlight lit the ledge chiseled into the earthen wall. Even though Lark had already seen it once before it still did not stop her from shrieking in horror.

The light illuminated the stark white profile of the skull, its teeth bared in greeting.

Baker had left a couple of hours ago, but had ordered one of his officers to watch the castle in the unlikely event of Lark's return. An unmarked car was parked on the side of the road by the fence of the property.

Thomas had seen the car and immediately felt a hot spear of anger shoot through him. Damn the detective for causing him to doubt Lark for a brief moment. Although the moment had been only a fraction of a minute, it was a time longer than he had wanted to feel the bitter pain of the man's spiteful words.

He had pushed away from the window after spotting the vehicle and his resolve had strengthened immediately. He was more determined than ever to not only find Lark, but prove her innocence.

His grandmother was not only worried about Lark, but also about him. Or more accurately what he might do if the irritating detective returned or one of the others started in on Lark again and her suspicious absence. Alicia decided to keep an eye on him and had taken it upon herself to follow him wherever he went. Now she was trailing him out toward the barn.

'Where are you headed now, young man?' she asked, not even out of breath with following his long strides.

'To the barn.'

'Well, I would say that is more than obvious, Thomas,' she said flatly. For the first time, his grandmother was starting to show her irritation with him. 'But why are you headed to the barn?'

'Because David's in there and I want to talk to him.'

'Don't go in there and jump down your cousin's throat, because if you do, you damned well won't get any answers out of him. Or anyone else for that matter.'

'I understand that, Grandmother,' Thomas assured her as he neared the large barn. 'But we're running out of time.'

Entering the barn, they could hear David talking softly in a soothing manner to a skittish horse as he bent over the animal's legs. He lifted one of the horse's legs to check its shoe.

At the sound of their approach, David turned his head toward them. When he saw who it was he let the horse's leg go and straightened. He started to smile in greeting, then apparently noticed their serious expressions. 'What's happened now?'

'Lark's gone and I need to ask you a few questions,' Thomas answered bluntly.

'I don't understand,' David said with a shrug of his shoulder. 'Did she leave?'

Alicia stepped between them so it wouldn't appear that they were both against him. 'No, she's disappeared and we are gravely concerned for her safety.'

'Disappeared? You mean someone kidnapped her?' he asked.

Thomas ran his hand through his hair in frustration. His eyes felt like sandpaper from fatigue and worry. 'We don't know. If she did leave she didn't take anything, but some time in the middle of the night she just disappeared.'

'Have you contacted the police?' David frowned as he looked from his grandmother to Thomas.

Alicia snorted inelegantly. 'I guess you could say that.'

David's brow rose at his grandmother's retort. He turned to Thomas for an answer. Thomas's expression matched Alicia's.

'Baker showed up here this morning wanting to talk to Lark. When Grandmother went up to go get her, that's when we found out she was missing.'

'That chicken-necked detective thinks she ran off,' Alicia added angrily with a wave of her hand. 'And he's put a warrant out for her arrest.'

'Damn.' David's eyes widened as if he couldn't believe what he had missed out on. As he shook his head in disbelief, Thomas thought he also looked relieved that he had missed all the action. 'So what are you going to do now?'

'We are going to find her,' Thomas said with more confidence then he really felt at that moment. 'That's why we wanted to talk to you.'

'Why me?' David asked.

'You weren't exactly thrilled that she had come here to help Grandmother.' Thomas regretted the brief look of hurt that passed over his cousin's face, but Lark's life could very well be in danger and they didn't have time to worry about people's feelings at the moment.

David held his gaze for a moment as his lips thinned into an angry line at Thomas's statement.

Finally he broke the look and shook his head as if he realized why his cousin had to say such a harsh fact. 'Look, I admit that at first I did not want her here. You didn't either for that matter, Thomas. But after I got to know her, I actually kind of started to like her. You were with us the last time I talked to her, when you guys were questioning me the first time,' he said with a pointed look. 'She and I actually ended on a good note.'

Thomas looked ruefully to David. 'I'm sorry about all of this, David. It hasn't exactly been the easiest of times lately.'

'I know,' David answered, reaching to give Thomas a reassuring squeeze on his shoulder. 'Look, if you need any help with this, let me know, Thomas. After everything that has happened lately, I don't want to see anyone else get hurt.'

'Thanks, David,' Thomas murmured. 'I couldn't agree with you more.'

Thomas and Alicia started to walk away when a thought occurred to him. He turned back to his cousin. 'Do you have any idea where Natalie is?'

'Satan's gone,' he answered with a wave toward the horse's stall. 'You know how she loves that horse, I bet she's taken him out for a ride.'

Thomas nodded as he mulled that thought over. 'Would you let one of us know when she makes it back here?'

'Of course.'

Thomas again turned and started walking to the big door of the barn to leave. As David watched his cousin leave he wondered what kind of spell the psychic had cast over him. He still harbored some doubts about the woman, but didn't think she was capable of murder. Then again, he couldn't think of anyone he knew who was capable of such a thing. He watched his grandmother and Thomas head back toward the castle, and an uneasy feeling settled over him. David called to Thomas from behind as he left.

'Good luck, Thomas. I think we're all going to need it before this is through.'

'I don't understand. Why do you think she brought me here?'

Lark had to force away the dark veil of fear that was enveloping her to ask the question to the voice. The sensations she picked up from the figure disturbed her deeply. Strong waves of pain moved through the person, the intensity so great it crowded out rational thoughts.

Leaving no room for sanity.

Still, she had made herself talk to the person even though her fear made her want to cringe away and hide.

'To right what was wrong.' The voice answered her almost desperate question simply as if it concerned the weather instead of murder.

Frustration started to force away Lark's fear, giving her the courage to keep pushing. She was trying to identify the voice by speech patterns and was dismayed to find none. Of course, she thought, it would help if the figure talked more.

So she tried again. 'What wrongs? Are you talking about the murders?'

The silence hung heavy in the darkness around them. Lark felt the figure's pain, and now more strongly, the guilt.

'So many things have happened that shouldn't have,' the figure murmured in a soft whisper.

Lark could now distinguish certain movements as the person shifted in the shadows. She started to ask yet another question when the voice cut into her thoughts.

'It should not have happened, but it did. Sometimes I wonder if we're not all cursed.' The voice sighed heavily. 'For years I've tried to free her spirit. I could hear her steps, moving aimlessly, as if she were lost. Searching for something. Perhaps peace. But most of all, I felt her pain till it became my own.'

Images of Lark's dreams entered her thoughts. Following the tall figure of Theorosa through the tunnel. Her face turning towards her to make sure she was following. Had Theorosa brought her here to ease this person's pain?

How was Lark supposed to accomplish that?

The voice hesitated, then continued in the same low whine, now filled with ragged desperation. 'Then it happened.'

Lark waited for the person to continue, then realized she was expected to prompt the individual. Finally she was getting the person to talk. 'What happened?'

The vague image of the figure started to pace with agitated steps. Lark hoped the person would step into the light. Yet, despite the individual's anguish, the captor remained careful and avoided the thin light from the flashlight beam.

'I had heard her and I hoped she was calling to me. When I looked out the window I saw Theorosa running to the river in the storm. I knew she was in danger and I needed to protect her, so I went downstairs to help her. When I went outside to find her she was gone again. Like she always is. I tripped over a short limb and, I don't know why, but I picked it up and started carrying it with me.'

The voice rose, shaking as the person continued. 'The storm scared me. The lightning was flashing around me and the thunder boomed so hard it felt like it was shaking the ground beneath my feet. I covered my ears and ran back into the castle. As I came in the front door, I ran right into that horrid man.'

'Jeffrey,' Lark murmured. Her eyes widened in shock as she realized she was hearing the confession to his murder.

'He scared me. The lightning flashed in the window behind him, illuminating him like a dark ghoul. He turned away and ran back into the library. He started to reach for the poker at the fireplace, and I . . .'

A heavy sob trembled from the figure. 'I hit him. I had no other choice, but to hit him. He was going to hit me with the poker. I had to protect myself.'

'Is that what happened with LeAnn too?' Lark asked. She was pretty sure she was hearing the truth, but she couldn't be completely positive. The figure was suffering from great emotional pain and guilt, that was clear enough, but there was also the sound of mental suffering.

The figure's restless movement stopped suddenly. The voice dropped to a low hiss. 'I don't want to talk about that bitch.'

The sensations of anger coming from the person were so strong, causing Lark to move sharply back as if she had been slapped. The harsh hiss of the voice made Lark think of Natalie. The blonde's ice cold eyes flashed into her mind and Lark bit her lip as her fear washed over her. Natalie was manipulative and vile enough just being herself, but if insanity had pushed her over the thin line of rationalization, Lark knew she was very much in danger.

The figure started to move. Suddenly Lark knew what the person was going to do and she gasped with renewed fear. She started forward on her knees toward the flashlight. Her captor darted quickly over and snatched up the light, instinctively drawing it upward to her chest.

The bright beam illuminated the face of the person who had left her here alone in the black ink of the tunnel. The light contrasted and distorted her features in stark black and white. Lark sucked in her breath as she recognized the person in the same instant the light flicked off, throwing them both into complete darkness once again.

Biting her lip, Lark fought the urge to scream after her captor. She could hear the figure scuffling her way through the darkened tunnel with familiar ease.

All too quickly she was left with silence. She was left alone.

Thomas pulled the door open for his grandmother, then held it for her as she passed through.

'Let's go back up to Lark's room and search it to see if we can find anything,' he said, his voice low and tight with tension.

Alicia flicked a worried glance toward him and nodded. She preceded him to the stairway and they started climbing the steps together. Moving down the hall, Thomas hesitated only a small moment before opening Lark's door. If he allowed himself, his concern for her would overwhelm him and he would start trembling as he almost had when he first heard she was missing.

He quickly scanned the room, surveying the general condition. As before, the room was clean, the bed unslept in. Except for the pile of clothes.

'Where do you want me to start?' Alicia asked from behind him.

Thomas ran his hand through his hair distractedly. He mulled the question over for a moment, then his gaze pointed toward the wardrobe. Perhaps his grandmother would have a better idea of what in Lark's wardrobe may be missing. At least they would have a general sense of what she was wearing.

He waved toward the wardrobe with his hand. 'If you don't mind, start with her clothes. I know neither one of us is that familiar with what clothes she brought, but maybe you can figure out what is missing.'

Alicia gave him a speculative look. He could tell by the look on her face, she knew that of the two of them, he was probably more 'familiar' with her.

She opened the door and started to inspect the contents. Thomas turned back to the pile of clothes. He knelt over them as he poked tentatively at her shirt. Nothing caught his attention. He did the same with the blanket. The clothes were obviously those she had worn last night for their dinner and the blanket was the one they had made love on.

Rising with a sigh of frustration, Thomas started to walk toward the bathroom but something on the dresser top caught his attention. Changing directions to move to the dresser, he stopped and stood with his hands on his hips as he let his gaze move over the surface. He frowned at the glass resting there. It was half full of water as if she had decided to get a drink before going to bed. He studied it for a moment, then looked toward the window.

Shifting slightly, he realized that Lark might have been standing at the window when she set the glass down on the corner of the dresser. If, and he knew it was a big if, but if she had seen something, what had it been?

Moving to stand at the window, he frowned as he looked around the grounds of the castle. Briefly he considered the bridge, then threw that idea out just as quickly. He would check later to make sure, but he truly doubted that she went there. He again wondered if some of Lark's abilities had rubbed off on him.

Studying the grounds, Thomas remembered the storm of last night. What if Lark had been standing at the window sipping at her water when she saw something illuminated by lightning. His gaze moved to the glass where it sat on the corner. She would probably would have set it there if she was in a hurry. As if reconstructing her movements, Thomas turned slightly and his gaze found her night gown at the foot of the bed. The filmy material was thrown to the floor much in the same manner the blanket and clothes had been.

He moved to the foot of the bed and started to kneel beside the night gown when a voice tight with anger stopped him.

'I wouldn't touch that if I were you, Blackwell. I could arrest you for tampering with evidence.'

Thomas straightened and met the hard gaze of Detective Ron Baker with one of his own. 'Did you finally figure out there was more to this than you had first thought, detective?'

'My opinion hasn't changed,' Baker said. His words squeezed through the thin line of his lips as he glared at Thomas. 'It is my firm belief that your girlfriend took off because she knew we were getting close to nailing her with two charges of murder.'

'Detective, you told me once to give you credit for investigative ability,' Thomas said quickly, his anger heating instantly white hot. Never had anyone affected him with such a negative response. 'Well why don't you start using some of that alleged investigative ability to see the big picture here.'

'I plan to do more than that,' Baker said, flashing his familiar unfriendly smile. He reached into the pocket of his jacket and pulled out a folded piece of paper. Thomas immediately recognized it for what it was. The detective apparently noticed the direction of Thomas's gaze and he chuckled with relish. 'This is a search warrant, Mr Blackwell. My officer and I will be conducting a search of Miss Delavan's room and anywhere else we deem necessary in regard to our investigation into her escape.'

'Escape?' Thomas said incredulously. He waved away the man's words with a dismissive hand. 'How can someone "escape" if she has never been charged, or jailed for that matter, in the first place? What's going on? You have no idea what happened or why, so now you're trying to pull rabbits out of a hat?'

Baker shifted forward, his scowl dark, before he stopped himself, forcing his animosity under control. 'Don't push me, Blackwell. I've about had it with you and your influences. I don't care if you call the mayor yourself, this time your money isn't going to keep your so called psychic's ass out of jail.'

'Is that it?' Thomas searched the man's gaze, hoping he wouldn't see the answers in the man's eyes, but did. 'You've made this your own personal vendetta against anyone who happens to have good economic standing and community respect? Because of your prejudices you're going to charge an innocent woman with crimes she didn't commit? For all you know she may be lying dead out there somewhere. Another victim.'

Thomas took a shaky breath as he fought for control. Even as his hands tightened into fists, he felt that control slipping away from him. His chest tightened with stark fear as an image too vivid for his heart to take filled his mind's eye. His voice raised in accusation at the detective. 'Is that what it's going to take, Baker? Another victim? If your investigative ability does find Lark dead because you wouldn't even make the effort to look for her, would that finally make her innocent in your eyes?'

'You've pushed me too far this time, Blackwell,' Baker seethed through clenched teeth.

'I haven't even begun to push.' Thomas's fury was so intense he could barely see straight. He focused on the door and headed straight toward it, knowing that leaving the room would be the only thing to keep him from pounding the obstinate look from the detective's face.

He strode toward the door, and Baker shifted to block his exit. Thomas shoved past the man with his shoulder as he left. Out of the corner of his eye, he saw the detective's momentary look of surprise before he quickly directed his anger at the officer who had been the unfortunate individual to accompany him.

Moving down the hallway, Thomas half expected the detective to race after him, tackle him and handcuff him. After a moment it was clear Baker had decided not to follow. Instead he heard his grandmother's soft steps behind him. She called to him and he felt the tears well in his eyes at the sound of the concern in her voice. For the first time in his life, he ignored the woman who had raised him and continued walking down the hall. He didn't want her to see the fear and pain he knew must be in his eyes.

'Do not ignore me, young man.' Alicia's voice was stern and demanding.

Her tone had the effect she wanted. Thomas stopped, but refused to turn around. He felt her hand on his arm as she moved to stand beside him. He continued to stare ahead of him, focusing on the vivid colors of the stained glass window at the end of the hallway.

Out of the corner of his eye, he could see his grandmother studying his profile. Moving closer she wrapped her arm around his waist to give him a gentle squeeze.

'I won't apologize for losing my temper, Grand-mother,' he said without looking at her.

Her low chuckle caught him off guard and he turned to look at her. Her eyes softened as she held his gaze. Alicia raised her hand and brushed a tear from his eye.

'I didn't expect you to,' she murmured. 'It was bound to happen sooner or later.'

Thomas shook his head and frowned as he remembered how close he had come to losing it. 'I've never been that angry before in my life, Grandmother. I don't know how it happened or even why.'

'I know,' she answered simply.

'Baker probably has that effect on just about everyone.'

Alicia laughed softly. 'He probably does at that, but I don't think that applies to someone who is worried about the person he loves.'

Thomas turned toward her, his eyes widened at his grandmother's unexpected insight. His look was incredulous, causing Alicia to pat his cheek with her hand.

'Don't look so surprised, Thomas. It happens to the best of us.'

Thomas started to deny his grandmother's statement, but the words refused to leave his lips. The first time he had seen Lark he thought she was beautiful. When he had found out what her business was with his grandmother, he had been concerned that her beauty hid something less honest. Her quiet grace, her resilience, compassion, and honesty had swayed him toward her.

He opened his mouth to say something to Alicia, then closed it when nothing came to mind.

Alicia had watched the various emotions play across his face, her smile widening when she finally saw acceptance. She took his hand and squeezed it gently.

'It shouldn't be that hard to admit, sweetheart.'

'I know.' He shrugged his shoulders, then turned to meet her gaze. 'I know it in my heart, Grandmother, but it's too painful for me to say it out loud. She's missing, her life possibly in danger. Two people have been killed already, I don't know if I could handle it if she were the third.'

'Thomas, don't say that,' Alicia admonished quickly. She took his face in her hand and pulled him closer till they were almost eye to eye. 'Lark's missing. She is in danger, I won't deny it, but we are not going to give up on her yet.'

Thomas cut her off. 'I have not given up on her. I will never give up on her. We need to find her and we have nothing. Baker keeps throwing up stone walls and the likely suspects are people we would never have thought capable of such things in the first place.'

'I know, sweetheart. I know.' Alicia pulled him into her embrace, making him lean over to accomplish it.

Thomas allowed his grandmother to hold him in the way she used to comfort him when he was a child. He closed his eyes and inhaled the sweet scent of her. Giving her a squeeze, he pulled away and gave her a small smile. He didn't say he was thankful to her. She would know he was.

Alicia straightened, suddenly all business as she quickly turned away. But, not before Thomas caught the mist in her eyes as well.

They were half way down the stairs when the front door flew open. David burst in, his head turning one direction, then the other as he searched for them.

'David, what is it?' Alicia called from the staircase.

He looked up at them, his expression anxious, but excited. 'She's back.'

'Lark?' he asked. Thomas felt his heart surge with relief as he started forward without waiting for the answer.

'No, Natalie.'

Thomas stopped, the elation draining away from him. David frowned at his cousin's expression.

'I'm sorry it wasn't what you thought, Thomas.'

Thomas started down the steps without saying anything and headed toward the door. The trio hurried toward the barn. Thomas watched as Natalie rode up to the barn on the black stallion and dismounted. He focused on the tall blonde and his voice drifted back to David and his grandmother as they followed.

'The only person who's going to be sorry, is the person responsible for this when I find out who it is.' Thomas watched Natalie lead the horse into the barn. 'And make no mistake, I will find out who did this.'

Lark felt helpless. Her tears had long ago dried on her face as she had pulled her knees in front of her and cradled them within her arms. Wrapping herself into a ball, she felt tiny and insignificant. The terror of the blackness was wearing on her, but she was too scared to fall asleep.

Could any nightmare be worse than what was happening to her right now, she thought without humor.

How long ago her captor had left, Lark had no idea. She had long since lost any concept of time, let alone night or day. Her frantic thoughts suddenly focused on the realization that she was rocking herself on a dirt floor of an unlit underground tunnel and not doing anything to try to help herself. Anger shot through Lark hot and quick.

She'd be damned if she was just going to sit on her butt and let that maniac keep her in the dark.

The unintended pun hit her and she chuckled. Rising to her feet, she didn't bother to wipe the dirt from her seat. Lark held her hands out in front of her and simply walked in the direction she remembered the hallway to be.

What did she have to lose?

CHAPTER 16

Natalie was busy loosening the cinch strap of the saddle, unaware of the trio entering the barn. She worked quickly and efficiently with practiced ease from many outings with the large stallion.

Thomas could see a good angle of her face as he silently approached her while she worked the ritual of taking care of the horse. Unaware that she was being watched, Natalie was talking softly to the horse as she performed her responsibilities. Her normally harsh, cold eyes were warm as she caressed the animal, her features gentle as she smiled naturally.

He shook his head at this side of the woman he had never seen, though he had known her for several years. It was obvious in her expression that she truly cared for Satan. That she could be herself with the horse, more so than she ever had been with the people she encountered.

Thomas couldn't shake the small amount of pity he felt for her. What could cause a person to become so cold with her own friends and acquaintances? With a small feeling of remorse, he realized that

Natalie had never really talked about her family and he had never pursued the subject she so obviously had not wanted to discuss at the time.

Forcing himself to push away his pity, Thomas reminded himself that a woman was missing, her life very much in danger if they did not find her soon. Already two people had died at the hand of the person who had more than likely taken her.

'Here, let me help you.'

The saddle was lifted from the horse's back easily and was taken over to the saddle rack in the tack room. From her side of the horse, Natalie only saw the hands take the saddle. Thomas's lips twisted up in grim humor at the look of surprise that swept over her face.

Natalie's eyes widened as she stared at the spot where the saddle had been, then slowly she looked up toward him. When her gaze met his, her eyes hardened even as she smiled enchantingly at him. Once again he was reminded how easily her attitude could change. Especially when it could prove to be beneficial to her.

'Thomas,' she purred, her hand caressing the silk of Satan's back in a provocative sweep as she moved around the animal toward him. 'What an unexpected pleasure-'

Natalie's smile, to her credit, dimmed only a little when she found both David and Alicia with him.

'I see you brought company,' she murmured, looking back to him with one delicate brow raised in question.

'Where have you been, Natalie?' Thomas asked, his voice sounding more harsh than he had intended.

If his tone had offended her, Natalie didn't show it. She merely shrugged as she waved a dismissive hand toward the land past the corral. 'I took Satan for an early morning ride. I love to watch the sun come up over the pasture.'

'Did you see anyone?' Alicia asked as she stepped toward them.

'Not really,' she answered. The blonde crossed to the tack room, brought back a hand brush and began brushing down the slick sheen of the tall stallion's coat.

Natalie had made it more than plain several times that she had not liked his grandmother bringing Lark here. On more than one occasion he had caught the look of loathing in the blonde's ice blue eyes as she watched him and Lark together. Just how far would she go to keep them apart?

Thomas moved beside her so he could study her expression when he said his next blunt statement. 'Lark's gone. You wouldn't happen to know anything about that would you, Natalie?'

Her gaze flicked to his only briefly as if she were testing to see whether he was joking with her or not. At the serious look of his features, she snorted rudely.

'Did the little scam artist finally turn tail and run?' she said.

'No,' Thomas answered softly. His quiet tone more chilling than if he had yelled at her. 'All her belongings are still here. She's disappeared and we're assuming she has been kidnapped.'

'Then why are you talking to me, Thomas?' Natalie's eyes had flashed briefly with what he had interpreted as fear before she regained her normal cool demeanor. She straightened to face him, her eyes hard and unfeeling. 'Isn't this a matter for the police? Why not call them?'

'We already have,' Alicia added with a stern tone to her voice. 'However, we are concerned with Lark's safety. As I'm sure you are also.'

Natalie's brow lifted again, this time in mock surprise at the last part of his grandmother's statement. She rolled her eyes, then returned her attention to the completion of her task. She took the remaining items to the tack room to put them away, returned to the horse's side and started to lead him away to his stall. Her actions made it clear that she felt her part in the conversation was over.

Thomas followed doggedly and purposely stood in front of the gate, causing Natalie to move around him to leave the confines of the stall.

'Lark could be in danger, Natalie,' he said quietly when she stood shoulder to shoulder with him. 'Two people have been murdered already. If you know something that could help us find her, then you had better tell me now, because if I find out that you had anything to do with any of this, you'll wish it was you missing and not her.'

Natalie's ice blue eyes crystallized with her dislike not only for his subject, but his intimidation. Her lips thinned into an angry line. 'Like I said, maybe you should leave this matter for the police to handle, Thomas. I can't say I'm too distressed that she's gone. Personally, I think you've all been taken in by her. She's off somewhere enjoying the sun while she laughs her ass off at how easily she took you guys.'

'She never "took" us for anything,' Alicia reminded her.

The cool attitude of the blonde showed her opinion of Alicia's statement, but even Natalie was smart enough not to cross Alicia Blackwell. 'Regardless, I think you guys are overreacting to her disappearance. You heard what the detective said about her before. She was charged with that kid's murder.'

'And they caught the real murderer,' Thomas interjected, 'and he confessed to the crime. That's how she was cleared of the charge.'

Natalie looked quickly at David and held his gaze for a moment as if she expected him to come to her aid. When the man crossed his arms, his expression not exactly the friendliest she had ever seen, the woman seemed to become increasingly agitated.

'Look, so she's missing. I feel bad about that,' she said, the last part spoken while she gave Alicia a pointed look, 'but there is nothing I can do about it. I don't have any idea where she is, or what, if anything, has happened to her.'

'I'm sure she'll appreciate your concern,' David said without humor.

She gave him a heated glare. 'I thought you weren't exactly pleased that she was here. I would think you'd be glad she had taken off.'

'First of all, we don't think she "took off", Natalie,' David answered with a hard look. 'Second, I don't like to see anyone hurt, no matter who it is.'

'Well, good luck tracking her down.' She turned on her heel and started to stalk away from them. She threw a parting shot over her shoulder as she headed for the barn door. 'I personally think you are all being taken for a ride.'

'She would know about that,' Alicia murmured softly.

David and Thomas exchanged surprised glances before turning their gazes toward their grandmother. Alicia wasn't usually one to make such sarcastic observations. No matter how accurate.

Watching her walk away, Thomas remembered the telling looks that had passed over Natalie's face. She had showed reluctance at one point and fear. He knew her feelings did not go deep enough to register fear for Lark's safety. No, something about her agitation made him wonder about what she might be afraid of. He truly did not think that she was capable of murder, but then again, what sane person was? Still, she might know something that she wasn't telling.

Thomas started after Natalie and grabbed her by the arm. All his senses were telling him that they were running out of time. He turned her toward him as he leaned in her face.

'What are you afraid of, Natalie?' he demanded without preamble.

Her eyes widened and her guard dropped, letting him see for the first time the emotions running underneath. Again, they flickered with fear and anger. Her mouth opened, then closed and she shook her head.

'Don't you know what you could be charged with if it was found out that you knew something about these murders and didn't come forward?' Thomas shook her for emphasis, his eyes cold with anger and fear for what could happen to Lark. 'How would you like to be charged as an accomplice to murder? Obstruction of justice? Hell, why not charge you with murder? You had more motive than Lark ever thought about having.'

He paused, letting the words soak into her agitated thoughts. His chest felt tight as he took a deep breath to calm himself. He lowered his voice. The soft tone only thinly veiled the anger simmering beneath. 'If anything happens to her, Natalie, I'll make it my personal goal to ensure not only whoever is responsible faces justice, but anyone else who hindered this in any way.'

'I did not kill them,' Natalie stammered, her eyes widening with the alarm his words seemed to cause once they penetrated her thoughts. 'I didn't mean to . . . I did not have anything to do with either of the murders.'

Her eyes darted away from his at her slip and she refused to look at him as she jerked her arm out of his grip.

'Didn't mean to do what, Natalie?' he demanded.

'Nothing,' she snapped, then realized how telling the statement sounded and decided quickly to amend it. 'I meant that I did not kill them. Damn it, Thomas. I can't believe that we are even having this conversation. I can't believe you are actually standing there accusing me of this. Murder of all things. After our relationship, how could you think I was capable of doing something like that?'

Thomas studied her look of self righteous indignation. Her tone, and more telling, her actions did not ring true with him. She protested a little too much and she had lost her normally cool demeanor a long time ago. His brows dipped into a frown as her eyes darted away from him, then as if she realized how guilty she looked, she forced herself to meet his gaze. No, he didn't think she had murdered Jeffrey or LeAnn and she probably did not have anything to do with Lark's disappearance. That would seem too easy. But, she was agitated about something she wasn't telling him.

'I'll admit that because of our relationship I don't think you are capable of murder,' he agreed. 'But you're holding something back. The detective might like to take a little time to talk to you. Maybe he could get you to drop this act and tell us what you're trying to cover up.'

'I'm not covering up anything,' she shouted. Natalie backed away from them, looking like a wolf being backed into a corner. She flicked her gaze from one Blackwell to another as she continued moving away from them.

'Then why are you acting so nervous?'

The unexpected voice from behind Natalie caused her to jump and wheel around to face the source. Detective Baker rocked back on his heels as he studied her pale face. The blonde started visibly shaking as her eyes widened with fear.

'What . . . what are you doing here?' she asked in a hoarse whisper.

'I would say the more important question is what have you been doing here, Miss Brown?' the detective's hard gaze never wavered from hers, his expression unrelenting as he waited for her to answer. 'You seem to be acting quite guilty for someone who claims to be innocent.'

'I . . . I haven't done anything,' she stammered as she wildly shook her head.

The woman's agitation seemed to build and grow on itself as she returned their looks. Alicia and David looked bewildered at her expression. Never would they have thought her capable of doing anything as horrible as murder, but her actions made it obvious she was scared of them finding out her involvement in something.

She backed away another step. 'I haven't done anything. Why are you doing this to me? Thomas? Alicia?'

Natalie looked from one to the other almost desperately. For one small moment, Thomas almost felt sorry for her, but then she surprised him by spinning on her heel and running. Before he could pull himself from his shock, the detective bolted after her and grabbed her by both arms and hauled her back against his chest.

Natalie seemed to go limp as he held her and led her back toward them. She started to sob, her make up quickly turning to a smeared mess as she leaned heavily against Baker.

'I didn't know it was going to happen, I swear it.'

Thomas was stunned by her words. He looked at Natalie, realizing how very little he really did know her. 'You didn't know what?'

She continued to cry, her head falling forward. Her voice was tight, her words choking from her lips. 'I put the mushrooms in the salad. I swear I didn't have anything to do with the murders. I didn't even know about them till you found her, Thomas.'

'How could you, Natalie,' Alicia said, her voice full of pain and pity. She shook her head with sad disapproval as she studied her. 'You could have killed her. Didn't you realize that?'

Natalie lifted her head, squeezing her eyes shut for a moment as her lips crumpled into a rough sob. She opened them, her lids already swelling and her eyes red from crying. 'I didn't want to kill her, Alicia. I knew how much to give her. I only gave her enough to make her sick and hallucinate. I wanted you to realize how crazy it was to bring her here in the first place.'

Baker released one arm, but continued to hold the other while he spoke. 'Whose salad did you put the mushrooms in?'

'Lark's,' she answered, then sniffled loudly.

'How did you know you wouldn't kill her?' he asked. He may not have liked the new direction his investigation was taking, but he was professional enough to do his job.

She turned tear filled eyes toward him. 'I've been around animals all my life. I've helped take care of them. I knew where to find the mushrooms and it took only a little research to figure out how much to give her. She would have needed to eat considerably more to ingest a lethal dose.'

Thomas remembered the day he and Lark had come back to the castle to find Natalie working with their vet. She had already started the horse on an antibiotic by the time he had arrived. The vet had said she missed her calling. What had she said about if she ever had to face a case of animal abuse? That she would be forced to kill the abuser?

Words that many, including himself, had so carelessly thrown out. How often did we think someone would actually mean them?

'You would never hurt an animal?' Thomas asked, 'but you would poison a human?'

Natalie's light blue eyes were the color of Arctic ice as she turned toward him. The color darker in contrast to the red rimmed edge of her eye lids. A tear spilled over her lashes and fell slowly over her cheek as she looked at him. He could see the naked hurt in her expression.

'At least animals never hurt you. They give you love unconditionally and without having to be asked. They would do anything to make you happy, including giving their lives to protect you. People use you, then throw you away. You can never depend on them to truly love you.'

Thomas shook his head as he turned away from the woman he had thought he once cared for. Disappointment layered over his thoughts and his heart was saddened by what he had seen in her eyes. No doubt Natalie had experienced many hard things that helped condition her into what she had become. Still, he didn't feel that was excuse enough for what she had done. Life was what you made out of it. Bad things happen to people all the time, in all walks of life. A person should learn from the experience and go on. Let the knowledge gained from the experience make them ultimately a better person.

Not let it be used as an excuse, he thought as he started walking away.

'Thomas, I did it for you,' she called desperately after him, a sob ripping from her throat. 'Thomas!'

Angry at her for trying to use him to get at Lark, he turned back to her. 'No, Natalie. You did it for yourself.'

Thomas started again toward the castle. His heart was heavy as he started up the steps. Natalie had continued to call after him till she started crying again. Alicia remained with her. No matter what she had felt for her before, the woman needed help and Alicia had never been one to turn her back on anyone. He felt like a heel for not having the strength of character that his grandmother had, but something of more importance was at stake.

Lark's life.

David followed him up the steps. Thomas stopped for a moment and rubbed his hand through his hair as he frowned at the scene that was going on behind him. His cousin moved to stand beside him and clasp him with his hand on his shoulder.

'This hasn't been easy to take, has it?' David asked softly, his voice filled with understanding.

'No, it hasn't,' he answered tiredly. 'And I wonder how much worse it's going to get before the evening's through.'

'So what are you going to do now?'

Thomas took a deep breath as he mulled the question over. He looked toward the castle, his eyes moving up the carved stone till his gaze stopped on Lark's room. He found it telling that in such a short time the room had become known as her room and no longer Theorosa's that all of the Blackwell family had grown up with.

'I'm going back up to Lark's room and see if I can figure anything out.'

Together they entered the house and started up the staircase toward the bedrooms. A few of Baker's men paused to look at him, but didn't stop them as they headed down the hall.

Stepping through the door, they found another officer going through Lark's room carefully. He stopped and looked at them. 'Is there something I can help you with?'

His words may have formed a question, but his tone was dismissive as if he wanted them out as quickly as possible so he could complete his task.

Thomas held the policeman's gaze. 'I would like to take a look at Miss Delavan's room for a moment.'

The man straightened the rest of the way and gave them a business-like smile that left no room for friendliness, though his tone never approached offending. 'I'm sorry, Mr Blackwell, that just won't be possible, I'm afraid.'

'Look, officer,' Thomas glanced down to his badge. 'Officer Malone, I only want to look out that window. I will not touch anything, I give you my word.'

Malone frowned at the unusual request. 'Look out the window? May I ask why you would like to do that?'

Thomas nodded toward the window. 'I know this must sound crazy, but I was wondering just what exactly she could see while looking out that window. I only need a quick glance, then I can leave you to your work.'

The officer continued to look disbelieving. Thomas could tell that he was reluctant to refuse his request probably because he had heard of the alleged

Blackwell 'influence' in the community. 'Well, okay. But only a quick look. Baker would have my ass if he knew I even let you in here.'

'Thanks, Officer Malone.' Thomas gave him a quick smile and stepped over to the window. His gaze scanned quickly over the view. The neat clipped grass of the lawn flowed toward the trees surrounding the castle. The bridge stood isolated within the trees to the left of the view from the window. Then something caught his attention.

The cemetery.

The blackened gray columns of some of the more imposing tombstones were barely visible from the clearing in the trees. But what had caught his attention was the large stone statue of the angel perched on top of the mausoleum. What was it Lark had jokingly said about her dream the other night at dinner?

Thomas searched his memory, remembering not only how beautiful she had been, but how her body had felt against his. At the all too real images, his body reacted and he forced his thoughts back on track. She had said that in her dream she had been following Theorosa through a tunnel. His gaze moved back to the stone angel on top of the mausoleum. She had said that Theorosa had been an angel. Would she have gone there to find out something about Theorosa?

He pursed his lips in thought as he studied the large statue. It was only a hunch, but it was a lot more than they had had only a few moments ago. Thomas turned away from the police officer with a distracted wave. 'Thanks for letting me take a look, Malone.'

'Not a problem, Mr Blackwell,' he answered giving him a speculative look.

David watched his face as he left the room, then fell in step beside them as they headed down the hall. He glanced back over his shoulder as if checking to make sure Baker's man wasn't listening in on them. 'You saw something, didn't you?'

'Well,' Thomas paused, as he continued to mull the cemetery and Lark's disappearance over in his mind. 'It wasn't so much what I saw, but what I might have figured out.'

'And are you going to let anyone else in on this big revelation?' David asked as they moved down the hallway.

'As a matter of fact,' Thomas started, then stopped at the sight of door standing wide open to John's and Stephanie's room. He could hear a low muttering and muffled sounds as if someone were throwing things around the room.

Both David and Thomas changed direction and moved toward their cousin's room. Stepping to the door, they found John muttering to himself as he tossed things out of the drawers of their dresser. They watched in silence, too shocked to speak for a moment at the sight of the normally bland man they had known for quite some time tearing about the room.

Thomas was the first to recover as he spoke. 'John, what is it? Is there something wrong?' He glanced quickly around the room and realized his cousin was nowhere to be seen. 'Where's Stephanie?'

John froze at the sound of his voice. His back was to them, but they still could see the shudder move through him. Slowly he turned toward him and Thomas again felt a sharp moment of surprise.

The man's face was red, either from exertion from his search or worry. Sweat beaded on his upper lip and his forehead and his chest heaved as he struggled for air. He raised a shaking hand to wipe the sweat from his lip and make an attempt to smooth the wild strands of his hair as he faced them.

He tried to smile, but failed when his lips started quivering from his nerves. 'Thomas. David. What can I do for you?'

'Are you all right, John?' David asked, the concern in his voice matching that of Thomas.

'Fine. Really, I'm fine,' John answered all too quickly. His gaze darted about the room, never quite meeting theirs as if he had been caught in the act of some petty crime.

Of course, Thomas thought, as he glanced about the mess of the room, John's 'search' could be considered on the verge of ransacking. As if reading his thoughts, John leaned over to pick up a pillow and toss it back on the bed.

He smoothed a hand over his rumpled suit and cleared his throat. 'I . . . I was, uh, looking for something. I can't seem to find it.'

'I guess you could say that again,' David said in an attempt to lighten the man's tension. He too looked around the room and frowned at what he saw. 'Where's Stephanie? I thought she was sick?'

'Yes, she is.' The words tumbled out of his mouth and he jumped as if startled by the squeak of his own voice. 'I mean, she . . . she was. I think she went for

. . . for a walk. Yes, she went for a walk. Said . . . said she was feeling much better. So she did.'

His eyes darted around the room, then settled down toward the floor as he stuck his hand in the pocket of his wrinkled jacket. John appeared to not quite know what to do with himself.

Thomas's gaze never left John's as he listened to his exchange with David. He purposely let the silence hang for a few moments before he spoke. Again, John jumped at the sound of a voice. 'Miss Delavan is missing, John. We discovered it this morning and, quite frankly, we're worried about her.'

John's red puffy face paled at his words and his eyes widened in disbelief. His mouth fell slowly open, then shut for a few moments as he tried to talk. He looked like a fat, rumpled fish out of water.

He clutched his hand to his mouth as if he were going to be sick, then turned away. He moved toward a chair and sat heavily, his face still registering his shock at Thomas's statement. 'Oh, dear goodness, no. It just can't be.'

Thomas thought the man's behavior was strange before, but it became even odder. Thomas's brow dipped into a frown as he studied him. 'What's wrong, John? Is there something you need to tell us?'

'No. Yes. I mean, how horrible,' he stammered as he tried to recover.

David and Thomas exchanged worried glances. The two men stepped into the room, carefully moving through the mess covering the floor. A filmy pile of yellow caught his attention and he bent to retrieve it. Thomas picked up a shirt that he recognized as one of Stephanie's and held it before him. It was ripped in jagged strips in some places and smudged with what looked like dirt.

Thomas held the item with one finger and moved it toward David so he could look at it. 'You're not telling us something, John.'

The man's eyes nervously flicked toward him and he wheezed for a moment. 'I do . . . do not have any idea what you're talking about, Thomas.'

'Damn it, John.' The words were hot with the anger that flared through him. He started toward John but David gripped him by the shoulder, stopping him. Thomas threw his cousin a pointed look but made no move to step forward. He returned his attention to the pitiful shell of the man before him.

'John, Lark's missing. Two people have been killed here. That person may very well have her. Where is Stephanie?' he demanded.

'She's . . .' Thomas's demand had prompted him into answering immediately till his insinuation sunk in. John's eyes widened as it slowly worked through his frantic thoughts. His mouth fell open as he slumped back into the chair, staring at Thomas in shock. His eyes moved from one point in the room to another as he seemed to be adding things up in his mind. By the sickly pallor of his complexion, Thomas had to guess that the man's conclusion was not a good one.

Apprehension tightened around his chest, not only for Lark, but now for his cousin. He repeated the question to the shaken man, this time more softly. 'John, where is Stephanie? If we're going to be able to help her, and Lark, we need to find them as soon as possible. If Stephanie was involved in Jeffrey's and LeAnn's murders, then we need to get to her before she does something to Lark.' ,

John shook his head as if he wanted to deny what Thomas was telling him. But both David and Thomas could tell that the man couldn't allow himself to overlook what had been going on.

His voice was strained and hoarse. 'Ever since our daughter's death, Stephanie seemed to feel responsible. I tried to tell her that it had been an accident. Just one of those things we never count on happening to us, but she wouldn't listen. Then I noticed she didn't talk about it any more and I began to relax. I thought she had finally come to terms with the death and had started to go on. But she was sick,' he choked the words out as he lifted his hand to wipe his tears away. His hand shook so badly he gave up and settled with gripping his hands together. He clutched them so tight, his knuckles were white. 'I honestly had not realized how sick she had become. I swear it.'

John's terror filled gaze flew to Thomas's guiltily. 'I swear I did not know or I would have taken care of her.'

Thomas felt pity for the man before him. His whole world was crashing down around him. He also felt pity for Stephanie and he shared John's guilt. Why hadn't her own family realized how much pain she had been in?

He cleared his throat of the grief working its way up and directed his attention back to John. Thomas forced himself to push aside his feelings for a moment. If Stephanie was as sick as it had appeared, then they needed to find the two women immediately.

'John,' he called to the man softly, pulling him from his guilt and misery. 'Do you know where she is?'

'I don't know, Thomas,' he answered, his voice distant and flat with shock. His eyes took on a far away look as if he were pulling away desperately from the reality that was crashing around him. 'Stephanie always seemed to enjoy visiting Alicia. Her moods would brighten considerably whenever we came to stay. That's why I would never tell her no when she asked to come here. Then you found the historian dead and a part of me began to wonder. I felt as if I were betraying her by even thinking that she could have had anything to do with it, but still a small part of me wondered. It never failed. Whenever we came here at some point I would wake up and she wouldn't be in the bed beside me, but I figured she was down in the kitchen. Then that night . . . I woke up and she was gone. I didn't think much of it because the next time I woke up, she was back beside me.'

'Why didn't you tell the police this?' David asked. His expression was worried, but disappointed.

John's voice gained some of its strength and his gaze hardened with his anger at David's question. 'She's my wife, damn it.'

'Do you know where she is?'

John closed his grief stricken eyes and shook his head sadly. He let his face fall into his hands as his shoulders hunched over in pain.

Thomas took a deep breath at the sight before him. He turned away, meeting David's gaze. 'I think I have an idea where they are.'

The two men strode out of the room and down the hall toward the stairway. They both remained silent, unsure what to say, how to express what they had witnessed, or what they had learned.

'Where are we going?' David asked as they headed out the back door of the kitchen.

'The cemetery,' Thomas answered, his voice sounding more cool and controlled than he felt.

Fear gripped him as they jogged toward the graveyard hidden now by the trees. Grief and remorse may have been more than his cousin Stephanie could handle. He didn't want to think about her being responsible for two murders, but had to. Stephanie was insane. His heart clenched at the thought. And now Stephanie had Lark.

As he quickened his pace, Thomas prayed they wouldn't be too late.

CHAPTER 17

Fear.

Lark had known fear in her life. When the visions had first started coming on, the intensity with which they had overtaken her had caused fear. Seeing a woman die, even if it was only in her mind, had caused fear. Being inside a jail cell watching the prison door slam shut with a metallic ring had caused fear.

Then, the fear had been a powerful emotion. An emotion that had seemed overwhelming at times, life altering, but not life threatening.

Now Lark knew that fear was palpable. She could feel it as her hands scraped against the earthen wall. She was trying to find a way out of the underground chamber and the hidden tunnel. She could smell it in the death and decay permeating the dirt around her. She could taste fear as it caused her mouth to dry, forced her to swallow against the bile that burned within her throat. She could hear it in the ethereal silence around her, broken only by the sound of the harsh walls skinning her tender palms.

She sensed it within her as she fought desperately to save herself. To escape from Stephanie before the woman, sick with insanity, returned.

Lark took a shaky breath, the sound ragged to her own ears. There was no light to help guide her way and she was forced to feel her way in the pitch black of the tunnel. With excruciating slowness she put one foot in front of the other. Her hands skimming along the wall were already burning, but she ignored the pain.

Holding her hands in front of her, Lark let the curves of the tunnel wall guide her to a destination. Where she was headed, she did not know, but only cared that it was as far away as possible from the chamber with its gruesome occupant.

At least she was fighting for her life, she reminded herself as she put her right foot in front of her left. She'd be damned if she was just going to roll over and wait for something to happen.

She thought again of the skeleton lying in the dug out ledge of the wall. At one point she had wondered if Stephanie had killed someone else, then she had realized with a heart wrenching lurch the identity of the skeleton. Lark paused for a moment as she shook her head, why hadn't she figured it out earlier? The fragile bones so small in stature, the light, longish hair that fell over the stark grinning face.

The skeleton was that of Melissa, Stephanie's beloved daughter.

'The poor woman,' Lark murmured softly. It occurred to her that her compassion for the obviously ill woman could be misplaced and, more importantly, dangerous. After all, this was the same woman who had already proved more than once that she was quite capable of killing someone.

A noise pulled Lark from her thoughts and she froze. Straining, she tried to hear it again to determine which direction it was coming from. She could hear it, a light scraping noise. No, she thought, it was a shuffling sound, like the shuffling of feet in the dirt.

Her heart started racing frantically as she continued to listen. The cavernous walls of the underground tunnel distorted the sound, making it bounce around her, confusing her. Her hands started shaking as she tried to decide what to do.

Keep going forward, she ordered herself. She pushed on as fast as she could. The rough surface of the earthen walls bit and cut into her already raw flesh and she felt the warm caress of blood on her wrists from her wounds.

Suddenly a light flashed on behind her and she swung toward it. Stephanie's face was ghostly white in the kerosene lamp as she moved toward Lark. The light gleamed off the knife she carried

'Did you get lost?' the woman asked innocently. Her tone was light, friendly, as if they were discussing the weather, not that she was carrying a long bladed knife and that Lark was escaping from an underground chamber with a dead body in it.

Lark looked to either side frantically, realizing that Stephanie's lamp light only reached so far. She had no choice but to run into the pitch black void ahead of her.

She pivoted on her foot and started racing through the darkness in the tunnel, all the while aware of Stephanie following her. The woman continued to call to her in a haunted voice as she calmly made her way through the tunnel.

Lark forced herself to slow because of her lack of vision. She flicked a fearful glance over her shoulder still seeing the halo of light behind her in the tunnel. She turned back as she again picked up her pace and hit an overhang head on. Literally.

Bursting pin points of color flared in front of her eyes. Lark found herself lying on the ground of the tunnel, unsure whether her eyes were open or shut since she could not see anything. She groaned as she lifted her hand to her forehead where she felt a warm stickiness flow over her skin and into her hair. Touching the spot tenderly, she realized she had a nasty cut, but it was more than likely superficial.

Which, she realized as she tilted her head to look behind her to see the fast approaching light, would be the very least of her problems if she didn't get out of there.

Lark sat up quickly. Too quickly, she found out, as her vision blurred and her center of balance felt off kilter. She swayed to her knees and started to rise. A sharp pull on her hair caused Lark to cry out in pain as she was hauled to her feet by Stephanie's fierce grip.

Damned if she wasn't going to get it all cut off if she made it through this.

'How dare you try to take off on me,' Stephanie hissed in her ear from behind her. She gave Lark a jerk as if to punctuate her displeasure. Then she brought her knife in front of Lark's face. 'She brought you to help me, remember?'

'I don't know what you want, Stephanie.' Lark tried desperately to make her understand. 'Nobody brought me here.'

'Well, of course she did.' Stephanie chuckled good naturedly as if Lark wasn't seeing what was so obvious. 'She brought you here to right what was wrong.'

'Who?' Lark demanded hoarsely, the woman's insanity was becoming more threatening with every minute that passed. Lark didn't think she could have been more scared. 'Who brought me here? What went wrong that I'm supposed to right, I mean fix?'

She was even starting to talk like her. It did not bode well for her deductive reasoning, she thought almost hysterically.

Lark twisted in Stephanie's grasp and found the woman frowning at her question. Stephanie shrugged as she looked back to her. 'Well, Theorosa of course.'

'Theorosa?' Lark asked incredulously, her voice barely above a whisper. Surely the spirit had not shown up in Stephanie's dreams too and told her to kill Jeffrey and LeAnn.

'Yes, she understands the pain of the death of a loved one,' Stephanie answered simply. She yanked at Lark to head them back toward the underground chamber. 'She not only was persecuted for something she did not do, but she also lost the man she loved. Just like I lost my Melissa. Melissa was the one bright spot in my life. Nothing has meant anything to me since then, until now. Until you.'

'Me? No . . . please,' Lark stammered, disbelief clutching her heart. 'You didn't kill them because of me?'

'Not "because" of you,' Stephanie reassured her with a smile. It quickly faded into a sullen frown. 'That man scared me. He was going to hit me.'

'But LeAnn?' Lark felt a sob rising in her throat. How could she protect herself when the woman had no reason left within her?

'Oh, her.'

Stephanie's frown deepened into a scowl. Her jaws clenched with anger as her eyes blazed with the memory of the woman. 'She followed me. She tried to stop me from seeing Melissa. She told me she was going to tell Alicia so they could put me in jail where I belonged.'

Stephanie's expression crumpled into sobs as she gave Lark a beseeching look. Her eyes were filled with tears. She clutched her hand to her cheek. 'That nasty woman slapped me. She tried to scratch at my eyes. She screamed at me and told me I was evil for taking away the only man she could love. I didn't know what to do.'

'So you hit her?' Lark prompted softly. She closed her eyes as she shook her head with pity. If circumstances had not forced her, Stephanie's insanity probably would never have taken a life.

'She was going to take Melissa away from me.'

They were standing back in the cavern, the kerosene lamp illuminating the room. Stephanie abruptly let go of Lark's hair and stepped away from her. She paced for a moment as if thinking, her brows bent in a frown as she bit at a finger nail.

She stopped as if suddenly noticing Lark. She stared at her for a minute with a bewildered impatient look on her face. 'Well, get on with it.'

Lark stiffened at the vague demand. She eyed the woman warily. 'Get on with what?'

Stephanie rolled her eyes and waved a hand toward the skeleton. 'You were brought here to right the wrong, remember? So, do it.'

Lark's eyes widened with shock as it started to sink in what Stephanie thought she was brought here to do. She looked uneasily toward the small skeleton cloaked in the shadows of the ledge. She shook her head with disbelief, then turned slowly back to the woman to find her watching her with an earnest expression. *You were brought here to right the wrong.*

Stephanie wanted Lark to make her daughter come back from the dead.

And the person in question was very dead, she thought as she turned her gaze back to the skeleton. A shudder of repulsion thundered through Lark. Her mind raced frantically for a clue on how to deal with the woman. She knew without a doubt that if she tried in any way to tell Stephanie that she couldn't bring her daughter back, she would be dead in the span of a heart beat.

Stephanie offered her an encouraging smile and gave her a prompting wave of her hand toward the skeleton.

Numbness showered over Lark. Shock and terror thinned into calmness of nothing. She stared at Stephanie's hopeful insanity realizing she had no choice but to placate her till she could think of something else to do.

Turning toward the skeleton of the dead girl, Lark took a deep breath. Squaring her shoulders she paused, letting the silence fill the room. With a dramatic flare, she flung her arms up in front of her, then raised them slowly above her head.

'I call to the spirits that protect the innocent souls of those lost without resolution . . . I call to you . . . Theorosa.'

Thomas and David ran through the thick belt of trees that surrounded the cemetery dodging low branches and the thorny limbs of bushes. Thomas slowed as he entered the clearing, his breath coming in short pants, more from fear and dread, than exertion. He scanned the graveyard and found it still, unmoving.

His gaze continued to study the area, then stopped at the gate of the iron fence standing wide open.

'She's been here,' he said to his cousin.

'They're probably both here, Thomas,' David added with a solemn expression.

Thomas nodded distractedly, then headed toward the fence. He paused for a brief second as he stood in front of the gate. He started toward the mausoleum.

'I assume since nothing's been recently dug up, there is only one place they could go to.'

Thomas turned toward his cousin with a pointed look of exasperation.

David shrugged, holding his hands in front of him. 'Hey, I'm just trying to help.'

'Why not be a little more quiet about it,' he suggested, then turned back to the heavy doors of the huge building.

He stood at the entrance unsure which door to enter. Looking at the doors, he found one slightly ajar and felt a momentary sense of elation. He opened the heavy metal portal as slowly and quietly as possible till he could look cautiously inside. As light from the sun behind him spilled into the interior, Thomas found it empty. Of people who were alive anyway.

Stepping in, he motioned for David to follow and they proceeded softly across the hard floor. Thomas's eyes narrowed as he spotted the tracks of foot prints in the layer of the dust covering the floor. The Blackwells had not had a death in the family since the tragic drowning of Melissa, leaving the room to gather the dust of time. All memorials were placed outside because of the family's, more specifically Stephanie's, reluctance to enter the building. Out of concern, they had complied with her wishes.

Silently he pointed to the tracks for David to see. They both nodded and began to follow them around the corner. The prints proceeded into the next addition, but Thomas stopped when he noticed a large number of them stopped at the wall.

Frowning, he studied the foot prints on the floor as they disappeared into the wall. How was that possible, he wondered?

David tilted his head as he too looked at the unusual find. 'I don't get it.'

'I don't either,' Thomas murmured.

Kneeling in front of the wall, he studied where the floor met the wall. His eyes widened with realization as he found the almost concealed space where the one section of wall did not meet the floor. Just like a door.

'I'll be damned,' Thomas exclaimed as he turned to look up at his cousin. 'It's a hidden door.'

'A secret door?' David asked incredulously. He bent to see what Thomas had found. 'I never knew about it, let alone heard rumors, did you?'

Thomas shook his head. 'I don't think Grandmother even knows about it.'

David straightened to study where the ceiling and the wall met. 'I wonder when it was put in?'

Thomas's gaze moved over the section but couldn't find any sort of knob to open it. There would have to be a disguised mechanism then, he assumed. He started running his fingers along the wall. 'If I remember right, Grandmother said this section was built during the prohibition era. Which could explain the hidden door. More than likely there's a room behind it.'

'I guess a cemetery would be a good place to hide your bootleg from the feds,' David murmured as he worked the wall above where Thomas crouched.

'Personally I could think of a few better places.'

Thomas's fingers slipped over a ridge and he felt a slight catch. He smiled up at David. 'I think I've found it.'

He pulled his finger over it till it moved. They watched in disbelief as the door swung silently open away from them. David had been partially correct. There was a room inside the secret door.

There was also a hallway leading into an underground tunnel.

Lark continued to hum something she hoped sounded like a chant. She was trying desperately to buy herself some time as she pulled on every memory she could think of from all the sappy psychic and ghost movies she had seen over the years.

'Oh, restless spirits . . . hmmm . . . help us to . . . uh-' Lark's voice faltered when she couldn't think of a single thing to say. Obviously she hadn't watched enough morbid movies in her life.

She flicked an uneasy glance toward Stephanie to gauge her reaction and hummed a few more bars to her nonsensical chant. The woman was swaying almost hypnotically to the chant with her hands crossed over her heart and a patient smile on her insane face.

At least one of them was getting into this.

Lark quickly returned her attention to what she was doing, which was a struggle since she had no idea what she was doing. 'Help us deliver Melissa from . . . uh . . . the ethereal plane where she awaits us.

'I . . . uh . . . beseech you to . . .' To what? Lark's mind raced as she sputtered and stammered a few more repetitive and chanting verses.

Stephanie's eyes opened and she looked hopefully, expectantly toward Melissa's skeleton as if she expected muscles and flesh to start forming on the thin bones. Her eyes widened at the obvious lack of change. Her lips started to crumple and quiver. Whether it was from anger or despair, Lark had no idea. She only knew the charade was over.

The hope Stephanie had built over so many years after her daughter's death, slowly started to shatter before Lark's eyes. Overwhelming grief filled the woman's eyes and tears flowed down her face as she moved toward the ledge. She tentatively touched the bony cheek of the skull as if her love only could undo

367

the girl's death. Her head dropped as a sob tore through her throat and wracked her body. Her shoulders shook with the emotion.

Lark felt tears well within her own eyes as she watched the woman's hope drain from her. Stephanie must have clung desperately to the notion that her daughter could be returned to her. For years it must have been the sustaining link that she had to cope with the emptiness inside herself.

Stephanie swung toward Lark, startling her. The look of sheer hatred and anger in the woman's wild eyes caused her to back away in terror. Stephanie advanced slowly toward her.

'You were brought here to right the wrong. You were supposed to bring my little girl back,' Stephanie spat the words at her as her voice slowly rose to a scream. Spittle flew from her mouth as she shouted at Lark and jabbed an accusing finger at her. 'You were supposed to bring her back and you failed.'

Lark shook her head at the accusations. She held her hands in front of her as she backed slowly away. 'Your little girl died in a tragic accident. It was no one's fault, Stephanie. It was not your fault.'

'She was such a beautiful child,' Stephanie sobbed, her eyes swollen with her tears.

'Yes, she was,' Lark soothed, keeping her voice low and calm. 'But no one can bring her back. I cannot bring her back.'

'No,' she wailed, leaping toward Lark with her hands held in front of her like claws.

Stephanie pounced on Lark, giving her only enough time to grab the woman's wrists before they connected with her face. The two struggled in the grit of the cavern floor. Lark tripped over a rock and fell on her knees. Stephanie grabbed her hair and pulled, causing Lark to scream in pain. Lark reached behind her and clawed at the woman's hands, forcing her to release her. She started to twist away when Stephanie shoved her roughly to the ground. Lark landed on her back, the air whooshing from her lungs.

Before she could take a breath, Stephanie wrapped her hands around her throat and started squeezing the life from her.

Thomas thought about going back to the castle to get a flashlight, then decided against it. They would be wasting precious time and, as far as he knew, they didn't have time. They had to find Lark before his cousin killed her.

'How do you expect us to find her, Thomas? We can't even see our hands in front of our faces,' David objected as he followed his cousin.

'I don't know, but we have to try. They're down here somewhere, we have to keep going till we catch up with them.'

'Then what do we do?'

'I don't know,' Thomas answered quietly. He would not have guessed that anyone staying at the castle could have been capable of murdering Jeffrey and LeAnn. If he had to think of someone, he would have thought Natalie more capable of it than Stephanie. She had always been one of the more timid and gentle Blackwells. But now they knew what insanity could drive an individual to do.

He took a deep breath as he continued through the tunnel. 'I guess if we find them, we try to reason with her. Try to talk to her.'

'But if what John says is true, she may not be able to understand reason,' David offered.

'I know, but we can't let her hurt Lark.' He made the statement, the realization of what it would more than likely entail causing his chest to tighten with dread. Never in his life would he want to harm his cousin. He loved her and wanted to get her the help she desperately needed.

But he also loved Lark.

Stephanie's hands squeezed tighter around Lark's throat. Lark could feel the pressure tighten, shutting off her wind pipe. Her attempts to breathe became only pathetic hisses of air.

Lark's heart slammed within her chest not only from the lack of oxygen, but from the terror that gripped her as tightly as the woman trying to kill her. Lark would never have recognized the face hovering above hers as that of Stephanie's. Her eyes were red and swollen from her grief and tears. The once pleasant wrinkles that covered her face had become crevices as she gritted her teeth with the rage that consumed her at the disappointment she had been forced to face today. Her teeth were white in the slash of red that was her mouth, contorted with her efforts to strangle Lark.

'You failed. Melissa's dead,' she repeated over and over, her jaws clenching.

The wave of terror that had washed over Lark, started to recede. This must be what dying is like, she thought. The black sand of unconsciousness started filling the circle of her vision. Her thoughts focused on Thomas. She could see his beautiful brown-gold eyes. Tiger eyes, she had called them. Her lids fluttered as she tried to fight the sleep brought on by the lack of air. She loved him, she realized. A tear slipped from her eye and slowly fell down her cheek. Would she ever get to tell him? Would the love they could have shared never happen because she had made the mistake of feeling compassion for the woman who now was squeezing the life from her?

The circle of her vision was growing smaller and smaller as she clutched desperately at Stephanie's wrists and tried to pull them away. She stared helpless with disbelief at the insanity before her. A movement just behind Stephanie's head caught her fading attention and Lark glanced toward it.

Her eyes widened. She felt the blood drain from her reddened face. The vision from her dream stood behind them. Theorosa in her beautiful flowing dress of ivory. Her long thick hair hung over one shoulder. She was as beautiful as her painting, even more so. Her dark eyes held Lark's with an intensity as strong as a physical touch.

You came to help me, now I must help you. The words spoke softly, gently into Lark's fading consciousness. *There has been too much death here already.*

Lark simply stared at the apparition, feeling the woman's thoughts merging with her own. There were so many things she wanted to ask her. So many things that needed to be revealed.

Lark blinked slowly, trying to form the thoughts, the words in her mind, but couldn't. Consciousness and life were fading away from her. She felt herself start to slip away into calmness and acceptance.

No, the word flared in her mind. She could not accept death. Not yet.

Opening her eyes, she looked toward Theorosa and found the beautiful woman smiling at her as she nodded her head slightly. The image of the tall woman stepped forward out of Lark's line of vision and apparently into Stephanie's.

Stephanie gasped. Her attention was now elsewhere and she released Lark's throat and started backing away, screaming. 'No. She has to die. She failed. She didn't bring my beautiful Melissa back to me. Do you hear me, she failed.'

At the moment Stephanie released her grip, the air whooshed into her starved lungs. The sweet feel of it was followed quickly with an incredible urge to be sick. Lark's stomach turned and she swallowed against the bile in her throat. She rolled away from Stephanie. Gasping for gulps of air, her vision started to clear and she wearily tried to push herself to her knees. Still, she was too weak and remained huddled over as she continued to fill her lungs, quickly rushing much needed oxygen to the rest of her body.

Unable to keep herself up, the last of her energy draining from her, Lark fell back to her side heavily. She tried to keep her eyes open, terrified that if she succumbed to unconsciousness it would bring death with it. She had too much to live for. How much she yearned to tell Thomas she loved him.

With that thought in her mind, she slipped into the sable darkness, no longer able to keep it at bay.

Thomas heard shouting, then a woman's scream. The terror filled sound of it ripped at his heart and he froze for a moment. His heart pounded within his chest and his breath broke into ragged gulps.

Was it Lark?

Although he had not been able to discern what had been said, he could tell by the sound that they were not too far away from the women. He started forward at a faster pace, heedless of the rough walls raking at the palms of his hands.

Another scream and the sound of a person wailing bounced through the tunnel toward them and Thomas felt his fear building with each step.

'Heaven help us,' David said, his voice filled with the terror Thomas felt himself.

Don't let us be too late, Thomas silently prayed. How was he supposed to help her when they could not move much faster than a slow walk? Still he pushed on, praying fervently for Lark's safety. Her life.

A rush of cold air moved over Thomas just as he rounded a curve. He shuddered at the icy feel of it washing over him, but shoved those sensations aside when he spotted the glow of a lamp ahead of them.

Focusing on the light, he rushed forward, heedless of what hidden obstacles might stand in his way. He ran, his heart pounding with fear, as he headed toward the sounds of a struggle.

Reaching the entrance of the chamber, Thomas slid to a stop, his pounding heart felt as if it had stopped when his eyes found Lark's unmoving form. He moved a small step, his jaw clenching to fight back the sob that threatened to escape his throat. He barely spared his cousin Stephanie a glance where she huddled against the wall crying hysterically.

He moved to Lark's side and knelt slowly beside her. His hand hovered for a fraction of a second over the bloody tangle of her hair before he stroked her. Thomas's eyes filled at the dark bruises circling her throat where Stephanie had strangled her. Blood still glistened from the cut on her forehead and had run down her cheek. Her lips were slightly parted and Thomas mourned the loss of never being able to feel them against his ever again.

Softly he stroked her cheek, then timidly touched the curve of her lower lip. She pressed her lips together as she swallowed, causing Thomas to jerk his hand back. When he realized that she wasn't dead, his lips spread into a wide grin and the tears spilled happily from his eyes.

Lark's lids fluttered, then opened uneasily. She looked groggy and disoriented as her eyes looked around her. Her gaze then settled on his face and she tried to smile.

'Lark, sweetheart,' he murmured, his heart pounding once again, this time for the elation that soared through him.

Lark tried to speak, her voice no more than a hoarse rasp before she swallowed and tried again. Her brow dipped into a frown as she was forced to concentrate in the effort to talk.

'I love you, Thomas.'

The words were no more than a rough whisper. Before he could say anything, her eyes closed and her head fell back to the side. Thomas gripped her by the arms with terror. Relief flooded through him at the sight of her chest moving with her breathing.

He let his head fall for a quick prayer of thanks. For the first time the sobs of his cousin Stephanie pulled at his thoughts. Thomas turned to find David cradling her within his arms as he rocked her and gave her soft words of reassurance.

Thomas met David's gaze. The look of remorse and pity reflected that of his own. Thomas looked away as he shook his head sadly. He held no anger or contempt in his heart for Stephanie. She had suffered the worst loss of any parent. The loss of a child. Melissa's death had been more than she could take and now the only thing left was to give her the help she so desperately needed.

A noise pulled him from his thoughts and he glanced toward the tunnel which they had just emerged from. A bouncing white beam of a flashlight washed against the wall and he could hear several voices approaching them.

The first to enter was Detective Baker. His dark scowl scanned the room quickly, then relaxed slightly when he saw that the scene was under control. Behind him, Stephanie's husband John shouldered his way past the detective, looking frantic till he saw his wife.

'Stephanie,' he choked as he moved toward her.

At the sound of his voice, Stephanie raised her face from David's chest and looked up to her husband. Her grief was overwhelming, her face ruddy with tears and despair. Her eyes held his beseechingly and she continued to sob. 'She's dead, John.'

'I know, honey,' he answered softly, as he knelt to pull her into his arms. He rocked her gently as he stroked her hair. 'I know. But now it's over and we can get you help.'

Thomas watched them, his heart aching for the two of them. He turned back to Lark as he continued to touch her cheek with his fingers. He had been afraid to move her, not knowing the full extent of her injuries.

A loud booming voice echoed through the tunnel and Thomas recognized Henry's roar of displeasure. The doctor practically ran into the room, the kerosene lamp he held swinging with his abrupt stop. The doctor's gaze quickly assessed Stephanie and he moved on, knowing that she was all right. He took one look at Lark and hurried over.

He knelt beside her and immediately felt for a pulse. Henry felt one just as Thomas told him she was still alive, just unconscious. 'She looks pretty much the worse for wear, but I think she's going to be all right.'

Henry lifted her lids to look into her pupils and grunted noncommittally. He gently prodded her gash and the other wounds to her head. 'She'll be fine, Thomas, don't you worry, but I think she needs to go to the hospital, just so we can make sure.'

'Of course,' Thomas murmured with relief.

Baker's officer was already heading back outside to use his shoulder mike to radio for an ambulance when Thomas turned to look over his shoulder. Baker stood with his hands on his hips as his gaze moved around the interior of the cavern. It stopped at the sight of the skeleton.

'What the hell is that?' he asked, his brow raised.

'I don't know, but I'm sure Lark can tell us later,' Thomas answered.

'Thomas,' Henry spoke, touching him gently on the shoulder. 'If you'll be so kind – pick her up, we'll get her out of this hell hole and get her taken care of.'

'What about Stephanie?' he asked, frowning with worry.

Henry gave him a quick pat. 'I'll help John take care of her.'

Thomas nodded and turned back to Lark. Her skin was pale, almost white against the crimson of her blood. He lifted her as carefully as possible into his arms and stood. David took one of the lamps and walked with him as he carried Lark out the dark tunnel that had been her temporary prison.

They climbed the stairs of the narrow hallway. Stepping through the secret door, Thomas had never been so thankful for sunlight. David held the door open for him as he stepped through the large metal doorway.

He heard his name being called and Thomas looked up to see his grandmother running toward him, her gray hair wisped around her face, her eyes filled with worry as she looked from him to Lark.

Alicia looked back to him, her voice quiet, barely above a whisper. Fear laced through her words. 'Is it over?'

Thomas nodded, the impact of her words lifting a heavy weight from his shoulders. 'Yes, Grandmother. It's over.'

* * *

Five stitches to her forehead, x-rays to make sure she didn't have a concussion, both her hands bandaged, and an exam so thorough that Lark's patience was starting to wear thin. She had awakened on the exam table and had immediately asked where Thomas was.

The doctor had smiled knowingly, then gently pushed her back on the table so he could finish. He explained that her young man was waiting outside for her. And that he was almost as impatient as she was.

Lark had not found the doctor's attempt at humor funny. She just wanted Thomas to take her home so she could shower the filth off herself and go to bed. This time she didn't care who knew, she was sleeping with his arms around her.

That's exactly what they did too. After her shower, she had cuddled up to the smooth warmth of his chest and had fallen into a deep sleep with a smile on her face. A moment of fear had gripped her though, when she awakened late the next morning to find his spot next to her empty. Looking at the clock, she realized that he must have left as silently as possible so she could get the rest her body needed.

Her gaze settled on the pillow with the indent where his head had rested and she smiled softly. A blush pink rose lay cradled in the hollow. Smiling, Lark picked it up and held it to her nose to inhale the soft fragrance of the bloom. The silk of the petals brushed against her lips and the memory of his lips against hers filled her. The thought of his touch on her skin caused the heat to center low in her belly.

Carefully pushing herself to the side of the bed, Lark took the rose with her as she stood and headed toward the bathroom to get dressed. She remembered the last few fading moments of when she had been hurt by Stephanie, the one burning thing she had had on her mind was to tell Thomas she loved him. The trip from the hospital was a blur. She had been so exhausted that she had fallen asleep almost instantly. Lark frowned as she tried to recall the evening. Had she told him she loved him?

She could not remember telling him. Lark finished the last touches of her make up and headed toward the bedroom door. She had one thing and one thing only on her mind.

She would find Thomas and tell him she loved him.

Leaving Thomas's room, Lark headed for the stairway. She moved slowly down the steps, her movements hampered by her sore muscles and the pain that sliced through her head if she shifted too quickly. At the foot of the stairs, she headed toward the kitchen when the sound of voices from the parlor caused her to change direction.

Stepping to the doorway, she hesitated. Quickly her gaze found Thomas sitting in a chair and she took a moment just to drink in the sight of him. He turned his handsome face to her and smiled when he saw that she carried the rose he had left for her. Lark was content to stare into his tiger-brown eyes as he mesmerized her with the feelings she saw reflected within them.

Thomas rose and walked to her to take her hand and lead her back to the chair. At the feel of his touch on her wrist, Lark felt a delicious warmth that spread through her heart. She took the seat he offered and reluctantly let go of his hand. He remained beside her though and she turned her attention to the others sitting in the room.

David sat with his grandmother on the sofa while Henry sat in the wing-back chair to Alicia's right. Detective Baker had stood at the sight of Lark and remained standing even after she sat.

'I hope I'm not-' Lark's throat was so sore from the attempted strangulation, her voice was raspy, uneven as she tried to get the words out.

'You are not interrupting anything, dear,' Alicia stated quickly to reassure her. She flicked a worried glance toward Henry before she returned her attention to Lark. 'I think Henry would agree with me that it's best if you try not to talk, if at all possible.'

'I most certainly do agree,' Henry added with a stern look toward Lark.

Baker rolled nervously back onto his heels as he shoved his hands into the pockets of his jacket. 'I'm glad to see you looking so much better, Miss Delavan.'

Lark's brow rose at the change in the detective's attitude toward her. If she didn't know any better she would almost think he was being nice to her. Her air must have been cut off longer than she thought.

At her perplexed look, the detective had the decency to look chagrined. He kept looking toward the toes of his shoes as he continued. 'I . . . uh . . . I wanted to let you know that in the light of everything, we've eliminated you as a suspect.'

'How incredibly astute of you,' Thomas muttered.

Baker's gaze hardened at the statement and he looked at Thomas for a moment, before he returned to Lark. 'Look, I just wanted to . . . to apologize for being so hard on you during all of this.'

Lark started to speak, but her throat hurt too much, so she gave him a dismissive wave of her hand to show she had no hard feelings.

'Yeah,' he watched her gesture, his stance relaxing slightly. 'Anyway, the DA is waiting for the test results on Mrs Tarrant, Mrs Blackwell, before he decides whether to press charges.'

Lark looked toward Alicia questioningly. Alicia nodded her understanding. 'Stephanie is in the hospital right now, Lark. They are taking care of her.'

Lark closed her eyes in thanks. Yes, Stephanie had tried to kill her. To strangle the life from her, but it had been the insanity that had caused her to do it. The death of her child had been too much. The years of hope and her repressed grief had crashed around her, driving the woman over the edge of reason.

Opening her eyes again, she looked back toward the detective. Against Henry's wishes, she forced out a raspy word of question. 'Natalie?'

'She's out on bond,' Baker answered quickly, before she could try again. 'She said she had not been trying to kill you with the Panther Mushrooms, only warn you away. Although it was obvious by the small amount she used that it would have been impossible to kill you, it's still illegal to use that particular threat tactic. She has a clean record, so she won't be facing much, if any, time. Probably just probation, but don't worry. I have a feeling she won't be coming around here any more.'

'You can be sure of that,' David stated.

'I know it's hard for you to talk,' Baker started, turning toward Lark. 'But did Stephanie tell you anything about the murders?'

Lark nodded. She held her throat with her hand as she worked to speak. 'She said that she had been visiting her daughter Melissa. She would have to go in the middle of the night so she could sneak away from John without his knowing what she had done with their daughter's body. She was coming back into the castle that night when Jeffrey surprised her. I guess she scared him too, because he started to get a poker from the fireplace, so she hit him.'

'What about you?' Henry asked, his look incredulous.

Lark shrugged. 'She had no way of knowing that Natalie had fed those mushrooms to me.'

'And LeAnn?' Baker prompted.

'LeAnn loved Jeffrey and was very upset about his death.' Lark frowned as she remembered Stephanie recalling the events of that horrible evening. 'LeAnn must have figured things out and started following Stephanie. She followed her into the tunnel and found Melissa. She threatened Stephanie that she was going to tell Alicia and that they would put her in jail where she belonged. Stephanie could not handle the thought of being separated from her daughter. Then LeAnn slapped her and they struggled. They must have struggled in the entry way of the mausoleum. That's where the dust smudges came from.'

'So she was basically provoked in both situations.' Baker nodded as he mulled over that. His brows lifted as he remembered something else. 'What about the skeleton? Is that the daughter?'

Lark nodded as she hugged her arms around her. Fear still filled her when the image of the small skeleton appeared in her mind.

Alicia shuddered, then turned toward the detective, her eyes sad and filled with tears. 'When will we be able to have her back?'

'I'll call you as soon as they release her from the coroner's office,' he promised. Baker's expression was a mixture of compassion and understanding, an unusual combination for the man who had been nothing but negative with them before. 'Then you can give her a proper burial.'

'Thank you,' Alicia murmured as she wiped at her eyes with a tissue.

Baker rocked back on his heels, then pulled his hands from his pockets. He started toward the door of the parlor. 'I need to get back to the station. Miss Delavan, we would like you to come down and fill out a statement for us, if you would, please. I know you've been through a considerable ordeal, so tomorrow would be fine.'

Lark held his gaze for a moment. In his own way, the detective was trying to make amends with her. She smiled and nodded at him. Baker returned her smile with a genuine one of his own. He started to turn when Thomas called to him.

Thomas stepped to stand in front of him. He offered his hand to the detective. 'Thank you for all your help.'

Baker took it and gave him a firm shake. 'You're welcome and I thank you. The both of you,' he added as he looked around Thomas to Lark.

Thomas waved his hand toward the door as he

started walking with the detective. 'We appreciate your coming by, detective. Let me walk you out.'

Lark felt a momentary sense of loss as Thomas left with Baker out the front door. Alicia's voice broke into her thoughts and she turned back toward his grandmother. Alicia smiled knowingly.

'Lark, I am so sorry that I brought you into all this mess,' Alicia said, her frown filled with worry. 'I only wanted to help Theorosa and now it will never happen.'

Shaking her head, Lark smiled. 'But you did help her – we did. You and I.'

'What do you mean?' Henry asked, leaning forward in his chair expectantly.

'I saw her when-' Lark swallowed at the pain in her throat, then continued. She left out the part about Stephanie choking her, afraid it would upset Alicia. 'I saw her briefly and she helped me. She distracted Stephanie so I could get away.'

'You saw her?' David asked his voice sounding doubtful, but the look in his eyes showed his belief in her.

Lark nodded. 'She didn't speak to me, but I felt her words within me.'

'What did she say?' Alicia was clutching at the ruffled neck of her light yellow shirt.

'That there had been too much death at the castle already,' Lark answered. She remembered the questions that had filled her mind, but she had been unable to ask.

'Do you think she's at rest now?' Alicia's expression was hopeful.

'Yes, she is.' Lark smiled. Theorosa had not wanted tangible evidence to prove her innocence.

The only thing she wanted was for the family to know she had not killed David. Lark took a shaky breath and met Alicia's gaze. 'Theorosa knew she could never have justice, but she could have truth. The truth is that she did not kill David Blackwell, someone by the name of Carolyn did it.'

Alicia gasped, then looked quickly toward Henry. At his questioning gaze, she cleared her throat. 'Carolyn was the mistress.'

She looked toward David to read his expression. David took his grandmother's hand and gave it a reassuring squeeze as he smiled at her. 'What happened then has no effect on the present.'

Alicia smiled and leaned toward him to kiss him on the cheek.

Lark watched the exchange, knowing if Theorosa was watching that she would be pleased. Suddenly a breeze moved through the room carrying with it the light scent of spring flowers. Everyone in the room frowned. All the windows were shut and the front door was closed, yet the breeze was strong enough the ruffle their hair and whistle about the room.

Ever so softly a voice rode in on the wind and said only one thing.

Thank you.

Lark left the parlor in search of Thomas. After the strange occurrence, everyone had been stunned into silence, then the others had all started talking at once. Lark left them talking about the incident. She had something important to do.

To find Thomas.

Opening the front door, she found him watching the detective drive away. She stepped out onto the front porch and walked toward him. He turned toward her and at the sight of her started smiling. He held his hand out to her and she joined him gladly.

They heard his grandmother call out to him from inside and they looked at each other, their thoughts mirroring each other's. Thomas grinned. 'Let's go hide for a while.'

Lark nodded and they moved down the steps. Thomas led her toward the garage where they closed the door behind them. His BMW convertible was parked inside with the top down. Thomas opened the door and pushed the seat forward so they could climb in the back seat.

Once she was beside him, he pulled her to him. Thomas touched his lips softly to hers. Desire flared within him at the silky softness of her lips against his. His hand instinctively moved to her neck to caress her when she tensed at his touch. Thomas pulled back and he looked at the slightly swollen purplish ridge circling her neck. His jaws clenched as he realized how easily he could have lost her.

Thomas looked to her eyes and found her watching him. He smoothed his thumb across her cheek. Lark started to speak and he stopped her by placing his finger across her lips.

'Lark, I know there's nothing keeping you here now and that you'll probably be heading back to your job.' He searched her eyes, not knowing exactly what he was looking for. 'But I have to tell you something,' he added.

'I almost lost you and it scared me. Now I wonder if you're going to leave. When I think I might never see you again, it terrifies me. There are lots of opportunities for accountants here, or I can always find a law practice where you live. It doesn't matter to me. The only thing that matters to me is that you are with me.' Thomas took a deep breath and offered her a nervous smile. 'I don't know how to say it, so I guess I'll just say it. I love you, Lark.'

Lark smiled in answer, cupping his face with her hands and kissing him. Thomas moaned as she opened her lips to him and he explored the heated warmth of her. She pulled back and looked into his eyes. Lark tried to speak, but her injured voice broke.

Thomas hushed her softly. 'Do you want to tell me you love me too?'

Lark shook her head. At Thomas's crestfallen look, she grinned. She shifted to stand beside him on the floor board of the back seat. He leaned back to look up at her as she started unbuttoning her shirt. Throwing it aside, her skirt went next, then her sandals till she wore only the thin lace of her bra and panties.

Lark stepped into the seat and sat on the canvassed fold of the top where the roof folded back into the trunk. The fold cradled her bottom like a hammock as she looked at Thomas.

'I want to show you,' she said, her voice no more than a whisper. The husky rasp of her voice washed over him and he felt himself respond to her.

Thomas's gaze moved over her long legs to the swell of her breast curved over the lacy cup to her smiling eyes. He didn't see the cuts, bruises, or the bandages, only her beauty. He looked into her eyes and saw his answer and his heart swelled. Quickly he removed his clothes and wrapped his arms around her. They made love on the back of the car. They whispered soft endearments to each other. They touched each other's bodies in ways that they would never grow tired of.

They touched each other's souls.

THE EXCITING NEW NAME
IN WOMEN'S FICTION!

PLEASE HELP ME TO HELP YOU!

Dear *Scarlet* Reader,

Good news – thanks to your excellent response we are able
to hold another super Prize Draw, which means that **you
could win 6 months worth of free *Scarlets*!** Just return
your completed questionnaire to us **before 31 January
1998** and you will automatically be entered in the draw that
takes place on that day. If you are lucky enough to be one of
the first two names out of the hat we will send you four new
Scarlet romances, every month for six months.

So don't delay – return your form straight away!*

Looking forward to hearing from you,

Sally Cooper

Editor-in-Chief, *Scarlet*

*Prize draw offer available only in the UK, USA or Canada. Draw is not
open to employees of Robinson Publishing, or of their agents, families or
households. Winners will be informed by post, and details of winners can be
obtained after 31 January 1998, by sending a stamped addressed envelope to
address given at end of questionnaire.

Note: further offers which might be of interest may be sent to you by other,
carefully selected, companies. If you do not want to receive them, please write to
Robinson Publishing Ltd, 7 Kensington Church Court, London W8 4SP, UK.

QUESTIONNAIRE

Please tick the appropriate boxes to indicate your answers

1 Where did you get this Scarlet title?
Bought in supermarket ☐
Bought at my local bookstore ☐ Bought at chain bookstore ☐
Bought at book exchange or used bookstore ☐
Borrowed from a friend ☐
Other (please indicate) _____

2 Did you enjoy reading it?
A lot ☐   A little ☐   Not at all ☐

3 What did you particularly like about this book?
Believable characters ☐   Easy to read ☐
Good value for money ☐   Enjoyable locations ☐
Interesting story ☐   Modern setting ☐
Other _____

4 What did you particularly dislike about this book?
_____

5 Would you buy another Scarlet book?
Yes ☐   No ☐

6 What other kinds of book do you enjoy reading?
Horror ☐   Puzzle books ☐   Historical fiction ☐
General fiction ☐   Crime/Detective ☐   Cookery ☐
Other (please indicate) _____

7 Which magazines do you enjoy reading?
1. _____
2. _____
3. _____

And now a little about you –
8 How old are you?
Under 25 ☐   25–34 ☐   35–44 ☐
45–54 ☐   55–64 ☐   over 65 ☐

cont.

9 What is your marital status?

Single ☐   Married/living with partner ☐

Widowed ☐   Separated/divorced ☐

10 What is your current occupation?

Employed full-time ☐   Employed part-time ☐

Student ☐   Housewife full-time ☐

Unemployed ☐   Retired ☐

11 Do you have children? If so, how many and how old are they?

_____

_____

12 What is your annual household income?

under $15,000	☐	or £10,000	☐
$15–25,000	☐	or £10–20,000	☐
$25–35,000	☐	or £20–30,000	☐
$35–50,000	☐	or £30–40,000	☐
over $50,000	☐	or £40,000	☐

Miss/Mrs/Ms _____

Address _____

_____

_____

Thank you for completing this questionnaire. Now tear it out – put it in an envelope and send it, before 31 January 1998, to:

Sally Cooper, Editor-in-Chief

USA/Can. address
SCARLET c/o London Bridge
85 River Rock Drive
Suite 202
Buffalo
NY 14207
USA

UK address/No stamp required
SCARLET
FREEPOST LON 3335
LONDON W8 4BR
Please use block capitals for address

SHPRO/10/97

***Scarlet* titles coming next month:**

MIXED DOUBLES Kathryn Bellamy
Ace Delaney – the bad boy from *Game, Set and Match* – is back! On the surface, Ace and Alexa Kane have nothing in common, but somehow fate keeps throwing them together. Has Ace finally met his match?

DARED TO DREAM Tammy McCallum
Lauren Ferguson never imagined that her obsession with Nicholas Kenward's medieval portrait would lead her into adventures beyond her dreams . . . Yet suddenly she's spiralling through time into Nicholas's arms.

MISCONCEPTION Margaret Pargeter
Margaret Pargeter's back . . . and she's writing for *Scarlet*! Guilty and confused, Miranda knows better than to protest at Brett Deakin's high-handedness. If she ignores him, surely he'll get the message? But he doesn't – he proposes that Miranda becomes 'Brett's bride'!

THE LOVE CHILD Angela Drake
Alessandra loves Raphael, but her obsession is destroying their impetuous marriage. Saul and Tara love each other, but worry about Alessandra is driving them apart. Then there's Georgiana who's determined to punish Saul *and* the women he loves . . .